Archibald Clavering Gunter

Mr. Potter of Texas

A Novel

Archibald Clavering Gunter

Mr. Potter of Texas
A Novel

ISBN/EAN: 9783337000981

Printed in Europe, USA, Canada, Australia, Japan

Cover: Foto ©Andreas Hilbeck / pixelio.de

More available books at **www.hansebooks.com**

MR. POTTER OF TEXAS

𝕬 𝕹ovel

BY

ARCHIBALD CLAVERING GUNTER

AUTHOR OF

"MR. BARNES; OF NEW YORK"

CONTENTS.

BOOK I.

THE BOMBARDMENT OF ALEXANDRIA.

BOOK II.

ENGLISH JUSTICE.

3

CONTENTS.

BOOK III.

A WOMAN'S BATTLE.

BOOK IV.

MR. POTTER TAKES THE WAR-PATH.

MR. POTTER OF TEXAS.

BOOK I.

The Bombardment of Alexandria.

CHAPTER I.

THE DESERTED HOTEL.

" Sir, I have something to tell you ! "

" My heaven ! Is there a woman—an English woman in this accursed place to-night ?" ejaculates the young man to whom she has spoken, turning with a start and looking at her in amazed horror, but still holding in his hand a revolver, the cartridges of which he has been carefully examining.

" I have come all the way from Europe to say to you something of great importance."

" There is nothing of importance now but to save your life ! "

" My life ? Is our personal danger so imminent ? "

" There is death to every European man or woman in this city to-night. And they deserted *you ?*" This last is · said in surprised astonishment, for he has noticed the unusual refinement and beauty of the woman speaking to him, the richness of her dress and jewels, though she is in the black of deep mourning, and the latent appearance of haughty command in her pose, notwithstanding there is in her manner and gaze, as she addresses him, a curious apologetic humility, as if she were ashamed of an indefinite something.

" They did not desert me ! "

" Then how in Heaven's name are you here ? "

" I saw them going away. The British Consul insisted on my leaving also ; but I refused. I said I must see you, I had come so far to do so. They telegraphed from Cairo that you would surely be here this morning, and I waited, expecting you, till too late ; then I hurried to the shore and found all communication with the ships cut off. What was I, a woman, to do in this strange city, not speaking an Eastern language? My dragoman brought me back again to the hotel, and then even he became frightened and left me. The sun went down, the gas burners would not light, and so I cowered alone in this vast, deserted, tenantless hotel, till I heard a step, and, following it, afraid to make a noise, but more afraid of missing help or aid, saw you light that candle, and, thank God ! looked upon an English face. I have seen your photograph. You are Charles Errol, son of Ralph Errol, of Melbourne, Australia."

" Yes, and you are——? "

" Lady Sarah Annerley ! "

" Lady Annerley ? here—to-night—in Egypt ? " mutters the young man, astounded; for the name she mentions is one that has often appeared as a leader of rank and fashion in all newspapers that chronicle the doings of the aristocracy.

" Yes," she replies, " Sarah, widow of Viscount Annerley, and daughter of the late Sir Jonas Stevens. I must speak with you for half an hour ; I have come from Europe for that purpose ! "

" Half an hour ! If we stay here half an hour I shall be dead—and you——" He gives a horrified gasp at the thought that comes into his mind, for the more he appreciates the fresh exquisite patrician loveliness of the woman the more he is amazed and dismayed at the frightful nature of the danger that he sees surrounding her. " Don't you know," he continues rapidly, as if time were very precious, " that at this moment we are probably the only English man and woman alive in Alexandria to-night ? That the instant the English admiral opens his guns upon the Egyptian batteries it will be the signal for these Eastern fanatics, who think themselves blessed by Allah in the deaths of unbelievers, to kill with fantastic atrocities every European that is not in safety on board the ships that fled from the harbor to-day ?"

For the time that this man is speaking to this woman is at eleven o'clock upon the night of the 10th of July, 1882, when every European inhabitant of Alexandria who could escape from that Egyptian city had fled for his life as best he might from Moslem revenge and hatred; deserting his home, occupation and worldly goods. All these had taken refuge upon the ships which had sailed away, their decks black with fugitives, leaving the harbor deserted save by the British squadron and a few foreign men-of-war; for the English Admiral had that day given notice to Arabi Pasha, who, half as rebel, half as patriot, controlled the Egyptian armies, that he would the next morning bombard the forts and batteries of Alexandria.

The place where this man and this woman are muttering to each other with pale lips is a deserted parlor upon the first floor of the abandoned Hotel de l'Europe ; the light by which they see each other that of a flickering candle, for the gas works of the town have been deserted and the city is in darkness. Around them, as if to emphasize their loneliness and desolation, are articles of dress and open trunks, and furniture littered with robes, bric-à-brac, and even jewelry ; showing the haste with which their European owners have fled for life and liberty from this Eastern political sirocco of destruction and death.

"Why did you not go with the rest in the steamers ?" Errol continues hurriedly.

"I have been here but three days. They said every Englishman must come down from Cairo to escape. I expected you each hour."

"And I—that cursed dragoman !—why could he have kept me ?—what object ?" cries the young man striking his forehead. " A week ago I sent him into Cairo from Memphis and he said, ' Everything quiet,' so I took my time."

"I thought you would surely be here this morning."

"And so I would, but our train was stopped by the black troops that scoundrel Arabi has in reserve at Kafr-el-Dawar. I had to tramp it in, seventeen hot and dusty miles. I should never have found my way here but for little Osman, who knows every by-path in Egypt. How that puny Armenian beggar stuck to my long steps to-day is a mystery. However, I've hung on to these and they may help us." With this the young man resumes the inspection of his arms that Lady Annerley has interrupted, carefully testing the lock of a Remington sporting rifle that is covered with the dust of his long tramp.

"But I must tell you," says the woman, laying her hand upon his arm with a curious pathetic intensity, "I must tell you !" and would go on but he interrupts her by :

"My Remington seems to be dirty, give me a piece of rag !—your handkerchief, anything—tear a piece from that silk skirt; the owner 'll never miss it !"

And Lady Annerley obeying him, he continues: "Hold the candle up, please, so I can get a better look at the lock ; this thing may save you as well as me."

As she does so she begins again: "This information I came from Europe to tell you concerns your father——"

But the click of the breech-loader interrupts her as the young man tests it and he remarks : "My father can wait, his life's not in danger ; yours is—" and then *very* suddenly : "Blow out that candle !"

"Why ?"

She gets no answer to this and gives a little suppressed shriek, for Errol has blown it out himself.

"Why did you do that ?" she asks faintly.

For answer the young man points out of one of the windows. Lady Annerley has been so engrossed with what she has to tell that she has not heard the peculiar cries of a Moslem populace, the clank of arms, and the tramp of marching men that comes in at the window, growing louder and louder each second. She goes cautiously to the opening and looking out sees the street Mohammed Ali, that grand artery of Alexandria, full of commotion, noise and action. A regiment of Soudanese Arabs, followed by one of the black troops of Arabi Pasha, are tramping down the avenue to reinforce the batteries and forts of Ras-el-Tin. The blackness of Egyptian night that crushes the town with darkness compels the leading files of each company to carry torches, the flames from which illuminate and light up in vivid but ghastly brightness the swarthy faces, Eastern features and flashing eyes of these barbarians, making them look more like devils than men ; and as they pass with slashing gait and hideous cries and Ethiopian jabber, the light of battle in their eyes and lust of blood in their hearts, this delicate English lady, who has never in her gentle life seen even a blow in anger, shudders as she looks on them and mutters, " Heaven help me ! " and, for the first time, her peril comes home to her.

Errol, who has stolen to her side, whispers : " A light would attract their attention—now they think the Frankish hotel deserted. Better darkness than those devils ! " and draws her from the window. He can feel her shiver, and asks with some concern : " You have not caught the fever ? "

" No, I think not."

" But you shivered—you are not so frightened as all that ? "

" No."

" You can't be cold this burning night ? "

But she, sinking into a chair, does not answer him ; for it is the first time Lady Annerley has felt the touch of Charley Errol's hand, and it has given her a sensation that is neither fear, nor cold, nor even that of an Egyptian fever ; but something she cannot describe, nor define, nor liken to anything else she has ever experienced before : for Lady Annerley though a widow has never as yet loved any man.

While she is silent, the young man is thinking how to save her. Before she came to him he had intended, aided by the darkness, to make his way by stealth if possible, or fighting if necessary, to the shore. Then, if unable to find a boat, to swim off to one of the English gunboats in the harbor ; for when a boy living in semi-tropical Australia he had become swimmer enough to make such an attempt not only a feasible but an easy performance. Now he is conscious that any such plan is only practicable by abandoning this woman, who can at this moment look for her protection to no other aid than his. To desert her never even enters his honest, brave Anglo-Saxon head, therefore he is racking his brain for some other scheme that promises safety to her as well as to him.

" Of what are you thinking ? " says Lady Annerley, breaking the silence that has become all the more noticeable, the noise of the passing troops and accompanying rabble having died away in the distance.

He is too generous to tell her how she has affected his chance of safety, and replies simply: "Of a way to give us both a chance of life!" The next instant he whispers "Hush!" Then she hears the click of his revolver as he cocks it and a coming feline footstep in the gloom.

"Halt or I fire!" says the Englishman.

"It is only I, Sahib. Is the Frankish gentleman frightened?" murmurs a soft musical Eastern voice with a slight Armenian accent.

"Oh! it's you, Osman! What made you so long? Have you found anything downstairs to eat?"

"None, Sahib, the Frankish proprietor has locked up his cellars and kitchens, and run off to the ships; but there is a *café* a few hundred yards away, kept by a Levantine who loves his property too well to desert it by anything but death—we might find something there!"

"All right, we must get there somehow. I haven't had a bite since I left Cairo last night."

"I have a bottle of wine and some crackers in my room; the proprietor sent them to me before he left," suddenly says Lady Annerley.

"By George, that's awfully jolly!" exclaims Errol. With a little wine, I don't care of what brand or vintage, and a bite of anything I'm a new man." Then he suddenly pauses and says: "Forgive the selfishness of hunger, but you must need the things yourself, Lady Annerley!"

"Not at all," she replies. "Martin and I ate all we wanted two hours ago!"

"Martin?"

"Yes, my maid. She remained with me; but is now cowering in my room. The lonely darkness has frightened her. I don't need anything so much as your strength and protection, Mr. Errol. I'll get the wine and eatables in a second, my room is only two doors away," and before he can stop her Lady Annerley hurries off, leaving Errol and his Armenian dragoman together.

"The Sahib has a lady in his care?"

"Two, apparently!"

"That is bad; to-night is a very bad time to be troubled with women."

"Nevertheless I shall not desert them. Osman, in the two months I have had you for my dragoman knocking about Egypt, your ingenuity has got me out of a good many difficulties ; help me to get these women on a ship to-night, and I'll make it the best paid job you ever had."

"Impossible, Sahib! The boats in the harbor are all guarded by order of Arabi Pasha. All the Franks have gone away on the ships dreading the vengeance of our populace. A good many Egyptians have fled from their homes fearing the cannons of the English. To-morrow will be a great day in Alexandria!" This last is said with a cat-like glitter and sparkle in his restless Eastern eyes; but the room is dark and Errol does not notice it, as these remarks of Osman have given him an idea that may lead to safety.

"A grand day in Alexandria!" repeats the dragoman, as if in meditation, for there is no greater scoundrel in this world nor the next than this same Osman Ali, half Arab, half Armenian, and whole rogue, called by his tribe *Backsheesh* Osman, *Anglicè* "Begging Osman," and he has some rather curious ideas as to what his occupation will be upon the morrow in Alexandria.

The next instant Errol interrupts his meditation saying : "You tell me a number of Mohammedans have left their homes for fear of the English guns?"

"Yes, Sahib!" returns Osman, who in his various wanderings has been in India and addresses his employer in Indian fashion. "They will not return to their houses till after the fight is over; they are in the country hiding."

"Can you not get one of these deserted Moslem houses for me and these women? In the home of a believer the rabble would never seek for European refugees."

"Ah, yes, they would not search for you there unless some one told them! What a mind the Sahib has! But to find a deserted Moorish house this dark night—it will be very difficult and expensive."

"You know every nook and everything else about Alexandria, Osman. Get me the home of a follower of Allah. We'll risk the English guns, but not Arab massacre. Set about it at once!"

"The night is dark. It is dangerous to tread the streets."

" Do it ! "

" Yes, Sahib, to-morrow morning."

" Now ! At once !." -

" It will be so expensive ! "

"Curse the expense ! Don't you see these ladies' safety depends upon it ?   Do as I tell you ! " and Errol's voice has a ring in it that stops any reply from Osman Ali, whose white teeth as he smiles glitter in the darkness.

" Can't you light the candle, Mr. Errol ? Those awful soldiers must be far away, and I cannot see to come to you with the refreshments," floats to them from the door in Lady Annerley's musical voice.

Osman goes quickly to the windows, pulls their draperies over them, and says : " The light will not betray us now ; " then, as Errol strikes a match and the candle illuminates the room, gives a little start and suppressed cry as Lady Annerley comes out of the darkness ; for this delicate, fragile Moslem imp is very susceptible to female loveliness, and for half a moment imagines that he sees a genuine houri stolen from Paradise.

For though English, Sarah Annerley to-night is an Eastern picture.   The heat of Egypt in mid-summer compels a tropical lightness of costume, and her dress, though black, is fragile in texture, and sweeps and clings to her perfect figure, outlining and developing each charm of movement or pose.   In it she looks like a statue of jet, save where the transparent tissue of her gown makes it ivory by revealing the whiteness of her gleaming arms and graceful neck, which supports a face of delicate, refined, aristocratic, womanly beauty ; its haughtiness relieved by a trace of passion, its passion redeemed by a brow of intellect.   All this is made charming, radiant, and vivid by a pair of grand dark eyes through which the soul says two things : " I shall love but once, for I shall love forever."

Her gaze is fixed on Errol and her beauty seems to come more strongly home to him than in the few excited minutes in which he has seen her before.   Both the Englishman and the Armenian gaze in silence at Lady Annerley as she comes toward them, followed by her maid, a Scotch girl, who crouches along in a distracted

sort of way bearing a bottle of Rhine wine and a can of
English biscuits. "Martin," says her mistress suddenly,
as the girl with a slight shriek stumbles over some of the
robes that litter the room, "there is no danger. These
gentlemen are here to take care of us. Pass them the
wine!" but the next instant, apparently changing her
mind, she assists Errol herself, leaving her maid to
do a like office for Mr. Osman, who smacks his thin
lips over the drink forbidden by Allah, and munches
Frankish crackers with a very good appetite, for he as
well as his master has had nothing to eat since the evening before when they left Cairo.

This is perfectly apparent in Errol's case, as that stalwart young Englishman finishes up the biscuits and
pours the last drop of wine down his throat in less than
five minutes after he gets his hands on them.

Lady Annerley stands silently looking at him as he
sits lolling back over a sofa, his rifle lying across his
knees. His legs and feet in their stout walking-boots and
knickerbockers are thrown lazily over a silken gown that
an Italian lady had tossed aside as she fled for safety
the evening before. His long, athletic arms in shirt
sleeves, rolled up above the elbows, display his big
white muscles, as he eats and drinks in a manner that
shows that it is only starvation makes him forget the
great fatigue and exertions of the day.

He has thrown aside his coat, the night being hot ;
and apparently eats and thinks at the same time. The
instant he has finished the first, he says quickly:
"Osman, go out and get two donkeys for Lady Annerley
and her maid to ride. We must leave this hotel at
once.!"

"Donkeys will cost a great deal of money to-night,"
returns the dragoman.

"All right! Buy the cursed donkeys! Here's five
hundred francs," and the young man crosses to his coat
that lies over one of the chairs in the room, looks in one
of its pockets, starts as if astonished ; then hurriedly
rummages in every one of them, apparently startled, and
after a quick search of his trousers and vest, and a hurried look about the floor, says in a broken, horrified
voice: "My pocket-book's stolen! My God, to be alone
in this city to-night without money !"

"I have plenty of that," cries Lady Annerley. "I've a thousand pounds in Bank of England notes, and a few thousand francs in French gold and Egyptian silver in my room, besides my diamonds," and she points to her ears where a couple of brilliants of large size and first water sparkle, and give out fire even in the dim light of the flickering candle. At the mention of this considerable sum of money a grim smile crosses Osman's features, but he says nothing, only gazes upon the diamonds intently.

The English lady has turned to go to her room, but the Australian gentleman stops her, saying hurriedly and somewhat doggedly: "I would rather not borrow your money."

"But you must! You can't get it from any one else. The consuls have gone. The banks are closed and their treasure taken away on board ship. Mine was the last check paid by the Anglo-Egyptian bank before it closed its doors; besides this money is partly for my use, the donkeys were intended for my service."

"Still I'd rather not."

"But /ou shall!" says Lady Annerley. "I demand it. Take it to save us both!"

This discussion is interrupted by Osman, who comes to the side of Errol and suggests : "Why not use your first plan? Make your way to the harbor and swim to the English war ships——"

"*And leave these ladies?*"

"These ladies shall be my care. I can hide them better without you than with you. They shall be safe, I, Osman Ali, swear it by the beard of Mahomet!"

"Impossible! I were not a man if I deserted women to-night!"

"You had a way to save yourself and gave it up for me, a stranger to you? Mr. Errol, make use of it at once! I am not afraid. I can take care of myself, this man has sworn to save——"

She doesn't finish the sentence, for as she turns to look on the man in whose honor she is about to trust, he cannot for an instant control his features, and a grin of such fantastic joy flits across his Oriental face that the words die out on Lady Annerley's lips, a sickly terror giving place to any faith in the promises of Osman Ali.

This is emphasized by her maid who gasps : "Oh, my lady, don't let him leave us alone with the heathen!"

"We are wasting very precious time. Under no circumstances could I leave English women alone to-night ; not if I knew my life depended on it ; " and Errol as he says this tosses back from his forehead the yellow Saxon locks that make his blue eyes seem so handsome to Sarah Annerley. Then he goes on sternly : "This discussion must stop at once ! To end it I will borrow your money and if anything happens to me, my father, who is one of the richest men in Australia, will repay you ! "

" Your father is rich—and *happy ?* " gasps Lady Annerley.

" Certainly! Both ! He's one of the jolliest chaps in the world ! Why not ? "

" I—I did not know—I never saw him—I will get you the money—and am but too glad that it may be of use to —to us ! " With this Lady Sarah leaves the room in a dazed sort of manner, as if she almost doubted Charley Errol's words.

The maid runs out after her, and as she searches for her purse Lady Annerley hears her abigail whisper in her ear : " Oh, my lady, don't—don't trust that Egyptian. His smile makes me sick."

" Don't be afraid, Martin ! " says her mistress sharply as she puts the money in her pocket, " I have perfect confidence in Mr. Errol ! "

" So have I, marm ! " returns the abigail. " He's that handsome that I could trust him with my life, couldn't you, my lady ? "

" Perhaps ! " mutters Lady Annerley and gives a curious little sigh.

This is interrupted by Errol who knocks on her door, saying : " Excuse me, can I come in ? Osman tells me it is better that you both arrange your toilets so as to look like Egyptian women in the street."

" Come in at once ! Martin, open the door ! " says Lady Annerley, but here gives an exclamation of surprise and her maid a shriek of fear ; for as the abigail does her bidding a tall figure draped in a long dark Egyptian cloak, his feet shod in yellow Turkish slippers and his head covered and concealed by a bright Arab turban, strides into the apartment carrying the lighted candle in his hand.

" Don't be afraid, Lady Annerley," laughs Errol, with an attempt at mirth, " I've gone into the Eastern costume also; Osman said it was safest and I picked up this rig about the hotel.   George ! isn't it horribly lonely ? Not a soul but us in this great empty caravansary."   And the laugh dies away as the young man thinks of the task he has set himself to do this night.

" Here is the money ! " remarks his charge, giving him her purse.

" A couple of thousand francs 'll be sufficient ; keep the rest, Lady Sarah," says Mr. Errol, helping himself and returning the balance.   " My arms and cartridges are weight enough for me after the tramp of to-day. Now !" and his voice becomes that of authority, for Charles Errol has generally been a leader in most of the affairs of his life, from stroke of the Oxford crew to bossing the sheep-herders upon his father's great ranges in Australia.   " If I am to command I must have obedience ; upon it depends our lives !   This is no masquerade for fun ! "   For the maid having regained her confidence by faith in an Englishman's presence and promise has giggled a little at the sight she makes muffled up to the eyes in a long wrap, which gives that hideous appearance peculiar to Eastern women on the streets.

" I am perfectly aware of that," says Lady Annerley, arranging the draperies she has thrown around her and veiling her face closely. " Martin, be quiet ! "   This last is said very sharply, for the young Scotch girl is apparently still amused at the appearance she makes.

" All right," says Errol.   " I want you both to pin a little piece of bright ribbon on your arms, for if we get mixed up in a crowd in the streets I must be able to recognize you at a glance, for neither of you must say a single word—an English exclamation might destroy us.   Now I'll go off and see if Osman has got the donkeys.   He told me he had money enough in his pocket for that." With this he gets to the door but suddenly returns, and laying his revolver beside Lady Annerley, says : " While I'm away you may feel safer with that to your hand ; it is in perfect order and loaded.   I shall hardly be gone more than a minute, however, and you'd better utilize the time by putting on a good stout pair of boots."

"Boots!" echoes his fair charge, blushing slightly and stealing a glance at a small foot that she suddenly withdraws from view. "Why, my feet are——"

"Are in slippers, and we may have some hard walking to do." With this Errol gets to the door and then suddenly commands, "Both of you put on boots!" and is gone.

"Isn't that a man?" mutters Martin in admiration.

"Stop talking and put on my boots," says her mistress. "Let this man who risks his life for us see that we obey him."

"Yes, my lady," and the maid kneels down to do her duty that is interrupted by a shudder and a shiver every time her eye catches sight of the loaded revolver. For Martin's is a mind to which the physical only appeals, and a revolver is a great physical fact to Martin's intellect this night. She is kept at her labor with such vigor by her mistress that when Errol returns a minute or two after, Lady Annerley and her maid are both bundled up to the eyes, and as like Eastern women as English women can be. As they are about to leave, the young man suddenly says to his charge: "I can give you a minute or so more ; most of the crowd have followed the troops away from the door. Put a change of linen for yourself and maid and any articles of personal value to yourself in a small valise."

"And have you carry it, burdened with arms as you are ? No, I can get along without them !"

"This affair may last for days, perhaps weeks; you must take them. Besides, if you do not, everything you value will be lost to you, for I expect this hotel will soon be nothing but ruins."

"Then Martin must carry it."

"All right, as I must have my arms free in case of accident ; please do as I tell you!" whispers Errol.

"How thoughtful you are of me," returns Lady Annerley, musingly, and then she calls her maid, and the two together select, by the light of the dying candle that is now flickering its life out down in its socket, some articles for their immediate wants, and a few jewels and

2

souvenirs that Lady Annerley values either for their association or intrinsic worth.

While the women do this, Charley Errol and Mr. Osman Ali outside in the deserted hall converse in hurried
whispers as to the best plan for safety after leaving the
hotel.

"I am ready to go now," says Lady Annerley, coming
to the door and looking with a shudder into the gloom
of the great corridors.

"In a second," returns Errol, feeling that his revolver
is ready to his hand.

"Oh ! Don't stay any longer. Don't! *Don't !*" This
last is a cry of agonized terror from Martin, for the candle has suddenly with a great flicker gone out, making
the place more dark and the lonely stillness more impres-
sive than before.

"Come !" says Errol, taking Lady Annerley by the
hand. "Osman, stop that girl's mouth and follow me ! "
and would go toward the grand staircase and entrance to
the hotel, but the dragoman stops him by "That way is
death. There is a crowd of Arabs at the door, I have
seen them. Follow *me*, Sahib ! "

With this he leads Martin, trembling and shuddering,
along the great empty corridor, and pursued by Errol,
who gropes his way after the slight noise Osman makes,
feeling for obstacles in the darkness with one hand and
half-leading, half-supporting this woman he is striving to
guide to safety with the other. After a moment they
turn from the great hallway of the hotel and take to the
by-ways and small passages, occasionally stumbling over
trunks, furniture and deserted baggage ; accidents that
produce faint shudders and shrieks from the maid-servant and low blasphemies from Osman, who claps his hand
over her mouth and curses her and her parents and her
tomb that will be and her offspring who may be, in all the
tongues and dialects of the East ; for this faithful dragoman is now very anxious to save his charge from the
fury of the Moslem rabble he has heard ascending the
grand stairway of the hotel in search of Christian loot
and plunder. All this time Errol says no word, but
Lady Annerley can feel that he saves her from every
accidental collision or bruise even to his own hurt, and
whispers : "You are more needed to-night than I am ;

please think of yourself a little, not of me all the time."

And so they stagger along blind passages and cross passages, opening wrong doors and groping into wrong corners and running against, as Errol thinks to himself, "everything in the hotel," until at last they come to a little stairway leading to a small unused side door known to Osman, whose calling makes him familiar with the hotel, and cowering silently down the steps they open the door, and peering cautiously about, steal out with bruised limbs and torn garments into the open air and streets of Alexandria.

CHAPTER II.

THROUGH THE STREETS OF ALEXANDRIA.

THERE are not many people upon the Place Mohammed Ali. The great square seems deserted, though the trees still rustle as dreamily and the fountains play as cheerily as when, a few days ago, its grounds were made merry by the cries of children and the hum of the busy life of a great city. From this heart of the Frankish quarters all Europeans have fled, and the Mohammedan population are chiefly gathered upon the shore of the harbor and about the fortifications, which are busy with the marching of troops, the transportation of ammunition, and the preparations for the morrow's battle with the enemies of the faith of Allah. This crowd has been augmented by a number of tribes of Bedouins, who, scenting combat, blood and pillage, have hurried from the desert into this city to add to the carnage, massacre and spoliation with which it is to be scourged.

Save the hum of preparation from the batteries, the town is generally silent and fearfully dark, even the harbor lights and beacons for the safety of mariners having been extinguished by order of Arabi Pasha. All this impresses itself upon Errol, as he stands for a moment regaining his breath and trying to see in what way to move.

Suddenly Lady Annerley crouches against him, the maid-servant gives a terrified shudder, and almost faints into Osman's arms, whose teeth now chatter too much for execration ; while Errol mutters to himself, "My Heaven! what horror is this ?"

For from the harbor rings out in their ears a shriek of such barbaric terror and abject Oriental dismay that it seems to bear carnage and death in every individual cry. Looking out onto the harbor Errol sees the great white electric search light from an English man-of-war thrown upon a thousand or so of these sons of the desert, who, having never encountered modern science before, think it some new and fearful engine of war, and flee from it with that augmented terror and dismay that ignorance always carries with it.

Unnatural as a laugh is at such a moment the Australian bursts into a hearty guffaw, and pointing out the matter to Osman, says, with Anglo-Saxon bluntness : " If your fellows run away from the light to-night, by George! how they will skip from the guns to-morrow ! "

This is unwise at this moment, for it makes Osman hate him personally, not generally. He had only hated him as an Englishman before, now he hates him as an individual. The only thing about an Englishman an Oriental does not hate is his money ; though their English masters somehow never seem to believe this until they have carelessly let themselves and their women and children be massacred by their Eastern slaves and brothers ; as many graves in Africa, China and India, and plentiful mourning and tears in English country homes and London town houses have so often shown.

The Oriental gives a little snarl and shakes the Scotch woman rather roughly to her feet. Then remembering himself, he says : " Sahib, the donkeys are round the corner in the little street. Come quickly."

They hurriedly follow him and find he has told the truth. Two little Egyptian vicious brutes with women's saddles are waiting for them. Upon one Osman almost tosses Martin, while Errol carefully and perhaps tenderly places Lady Annerley upon the back of the other animal. Then, Osman leading the way alongside of the maid and Errol walking at her mistress' bridle, they plunge into the dark labyrinth of back streets that lead to the northward

between the two great thoroughfares of the Arab quarter
of the town, the streets Ras-et-Tin and Mosque Ibrahim, making. for the *Café* Sphinx, kept by a Levantine
Greek named Constantine Niccovie, a chum, companion,
and bird of the same feather as Osman.

These streets are so deserted that Lady Annerley, who
has not spoken since she left the hotel, thinks she may
venture to say a word, and looking at the young Australian very kindly whispers : " A curious introduction this
one of ours has been."

" Very ! " returns Errol, " and now you will perhaps
have time to tell me that for which you risked your life
to remain in Alexandria—My heavens ! you are fainting,
this strain has been too great ! " and his arm quickly supports her, for she is reeling and trembling and would fall
from her saddle but for his assistance ; for the woman is
thinking to herself, " How this man will hate me when I
tell him, as I must some day.—But not now—*not to-night!*
No man on earth· would be noble enough to save me
after I told him THAT ! "

As Osman plods along beside the Scotch girl he is meditating in great glee. He has saved from general pillage the English lady's money and diamonds for his own
individual loot. They shall be all his and more ; for this
same Armenian has done a little sly dealing in human
flesh before in his time ; and he thinks that after the battle
Egypt will. once more be the Egypt of old. He knows
of a great pasha, who has a harem far away on the Nubian hills high up the great river, who has given many
purses before for Frankish women, and he slyly looks at
the Scotch girl beside him and sizes up hèr good points
and values her as an Arabian horse-dealer does his beasts.
Then he gives a great start and his eyes open wide
with greed of gain as he thinks of the beautiful English
lady, who rides behind him, in a way that would make her
shudder and writhe even more bitterly than her thoughts
are making her do now as *Backsheesh* Osman dances
along the street with a cat-like step and chirps to his donkey : " *Yal-lah! yal-lah!* " in his merry Egyptian way,
then mutters to himself, as if intoxicated with some un-·
canny joy : " IT WILL BE A GRAND DAY IN ALEXANDRIA
TO-MORROW ! "

Thus they grope their way along the close. narrow

Eastern alleys, whose Arab houses sometimes nearly
meet overhead and which would be dark at mid-day, but
are now so black that the party stumble over half-starved
Pariah dogs, who snap and snarl at them for driving them
from the scanty subsistence for which they are wallowing
and nosing in the garbage and filth such as only the back
streets of an Egyptian town can have, the uncleanliness
of which fills the nostrils with fetid odors and the air with
pestilence.   Till at length, turning into a wider street,
after passing a few *fellaheen* beggars to whom Osman
gives kicks instead of *paras*, and an Arab boy who is
lamenting some loss with the loud, exaggerated execrations peculiar to the fantastic rabble of the Orient, but
who stifles his curses and cries and pricks up his ears at
the sight of the two donkeys who give each a little
whinny, they find themselves at the *Café* Sphinx.

Though they think themselves unobserved and unnoticed, the Arab urchin ever since he saw the donkeys
has followed them stealthily in the shadow ; and to him is
due a woful surprise for the whole party, even including
the Arab boy himself.

The *Café* Sphinx fronts upon the street of the Mosque
Ibrahim.   It has an appearance of being half-European,
half-Turkish, and is in a house of Eastern construction
which contains at the back a little court-yard.   Into this
yard Osman leads the party, bidding Lady Annerley and
her maid to remain seated upon the donkeys, as their stay
will be very short.   Thinking them perfectly safe in their
seclusion, Errol follows Osman into the *café*, for it is
absolutely necessary for him to obtain a supply of provisions sufficient to victual the Moorish house that Osman
has assured him can be obtained for their temporary
seclusion during the bombardment, and any riot or bloodshed to which it may give rise.

So, after going through a little dark doorway, in the
wall, the Australian finds himself in a small room
made dingy by dirt and age, and in the presence of his
dragoman and the Greek Levantine who is the proprietor
of the place.   Further on beyond them he can see à larger
apartment, the *café* proper, which is arranged on one side
for Eastern customers with divans, mats and rugs, upon
which the guests may loll in Turkish fashion.   On the
other side there are a lot of tables with common deal

chairs about them similar to those seen in third-rate beer
halls in European cities. This portion of the room is
apparently intended for Christian customers. The whole
place is illuminated by a couple of oil lamps that are
now turned low ; they are probably temporary substitutes
for the gas brackets which line the sides of the room,
but are useless upon this night. Over this dingy scene
hangs the odor of stale beer, bad wine, and worse tobacco. It is now, however, Errol is happy to see, empty ;
its European patrons having fled the town, and its
Egyptian customers having gathered upon the docks and
quays of the harbor to see what the infidel war ships are
doing.

The owner of the establishment has a semi-European,
semi-Oriental appearance like his *café*. His trousers are
greasy and Egyptian, his coat French and buttonless, he
wears ragged English side whiskers, and a shabby Turkish turban about his round head that contains two flashing dark, treacherous eyes ; a large hooked nose and ʃ
pair of very red lips, that are in strong contrast to hi
pale cheeks and white teeth. His *salam* is dignified, his
gestures effusive and vivacious ; when in repose he is
Turkish, when in action, Frenchy.

As the Australian enters, Mr. Osman and Mr. Constantine Niccovie are holding deep converse together in some
unknown dialect, with great elevating of the eyebrows and
much gesticulation of the hands and arms. On seeing
him Constantine stops suddenly, and says effusively in
very imperfect but intelligible English :

" The Sheik Errol, I think you am ? "

" That is my name," replies the young man.

" My house and all my family are yours—all yours! "
returns the Levantine with a solemn *salam* to which Errol
replies with English brusqueness by asking Osman if he
has told the man what they want.

" Certainly—all, Sahib," is the dragoman's answer.

" Osman Ali, whose breath is sweet with truth, is my
instigator, and says you are the defender of women. I
would give my life for women also, were it so decreed.
You wish provisions ? You shall have them ! But food is
high. This is a time of scarceness. We are going to
have a famine, still I shall charge you nothing ! *nothing !*
NOTHING ! ! " This last is almost a shriek as Constantine

has become French and effusive and he seizes Errol's hand
crying : " Behold my prices! " and then runs through the
list of articles needed, asking for them something over ten
times their value.

Errol, who has no time to haggle or barter, pulls his
hand out of the Levantine's greasy clutch and says simply : " Bring them at once ! "

At this quick bargain Constantine goes for the articles
mentioned, cursing himself for not having demanded
more, while the Australian turns to his dragoman and
says : " Have you succeeded in getting a Moslem house
for my purpose ? "

" Yes, Sahib. Allah has been good to us. Abdallah
Yusef, the Moor, fearing the Frankish cannon, has fled
with his harem, family and slaves to his villa at Rosetta.
Constantine Niccovie who has a kind heart has the key
in his possession. Abdallah's *bowab*, his house-porter,
is now drunk with wine and fear and hiding in the cellar
below us. Constantine will lease unto us the home of
Abdallah, who is respected by all true believers and whose
house is safe from their molestation, for five thousand
francs."

" Five thousand francs for a few days ? It is an awfully
steep price," mutters Errol.

" So Constantine himself says, but his conscience
hurts him at leasing the home of another man. The
money will be paid to Abdallah, every *para* of it, and Abdallah might curse him if the price was not sufficient.
But I'll see the Levantine and ask him to reduce his
terms." With this Osman disappears in pursuit of Niccovie, chuckling to himself : " What matters it how much
these English pay *now?* To-morrow we will have their
all and more too ! " for the dragoman has got slave-
dealing running in his head again.

Errol turns and opening the door looks at his charges.
The court-yard is silent, and Lady Annerley and her maid
are resting quietly in their saddles. He steps out to the
English lady, and knowing how anxious she must be,
whispers to her : " Everything is going finely. We
have the provisions we need and I shall soon get a place
of undoubted safety for us all, but these Eastern beasts
are extortionate. I fear I must borrow from you
again."

" Borrow from *me* ? Mr. Errol, are you not lending to me perhaps your life ? Please keep all for me ; spend it all if you please, and then I still am the debtor," and she slips her purse into his hand.

" Thank you for your confidence, Lady Annerley," says the young man and turns back to the house again, speaking a word of encouragement on his way to Martin who sits her donkey in a stony kind of paralyzed fear.

He is met at the door by Osman, who says with a deprecating shrug of his shoulders : " It is no use; Niccovie is a man of honor and he declares his conscience would smite him if he did Abdallah the wrong to abate a franc of the five thousand. Take his offer. Think of the women ! "

" All right. I've no time to haggle. Give him his money," and Errol hands over the sum to the drago-man, but concludes rather suspiciously: " How the deuce does Niccovie, who you say is a Levantine, dare to stay openly in Alexandria at such a time ? "

" Oh—ah—Constantine Niccovie is a man of business and would risk his life to do a good turn in trade, he is so brave!" answers Osman, going with the cash in pursuit of Niccovie, who is still busied below getting out the supplies for which they have bargained. He does not however tell the Australian that the Greek Levantine is a Renegado who has but lately taken himself to the faith of Mohammed, and is as safe as any full-born Moslem who is crying to Allah and cursing the Franks this night in Alexandria.

A few moments after both the Armenian and the Levantine come out of the cellar with the supplies, which Errol examines and finds fairly good, and enough to provision the party for a week.

" How the deuce are we to carry all this ?" he asks, and is rather grateful to Osman for the suggestion that the donkeys are strong and sturdy.

" I paid a grand price for those beasts, Sahib," says the dragoman proudly, and mentions a sum that makes Errol open his eyes.

However, he merely remarks, "I'll settle for them when we get to Abdallah's house," and goes about arranging several little details with Constantine, the Greek,

an occupation which is interrupted very suddenly and
unexpectedly by a piercing shriek from Martin, outside
in the court-yard, and Lady Annerley's hurrying into
the room in a dazed kind of way and whispering to him :
"There is something the matter about those donkeys.
Two men and a boy have just dragged my maid off
hers, and—"

But she says no more, for here the door is opened
suddenly and two Nubian policeman appear, one of them
dragging in Martin by the arm, who says : " Don't !
don't ! " in a pathetic, pleading tone, and holds her
hand up to her head as if she expected the man to
cuff her ears.   They are followed by the Arab boy, who,
though his eyes are still red with the tears of his late
lamentations, gives a grin of joy, points to Osman and
cries : " Behold ! There is the jackal who in the darkness stole from me the bread of life, the two prettiest,
strongest, and fleetest donkeys in Alexandria. May the
curse of Allah blight his eyes, and the dogs of the desert
defile the tomb of his father ! "

For a moment, under this invective, the dragoman
starts and drops his eyes, but after exchanging a glance
with Niccovie his coolness comes back to him, and looking
up and seeing that his accuser is but a boy, he turns upon
him, and not to be outdone in invective fires at him,
embellished with a quantity of threatening gestures :
" Thy tongue be cut out ! Thy mother was a liar, and
thy father likewise ! These beasts I bought in the market to-day, paying for them in the gold of this Frankish
sheik of whom I am his dragoman! "

At this the two policemen look at each other and
then at the two women and Errol, and one says fiercely :
" These people are here for no good ! They are our
enemies ! "

And the other replies : " Let us drag them all to prison !
To-morrow these unbelieving dogs shall have Eastern
justice! "

However, their cause is in Mr. Osman Ali's hands, and
he being truly anxious to save his prey for himself, it is
not likely to be lost for want of any of the delicate diplomacy of the East. On hearing these words, the dragoman instantly steps forward and producing a number of
gold twenty-franc pieces, says : " This scamp's words are

as deceitful as the sands of the desert! The donkeys are mine by the will of Allah!"

"They are not yours, you spawn of liars!" cries the boy. "They belong to me, by Allah! They know their names and answer to my voice. One is called *Boozch*, because he is frisky like strong liquor, and the other is named *Doorrah*, because he cries like a parrot." With this the boy calls out loudly: "*Boozeh!*" "*Doorrah!*" and the beasts put their heads in the door, and whinny and bray in apparent recognition.

This, however, is all thrown away upon the Nubian policemen, whose eyes have never lost sight of the money ever since Osman has produced the gold.

These coins he chinks about in his hand and goes on quietly, as he feels pretty sure of his ground now: "That the boy lies is proved by *this*! Is it likely that I, Osman Ali, a man of distinction and wealth—" here the Armenian drops the money slowly from one hand to the other, every chink of the coins being responded to by a greedy, grasping, dog-and-the-bone glance in the eyes of the two guardians of the law.

"Don't look at his gold!" shrieks the Arab *gamin* in despair.

"Wealth so great," continues Osman unmoved, "that I can give two faithful officers of the law a thousand *piastres* apiece as a mere matter of charity and good will—would I steal a couple of donkeys, the price of which is to me as the dust of the earth?" And saying this he drops the golden shower into the policemen's outstretched hands.

This is backed up and enforced by Constantine effusively uttering, "And you know me also! I am Niccovie, whose house of entertainment has given you many refreshing drinks and will give you many more, please Allah! This man is Osman Ali, a man whose breath smells sweet with truth like the roses of Sophia!"

"Is it likely that I should be a thief?" almost sternly demands the dragoman of the two officers.

"No; *Enfendi*," is their reply.

At this moment Constantine suddenly cries out: "Ah! another proof of innocence! The false accuser flies!" For the Arab boy, seeing the scales of justice weighed down by gold turn against him, has made a sudden bolt for the street.

This unfortunate is now seized by the policemen, and one of them whispers in an undertone to Osman as they return to the court-yard dragging the urchin with them.

Now this affair has hardly been understood by Errol or Lady Annerley, nearly every word of the excited conversation being in Arab dialect; and the dragoman hurriedly explains it by saying that the avaricious little spawn of the streets had demanded increased payment for his donkeys, and he had given a couple of hundred francs to settle the matter, an elucidation that is perfectly consistent with the gestures used and the money paid on the occasion.

Had either of them understood it, the Arab boy would doubtless have fared better, as the argument of Mr. Osman would have scarcely convinced any unprejudiced mind of his innocence. They have little time to think over the matter, however, as the noise from the populace about the harbor becomes greater, and a battery of artillery rattles hurriedly down the street; one of the English gun-boats having produced an excitement by throwing up some rockets as a signal. They hurriedly place the provisions upon the donkeys, and are just setting out when Osman mutters a few words to Errol and darts back into the house where Constantine Niccovie still remains, he neither having come out into the court-yard nor assisted in loading the beasts of burden.

"Oh, why does he keep us here waiting?" whispers Lady Annerley, who has become nervously anxious ever since the policemen have made their appearance. "Why has that man gone back into the house?"

"He said he had forgotten the key to Abdallah's," is Errol's reply.

"The key? Why, I saw it in his hand!" she goes on impulsively, and then suddenly stops, shivers and exclaims: "Oh, heavens! What is that?" For from that corner of the little court-yard which is shrouded in the deepest gloom there comes a sound of stifled suffering, and then a shriek of intense agony such as this delicate English lady has never heard before.

This shriek is echoed by Martin, whose nervous system, never very strong, has now got into a fearful state.

"By George! They are beating somebody!" says Errol.

"Oh! it's that poor little Arab boy!" cries Lady Annerley, slipping out of her saddle. "Oh, Mr. Errol, hurry! Save him! Save him! If you don't I must!" For here another cry of intense anguish, in a young, fresh, childish voice, cuts into the still night air.

Thus adjured, the Australian runs to the far corner of the court-yard, and finds the two policemen, after the manner of Eastern justice, are inflicting a summary *bastinado* upon the feet of the boy who has accused the dragoman; having received a hint from Osman to that effect.

He pulls them away and cries, "Stop!" which they don't understand, and gives them money which they think they do comprehend, for the next instant as Errol turns away their canes are beating with greater vigour upon the upturned soles of the helpless Arab boy, and his cries are more piteous than ever; for cruelty to another is often purchased in the East: mercy, never!

Errol hastily dashes one of the torturers aside, and is about to seize the other when Lady Annerley is between him and the man, and fighting the wretch away with her delicate hands, bends down over the victim of their cruelty, sobbing herself when she sees the little sufferer's anguish.

"Lift him up!" she cries to Errol, and turning to the men: "Don't you touch him again, or I will kill you!" There is something in her spirit that makes the Nubians' eyes droop under her glance, and she turns again to the Australian and begs him to carry the boy into the house; for the child's eyes are closed though he gives out faint gasps and sobs.

"I could not go away from him without seeing how badly he is hurt!" she murmurs. "Please bear him gently."

And Errol doing her bidding, in the dingy room of the dirty *café*, this great English lady, unmindful of the dangers of the night and place, bends over and revives with strengthening wine and kind words and soothing gestures, which do him even greater good, this little victim of man's injustice.

The young man looks on silently a moment, and muttering, " She is braver than I am," steps out to Mr.
Osman, who has been brought into sight by the noise,
and bids him see that the policemen go away at once
and molest the boy no farther.   This the dragoman with
a rather shamed face does at once ; for Osman Ali has
some doubts of how much his master guesses of the truth
of this affair.   .

Meantime Lady Annerley, calling her maid, bandages
with her own handkerchief the bruised feet of the little
boy, who looks at her in an unbelieving kind of way with
eyes that have become perhaps too knowing in his
early immature struggle for existence.   And the tears
fall upon him from the beautiful woman who is bending over and comforting him and saying kinder words
to him than he has ever heard before ; for this Arab
gamin in the streets of Alexandria has picked up a smat-
tering of most languages, English among the rest.

At seeing this unusual sight Mr. Constantine Niccovie
turns away with a shrug of his huge, stalwart shoulders,
for the Levantine is big and bony in stature ; while Osman
looks at Lady Annerley from a distance, a supercilious
sneer floating now and again over his delicate, cunning
features, as he thinks: " This haughty beauty will to-morrow need her tears for herself ; perhaps even she may
some day suffer the same chastisement as this boy she
comforts."   For Mr. Osman Ali in his Eastern experi-
ences has discovered that the *bastinado* is by no means
banished from the harems of the great, and he thinks
that if things go to-morrow as they should do, before
long this beautiful English lady may be one of the veiled
ones in the *zarina* of a great pasha who lives far from
civilization and who is very rich and pays immense prices
for Frankish *odalisks*.   For with all his acuteness this
Armenian scoundrel is not analyst enough to know that
this woman he speculates upon could be and would be a
slave to but one thing upon this earth ; that is her own
passion.   .

Thus criticised and commented upon, Lady Annerley
continues her labor of mercy until the little sufferer's
sobs die away, and he looking at her whispers in her
ear : " *Backsheesh* Osman stole my donkeys ; they beat
me for telling Allah's truth ! " .

"If they are yours they shall be returned to you," answers the lady. "Do you know the house of Abdallah
the Moor?"

The little fellow nods to her in reply, stifling a sigh.

And she, knowing she can trust him, says : "Come for
them to his house to-morrow. To-night we have need of
them!" With this she slips into his hand a lot of gold
and silver change, just as Errol comes to her and says
quietly but decidedly: "My lady, we must wait no
longer."

As she rises from the little boy's side, a single tear that
still lingers in her eye falls upon his upturned face,
which never ceases to watch her until the party, headed
as before by Osman, pass out into the darkness of the
city. Then the donkey boy, feeling not altogether safe
with money in his pocket in the presence of Mr. Constantine Niccovie, hobbles groaning and staggering with
pain into the darkness also ; and finding a sequestered
corner of a dirty but quiet alley, sobs himself to sleep ; a
subdued pathetic smile coming over his pale suffering
face as he mutters after the poetic manner of his people:
"The tears of the beautiful Frankish lady are pearls on
my face."

And Sarah Annerley has, in her five minutes' womanly
kindness for this poor little kick-about ragamuffin of the
streets of Alexandria, done a better stroke of work for
herself than even she dreams of or imagines.

CHAPTER III.

THE FIRST GUN.

TURNING from the *Café* Sphinx, the English party
make their way through the narrowest streets of the
Arab portion of the town, for Osman thinks it best to
avoid the thoroughfares which become more crowded
with people as they near the harbor. The dragoman
leads them in a generally northwestern direction, and,
after dodging across the larger streets of La Douane and
Marina, in a little time they come to the house of Abdallah
the Moor, which is situated on a somewhat broader alley

than those in the neighborhood, and just where the Turkish quarter and the Arab portion of the town meet each
other.   In the darkness Errol can only see that the ex-
terior of the house, which is of moderate proportions, is
Eastern in appearance and design.

Osman unlocks and opens the outer door, which the
Australian notes is by no means strong enough to resist
a violent attack, as its woodwork and lock are old and
its hinges rusty.   Then the Armenian lights a candle,
of which they have procured a stock from Niccovie ; by
its uncertain flicker they grope their way into the small
arched passage, where Errol pauses and says :

"From this time on I am commander of the garrison,
and I'll have the obedience of martial law.   Lock that
door, Osman ! "

This the Armenian does, though if the candle were
brighter they could see that his face has turned pale.

" Now give me that key."

" Had I not better leave it in the lock ? "

" No, my pocket is the place for it ! "

" But we might have to fly from here in a hurry ! "

"Give me that key !   Quick ! " and there is a menace
in Errol's voice that makes the Armenian dragoman
hasten to obey ; for his master has not been altogether
pleased with certain performances of Mr. *Backsheesh*
Osman since they have left the Hotel de l'Europe.

" Now go ahead with the light ! " And Osman obeying,
they all turn to the right and in a step or two emerge
from the passage into a small court-yard, which, after the
style of most Turkish dwellings, has a fountain near its
center, and a small pagoda or summer house in one
corner.

Here Errol tells Lady Annerley and her maid to remain upon their donkeys until he and Osman see if the
house is really deserted.   Together the two make a hasty
examination of the lower floor ; and, finding no one in
the rooms below, he bids Osman show him up the old-
fashioned stair-way to the door of the upper floor, which
is only fastened by an ancient Egyptian wooden lock
which the dragoman soon picks.   Then the two men disappear, and the two women wait for them anxiously,
listening for any sound from above that may indicate
they have intruded upon a Moslem household.

After a few minutes Errol returns and says: "I've looked over the whole establishment. There's nothing living in it but a cat, and she was happy to see us."

And he assists the women off the donkeys, which he leaves to contentedly graze about the court-yard that has a few blades of grass growing up between the flags with which it is paved.

Martin is about to enter the lower floor of the build-ing, but Errol says: "Upstairs, please! I can defend the stair-way in case of attack; besides, the rooms are more snug above, and Osman, who is a useful fellow, is making them as comfortable as possible for you."

Then he assists Lady Annerley up the old-fashioned stairs, for now the first excitement being over she be-comes weak and faint, and ushers her into the Eastern apartments. Here she turns and giving him a little laugh that is rather forced, says: "The first time I was ever immured in an Egyptian harem!"

To which Mr. Osman, who has been making the place look brighter, having kindled a charcoal fire in a brasier and lit enough candles to give a pleasant light, comes forward bowing humbly, and remarks: "The harems of believers are the places for beauty."

Perhaps there is a certain sinister expression in his glance that for the life of him this little fiend cannot conceal, or perhaps some latent impertinence in his smile; but Lady Annerley, who is usually kind to her inferiors, draws herself up haughtily and replies, "I am not accus-tomed to the compliments of servants;" while Errol cries out at him: "Hold your tongue, Osman, and get coffee and something to eat!" Which the Oriental does with a rapidity that is simply wonderful, bring-ing up the provisions that they have brought with them, and levying upon certain stores of dainties he finds left in the house, with an unscrupulous vigor that very greatly disgusts Abdallah the Moor upon his return to his home some weeks afterward. Consequently in a few minutes, during which Errol has arranged the rooms so as to give Lady Annerley and her attendant as much privacy as is consistent with his plans for their safety, Mr. Osman Ali gives a *salam* and announces, "Sahib, Allah has given us plenty." Then the whole four without ceremony, Lady Annerley seated on a divan, and waited

3

on by her maid and Mr. Errol, and the Armenian taking
good care of himself in a corner, do justice to the good
things the dragoman has provided.

Toward the conclusion of this Lady Annerley suddenly says with a smile : " Mr. Errol, I don't object to
cigar smoke."

" A-ah ! Why did you think I wished a weed ? "

This is answered by a little laugh from the lady, who
gives a kind of roguish glance at something the young
man has taken abstractedly from his pocket ; and looking down, Charley Errol finds it is a cigar-case.

" By George ! " he exclaims, " pardon the force of
habit," and is about to replace the article.

" I will pardon the force of habit when you carry the
force of habit to its legitimate end."

" How is that ? "

⊦ " Enjoy your Havana at once ! "

As Errol lights up and puffs the cigar smoke about
him he thinks to himself, in a dreamy way—for he is becoming very sleepy—she looks like a beautiful Eastern
picture, surrounded as she is by the Moorish interior, its
divans, rugs and tessellated walls, with their latticed windows, and Osman squatted in Turkish fashion as a background.

The next instant his eye catches something that makes
him wake up with a start ; he seizes his cigar-case, examines it hurriedly, and says in a very gloomy manner :
" There are only three left."

" Three what ? " suddenly asks Lady Annerley, who is
alarmed at the seriousness of his tone.

" Three cigars ! And this siege may last a week.
I'm in a deuce of a fix," mutters Errol, rather savagely.

" But you can get plenty to-morrow--I mean to-day,"
suggests his questioner, consulting her watch.

" Impossible ! If a shop could be found open, I dare
not take the risk of being followed on returning to this
house with you here."

" I—I am afraid you mean that for a reproach ; that
you feel burdened by the care of me," mutters Lady Annerley, turning away with a little sigh.

" Do I look like one of that kind ? " answers Errol, impulsively turning her toward him. " No ! but I feel my
responsibility too strongly to risk bringing danger upon

you for any selfish want of mine—even a cigar. Don't
you believe me and—trust me?"

"With my whole heart. God bless you!" As she says
these words some unknown impulse or emotion seizes
this woman whom all call haughty, and she tries to take
the young man's hand and kiss it in a contrite, humble,
ashamed sort of way that astounds him.

"Pough!" he cries, trying to make light of his service
though blushing with embarrassment, and perhaps with
pleasure, for Lady Annerley looks even more beautiful
when tender than when cold. "*I* should be the grateful
one. Look what your money has brought us—comfort,
and, I hope, safety." He glances about the apartment.
"Now, let's get settled for the night. Twenty-eight
hours, and hardly a wink since Cairo."

Errol emphasizes this remark with a fearful yawn, sleep
having got the better of etiquette, and makes the necessary arrangements for the disposition of the party until
daylight.

There are four principal rooms upon this floor of the
house. Lady Annerley and her maid are to occupy the
two to the left of the apartment they are now in; he will
sleep at the head of the stairs leading from the court-
yard which enters this one; and Osman Ali shall have
the other and smaller one on the right, an arrangement
which pleases the Armenian though he does not say so;
for connected with his apartment is a small stairway and
little door, opening into the street, which is common to
most Turkish dwellings for the private use of the master
of the house. This opening is concealed by several very
heavy tapestries, but the dragoman, knowing the usual
construction of Eastern mansions, has already discovered
its location and thinks it may be useful to him.

Mr. Osman immediately prevents any rearrangement
of the party by retiring to his room with an Oriental *salam*. Lady Annerley and her maid betake themselves to
the divans and rugs of their apartments, Errol charging her
as she leaves him to be sure and let him know if anything
disturbs her in the night; the lamps are extinguished
save one that dimly illuminates the large room which
Errol occupies; darkness and silence are again upon the
Moorish house.

All are asleep except the great English lady, who has

something on her mind that makes her sigh and moan and writhe as she tosses about upon her luxurious divan, and envy the regular breathing of Martin, who is sleeping the sleep of the just and the lazy. The tension of her brain increases the acuteness of her nerves—hearing, seeing, and all her senses become more powerful and more delicate. So it comes to pass that after an hour or two of excited meditation Lady Annerley feels sure she hears a noise coming from one of the two rooms to the right of hers. She says nothing to Martin, not wishing to alarm her, and passes quietly into the large apartment occupied by Errol. This is silent, but after listening a moment she thinks she hears the noise of a closing door coming from the chamber of the Armenian. To the entrance of this room she passes; but after waiting there some little time hears no noise, thinks it all must be her imagination, and is about to return to her own room, when remembering Errol's injunction, she turns to him to tell him what she has heard, and sees him by the pale light of the Turkish lamp lying across the doorway, his arms ready for service, the rifle under his head, and his revolver grasped in his right hand as he sleeps.

His breathing has the deep regularity of extreme exhaustion, and she hesitates to awake him, thinking the noise she heard is but a creation of her imagination. She will wait and warn him if she hears anything more, and she seats herself at his head and looks at him, thinking what a fine picture the young fellow makes with his six feet of manly beauty ; but here she starts, for he is muttering in his sleep of his home and friends in far-away Australia, and is saying kind things to his dear old father.

At this the tears come into Sarah Annerley's eyes ; she moans to herself : " His father for my father—perhaps now his life to save mine. How shall I tell him now when I like him so much as a—friend ! " And sitting in this meditation, she hardly notes that time passes by ; that the morning light comes in the little Moorish windows, the birds chirp and sing in the court-yard, and the tired Egyptian donkeys' bray and whinny outside as if hinting at breakfast, and all becomes bright and cheerful and sunny, until something breaks the stillness of the scene with one tremendous startling crash, and a con-

cussion that makes the house shake and tremble like
an earthquake, and destroys the sounds of waking life in
happy nature. With a wild cry Martin runs into the
room. There is a howl of agony from the roof to which
the Armenian had gone to say his prayers, looking to
Mecca, Allah and the rising sun ; and Errol, springing
up, cries : " *By George! the first gun in the bombardment
of Alexandria !* "

Osman's cry from the roof attracts Errol. He hastily
ascends and looks out ; then, after a moment, returns
and says : " Lady Annerley, come up—quick ! "

" There is no great danger, I suppose ? "

" No more than down here," and he assists her up the
narrow step-ladder leading to the roof, and as she looks
out over the scene that from their elevation is disclosed
to them, he cries in her ear, for the·thunder of the guns
is now deafening : " Is that not a sight worth the risk of
life to see ? "

" Yes," returns this English lady, who has never seen
war before, "beautiful and grand ! "

And so at this moment it is to Sarah Annerley beautiful and grand ; *the horror of it came to her afterward.*

To her right, slightly receding from a straight line,
but all the time running out toward the sea, is the Cape·
of Ras-el-Tin ; in its foreground the Arsenal, but further
on, it is lined with batteries that end in the great Pharos
Fort, and the lighthouse upon Point Eunostos. Behind
these are the walls, minarets and sloping roofs of the
Khedive's palace and this monarch's prison for female
loveliness gathered from the four corners of the earth
to satiate his passions, called the Harem. Their surrounding gardens of tropical trees, flowers and fruits,
their Oriental architecture give them a graceful Eastern
beauty in keeping with the romantic names of their
location, the gardens being called in the metaphor of
the East " The Abode of Pomegranates," and the prom-
ontory " The Cape of Figs." From almost her feet the
quays and landing places of the town, called " The
Marina," run in a graceful curve far to the left, which
suddenly changes to an almost straight line, then darts
out toward the sea, becoming a series of forts and batteries after it passes the long pier or mole which divides
the inner from the outer harbor. The nearest of these

forts to her is Gabari, then Silese, beyond these Massa-
el-Kanat, and the Meks Fort and batteries; and still
farther out to sea Adjemi and the Marabout fortifications commanding the channel of that name, which is the
largest, deepest and safest entrance to the roadstead of
Alexandria, and scattered all over the picture windmills
—windmills everywhere !

Between these two great lines of fortifications lies
straight before her the inner and outer harbor of the
town. The inner, bereft of shipping save a few Egyptian coasters, Mahmudiyeh Canal and Nile boats, whose
white lateen sails give picturesque romance to the scene,
is quiet, calm and peaceful as an Italian lake ; the outer,
torn up and churned into foam with flying shot and shell,
and covered with the iron-clads of England, their decks
cleared for action, their heavy masts and yards made to
look more powerful and massive by being relieved of all
their light rigging and loftier spars, their tops filled with
men and machine and rapid firing guns, and their great
turrets or black broadsides wreathed in the smoke and
flame of their enormous cannon, is a picture of grand,
awful, annihilating modern war. The town, shore, batteries, Khedive's palace and Harem are picturesque,
Eastern and ancient, and fly the flag of the Crescent of
Allah ; the ships of war are ugly, Western and modern, and fight under the Union Jack of England which
contains the Cross of Christ ; and both are going to do
some very savage, cruel and devilish work beneath these
banners.

There are four of these floating instruments of destruction bombarding the Meks batteries, and though they
are not all in full sight, from their position Errol judges
about the same number are at work upon the batteries of
Ras-el-Tin and the Pharos Fort. Fort Ada, whose guns
can be heard nearly north of them, is entirely out of their
view.

Far down the bay, opposite the Marabout batteries,
can be seen several small gun-boats preparing to make an
attack upon them, and about mid-way from the Meks and
Pharos Forts lies a broad black British iron-clad, very
large, but floating low in the water, having upon her deck
en échelon two great black turrets. Not being at anchor
she is about to fight under headway, and what is techni-

cally called "bow on." All this is perfectly apparent to both Lady Annerley and Charley Errol, that young man having carried with him all through the preceding night with British bulldog tenacity a large field glass such as denotes the traveling Englishman the world over, and which he now brings to bear upon the scene before them, which as yet is unobscured with smoke and is lighted up, illumined and made brilliant by the rising sun of Egypt, hot and blazing to-day as it is far to the south, where it is burning out the lives of travelers upon the deserts.

A little farther out to sea beyond the big iron-clad is a much smaller man-of-war, which appears to be nearly as much in danger as the larger one, though evidently not in action. This produces an exclamation of surprise from Errol, who, after examining her attentively with the glass cries: "Wheugh! Here's Yankee curiosity! Brother Jonathan's risking death to see what's going on!" For the vessel he is looking at flies the American flag, and is there to save life, not to destroy it, though the excitement of her officers has run the ship into the range of the Egyptian batteries, which are now returning rapidly and regularly in one continuous echoing roar the fire of the English guns.

A second after this Lady Annerley, chancing to look at the large English iron-clad with the great black turrets, exclaims: "What is that big fat ship doing? She's ——"

But her words are annihilated as almost her senses, for there comes into the air a crashing roar that dominates and makes seem silent the thunder of all the other guns; a hustling, howling shriek such as is sometimes heard in tropic hurricanes yells through the place; the houses of the town rock as in the cradle of an earthquake as all their windows fall crashing inward, while from an Egyptian battery a cloud of dust, sand and masonry flies up as if a gigantic volcano had opened its crater beneath the Moslem works.

After a moment Lady Annerley whispers with white lips, for all the other guns have become for the second still, as if in silent terror of this new thing they feel their master: "What awful noise was that?"

And Errol, who has now recovered his speech, answers: "That was the first eighty-ton gun fired in war. By George! that vessel over there must be the *Inflexible*."

This eighty-ton horror is too much for Mr. Osman Ali, who has been trying to force himself to regard the bombardment with a supercilious Egyptian smile, though at times his teeth have chattered. The Armenian now bolts down the stairway and hides himself in the cellar. Martin, who has so far occupied the second floor in a kind of comatose state, from which every now and again she has seemed to wake to give sometimes a shriek, sometimes a prayer, now sets up a cry of such plaintive despair that Lady Annerley thinks she is dying and goes down to comfort her.

Errol alone occupies the roof, and the smoke not being as yet too dense, directs his glass toward the Marabout batteries far down the bay, and sees something there that interests him so much he does not notice that Lady Annerley has returned to his side, until she shouts at him, for the firing is now at its height and the roar and racket tremendous : " What excites you so much ? "

" I'm just looking at one of the pluckiest things done at any time in any war ! "

" What's that ? Show me ! "

" Look ! " cries Errol, giving her the glass. " The chap who commands that vessel will get the V. C. if he lives through this."

And the English lady can see a little gun-boat unassisted and alone steaming into close range of the powerful batteries and big forts of the Marabout Channel.

" She'll be blown to pieces ! " screams Lady Annerley, who has seen enough to know that the Egyptian guns are being well served this day.

" Yes, if they hit at their first fire ; if not she may have the best of it. Her commander has brains as well as courage," says Errol, and explains to his listener that a light-draught gun-boat may get so close to the forts that they cannot depress their guns sufficiently to hit her ; then she will be comparatively safe. After a moment there is a tremendous salvo of artillery from the Egyptian batteries, and peering through the smoke, Lady Annerley cries in a voice hoarse with horror: " They've sunk her ! Heaven forgive them ! "

But Errol, seizing the glass from her, the next second shrieks : " By Heaven, she's safe ! I see her masts right alongside the Moslem guns. Give it to them! Blow 'em to the devil," dancing about and shrieking in excitement at the English tars as if they could hear him miles away, through all the clang and roar of a hundred guns. For this young man has got the lunacy of battle upon him now, and uses words and expressions in his frenzy that the lady by his side would reprove if she were not as excited herself.

Whether the tars on the distant gun-boat hear Errol or not, they act as if they do ; and from each of her tops such a storm of bullets flies into the Moslem batteries, whose big guns cannot be trained effectively upon the vessel below them, that they drive the Arab artillery-men from their works.

At which the Australian hurrahs himself hoarse and cries : " By George ! I'd much sooner stand against the household troops armed with the muskets with which they downed Bonaparte at Waterloo than against those few sailors and the inventions of Messrs. Gatling and Hotchkiss mounted on that vessel." .

Then the two Anglo-Saxons rejoice together in the triumph of their countrymen and Errol cries out enthusiastically : " I'll shake hands with the gallant fellow who commands that ship after this is all over ! " Next pauses and mutters to himself, " Perhaps ! " for he feels that the English captain's chance of life under the fire of the Egyptian guns is better than his, penned in this town surrounded by Moslem fanatics.

" I know what makes you solemn ! " cries Lady Annerley coming to his side. " Is it not awful ! You have seen some of the wounded ; so have I. There they are ! " And she points to a stream of men, some limping, some staggering along, others borne on litters, their uniforms bloody, their limbs bandaged, that begins to appear on the street " Ras-el-Tin," leading from the forts and batteries at Pharos and Ada. Now that it has commenced this stream never ceases, but all the day gradually becomes larger and larger, until, though it has begun with groups of twos and threes, it ends in the steady march of a horrible column from whose ranks come the groans, cries, and shrieks of suffering humanity.

So they go to the rear of the house again, where they are protected from view by a low parapet, and look at the bombardment, which becomes more and more awful each minute.

Midway between the two squadrons lies the low, big iron-clad, swinging her bow first to the one side and then to the other, as she with awful impartiality fires her immense annihilating missiles from her starboard turret into Meks and her port turret into the Pharos and Lighthouse Forts.

The position of the Moorish house enables Lady Annerley to look behind the batteries on this part of the Cape Ras-el-Tin, and gazing there as one of these awful shells comes into the doomed Lighthouse Fort she drops the glass, gives a cry of horror, and would perhaps fall did not Errol support her as she gasps : " All ! All ! It is too horrible !"

" What do you mean ?" inquires the young man.

" I mean," she says, steadying herself, " that that shell after going through the masonry of that fort struck one of the great guns upon its muzzle and threw it over upon the men working it ; they are now writhing, crushed beneath it. There were twenty-five. I had counted them before, and not one went away after that shot, *not one !* Oh, that awful ship is going to fire again ! Take me from the sight. I hate—I loathe the cruel flag she carries !" And this gentle English woman, forgetting her love of nation in her love of man, shudders and raves at this ship whose guns kill so many.

Looking at the destruction of these gigantic shells, Errol mutters : " This thing can't last long." But here he is mistaken.

Arabi with Oriental cunning has placed at these guns artillery regiments from Upper Egypt composed of fierce Nubian blacks and dauntless Arabs of the Soudan, barbarians who value their lives so little, perchance because they have so little to make their lives of value.

And these men, equally careless whether death comes to them by the naked steel of single combat, or the distant lightnings of modern artillery, stand to their guns and fight and die, and still fight on because they are Moslem and their enemies infidels ; and their faith teaches them they step with death from the Egyptian battlements into the Paradise of Allah and the arms of the houris of Mohammed.

And so the scene goes on to its grand and awful climax ; great rents now appear in the Lighthouse Fort and the batteries about it. The Khedive's palace begins to burn ; while over all, drifting in upon the wind, comes a dense cloud of cannon smoke that settles down upon the batteries and town, till it is as if the place were in a great thick fog, through which none can see but only hear ; for the ceaseless roar of cannon still crashes cruel as before, and all the time the stream of wounded from the Pharos Fort becomes denser and denser, and wilder screams and deeper groans rend the air.

And as the smoke drifts in and in, burying the place from view, the English guns lose their accuracy of aim, and every now and then shells come shrieking and moaning over the two watchers' heads and burst in the crowded streets of the town, making its populace wild with rage or frenzied with fear. But nothing seems to drive the Arab gunners from their posts ; and with dismounted cannon, crumbling bastions, and death and carnage all about them, these barbarians still fight and die for Allah and the Faith.

This hearing without seeing makes the day more awful. As Errol gropes his way through the smoke to the little stair-way, and half carries Lady Annerley to the rooms below, she gasps to him : " Please light the lamps. In this darkness I shall see it over again. Oh, the cruelty of that ship ! "

For the immense destruction done by the pride of the British navy, which the world who did not see it has applauded and called great, causes to the woman who has seen its fearful carnage nothing but shuddering, sickening horror.

CHAPTER IV.

THE OATH OF THE ARAB BOY.

ERROL leaves Lady Annerley sitting pale and dazed, listening to the crash of guns she cannot see, and finding his way to the cellar, drags out the Armenian and says to him, " Coffee ! "

"Not while the cannons fire ; the danger is too supreme !"

"Coffee, you miserable coward ! " and the Englishman kicks his dragoman upstairs.

These kind of kicks have cost many Englishmen their lives : they have kicked Indians in the old days in America and repented of it ; they have kicked Zulus in Africa and been sorry for what they have done ; they have kicked Hindoos and Chinamen in the far East and have died for their trouble ; but still in their blundering Anglo-Saxon way they will keep on kicking "*niggers*" until the end of the world.

However, Osman only answers with a snarl, and flying from the present danger of the Australian's foot into the distant danger of the Englishmen's cannon, proceeds to do as he is told.

The coffee revives and makes them feel better ; they all contrive to eat a little, and Errol enjoys the last of his three cigars ; for the young man has contrived to dispose of the other two during his morning view of the bombardment ; great excitement generally giving increased smoking capacity to the devotees at the shrine of nicotine. Then the thunder from the guns having died out in the direction of the Meks Fort, the noise being not so deafening, Errol hears the donkeys bray in the court-yard, and thinks they too may be hungry and perhaps thirsty, for the fountain is not playing outside to-day. Having an Englishman's love for the horse, and including asses in the same category, he hurries down to look after the beasts, and finding some fodder in the deserted donkey stable attached to the house—for Abdallah, like most Moors, enjoyed this means of locomotion—he gives them their food ; but when he turns to the fountain to let on the water he gets a start, for he discovers that the pipe has been cut. Whether this has happened by accident or design he, of course, cannot tell, but it is a serious matter in this hot tropical climate, and he goes upstairs at once to see how great the supply is in the upper rooms. This, he is relieved to find, is ample for several days, as the *mushrebiyehs*, or little latticed balconies of the house, contain several porous earthen jars of water placed there after the Turkish custom to cool.

Charging them all to be very careful not to waste this water, he carries some of it down to the donkeys, who whinny their pleasure as they drink it.

While doing this his attention is called to the smoke that still obscures everything about him, even in the court-yard; this smoke upon the side nearest the town has become yellow and golden. He goes to the door leading to the street, opens it a little to look out and discover the cause of this; and as he does so gets a sensation, for a soft Eastern voice says in very bad English: "Me come along for the donkeys of mine!"

"All right," returns Errol, to whom Lady Annerley has told what passed between her and the Arab boy. "Come in, quick!"

Then the urchin of the streets accepts the invitation, and astonishes Errol as he whispers:

"No care for donkeys—donkeys all right—lady, beautiful lady, all wrong! You have bad man upstairs!"

"Bad man? Whom do you mean? Osman?"

"*Backsheesh* Osman."

"A—ah!"

"Him go out last night!"

"Last night? Impossible! I had the key in my pocket!"

"Him go out last night! Me see him. My feet not let me sleep much," returns the Arab urchin, sitting down on the porter's bench near the door and caressing the parts afflicted.

"You are sure you saw him?"

"Sure! Him come to talk to other bad man."

"What other bad man?"

"Constantine, the Greek liar!"

"Constantine Niccovie?"

"Yes, *Giaour!* Too many people in the house. *Backsheesh* and the Greek come out and talk in the street. I lie in the darkness and hear them talk of the English houri whose tears fall like pearls."

"Well, what did they say?"

"*Backsheesh* say, 'The English dog, him whose voice is loud, but his brain fat and stupid, who walks about with his eyes open, but sees nothing.' That is you, my master."

"Curse his impudence! What did he say of me?" interrupts Errol, not at all pleased at this description.

"Him say, 'The *Giaour* dog smokes *six* cigars a day!'"

"Look here," returns Errol. "Don't you make fun
of me, young one. This is too vital! If you do——"

"May Allah judge me, it is the truth!"

"What has six cigars a day to do with this affair, any
way?—though I rather believe that's about my day's consumption. By George! I wish I had one now," continues Errol, feeling his pockets carefully in hopes he
has overlooked a stray Havana. "What did they say
next?"

"They walked away. I could not follow them, my
feet too sore—look!" Here the poor little fellow exhibits
to the Australian the bruises left by the Nubian policemen's canes.

"Yes, I see, you can hardly walk now. And you
heard no more?"

"Lots! They come along again, and Constantine, him
say the beautiful lady sell for a thousand purses and the
other one for a hundred."

"Sell for a thousand purses?" echoes Errol, not understanding the boy.

"Sell her to pasha way up there," and the child points
toward Nubia, "the great pasha, the gates of whose
harem are always open to Frankish beauties."

"Sell Lady Annerley!" gasps Errol, more in astonishment than in horror, for the idea is so new to him.

"Yes, sell the lady of the tears and kill you! Now
that Egypt is Egypt, and the infidels are fled, kill *you!*
That's what him said, kill—" The Arab boy suddenly
disappears into the donkey stable as Mr. Osman Ali, who
has come down to see what detains his master, turns
the corner of the court-yard and stands in the passage.

"What the dev—" begins Errol, but gets no farther,
for a loud knocking is now heard on the street door and
the voice of Mr. Niccovie loudly cries: "Open! It's me,
Niccovie! Quick, my life is dangerous!"

For a moment the Australian hesitates, partly from
astonishment, perhaps partly from fear. The next instant
he does as Niccovie requests, pulls the Greek in and
locks the door again. For Errol has the Anglo-Saxon

instinct to face danger rather than to fly from it, and he reasons to himself, " Just as well now as any time," being by no means afraid of a personal combat with both the Levantine and the Armenian united against him.

Mr. Niccovie has no belligerent intentions, however, and pants and gasps for breath as if he had had a hard run ; then after a moment seizes Errol's hand and begins effusively : " Grand English master, to you am my life, this house has saved Niccovie ! They has made a bonfire in the Frankish quarter ! Behold, the smoke am red ! " pointing toward the town from which the hum of commotion becomes greater as the noise of the bombardment which is dying out becomes less.

Errol now understands the reason for the tinted smoke that drew him to the door, and being anxious to get both his visitor and his dragoman away from the Arab boy's hiding-place he leads the two upstairs.

Arrived there, Osman, who has been jabbering to Niccovie in some unknown tongue, says to his master, " Constantine tells me that the English are driven back and their war ships sunk."

" Oh, the poor English, it am awful ! The soldiers of Allah, how 'em fight !" chimes in the Greek with unctuous enthusiasm.

" Impossible ! I don't believe you," says Errol, though his face becomes gloomy, for he knows there are no impossibilities in war.

" Now I am come to save you. The populace are not yet excited ; if you fly you may escape. I will lead you to the shore !"

" And leave the women ? "

" Yes ! We will be responsible for the ladies. Under our care —— "

" You need say no more," interrupts Errol. " I did not leave them last night. I shall still less desert them now."

But here Lady Annerley enters the room ; coming up to him she leads him apart and whispers : " Mr. Errol, I have heard what these men say. If the English have been defeated, your only chance of safety is to fly. Alone, you may succeed ; with me you are doomed."

" You—you insult me," mutters the young man. " Do you think me coward enough to desert women ? "

" No. I think you are very brave and truly noble.

But you and yours have suffered too much already for me and mine."

" What do you mean ? "

" While you were downstairs, foreseeing that you might live through this and I might die, I wrote this," mutters Lady Annerley, producing a carefully folded and tied-up packet which she gives to him. *"Treasure it as you would your life,* and when you have escaped, read it. It will answer your question."

" Certainly, if you ask it ; though I don't understand you," returns Errol, placing the packet upon his breast with such care that Osman and Niccovie, who have been looking at this interview from the other end of the room, say a few words to each other in Arabic under their breaths, and after this do not press Errol's departure, for they imagine this packet contains the English lady's jewels and money.

" Now you will go ? "

" Never, till you are safe ! "

" Even if I told you what would make you hate me ? "

" Hate *you ?* " There is a curious unbelief in this man's voice as he looks at her, for Lady Annerley's beauty is very great. " Hate *you ?* " Then his tone suddenly changes and he says to her sternly : " Don't you dare to tell me anything that would make me desert my duty ! " and so goes off to the Armenian and the Greek and cries at them : " You two drop this talk of my running away ! " while the lady stands gazing at him with a blush on her face, for there is something in Errol's tone which has set this woman's heart to beating very wildly.

At this command Osman says nothing ; but the Levantine stalks over to Lady Annerley, and giving her a solemn and ceremonious *salam,* shouts out : " That man is a bravo ! him a protector of women—me too ! Me Niccovie stay with him and save you all—*all*—ALL ! Me too am a protectionist !—for you." Here he makes some fantastic gesticulations, and seizes his greasy coat in the region of the heart, emphasizing his concluding remark with a glance of such comical gallantry that the English lady at first smiles, but a moment after blushes and then turns pale, giving a little shudder, half of indignation, half of loathing : for though Sarah Annerley could not

defiue it Mr. Niccovie's gaze has become that of a slavedealer valuing his goods.

Errol has not paid much attention to this last; he is
sitting down trying to pull his mind together as to what
course he shall take ; for though he doesn't entirely believe the Arab boy, whose revelations he regards as
monstrous, still he by no means trusts Mr. Niccovie and
Mr. Osman.

After a moment the former of these worthies gravely
squats down and produces a *nargileh* pipe and prepares
to smoke with the deliberate manner of the East, filling
it carefully from a package of Turkish tobacco he takes
from his pocket, and arranging its water bowl—which,
curiously enough, contains no liquid, perhaps from the
difficulty of carrying it in his pocket—with great care ;
all the time eyeing it with a kind of satisfied glance, as if
remarking to himself, " How cunning I am."   Just as
Niccovie is about to light it, he suddenly seems to remember something and exclaims :

" My friends no smoke !   I forgot me—I have cigars
in my pockets ! "   Here he pulls out some Havanas, takes
one himself and lights it, offers another to Osman, who
also smokes, and with a *salam*, says : " This is true Cu-
ban.   May it find favor in the Englishman's eyes ! " as
he offers Errol the choice from several weeds he holds
in his hand.

" And in his mouth too ! " says that young gentleman,
lighting up also, for he has been looking at the two
men with envy from the minute they have begun to
smoke.

Had the Levantine only offered a single cigar to him
or had he not smoked himself, perhaps Errol might
have been suspicious ; as it is, after a few gingerly taken
whiffs, he finds the cigar is so good a one for the East,
where true Havanas are scarce, that' he half thinks the
Arab boy must have told all fiction and no truth.

So the three sit smoking together ; the *nargileh* pipe
all ready for lighting standing unused upon a divan at
the side of the room, where the Greek has put it away.
Toward this, as they smoke, Osman's eye sometimes
turns with a twinkle as he notes how Errol enjoys his
cigar, while Mr. Niccovie's restless red orbs seem to
divide their attention between the beautiful English

woman and the Australian's repeating rifle, which Errol
has all day kept close at his hand. The first Mr. Niccovie's eyes regard with a smile of pleasure; the last
with an apprehensive glance, which changes into a sneer
as he looks upon the owner of the weapon enjoying his
cigar that is now nearly finished.

"You smoke not much," he says, as Errol throws
away the remnant. "Another?—take all!" and he empties his pockets of what cigars are in them upon a neighboring shelf. "Osman and me are contentment with a
pipe." Here he points to the *nargileh*.

"Thanks, very much," replies the Australian, and is
about to take another when Lady Annerley remarks:
"The guns from the harbor have died away long ago.
I think all fighting is over; come and see!" Errol
goes up to the roof and finds that the night is dark but
clear, and listens for such sounds from the water as will
denote the English are preparing to occupy the town.
Toward the sea there is no noise; but from the town
comes the hum of many voices and the tramp of moving
troops, as if the place was being strongly patrolled. The
fire is still burning in the Frankish quarter, but has
grown no larger since the afternoon. He goes down
into the main apartment and looks at his watch. Discovering it is nine o'clock at night, he finds himself hungry and tells Osman to get them something to eat.

While the dragoman is doing this, Martin, with one or
two mysterious gestures, gets Errol to her, and gives
him a piece of information which is one of several that
produce a resolution in the Australian's mind which
shortly afterward astonishes both the Greek and the
Armenian. The girl has been in a terrified stupor all
day, but she is now in an equally terrified state of alert-
ness as she whispers: "Don't you trust them two heathens. If you do, we're all dead!"

"What makes you think that?"

"This morning I saw Osman out in the street."

"In the street?"

"Yes, cutting the fountain pipe. It won't run now.
To-day there was five full water jars, now there are but
three. He empties them every chance he gets. And
the way them two looks at misses and I! See, that one's
at it now!"

And Errol, following the girl's gaze, sees one of the slavedealer's expressions on Mr. Niccovie's face, who is enjoying the pretty picture made by Lady Annerley as she, worn out by the excitement of the day, lolls upon a divan, and looks about in a dreamy manner as if she hardly thought the present was reality. Draped in the clinging, airy, black dress of the night before, the only one of the hundred toilets she had yesterday, she makes a picture Gérôme would love to put on canvas.

"Why didn't you tell me this before?" asks Errol, his face growing a little paler, for he has now corrobora-tive evidence of his dragoman being out the night before, and the truth of the Árab boy's story.

"The guns made me too frightened to think—too daft to talk. Oh, don't trust them—*don't!*"

"I'll keep an eye on them, don't you fear," mutters Errol, a very nasty look coming into his face as Mr. Osman announces, "Allah has blessed us with food!" Then they all proceed to make another picnic meal, Mr. Niccovie being in great spirits, and giving them a dis-sertation on how the English have been destroyed this day, Allah's soldiers being so brave. For them to die on the battle-field is to go to Paradise!

"Yes," says Errol grimly, "under the English guns they emigrated to-day in large numbers to heaven."

"But," continues the Greek, "though the English have fled Niccovie is here. Him will save you! Nic-covie to-morrow is dead! Niccovie dies for woman! Niccovie the protectionist! Niccovie the bravo! Poot Niccovie!" and he weeps over his own cruel fate in a comical, pathetic way that would make Sarah Annerley laugh were she at home by her fireside, but here it is so different, and the English lady sighs.

But Mr. Niccovie is now interrupted by Errol. The young man's rifle has been placed behind him; during the meal he has moved a little way from it to assist Lady Annerley. While the Greek has been making his loud-est harangue and greatest jabber, the Australian's ear has caught the click of the repeating mechanism. He turns slightly round. Osman is walking from the rifle, which has been moved slightly; Errol saunters to the weapon as if to change its location, and as he does so tests the lock and breech apparatus; his touch tells him they will not work. In perfect order when he had laid it down, the weapon must have been tampered with.

As he faces them both, for Osman has passed to where Niccovie sits, there is something in the Australian's face that makes the Greek rise suddenly from his divan with a cry of alarm ; for it is the look of a man who has given up playing a game he fears he will lose, and has taken to playing a game at which he knows he is sure.

" You infernal cads and sneaks ! " he begins, then suddenly cries : " Put up your hands or I fire ! " and his revolver is cocked and at the Levantine's breast, for that gentleman is feeling as if for a weapon.

Mr. Niccovie's hands go up, as also Mr. Osman's from sympathy. " Now ! " Errol says to Martin, " take the weapons from those men, if they have any."

" Oh, sir ! I daresn't, sir ! "

" I will guard you. Do it at once ! "

" Oh, sir ! I'm too frightened, sir."

" I will do it, Mr. Errol," says Lady Annerley, quietly, and without another word, though her hands tremble slightly, this belle of Belgravian mansions and Paris *salons* relieves the Greek and the Armenian each of a knife and a pistol.

" What shall I do now ? " she asks, moving away with the weapons.

" Lock them up in that cupboard."

She does this, but Errol can see she conceals one of the pistols in her bosom.

" Now ! " he says to the two men, who, after their excited Eastern way, are beginning to gesticulate and cry out innocent. " Not a word from you ! Into that room and sit down ! " And he marches them to the apartment the Armenian has occupied the night before. And they squatting in a corner he points out to them, he says to Martin : " Come to this doorway and keep your eyes on these scoundrels, and if they move, shriek ! *shriek!* That's about all you're fit for—SHRIEK !! "

The maid having obeyed him, he leads Lady Annerley to one side and whispers : " Please go down to the stable below—there is no danger, the street door has been kept locked. You will find your little Arab boy, bring him up here. I would do it myself, but it is necessary I keep near these men."

Lady Annerley, without a word, goes down to do his bidding, and in a minute or two returns with the Arab urchin, who is crying, and says he is hungry.

"You shall have something to eat after you answer my questions," says Errol. "What is your name, my little fellow?"

"Ammed."

"Ammed, do you believe in the Koran?"

"Aye! and in Allah!"

"Do you believe that false swearers against the life of man will be punished?"

"If I swear away a man's life Allah will curse me!"

As the Arab boy speaks there is an uneasy rustle from the other room.

"Then swear to me by the oath you value most whether you told the truth to me to-day!" Errol's voice is very low and solemn here and trembles slightly, and Sarah Annerley looking at him begins to tremble also.

"May Allah, Mohammed and Paradise never be seen by me," replies the boy very solemnly, turning and making obeisance to the East after the manner of the Moslem faith, "may my grave be defiled and my kindred be cursed if the words I spoke to you, *Giaour*, to-day be not the living truth! On my head be it!" And Errol knows he can believe, for the boy is trembling at his own oath. He turns to Lady Annerley and says hoarsely: "Do you take the girl and Ammed with you into your apartment, the one farthest from here, and wait till—till I call you."

"Think what you are about to do!" whispers the woman with white lips, for the man's face tells her he is going to kill.

"Take the girl and Ammed away from here!"

"Errol, remember you must answer to God for these men's lives!"

"Yes, and for your life also! I command here! *These men have condemned themselves!*" and he cocks the revolver and motions her out of his path.

"No! No!" she cries clinging to him. "Not even for my safety. Spare them! don't kill them! *It would be murder.*"

But at these words there comes a shriek of terror from the next room, a noise of rapid movement and a cry from

Martin. Errol forces his way past Lady Annerley and
dashes into the apartment of the Armenian, only to find
it empty and the arras torn from its wall, showing an
open door and flight of steps leading to the street; for
Osman Ali and Constantine Niccovie have fled from
their executioner by the same path the dragoman had
used the night before.

As the two sped along the street, one whispers to the
other : " To-night would have been too soon. See !
the law is still enforced ! " pointing to a strong patrol of
Egyptian soldiers that march past them.

This is true, for Arabi Pasha well knows the demorali-
zation that would come upon any army retreating through
a town that is burning and being pillaged ; and the only
road by which his troops can evacuate the batteries and
barracks of Ras-el-Tin being through the city, that commander is strongly policing the streets and keeping down
the conflagration as much as possible this night in Alexandria.

Charley Errol, seeing that his condemned criminals
have escaped him, barricades the door by which they
have left, returns to the main apartment, and says to
Lady Annerley, from whose face the horror of the last
few moments has not passed away : " Better open enemies than false friends.   I must think what is next to be
done."   And glancing about him, exclaims : " By George !
here's a lucky windfall.   That Greek scoundrel has left
me six cigars and his *nargileh* pipe."

CHAPTER V.

THE NARGILEH PIPE OF NICCOVIE, THE LEVANTINE.

SMOKING one of these cigars, which is very comforting
to him, the Australian sits down at once to repair, if possible, the damage Osman has done his Remington.   He
carefully overhauls his rifle, which is very simple though
effective in its mechanism, and finding the injury done
to it by his dragoman is slight, that scoundrel having
had but a moment to do his work upon the weapon, soon
has it in repair.

After testing the lock and repeating apparatus several times, he gives the rifle an affectionate glance, and mutters: "'Thank God, you'll do your duty if I but do mine." For he has grown to regard this gun as a friend, having tested it against small game that run from you, and against big game that come to you to kill you, and it has saved his life on other occasions than this ; and the English woman looking at him, says " Thank God " also. Do artisans in the great gun factories of the world often think how many times on their skill and faithful labor hang the lives of men and the honor of women?

The weapon being laid down with a sigh of relieved anxiety, Errol says suddenly :

" I had hoped in this Moorish house to remain concealed through any riot or tumult. Now, with those two scoundrels to point out my place of hiding, I must fight my way through." Here he muses with a perturbed countenance, and after a moment asks Lady Annerley if she can suggest any plan by which one man can defend two entrances at the same time.

" Why not barricade one ? " she suggests.

" Barricade one—with what? Divans, rugs and mats? " mutters Errol, looking about with scorn, for these, after the Turkish fashion, are the only furniture of the rooms.

" Then nail the door up, " says Lady Annerley, as if suddenly struck with the thought.

" A fine idea ! Nail the door up ! " echoes Errol with a glum laugh.

" I am glad you think it a fine idea. Let's do so at once," returns the English woman proudly ; conscious that she has solved the problem.

" That's right ! bring the nails and tools at once, " he laughs with a sneer at woman's thoughtlessness.

At this Martin interjects : " So I would, sir, if I warn't scared."

" What do you mean ? " asks Errol in astonishment.

" There is a whole work-house below," answers the maid. " I seed it there when I was trying to get out of the way of the cannon shot this morning."

The Arab boy, who, having been fed, has been too busy with the provisions to talk during the preceding interview, here corroborates Martin by saying sententiously: " Abdallah the Moor makes copper things."

"Ah ! A coppersmith ! We may find something useful." And Errol, taking a lamp, is downstairs in a minute, followed by the whole party except Lady Annerley,
who remains above to warn him if any one approaches
the little entrance which as yet is only secured by a lock.

Abdallah the Moor apparently has not been educated
to the use of modern tools. Errol finds little that will aid
him, except a small saw, a few copper nails, a strong pair
of shears capable of cutting heavy copper plates, a large
hammer, and a few pieces of wood of various sizes but
not large enough to be of service as a barricade. There
are also a number of tools peculiar to the working of
copper, the use of which the Australian cannot understand. After rummaging about, he pulls out a couple of
old-fashioned augers that have apparently been used in
odd jobs of carpenters' work about the house, and carrying them with him, he returns upstairs, the idea having
come to him that he will secure the small door to its
frame with large wooden pins, as he can find no nails
strong enough to withstand any forcible attack.

Then making an examination of the door at the street
end of the little stair-way, he finds it altogether too dilapi-
dated and decayed for his purpose ; though the one at
the head of the stairs is entirely suited to his purpose,
being between one and one-half and two inches thick of
strong seasoned oak. He is preparing to secure this
door when Lady Annerley, who has been watching him,
says suddenly, looking down the narrow stone passage,
through which the steps come up straight from the street :
"What a place for a *mitrailleuse*."

"Magnificent !" returns Errol grimly. "How I wish
I had a Gatling and half a dozen men to work it. What
made you think of a *mitrailleuse*, Lady Annerley ?"

"Why, I read in the newspapers that *mitrailleuses* were
useful for defending narrow places where men could not
avoid their fire.—Oh, Mr. Errol, what is the matter with
you ?"

For the Australian has jumped as if shocked by elec-
tricity and uttered a cry of joyous exaltation. "Lady
Annerley, I adopt your idea. This door shall be my
Gatling gun !"

With this he pulls out one of his Remington cartridges,
and comparing it carefully with the thickness of the door,

mutters to himself: "George, won't it surprise the scoundrels! That's a rum idea!" and other expressions of delight at the plan.

In fact he intersperses all through his work upon his killing machine remarks of a similar jovial nature, such as, "This *will* be an eye opener!" "How Niccovie will stare!" "This will make Osman *jump!*". "Here's a rib cracker for the Turks!" etc., etc., all the time, however, working as if it were for his life.

First he measures the door, which is of hard unyielding oak, strong enough to hold a Remington cartridge firmly and prevent its copper shell expanding when fired. Next he makes them all search Abdallah's tool-shop till they find an auger that has but a little greater diameter than the cartridges.

This being done, he examines his belt and pouch, finding he has nearly two hundred rounds of fixed ammunition beside six in the magazine of his Remington; for Charley Errol, rather expecting a row in Alexandria, had thrown away all his provisions to carry more cartridges.

He can spare fifty for his infernal machine, and bores that number of holes through the door, which is about eight feet high, thirty inches wide, and two inches thick throughout, having after the Eastern fashion no panels.

These holes he makes in five lines across the door, each line ten inches from the other, and the lowest one a foot above the sill. There are consequently ten holes in each row, the highest of all being about four feet and a half from the floor.

The lowest row he directs so as to rake the stair-way about a foot high for its whole distance, judging this will catch any one trying to reach the door by crawling. To the other lines of auger holes he gives a generally increasing depression till the top row will shoot so as to about strike the knees of men standing at the bottom of the steps. These orifices also converge at such an angle as to make a complete cross-fire upon this little narrow walled-in stair-way, those on the right shooting to the left, and *vice versa*. All this Errol does with a good deal of labor, for the wood is tough and the auger old-fashioned and rusty; and with a great amount of care, for he squints through each hole to see the direc-

tion is right, sighting at a candle• the Arab boy holds
down the stair-way. This being accomplished, he plugs
each of the holes with a Remington cartridge, driving
them home from the inside with a piece of wood till the
copper rims of their shells prevent their going in any
further and hold them firmly in their places, while the
bullets project slightly upon the side of the door facing
the stair-way.

Looking on this instrument, studded as it is with fifty
murderous knobs of cold lead, Errol gives a grim chuckle
and mutters : " They'll be cursed clever and devilish
lucky if they dodge that," and proceeds to put his firing
apparatus in order. He finds two good-sized plates of copper, each about an eighth of an inch thick, in Abdallah's
work-shop ; in these he punches fifty holes about a
quarter of an inch in·diameter, at such distances apart
that when placed behind the door each of these orifices
will expose the central fulminating cap of one of the
cartridges—a laborious job which he at length accom-
plishes by heating the plates with the aid of a brazier and
bellows the Moor had evidently used for the same purpose, and then cutting them as he wishes by a die and
sledge-hammer.

This being done, he takes them upstairs and fastens
the plates to the back of the door as firmly as he can
with the materials he can find. After this he closes the
door, locks and secures it in place as well as possible, and
puts a brace against the lower plate, not having any tim-
ber long enough to reach the upper one.

He then darts downstairs again and finds a small sharp-
pointed hammer, such as braziers sometimes use, and to be
sure this will work, tries it upon a cartridge, sacrificing
one to be sure. This he does in the cellar for fear the
noise will attract attention from the outside, and finding
it explodes under his blow, brings the hammer up to the
room above and placing it beside the door, announces that
the *mitrailleuse* is ready for action ; and the pride of the
inventor coming to him, almost wishes the Moslem beggars
would hurry up so as to test his mechanical skill. Next,
the back door being defended by the machine gun, he
tries to think of some means to make the fire of his rifle
that must protect the main entrance of the house more
deadly ; some means of knowing the exact location of his

enemies by *hearing* instead of *seeing*. Upon going down
to take a look at this front door, the jingling of the strings
of bells that adorn Ammed's donkeys comes to him from
the stable and with it an idea.

He hastily removes these from the beasts : they are
little sleigh bells strung on strips of strong leather, each
about five feet long, and three in number. The first of
these he stretches across the entrance of the passage
where it opens upon the court-yard ; for he has determined to make no fight at the outer portal, but to take
his shooting stand upon the little balcony overlooking
both the entrance to the court-yard and the steps leading
up from it to the second floor they occupy.

"The beggars can enter the rooms upon the ground if
they like. I have little fear of fire," he thinks ; "the
house is all stone and brick, besides—" he pauses and
whistles a little, meditating upon the Arab boy's evidence—"Mr. Niccovie and Osman would hardly wish
to burn up one thousand and one hundred purses of
gold, no matter what they might like to do to me." Then
mutters to himself : "George ! a new factor in military
engineering—Lady Annerley's beauty."

The first string of bells he hangs about a foot high, per-
mitting it enough sag to give out sound briskly to any
touch. The second row he places in a similar manner
across the stair-way leading up from the court-yard.
Testing them and finding them to work satisfactorily, he
takes the bearing of these strings by other objects nearer
to his shooting stand, so that he has their range pretty
accurately in the dark. Then he gives a grim chuckle
muttering: "The scoundrels 'll hardly crawl over those,
dark as it is, without my hearing ; " and coming to Lady
Annerley says : "Now I think I'm ready for them, but
it was hot work," then sinking down on a divan, wipes
the great beads of exhausted toil from his forehead.

All this has taken hours, though the young man has
worked like one possessed, the fire of invention in his
eye. In fact he has made them all work this night ; running his errands and doing his bidding like slaves about
the forge of Vulcan, even telling Lady Annerley to "jump
quick !" Which that lady has done very rapidly, for,
though Sarah has been accustomed to command, like most
women, she is delighted to obey the right man, if he only

orders her about in the right way.   Indeed, all this
night while the young Australian has been forging the
weapons that shall give her freedom, he has been forging
fetters about the heart of this great English lady that
make her a slave forever.

As Errol sits down with a sigh he mutters : " George !
I'd get a cigar if I were up to it," and the next moment
is astonished to find one of his windfalls from Niccovie
placed in his hand, and Lady Annerley standing before
him with a little burning coal, ready to light it at his
behest.

" I beg your pardon," he says.   " I meant the hint for
Martin, not you.   Pardon my laziness ! "

" I prefer to wait on you myself," she returns, blushing slightly.

" And why is that ? "

" Don't ask questions !   You're—you're too tired.   Oh,
how you have toiled for my safety this hot night ! "

Which is true, for the beads of perspiration are still
upon Errol's forehead, his arms ache, and his breath
comes in the short gasps of exhaustion.

Having said this she goes a little way from him, and,
sitting down herself, gazes at the young man in a pathetic and wistful manner, which is a very bad symptom
in women of Lady Annerley's temperament.

Errol finishes his cigar and, turning everything over in
his mind, remarks :   " Now I'm good for the front entrance I hope, and I have strong faith in the *mitrailleuse*
doing deadly work at the back door."

" Then it is time for you to go to sleep," says Lady
Annerley.

" Sleep ?   Why there's no telling at what moment we
may be attacked."

" For that time you must keep your strength.   I cannot fight, but I can watch.   Let me at least do some of
that."

To this Errol, after some grumbling, assents, lying
ready for action at her call.   For both of them, not
knowing what the Egyptian commander is doing in the
city, imagine their danger is now—not to come.

So Lady Annerley sees the early sun rise and get
nigh in the heavens on the second day of the English
attack upon the city.

When Errol opens his eyes she is still watching. He looks at his watch and cries :· " 'Twelve o'clock! Why didn't you wake me before? Now it is your turn, Lady Annerley, you must lie down. I'll look out for you. I'm a new man now. Please go to your room ! "

But she answers : " Not till you tell me what the movement in the harbor means !"

" Ah ! the English ships are still there ? "

" Yes."

" Hurrah ! Then I expect we're all 'right," and he dashes to the little stair-way, but, seeing she is following, turns and assists her up to the roof, and the two look out on the harbor together.

The Egyptian forts are silent and dismantled, their parapets in ruins, their guns overthrown, destroyed and deserted. The English fleet, on the contrary, are apparently in nearly as good condition as when they opened fire the day before ; though they all show scars from striking shots, and one has a large gaping hole in her smoke-stack. They are under steam, but all far away in the outer harbor, which surprises Errol, as there is a flag of truce flying from the Lighthouse Fort, and a small steam yacht with the Egyptian flag is alongside the Brit· ish ship that bears the admiral's pennon.

" We're safe," he cries.

" How do you know that ? Are you sure ? " asks Lady Annerley, her lips trembling.

" Of course ! They're arranging the terms of surrender. Our troops 'll occupy this town before night. Home again ! " and he begins to sing the old British ballad.

" Home again ! " echoes the English lady, and there are tears in her eyes. Apparently some also get into Errol's, for the song seems to choke him, and he murmurs, " Thank God ! " the two days' strain upon the young man having given way with a snap now he thinks they are safe.

After a moment he mutters : " You had better go down and rest. All is over ! "

" Not till I see the boats land. I couldn't sleep now."

" All right. I'll go down and get a cigar," and he does so, bringing up two.

Then the Arab boy comes and puts his head out of

the skylight, and looking at him smoking, says, plaintively : " Me no cigarettes ! "

To which Errol, in his happiness, responds by throwing
him the other cigar, and telling him to put that in his
mouth.

An invitation young Ammed accepts at once, puffing
away with the vigor of a veteran ; Errol informing Lady
Annerley he will buy the boy who has done so much for
them a whole herd of the best donkeys in Alexandria.

But Ammed declines his offer with barbarian brusqueness, answering : " It was not for you, *Giaour*, but for
the lady whose tears are pearls ! " and striding up to
Lady Annerley, makes her blush by patting her fair
cheeks and muttering, " Beautiful ! Beautiful ! "

She, however, smothers the blush in a merry laugh,
for they have got to laughing real laughs now, they are
all so happy.

Then Martin, assisted by the Arab boy, gets breakfast,
which they take still watching for the landing of the
English, no signs of which come.

The Egyptian yacht has left the ship of the British
admiral and returned to the shore ; the white flag still
flies from the Lighthouse Fort ; but no boats are launched
from the great iron-clads that hardly move under the
strong breeze that is producing quite a sea. Behind them
two American men-of-war roll and toss; they are not half
so big.

The town, however, is moderately quiet, though the
fire in the foreign quarter is still burning, and the ones in
the Harem and Khedive's palace are not yet extinguished.

Lady Annerley suddenly says : " It is now two hours,
and no move yet," then gives a sigh.

Errol does not answer her. He is sweeping with his field-
glass the outer harbor and trying to see the Mediter-
ranean behind the Ras-el-Tin Cape, as if searching desperately for something. After doing this again and again
he finally moves away from his companion as if he did
not wish to alarm her by his manner. Noticing this,
Lady Annerley strides after him and asks : " What is it
you wish to conceal from me ? "

" Nothing—I—I—— "

" Don't prevaricate ! I demand to know what is the
matter ! "

"Well, then if you insist—I—I don't see any troop ships here. There are no soldiers to occupy this place!"

"Oh, they'll come after—in a day or two."

"In a day or two we shall be——"

Though Errol does not complete the sentence Lady Annerley does. "You mean we shall be *dead?*"

"It looks that way!"

"But those iron-clads can send some men on shore?"

"Too few! They don't seem to dare risk it, even now that Arabi is evacuating the forts." Here he points to the long columns of infantry and artillery that are coming along the Street Ras-el-Tin, and from the barracks behind the Meks Forts, and are moving through the town to the gate called the Column of Pompey and the road leading to Cairo. "Those modern ships are full of steam-engines, not men," he continues. "You can't garrison a town with machines. One of Nelson's old liners could spare more sailors for shore duty than that whole fleet."

"Then you think our case desperate?"

"*Very!* It would be wrong to hide it from you now. Please go downstairs and get a little rest. I'll call you if needed; good-bye till—to-night!" Errol lingers upon the last word as if to-night will be the crisis, and she understanding him gives a smothered sigh, but says nothing, and leaves him to watch and see the hopes that, made bright this morning, fade one by one this evening.

Still no sign of movement in the English fleet; but the columns of soldiers leaving the town become heavier, more dense, and worse disciplined as they pass along. The advance guard were in exact military array, the center has been somewhat ragged and broken, with occasional stragglers that become more and more numerous; until the rear guard that passes now is nothing but an armed mob that, killing any officer who tries to control them, spread out in squads over the hapless town in search of loot and liquor.

The fires in the Frankish quarter become brighter and more numerous, and some appear in other parts of the city; the yells of the barbarian populace, augmented now by drunken soldiers and criminals from the prisons that have been burst open, fill the air, mingled with the cries of women and children ; while now and again musketry firing tells of violence and death.

And as night and darkness settle down upon this town that military rule has left to anarchy, they bring with them all the horrors of lust and drunkenness, riot and arson, pillage and murder, each exaggerated and made more cruel, because it is an Eastern mob of fanatics that do this bloody work ; for at this business they are supreme. The Apache Indian has done some good work in the torturing line ; Protestant ministers have made witches die very hard ; the Inquisition has invented some rare tormenting in its time ; but for cold-blooded, fantastic, atrocious cruelty on unbelievers, there never has been and there never will be such a conglomeration of fiends upon this earth as an " Allah be praised," impromptu Mohammedan mob.

Looking at this, Errol mutters, " God help us ! " gives a last appealing gaze at the British fleet that still never raise an anchor nor lower a boat, and anathematizes the head of the government, who has sent a navy to drive out Egyptian law, but no soldiers to prevent Christian massacre.

" Hang him ! " he cries, " this man of half measures, who values loutish votes more than innocent lives. His troops 'll come too late ! There'll be more men than me in this war who'll look for succor that 'll come *too late!* Curse him ! some day his country 'll say he died TOO LATE ! "

With this parting shot at him whose half-way policy has killed so many of those who have trusted in England's faith, the Australian goes downstairs to make his final preparations for the combat he knows this night will bring to him.

He inspects his arms and defenses, and finding they are all right feels wearied and tired ; for the day has been blazing hot. He lies down on an ottoman, thinking he will get a little rest if the noise outside will let him. The next minute he imagines he would like a cigar and remembers there is one precious one left. Looking for this treasure he finds it gone ; discovering the smoking stump of it in the Arab boy's mouth. That young urchin having enjoyed the first one so much, has appropriated number two, in the absence of his loved cigarettes.

Not having one, a cigar becomes almost a necessity; and Errol returns very much disappointed to his divan. "It would have been my last cigar, I imagine," he thinks, "and to be robbed of that—" But a moment later his eyes brighten as they fall upon the *nargileh* pipe that Mr. Niccovie had prepared for himself. He cries : "Here's luck. Pipes and baccy ! "

So it comes to pass, the Arab boy having finished *two* of the *six* cigars the Levantine left behind him, Charley Errol lights up and smokes Mr. Niccovie's pipe *about five hours before that gentleman calculated he would.*

After a whiff or two the young man pauses suspiciously; then mutters, "Pshaw ! Niccovie was going to smoke this himself;" takes a few whiffs more, and with these whiffs loses the wish to abstain. For he mutters : "This pipe's the most soothing upon earth," and going on smoking in a dreamy, happy sort of way, the terrors and anxieties of life pass from him, the room that was somber with foreboding and the lowering shadows of night becomes bright with hope and brilliant as with the noon-day sun; the tumult that comes from the town with a louder and more horrid din of shouts and cries and roar of flames is to him as the music of the spheres of Heaven ; and Charley Errol, who should be awake and watching, sleeps the sleep that has been prepared for him by Niccovie the Levantine.

A few moments after this Lady Annerley comes into the main apartment. Unable to sleep for the noise, woman's curiosity has suggested that she can find forgetfulness in discovering the precise thing that made Errol the night before think that for her safety Osman and the Greek must die. Approaching to ask him this, she finds him asleep, and with careful, noiseless steps crosses to the next room, thinking it best to let him rest for the exertions that the night may bring to him ; but as she goes favors him with a look such as this woman, widow as she is, has never given to any other man before.

In the apartment she enters, which is the one from which Osman and the Greek have fled, she finds the young Arab curled up on a mat.

Under her questioning Ammed tells her of the future fate these gentlemen had prepared for her and her maid.

At first she does not understand him, but finally the

5

shock to her pride and womanhood comes home to her,
and she shudders and blushes and hides her head in
shame ; but when Sarah Annerley lifts it up again a
dauntless resolution is in her face ; and the boy's revelation has given her a spirit to achieve many things this
night that under other circumstances she could scarce
have brought her hands to do.

This is hardly over when Martin's scared face is put in
the door and Martin's voice says : " Please, my lady,
what's the matter with Mr. Errol ? "

" What do you mean ? "

" Oh, mum, he's snoring awful ! "

" Then you'd better wake him up ! "

" I can't, mum ! I've been trying for a minute ! "

" Can't wake him up ? Nonsense ! " and Lady Annerley coming to the young man's side tries again and
again to bring him from his slumber, *without effect.*

Here the Arab boy, who has strolled in after the two
women, astounds her, for he walks to the pipe, sniffs it
once or twice, and remarks sententiously, " Opium ! "

" Opium !   What do you mean ? "

" Him smoke opium ! "   .

" Good heavens ! " for now the treachery of the Levantine comes home to her as she looks at the *nargileh* pipe
and cries : " He has robbed us of our defender ! Wake
him up ! Wake him up ! God help us, how shall I wake
him up—*in time?*" and wrings her hands as one distracted.

Here Ammed, who, like all who live in the East, is
familiar with the opium habit, suggests, " Coffee ! Black
coffee ! Strong coffee ! "

" Coffee ! Martin, you hear him ! Make the strongest
coffee possible ! For your life ! "

" I can't, marm, I'm too agitated ! "

" Then, idiot, run and get water ! Quick ! " screams
Lady Annerley, seizing in her own hand the package of
that precious berry.

But Ammed takes it from her, saying " Me know ! "
and the coals in the brazier being in a glow brews coffee,
hot, strong, black and full of grounds, with the skill of
an Arabian ; all the time giving directions in his lingo as
to further treatment.

Under his orders Lady Annerley and her maid force

Errol to a sitting position, propping him up with pillows, and then work his limbs to increase the circulation. Next, the coffee being ready, they pry open his mouth, and Ammed pours down his throat such a burning hot concoction of black grounds and blacker liquor that it might almost wake the dead.

Then the Arab boy yells, " Make the *Giaour* walk ! " And with a strength born of despair, for the noise of riot outside is getting nearer, this gentle English lady, almost unhelped by the maid, who becomes more useless the more her aid is needed, forces the six feet of inanimate bone and sinew to its feet and tries with desperate jerks and pushes to force it to move ; but it only gives a half stride, half stumble and falls upon the floor.

" More coffee ! " screams the boy, who has got to take pride in his work, and he is upon Errol again and gives him another dose larger and hotter than before, yelling to the women : " Beat his feet ! Whip the unbelieving dog to life ! " and suiting his actions to his words, falls to with all his infant might punching and pummeling the human log before him.

In this he is assisted in a more moderate manner by Lady Annerley and her maid. Still seeing no signs of returning animation, the Arab bolts from the room, returning the moment after with a lot of canes, perhaps used by Abdallah the Moor to keep order in his harem, and throwing one to each of the women shrieks, " Beat him ! *Beat him!* BEAT HIM ! " belaboring with every yell the limbs of the Australian.

This desecration of her hero's person horrifies Lady Annerley ; she screams, " Let him alone, you little fiend. Let us die in peace ! " trying to push him from his victim.

But he jabbers, " The only thing ! No time to wait ! See 'em do this before ! " and beats away until exhausted. Treatment that finally has its effect, for Errol rolls over and groans.

" Ah, he is coming to life ! Heaven bless you, Ammed ! " sobs the English lady who, womanlike, now praises what she had condemned and falls to supplement the work of the Arab boy by pattings that are caresses.

But Ammed cuts short sentiment by another long, strong dose of coffee, which causes the Australian's eyes

to open ; though after a moment he closes them again.
But he does not do so long, for the boy is at him once
more with switchings of the cane which make him open
his mouth and beg, " Go away and let me sleep ! "

" No sleep now ! Get up ! "

" I—I'm too tired." This is with a lazy sigh ; and the
opium smoker rolls over on the divan, for another dream of
heaven, despite the hell of noises upon earth that come
from the ravaged and looted town, and the tears and entreaties of the woman who begs him to rise up for her
sake.

But the next second Errol springs up with a yell of rage,
not pain ; the drug is too strong in him for feeling, only
he will not have his rest disturbed. For the Arab boy,
getting a chance when Lady Annerley's back has been
turned, has taken off Errol's Eastern slippers and fallen to
again with vicious vigor upon the soles of the sleeper.

" Now him on his feet, no let him lie down. Keep
him up. Him all right. More coffee ! "

Thus adjured the two women try and support the man
about ; but he staggers from them to a divan, muttering :
" Let me sleep but a minute ; and dream of—— "

But Lady Annerley will no more let him succumb now
than the Arab boy, for the sounds without make her desperate, and she flies at him. Despite his struggles they
all together succeed in getting more coffee down him,
and shake him, and prod him, and fight him till he snarls
at them with rage ; for it is not the man who speaks to
them, it is the drug ; but they are all at him again till he
sits up and has apparently more vigor.

Here Lady Annerley calls the Arab boy to her, for she
has already written a hurried message :

" Come to my aid.
" Sarah Annerley,
" House of Abdallah, the Moor."

And hearing from him the name of the street, adds it to the
note as she speaks to the child and says : " Ammed, you
are the only one of us who can pass through the town
this night with life. Will you take this note to the Marina and wait there till boats from the English come, and
give it to the first Frankish sailor that you see ? "

To this the little fellow answers : "Yes, lady, me
know."

" I can depend on you ? "

" As I live and believe in Allah ! "

Then charging Martin to keep Errol, who still gazes about as if dazed, awake and moving as she loves her life, Lady Annerley goes with the Arab boy down the stair-way into the court-yard, and so through the passage that leads to the front door, taking care not to disturb the two strings of donkey-bells she crosses. Here pressing some money in Ammed's hand, and bidding him " God speed," she opens the portal, and he darts into the street and disappears in the noise and tumult that seems now all about them.

Then she quickly runs back to the great apartment and gives a groan of despair, *for Errol is asleep again.*

"He said as how it would do him good," murmurs Martin complacently.

" Worthless wretch ! " shrieks her mistress. " Were it your life to save I'd let him sleep and you die. But it's his. They'll come and kill him while he lies there ! "

Then she flies at him and caresses him, and throwing pride away, begs him to rise up and live, if not for his sake for her own. She loves him. She will make him happy, her hero who has protected her so far. And then growing very desperate, for she has lost Ammed's help now and knows the time is shorter and the danger is more near, she beats and buffets this thing she loves, and cries over him, but strikes him all the same, until at last he opens his eyes again, and this time there is more sense in them ; the pupils are not so dilated. Then she gives him more coffee and begs him to move about ; crying that their lives depend upon his sense and power. This he does, for he has now thrown off enough of the drug to *wish* to be himself, and manhood comes in to help him fight his battle. So after more struggles, and more coffee, and then having deathly nausea and spasms of pain and vomiting, Charley Errol, pale, trembling, weak as an infant, the ghost of his former self, awakes from the opium sleep *just at the hour Constantine Niccovie thought he would be most under its power*, and hears a clang of arms and the noise of men creeping up the little stair-way by which the Greek had fled, and stealthily trying to force the back door that he has made a *mitrailleuse.*

CHAPTER VI.

A MOSLEM MOB.

AND the woman, hearing the noise also, whispers with white lips to the man : " Tell me what to do to save us ! " For Errol has staggered to his feet, but sank again exhausted and put his hand to his head and cried out : " My Heaven ! Too dizzy to see to fight ! "

"What shall I do to save us ? "

And he gasps back at her : " They must be standing now. Take the hammer. Strike the caps of the upper row. Quick ! " For finding no resistance the hand of Osman and Niccovie are driving the little door off its hinges.

Running into the room Lady Annerley pauses to beg God to forgive her for these men's lives, but as she prays she hears amid the varied blasphemies of the East her name and price for the pasha's harem, and she prays no more but strikes. And mingling with the awful rattle and tattoo of the crashing reports come groans and oaths and shrieks of agony.

For there was no time for retreat, and the heavy cartridges did deadly work on the Moslem crowd jammed in the sixteen feet of narrow staircase. Those that live retreat from this new engine of war ; the wounded drag themselves away ; only the dead remain.

Listening for another attack, this gentle English woman hears moans that tell her what she has done, and shudders. As she does so two or three pistol shots tear through the door, but are turned aside by the copper plates, and Errol staggering in gasps : " My strength's come back. The dizziness has gone. I fight *now !* " motioning her to the cover of the wall. Then a moment after he mutters : " The brutes are creeping up the steps now. Hear 'em ! " and falling down on his hands and knees, being too weak to walk, drags himself to the door and rakes with a volley from his lower battery the surface of the stairs. Shrieks and yells follow this discharge, but the next instant there is an awful impact on the door. Taking a beam of wood and dashing up, the attacking party have nearly knocked it off its hinges. Seeing their success, they draw back for another charge, and Errol listening waits, and as they come again, raps the ten center cartridges right into their column with fearful effect. Few outcries follow this discharge; the men, bending down to give greater force to the blow, have mostly been shot through the head. But Lady Annerley can hear the beam drop from their lifeless hands, and the few that fly slip in the blood and stagger over the bodies that clog up the stairs.

She shudders as Errol mutters proudly : " That was a settler, they'll not try to rush this door again ! " Then he makes her sit down in the shelter of the wall and goes off, walking wearily, but in a way that causes her a sigh of relief, for she can see that excitement is gradually dispelling the effects of the opium. A moment after he returns with a cup of water and says : " Drink ! The night is hot. You're deathly pale. You're not used to this ! "

" No," she mutters dismally, " I'm not used to killing people ! Oh my God, those wretched cries still rend my ears ! " then clutches the cup and drinks greedily.

While she does this, he, trying to console her, is saying : " The danger's over for a while now. Don't get nervous; " then suddenly pauses and whispers : " Hush ! " and listens with all his might.

Lady Annerley listens also and can hear the faint jingle of the donkey bells in the court-yard, and now knows why they were placed there. For Errol cries: " Good heavens ! They are attacking the front entrance ! Watch this door while I defend the front ! " and seizing his Remington, half runs, half staggers from her sight out through the main room to his shooting stand on the little balcony that overlooks the court-yard of the house.

Shortly after she can hear the sound of his rifle and the answering shots of their foes, and listens to them, half thinking that this is all a dream, and she will wake up in her lovely English home or her grand hotel in Paris ; for the past few days of her life have hardly seemed real to Sarah Annerley. This brings her to pondering on the curious fate that has brought her to Egypt, and to this man who is fighting her battle so truly, her father's sudden death in Italy, her hurried journey to catch Errol before he left Alexandria for Australia. She thinks ; " I

came here to tell him. Now I dare not let him know. I'll
get the packet back from him. I could not live to bear his
hate or contempt, now that I love him ! "

Thus working herself into an agony she mutters : " My
father when alive made my life unhappy ; now in his
death he has destroyed me ! " Next suddenly cries out :
" Curse him and his death-bed confession ! " and sobs
and beats her hands about, forgetting in the agony of
despair the din of battle that is around her.

But she is brought out of this spasm by an heroic rem-
edy, for some sneaking creature, a cowardly Egyptian
fellaheen, here fires a revolver at her through the door,
and directing his pistol at her noise, puts a bullet through
her dress, which is pretty close practice, as she wears a
modern costume. Perhaps he would fire again, but a
comrade's voice is heard beside him saying : " Unseeing
dog, would you kill a thousand purses of gold ? "

All this makes her spiteful. She springs to the door,
and rapping at the cartridges with hysterical vigor, gives
them a whole diagonal volley from right to left, wounding
or frightening both the men, for the two run howling into
the street.

Listening and hearing no noise upon the stairs, the
English lady tries to discover and count the shells that
have been discharged. There are only nineteen loaded
ones left. At this she becomes down-hearted. They
will not be enough if there is another strong attack, but
for the present no more come to face the fatal door.

The firing has also died away at the front of the
house ; she fears Errol may be wounded, and darts to his
succor, and as she does so a resolution comes to her that
has greater effect upon the lives of both than she imagines as she makes it.

As Errol lies down at his shooting stand, protected by
a light stone balustrade perhaps two feet high, the
open air of the court-yard drives away the effects of
the drug that is in his system ; his head gets clearer, his
nerves steadier, and his muscles stronger. He begins to
feel confidence in his shooting powers once more, for he
knows his weapon, and has used it before against *living*
things, which is much better preparation for such a fight
than any practice in the shooting gallery or even before
the butts in the open field.

He peers out into the court-yard which, shadowed by high houses, is so dark he can see nothing, though the sky above him is bright with the reflection of the fire that is now eating out the heart of the town. Bringing his Remington to bear upon the passage opening into the court where he has hung his first string of bells, he listens anxiously, for he must shoot by ear, not by eye.

Not a sound comes up to him, and he almost thinks the attacking party have gone back when he gets a sudden and awful surprise—the bells on the *second* string, the one on the stair-case not ten feet from him, sound an alarm. His foes, having crossed the bells in the passage-way while he has been defending the back entrance with the *mitrailleuse*, have all this time been silently creeping nearer and nearer to him, and are at the very threshold of the great room.

As this flashes upon the Australian his Remington flashes also, and in thirty seconds he pumps four shots into the crowd on the stair-way, who have suddenly stopped at the unlooked-for noise.

One man falls and two others stagger moaning away, while the rest skulk silently through the gloom, retreating across the court-yard to gain the passage to the street.

Here they come to grief again, for Errol has his rifle bearing upon the spot, and the moment he hears the bells hung at that place jingle, pumps three more bullets into the darkness that give him back a death-cry and some more Moslem groans. No danger coming to them when they had rung the bells upon their advance, the motley crew of Osman and Niccovie had thought these things, that now bring them destruction, an accident, and so failed to remove them.

One or two from a sheltered angle of the passage-way return his fire ; of the balance, those who are able do not stop till they reach the street.

Everything is silent for about a minute, then a voice is heard speaking to him out of darkness : "*Giaour*, you know me. I am Niccovie the Levantine, whose breath smells sweet with truth." *Bang!*—" A-a-a-aup ! "

This last is a howl of agony, with a twist at the end of it, such as dogs give on moonlight nights, for the Greek, becoming excited, had popped his head out of shelter,

and Errol, firing at the voice, had hit it and knocked three
teeth through the Levantine's cheek.

The Australian bursts into a roar of laughter, for the
shrieks and exclamations of Mr. Niccovie, though piteous,
are very funny ; but just here the young man gets a surprise himself, for the body of a gigantic Nubian lying on
the stair-way in front of him, that he has thought one of
the dead, rises suddenly up and fires a pistol straight at
him.   The distance is about ten feet, and Errol is lucky
to escape with a flesh wound in his left arm.   The Nubian darts into the darkness of the court-yard, and the
Australian brings his rifle to bear upon the passage
through which he knows the man must pass to escape,
and listens for the tinkling of the bells.   The moment he
hears them he shoots and the Nubian drops dead, a bullet
between his eyes.   Before he can fire again he hears the
sound of the string of bells being torn down and thrown
away as the attacking party have seen the fearful increase of danger this noise brings to them.

Then comes a lull, which Errol employs in binding a
handkerchief around his wounded arm, and finds the loss
of a little blood has driven the last of the opium from his
brain.   He recharges the magazine of his gun, and wipes
the perspiration from his forehead, for this fighting has
been hot, sharp work.

As he lies there Lady Annerley opens the door from the
main room and whispers, " Are you safe ? "

" Yes ! "

" Thank God ! "

" Go out of this danger !   Quick ! " commands Errol,
but she lies down also behind the parapet and watches
with him.

After a few minutes' silence Lady Annerley says under
her breath : " They have all gone away from the back
of the house, perhaps they have fled from here also."

" If I had a fire-ball I'd find that out ! "

" A fire-ball ; what is that ? "

And he describing it to her, she crawls into the house
and shortly after brings him her pocket-handkerchief
soaked in oil from the lamp.

Lighting this, Errol throws it into the court-yard,
where it burns itself out upon the flagstones, showing
that all but the dead have deserted the place.

"They are gone!" she cries joyously.

"Yes, for reinforcements. When they come back it'll be worse!" he returns grimly. Which is true, for Osman and Niccovie had not brought any great number of men with them, not wishing to pay too many, and thinking their booty sure and easy of capture. Disappointed in their first onslaught, they have gone to get enough of the rabble of the city to make their next attack certain of success.

After a moment's consideration Errol goes on: "I've too much to do to stay here and watch for them. I'll take the chance!" Then he crawls carefully down the stairs into the darkness, and after a minute Lady Annerley can hear the jingling of the bells as he replaces them in the position from which they have been torn, and gives a sigh of relief when he is at her side again for she knows his danger has been very great.

"Not a beggar down there," he says. He does not care to tell her of the three bodies he has stumbled over in the passage-way that made the bells jingle in his hand despite his caution. "Now, into the house! Quick! I've lots of work to do before the beasts return!"

"Work? You've had no food since breakfast. You must eat first!"

But he shakes his head.

"For my sake!" begs Lady Annerley.

"Well, if you'll help me, I'll work and eat together!"

And he goes about the business he has set himself to do, while she ministers to him, bringing him what dainties she can lay her hands on; then, blowing up the fire in the brazier, makes him coffee.

First, Errol rouses Martin out from her place of hiding, and putting the auger in her hand drags her to the door of the large room that opens upon the stairway leading up from the court-yard and main entrance. This door is equal in strength to the one that as a *mitrailleuse* has been so fatal at the secret portal in the rear.

"Bore this full of holes, too," he cries. "Point 'em downward!"

"The heathens might shoot me!" murmurs the maid hysterically.

"If you don't work I'll throw you out into the street, by Heaven!"

Thus adjured, Martin, sobbing, makes a strong attack with the auger upon the door, and soon has it full of holes.

While she is doing this, Errol, with his mouth full, and a cup of coffee beside him, is in the room from which Osman fled, replacing the discharged shells of his *mitrailleuse* with loaded cartridges.

This done, he returns to the large apartment, and finding Martin has made about forty holes in the main door, he plugs each of these with a Remington loaded shell, and secures them in place by some wire-netting he tears out of one of the windows and nails to the back of the door. Then he says to Lady Annerley: *If they come in a crowd and are too strong for me, or I am disabled, lock this door, and shoot the volley right in the wretches' faces. It'll be no good ten feet off!" For Martin has bored the holes in an hysterical way, and they point up and down and to all the points of the compass.

Next he looks at his watch, and mutters: " By George ! three o'clock in the morning. They'll be upon us soon !" and a second afterward suddenly turns to Lady Annerley, and cries : " Give me the pistols and knives that you took from the Greek and the Armenian !"

Lady Annerley silently brings him two daggers and one revolver.

" There was another pistol ! "

" That one is for me, at the last, if the worst comes !"

" You—you intend to—— "

" To kill myself ? Certainly !" mutters the woman, with pale lips but blazing eyes. " The Arab boy told me. They say I will sell for a thousand purses." Then she strides up to Martin and in a kind of hysteria laughs : " You will bring but a hundred—you are *cheap!*" then cries: " Take a pistol and at the last kill yourself if you are a woman ! "

To this her maid only answers by hiding herself in the darkness of the next room and sobbing more loudly.

Errol says nothing, seeing Sarah Annerley is determined and has a spirit to do desperate things when she is driven to despair by hopelessness and misery. A moment after, however, he takes her by the hand and whispers: " You're a brave woman, but keep cool ; remember, five shots for *them*—and the other only at the last—*the very last!*" •

Holding his hand, her hand trembles and her heart beats
faster and she remembers ; she says to him : "Charley—
I beg your pardon, Mr. Errol "—turning away her face,
for it is the first time she has called him by his Christian
name.

"That's right. We've been good comrades, haven't
we ? Call me Charley ! "

"Well, then, Charley," here she gives a great blush ;
" I gave you a packet ! "

"Yes, containing some revelation or other."

" If I die and you live, send it to your father unopened ! "

" Yes ! "

"If we both live, give it back to me ! "

" But you told me——"

" As you are a man, give it back to me ! for my happiness ! Pity me ! Give it back to me unopened and
unread ! " This she begs him with tears, and sighs, and
pleadings that astonish him, but are unnecessary, for he
returns :

"Certainly, if you ask it. The packet is yours, but you
said——"

" I'm a woman and have changed my mind," the last
with half a smile. Then she becomes very serious again,
and says : " Remember, if we both live, you have promised on your honor to give that packet back to me ! "

"Of course I will ! It is in my pocket in the other
room," he replies, for the night has been so oppressive
he has been working and fighting in his shirt. Passing
his hand over his eyes, after a moment he goes on :
" Now a promise from you. In case I die and you are
saved, just drop a line to my dear old father telling him
how I thought of him at the last."

" Don't fear ! " she returns. " I'll remember you who
fell fighting for me—for me whom you should—" but here
for the first time she notices Errol's wounded arm, and
Sarah Annerley gives way and dropping her head upon
his knee, bursts into tears, and cries "For me ! " and
kisses the man's hand, calling him her preserver and her
savior, though he ought to hate her, in a hysterical way,
which makes him fear the strain has been too great for
her mind.

Sitting thus in the gloom of the half-lighted room, th ;

roar of arson and riot rising to their ears from the burning city, to these two comes the horror of waiting—*waiting to be attacked.* They dare not sleep, though they are
cruelly tired ; they dare hardly breathe, they must listen
so intently for warning noises, for the court-yard is too
black for seeing ; they can only wait.

The ticking of Errol's watch at first relieves the
silence, and this has become monotonous and dreary,
when Lady Annerley suddenly whispers, " Hist ! " and
he mutters, " It has come ! " for at the outer entrance of
the court the little bells give forth their tinkling warning.

Errol crawls upon the balcony but can see nothing, and
desperately fires at the sound. To the report of his gun
comes the rush, not of a few men but of a hundred, and
he cries out for a fire-ball so he can see where best to
direct his shots.

But there is no time to make one now, and Lady Annerley desperately throws out the burning lamp into the
center of the court-yard.

Descending in a whirl of flame, this falls upon and
breaks over the head of an Arab, deluging his cotton garments with kerosene and setting him on fire ; while the
wretch runs about giving out horrid cries and screams
and lighting up the yard, showing it full of Bedouins,
Copts, Moslems, Turks, and Soudanese grotesquely armed,
the desperate scourings of the Moslem streets.

By the light of this human fire-ball Errol sees this fantastic crowd, with jabbering cries, forming in solid column
to charge the stairs, careless of the awful fate of their
comrade ; who, with shrill shrieks that pierce the air and
great bounds of agony, is burning up alive as he dances
the court-yard round.

This whole thing passes in a second ; the next the Australian turns loose his breech-loader on the head of the
column, and though each shot probably carries with it a
life, instead of stopping them it only makes them come
on quicker ; and, the magazine of his rifle being empty, he
runs to the head of the stairs. Firing his revolver at the
leaders of the rush, he, pursued by a volley, flies in the
door, and bars it, the English lady helping him. The next
instant the human battering ram strikes it with a bang,
and he cries : " Shoot 'em before their weight forces it ! "

With this she is at the door, the hammer in her hand,

exploding the cartridges that have made contact with the
door death, and he with Osman's dagger goes to work
upon them also.

As the bullets pierce the leaders of the rush and they
fall dying, others are forced, by the pressure of those
charging in the rear, against this door that spouts forth
destruction. And as they are stricken down, those behind
them are pressed against the exploding shells, until the
struggle to escape death becomes greater than the force
of those behind ; and panic seizes the mob, who run away.

Hearing this Errol tries to open the door to give them
a parting shot ; but cannot, there are too many dead and
wounded lying against it. However, some of these last
succeed in crawling away, and he gets the door open
wide enough to squeeze himself out, tumbling over the
body of a Turk, who jabs a knife in his leg and gasps,
" For Allah ! " as he dies.

On the balcony the young man, by the early morning
light, which is just streaking the east, shoots two or three
wounded who are escaping, for this stab has made him
merciless. Then he staggers in, for he hears a fusilade
coming from the back entrance to the house. Osman and
Niccovie have led their followers round, and are trying
to force it.

As he gets into the main room, Errol sees he must
bind up his wound or he will lose his strength. Knowing the door with its fifty shots cannot be forced immediately, he sits down and finds he has two ; one, the stab
in the calf of the leg, and the other from a bullet that
has come through the door, and being partially spent,
has glanced round his ribs. In the excitement of the
combat he has not noticed it before.

As he dresses them the fusilade ceases, and Lady Annerley comes to him, her beautiful face black with powder, but blazing with excitement, and cries proudly : " I
beat them off—alone ! " and then more sadly : " but fired
every cartridge in the door to do it."

" If they come again, I can spare no more ! " says
Errol, gloomily, inspecting his ammunition, " I need all
the rest for my rifle."

The next instant there is a yell from Martin, who has
taken refuge on the roof to get as far from this last fight
as possible. As Errol springs up to her cry the servant-

girl comes down the steps screaming : "There are men up there—*men!*" Cautiously putting his head through the scuttle the young man sees that she has exaggerated the matter but only a very little.

No one is already upon the roof of this house, but a number of men are on the top of the next one. It is a little higher than that of Abdallah's dwelling, and there is only fifteen feet of space between them. All this he can easily discern, for the morning is advancing rapidly.

As Errol brings his Remington to bear, a lithe-limbed Soudanese has taken a short run in order to spring across the chasm. The Australian has been accustomed to kangaroo-shooting, and as the man jumps he dies in mid-air. This unexpected attack makes his foes retreat for a moment, and gives the young man time to look around him. Instinctively his eyes turn to the water, from which their only relief can come, and he gives a cry of joy, for by the early morning light he can see armed boats' crews from the men-of-war landing on the Marina.

"What is it ?" asks Lady Annerley, who is standing below him on the stair handing him up some cartridges for his rifle.

"English sailors !" he cries. "We are saved !" but the next minute sighs : "I'm afraid they come too late !"

For he sees the crowd, increased by numbers the firing has drawn to the spot, preparing to jump onto the roof *en masse*, while, to keep his fire down, a fusilade is opened on him from several house-tops ; and as the bullets come singing by he recognizes the crack of the Martini-Henry rifle, and knows he has now against him Egyptian soldiers who have deserted from Arabi's army.

At this moment Lady Annerley cries from below : "They are forcing the back door !" and he, hearing the sound of the blows upon it, feels his hour has come—but only for a moment.

In the next that dogged, never-say-die, fight-to-the-death spirit that has won the Anglo-Saxon race so many battles and such glorious victories, when Hope has turned her back upon them and Death has set his hand upon them, comes to him, and he cries : "FOLLOW ME ! I'M GOING TO FIGHT OUR WAY TO THE ENGLISH BOATS !"

As his voice rings out these brave words, the woman

who has only loved him before now adores him. Hastily giving their assailants on the roof one or two shots to check their advance, Errol runs down the stairs and finds Lady Annerley waiting with Martin, whom she has just dragged from an inner room. The blows upon the door at the back of the house warn them that the front way is their only chance of exit. They climb over the corpses before the entrance to the main room and glide down the steps into the court-yard. Errol whispers to Lady Annerley, who is following him closely : " Get your revolver ready and come quickly ! " And they pass through the archway and into the street unobserved, and to their astonishment, unopposed. For no thought of their prey's flight having ever entered Osman or Niccovie's heads, they have left no men to guard the main entrance ; and the audacity of the attempt has so far made it safe.

CHAPTER VII.

THE AMERICAN MARINES.

IN the street, however, there are one or two rioters who on seeing them set up a shout, but run away, for this night's fight has made Errol a terror to his assailants.

" Now's our chance ! Run ! " he whispers, and begins to move quickly ; but she hangs back and says, " Where's Martin ? "

" If Martin is not here she is lost. By heavens ! they are in the house now ! " he exclaims as a yell of disappointed rage comes from the rabble in the rooms from which they have fled. " Come, it's our only chance ! "

Thus adjured, Lady Annerley darts after him, but the delay has been fatal. As they move along, a band of Arabs, Nubians and *Fellaheen* dart round the corner of the street and head off the retreat. At this Errol clinches his teeth and cries to her : " Follow me closely, I'll cut our way through ! " and runs toward them.

They fire at him, but their old matchlocks and superannuated pistols miss him. As he advances, he turns loose his Remington and wounds two. But now Lady

6

Annerley hears a noise behind her and looking back sees
they are surrounded; for another crowd of Moslems
headed by Niccovie in person are issuing from the house.
This only makes Errol hasten to meet the first party,
wishing to break through them before the others come
up.

None of the Arabs fire now, perhaps afraid of shooting
each other, perhaps because Niccovie cries out from his
bandaged mouth in Eastern jargon: "Don't kill the
woman, she is too valuable!"

If they don't fire, Errol does and drops another before
they get to him. Then he suddenly pulls Lady Annerley behind him into a retreating corner made by the joining of two houses, and thus having his enemies in front
of him, opens with his revolver. Two get to him a little
quicker than the rest; one a wiry Arab, the other a
savage-looking black. The Arab he shoots. As he does
so, Lady Annerley sees the black raise his scimiter to strike
the life she has learned to love, and a mist comes before
her eyes; but in that mist she sees her own revolver raised
and smoke coming from its mouth; and, as this clears
away, *the black is dead.*

To do this, she has to step a little out from the wall,
and some one coming behind her, seizes her round the
waist and drags her backward away from the man who
is fighting for her.

She tries to get her hand behind her to shoot the
wretch who now actually carries her along with brutal
jeers and mocking laughter; but in vain. And now
others join him, foolishly coming in front of her, and getting winged for their carelessness, for her arm is free
enough to shoot before her.

All this she does silently and hopelessly; the first, because she knows that to call Errol's eyes from his own
personal assailants will be his death; the second, because she sees that every moment more foes bar her
way to his protection. Till at last her five shots are all
gone and she despairs; for Niccovie's face is leering
into hers and the next instant her pistol will be torn
from her. Even now he speaks to her as if he owned
her. This makes her desperate, and the revolver's muzzle,
cold and chilly as the death it gives, is pressed against
her forehead, for the last moment is come, the last bullet

is hers. But as her finger presses the trigger his words buzz in her head : " Wait till the *very* last ! " She gives herself five seconds *more*, and in them *thinks* she sees the little Arab boy hanging to Niccovie's coat-tails and that a cheer is sounding round the corner ; and it is Anglo-Saxon, and she turns her hand, and the shot that was to kill her she fires into the Greek's smiling face. While as she does so a crashing volley sounds in her ears, and there are blue uniforms and English voices and rough but tender hands about her, and a dandy lieutenant shoots with one hand the man who holds her, and catches her as she falls with the other.

Panting and dazed, and only kept upon her feet by this young officer's arm, Sarah Annerley sees in the hurly-burly around her the blue uniforms make short work of the Moslem crowd ; the lieutenant shooting two as he holds her.

Now, all this makes quite a cloud of smoke and dust, and as it clears away she notes Niccovie holding a broken jaw in one hand, and a large sword in the other, pursuing little Ammed, who is dodging for his life. She cries to the lieutenant, " Save the boy ! "

He runs after the Levantine, calling to him to surrender ; but Niccovie only answers with another slash at the Arab urchin. Then the officer's great navy revolver gives a puff and, though thirty yards away, the ·Greek *renegado* gives a yell and turns round to find out what hurts him, but dies too soon to be quite sure.

During this Errol has staggered up to Lady Annerley, and they both sit down on a couple of stones, too exhausted to do anything but gasp for breath and wipe away the dust and sweat of battle. She looks at him, and, seeing no new wounds except a slight scratch upon his forehead, becomes very happy.

Heading his men, the officer soon clears Abdallah's home of rioters, chasing them from the rooms up to the roof, and then over the neighboring house-tops. Returning from this to the street, this young gentle, man (for he is hardly twenty-five), who has fought his fight in a rough-and-ready, free-and-easy sort of a way, produces a silk handkerchief, brushes the dust off his patent-leather boots, and becomes a dandy once more.

Approaching them he gives the English woman a mil-

itary bow, takes off his cap and says : " Lady Annerley,
I believe. Permit me to introduce myself," and producing a card-case, he presents :

Mr. Houston Potter,

U. S. Ship Quinnebaug.

As she has been looking at the young man, the lady
he addresses has discovered something in his fine face
that makes it familiar. She reads his card and all this becomes clear to her. She cries : " Why, you're Miss Potter's brother—the naval officer ! "

"Yes, I'm Miss Potter's *brother*," returns the gentle-
man, with a little laugh. " At home I'm Mr. Potter of
Texas' son ; in Europe, Miss Potter of Texas' brother.
The only place I have an identity is on the ship's books."

" The fate of being related to such distinguished people," smiles Lady Annerley, for Miss Potter is the reigning American belle in Europe, and the whole of fashionable France and England are bowing to her great wealth
and greater beauty. " You should be proud—" but
here she appears to be astonished, and cries : " You're
American ! "

"Certainly. These are American marines ! " and as he
points to his men she, for the first time, notes that their
uniforms are not English.

" You see," he goes on, " I'm not a marine, I'm a line
officer. I volunteered to come on shore on your account.
Ida, my sister, wired me from Paris by the telegraph
ship, the *Cheltnam,* which has picked up the European
cable, that you were here, and to look after you ; and I
might have looked after you a long time, had it not been
for little Ammed waiting for us at the Marina, giving me
your note and begging me ' Quick ! Save the beaut-ful
lady !' " With this he pats the Arab boy's head, who
gazes proudly at Lady Annerley, then grins in the lieutenant's face, and cuts a caper. For he has just strolled up
to them, grand in the possession of the sword of the late
Nicovie which he carries over his shoulder.

Here the lady says suddenly: "Excuse me, Mr. Potter, this is Mr. Errol, the gentleman who fought for me all night."

"Then," remarks the American, "I congratulate you on your champion. I've been admiring his handiwork up there," and he points to the house of Abdallah the Moor.

"You never learned that pistol shooting on the quarterdeck!" returns Errol as the two men shake hands.

"No," replies the American, "my father taught me that as a boy, in Texas. Can we smoke, Lady Annerley?" Then he produces his cigar case and offers one to Errol.

Permission being given, the two young men light up and the lieutenant says: "I must call my men back. They are fighting too much and killing too many. We only came ashore to save life, but the sights we saw as we forced our way here have made the men very savage. They've seen dead Christian women and wounded little children till they are ready to butcher every Moslem looter in Alexandria. Might I offer you my escort back to the house? You may wish to change your dress;" this last a little significantly.

"I've lots of clothes at the Hotel de l'Europe. Let's go there. Oh, for the luxury of something clean!" cries Lady Annerley. Then catching the lieutenant's eye she follows it, and looking at herself for the first time this morning, hangs her head and mutters: "Oh, how awful!" This is with a big blush that they don't see, her face being too dirty. For she is one grime of powder smoke; a lock of her beautiful hair has been singed off by the flame of the lamp that she threw into the courtyard; her dress is torn to rags, and there is a great red burn upon one of her shapely but now black and dirty arms.

"No," says Errol grimly, judging her thought. "You're not the woman of fashion of three days ago."

Here she takes a look at Errol and cries laughingly: "But you're worse!" for he is simply a background of dirt daubed with blood.

But the sight of his blood makes the laugh leave her voice, which becomes so tender that it attracts young Potter's attention as she goes on: "Wounded, and all for me!"

"Oh, I'm quite right," says Errol, getting on his feet, but so stiffly that the American puts his arm round him, for which Lady Annerley's eyes thank him.

Lady Annerley's thoughts having gone back to dress, next come to her maid, and she cries : "Oh, poor Martin ! she was left in the house ! "

"Your servant is all right."

"Thank Heaven ! " for in this moment of safety she thinks kindly even of Martin's fears.

"But your dresses are all gone."

"Gone ? "

"Yes. The Hotel de l'Europe and the whole Frankish quarter are nothing but blazing ruins ! " Here the lieutenant points to the smoke, and after a moment suggests : "If they are saved, your dresses will all be very black." Then thinks he has made a *faux pas*, and stammers a little as he says : "I—I beg your pardon, Lady Annerley. I—I had forgotten you're in mourning. Your father, Sir Jonas Stevens, died in Italy."

"Yes, only three weeks ago. I came here direct from his death-bed." As she mutters this the woman's eyes turn to Errol with a beseeching, appealing, apologetic glance. She says : "Remember your promise ! "

"Oh, about that packet ! "

"Yes, we *both* live now ! " and she looks at him as if that meant a great deal in their future.

"Of course, I'll get it for you. It's in my vest-pocket in the house."

Then they all stroll up the street and into the little court-yard ; the lieutenant, careless of his uniform, helping Errol, who walks quite stiffly, but says he'll be all right in a week. And the conversation becomes very animated and full of laughter, for the sun seems to shine very brightly in Alexandria this morning on Lady Annerley and Errol ; and they feel as if they have come a long and dangerous journey from a far country, where death has been close about them ; and the world they have come to again is a very joyous and happy one, as they listen to the whinny and braying of Ammed's donkeys in the stable, and the chirping of the birds in the court-yard. Then Lady Annerley tells Errol that he must come to Europe and she will give him the *entrée* to the world

of fashion—her world. This he says he'll do, after he
has returned to Australia to see his father, who never
leaves that country. For he is very much flattered and
rather delighted, as what young man wouldn't be with
one of the queens of the *beau monde* half begging him,
half caressing him to visit her.

But this mention of his father causes her to start and
say : " Your promise, *quick !* "

" Of course ! " and he turns toward the stairs.

She is about to go with him, but the lieutenant stops
her, saying : " The sights down here are bad, those above
are worse ; by daylight they would shock you ! "

" I'll bring it down to you ! "

" Perhaps I'd better go for you, you're not quite up to
much exertion," suggests young Potter.

" No, I can do it ; I've got some other things to
find," says Errol half way up the stairs, and seeing the
maid on the balcony laughs : " Hello, Martin, all right
after all ? "

" Yes, sir, I'm comfortable," grunts the servant-girl,
" except as my boots is bloody ! "

Passing on, Errol enters the house, while Martin remains on the balcony giggling at young Ammed, who is
getting his donkeys out of the stable and decorating
them with the strings of bells of which they have been
denuded, while Lady Annerley and young Potter chat
together in the court-yard below.

They are talking of his sister, and the lady is saying :
" Now you are to visit me also," when the noise of struggle and a smothered cry come from the open window,
and Martin on the balcony is yelling like one possessed.
In two bounds the lieutenant is up the stairs and in the
house ; two seconds after his pistol speaks.

Lady Annerley hurries after him, but he meets her at
the door and she notices his face is pale. " You'd better
not come in ! " he says in a low voice.

" What do you mean ? "

" These things happen so suddenly sometimes—in
war."

" It was Osman killed Mr. Errol ! " cries Martin. " I
saw it through the window ! "

" You idiot ! " exclaims the lieutenant, " you have
killed her ! " For Sarah Annerley, who had fought through

all the carnage and bloodshed of that awful night in grim silence, has now uttered a terrible cry and fallen senseless upon the pile of corpses in front of the door.

Calling Ammed to summon the sergeant in charge of his men, he picks up the English lady, carries her into the main apartment, and says to Martin savagely : " Get some water and bring her to. The man needs my attention first," then goes to look at Errol, who lies moaning in the next room, a terrible knife wound in his side. As he is making his examination, the sergeant comes in to him and touches his cap.

" I told you to clear the house of rioters, and you left a man in it ! " says the lieutenant sharply.

" Yes, sir, Mr. Errol's dragoman ! "

" How do you know that ? "

" He showed me the document by which he was hired. When I tackled him here he was quietly fixin' his boss' clothes ! " With this the sergeant of marines points to the Australian's coat and vest that lie near the wounded man.

" I shall hold you responsible for the absolute obedience of my orders. Get me the paper by which the scoundrel proved his story to you ! "

" How can I ? It's in his pocket and he's skipped ! " mutters the sergeant, bewildered.

" You'll find his body at the bottom of that flight of steps ! " replies Potter, pointing to the stairway leading to the private door.

As the soldier is about to go to Osman's body, the lieutenant calls him back and says : " On second thought bring me all the papers on the corpse—all ! "

Then the men carry Errol down to the Marina, followed by Ammed and Martin. Mr. Potter, by the aid of the Arab boy's donkeys, gets Lady Annerley to the boats also, though she is half fainting, half crazy, and wildly whispers things in the lieutenant's ear which make that young man open his eyes. On shipboard the surgeon looks at the wounded Australian and says he may live, but not in this hot climate.

So it comes to pass two days after this that, the P. & O. steamer *Calcutta* being ready to sail, Lady Annerley, pale, careworn, loveworn, the ghost of her former beautiful self, stands on the landing-stage to bid good-by to

the Arab boy and Mr. Potter. She has not the strength
to say much, but she pats the little *gamin's* head and
tells him he is to be educated (she has arranged this
with the English consul), and taking the officer by the
hand, she murmurs a blessing on him and the American
marines who saved her as they did many other Christian
women in those days of riot and carnage, in that hot,
looted Egyptian city.

Mr. Potter and the boy watch the receding steamer,
as her big propeller drives her through the anchored fleets,
en route for Brindisi and Venice, in her main saloon
Charley Errol of Australia, wounded nigh unto death,
and raving with the Nile fever, and a woman nursing him like an angel of mercy, and weeping over him
and begging him to live for her sake ; then wildly
swearing he shall not die—this, the only man she ever
loved.

The *Calcutta* fades from view, and Ammed, chinking
in his pockets the plethora of coin Lady Annerley has
put in them, says quietly : " The beau-ful lady's tears
are pearls, but she has no more."

" No," mutters the lieutenant, gloomily, " she's hit too
hard." Then he takes to meditating in a cynical way
upon the affair, thinking : " George ! she's been a widow
eighteen months—a widow with a title and twenty thousand pounds a year, and stood it out against every buck
and blood in London and Paris ; yet that Australian, in
one night's fighting, fought himself into her love—that's
luck ! " A minute after he gives a half sigh and mutters:
" Quackenboss, our sawbones, says they'll toss him over-
board between here and Brindisi. That isn't luck ! I've
half a mind to try and take his place. Wonder if this
cable would get me leave on the ground of family business." With this he produces a message and reads :

" POTTERSVILLE, TEXAS, *July* 14, 1882.
" To POTTER,
" U. S. ship *Quinnebaug*,
" Alexandria :
" Worried about Ida. *Texas Siftings* says she can marry a duke.
Send the girl home right off—I'm afraid she's getting into bad com-
pany.   DAD."

"The dear old boy ! " cries the lieutenant, and gives

a shriek of laughter, but it is cut short by the sergeant of marines who, saluting, says : "I've been on duty in the town, impossible to deliver these before. The papers found on the body of Osman, the dragoman ! "

Among these documents is the packet given by Lady Annerley to Errol, the Australian.

BOOK II.

ENGLISH JUSTICE.

CHAPTER VIII.

THE GIRLS HAVE COME!

THE *Calcutta* churns her way through the Mediterra-
nean, stops at Brindisi, and then goes on to Venice, and
somehow they get Errol to this place not yet dead. Here
a celebrated doctor, telegraphed for to London, meets
them and says: " No farther or he dies!"

And so, in a great *palazzo* on the Grand Canal that
Lady Annerley engages, they stop to fight the last round
in the Australian's battle for life ; which goes on in all
the terrible ups and downs, despairs and hopes, of such
awful combats.

But at last, with the nursing of love and the aids of
wealth, youth, a strong constitution, and modern science,
death is driven from the ring, and hope takes the place of
despair in the heart of the woman who watches. The at-
tacks of delirium become fainter and less frequent, and, as
she sees this, Sarah Annerley herself becomes better ; for
she has fallen down to a shadow of herself. As Charley
Errol gains strength, she regains beauty, until one morning in September she is her own radiant self, as Dr. Lampson feels the pulse of the young man in a cheery, never-
say-die manner peculiar to him, and says : " Killed any
more kangaroos in your deli—I mean your dreams last
night, Errol ? "

" No, not even a rat-kangaroo," replies the patient,
very languidly and lazily, as he stretches his long, ema-
ciated limbs.

" Ah, glad to hear it. Since you've given up killing, I think I may say that you'll live."

" Was it so near as all that ? " asks the young man, with a kind of wonder in his blue eyes that are made almost pathetic by the deep circles disease has drawn round them. " I didn't know that ! "

" No, you knew nothing. All you did day and night was to hunt kangaroos."

" George ! didn't I hunt them ! " re-echoes the patient. " I believe I've killed, in imagination, about all in Australia. There was always one big fellow who used to run about blazing, giving light like a torch for me to shoot them, and one night a ferocious old man-kangaroo had me down and would have murdered me, when she shot him over my shoulder."

" She ? " says the doctor, with an accent of surprise, feeling Errol's pulse again surreptitiously to be quite sure the fever has not again returned to him.

" Yes, she, the lady who comes every day—the one that makes this room look—well—look as it does ; " and the young man gazes at a bunch of Roman roses and Parma violets that lie on a table near him. " You didn't bring those, did you ? "

" I—I—you see—I brought—— "

" No, you bring only medicine. I know you, doctor ; you'll say I excite myself, though I've been sensible these three days, but sleepy, oh, how sleepy ! I've liked to be sleepy ; because when I was sleepy she came in and looked at me. If my eyes appeared to see, or I grew restless, she sneaked out again. Then I laid traps for her. I pretended somnolence, and she came in and cried over me and begged me to forgive her. What the deuce should I forgive the angel for ? Why, I hear her now ; she's there ! " cries the young man, struggling to a half-sitting position in bed and pointing eagerly, for at this there has come a deep feminine sigh from behind a light screen that shields a little corner of the room from his gaze.

" Confound you ! " grunts the doctor ; " if you don't keep quiet, young man, I'll give you a devil of a dose of quinine ! " pushing his patient down on to the pillows again.

" I won't keep quiet till I've seen her ! "

"Go to sleep!"

"Yes, with one eye open! Doctor, can't you see I'm better and strong?" With this he attempts to struggle up in bed again, then says, plaintively : "How—how sore my side is! My heavens, I must have been wounded!" sinks down and looks astounded.

Here from behind the screen comes Lady Annerley, who cries savagely to the doctor : "Don't be so rough with him!" and pushing herself between the physician and the patient, arranges the pillows and settles the young man's head upon them, giving his tossing blonde locks that have grown very long in his months of illness a surreptitious caress.

"There," she says smilingly, "now you've got your senses back again I shall not run away from you any more, as the naughty doctor has made me do—Charley!" As she murmurs the last she smothers it in a blush.

"You're awfully kind—*to a stranger!* Doctor, please introduce me. I—what have I done?" stammers Errol, astonished.

For Sarah Annerley has risen from his bedside and is standing like a statue of despair, murmuring in a broken voice : "He don't know me. My heavens, *forgotten!*" and then, before either of them can say. a word, she .is on her knees holding his hand, crying : "Don't you remember the woman you fought for, the woman you were wounded for, the woman you nearly died for; don't you remember Egypt and that awful night—and ME!!" Then mumbling over his hand she begs of him to "*think!* THINK!! THINK!!!"

The last "*think!*" is uttered outside the door, for the doctor is upon her like a whirlwind and has her out of the room, crying : "Lady Annerley, remember the patient!" Though as a man the doctor enjoys the sensuous beauty that this brune Niobe makes in her floating, gauzy dress that outlines her graceful pose as she pleads with her forgetful hero; and as a psychologist he is struck with curiosity that any one should forget, like Errol, the greatest crisis of his life; still as a physician he is horrified at the effect of such excitement on his patient. He says very impressively to her : "How dare you?"

"Oh, doctor, he did not remember me!"

"That'll all come back in time," returns the doctor

grimly. "Another outburst like that and I'll order you not to come into the sick-room at all."

"Not let me in—his nurse? You—you couldn't get along without me!" which is no exaggeration, for Lady Annerley has for two months been, as the doctor expresses it, "good as the whole staff of *Guy's.*"

"I shall try to, at all events. And now, Sarah, I want to have a plain talk with you," and he leads her from the door of the sick-room to a little antechamber, where the September sun comes in mellowed and tinted by the colored awnings, and the splash of the gentle ripples of the Grand Canal rising softly to their ears seems to punctuate their conversation.

"Ah, you're going to scold me! I know you are!" replies Lady Annerley. "You always call me Sarah when you are about to say something that is cross. Oh! you are not going to prevent my seeing him ; don't dare to think of that. I'll—I'll restrain myself. I'll—I'll do anything!" This last is said with a tone of abject humility that almost startles him. And then, as if picking up courage, she gives the grim doctor a kind of a half smile, and continues suddenly : "But we're outside the sickroom, and you can't bully me now!"'

"If bullying is asking questions, I'm going to do a good deal of it," says Lampson, taking a pinch of snuff, the abstinence from which in the chamber of illness has made him rather surly. "Why did you telegraph me to leave my big practice in London and come all the way to Venice to pull this young fellow through the fever ?"

"Because I had no faith in Italian doctors!"

"Quite right; neither have I!" assents Lampson. "But it'll be a pretty expensive little affair for you."

"I don't care how much you charge!"

"Ah! the arrogance of wealth; but I'll remember it in my bill."

Here Lady Annerley suddenly questions him : "Why didn't you ask me this two months ago, when you first came here?"

"Why? because," says the doctor leisurely, "I had too much to think of to save his life. Besides, I made sure you were engaged to be married to young Errol—are you?"

"Engaged to be married to *him*!" There is a kind of fear in Sarah Annerley's voice as she mutters this.

" Yes, it wouldn't be so awfully horrible as your tone indicates," says old Lampson with a chuckle. " He's not too old for you, and when he's fatter 'll be very handsome ; besides, all your money is in your own name ; your father, the late Sir Jonas Stevens——"

" Don't talk of my father *here !* " interrupts his listener in a gasp of grief that astonishes the doctor, for her dead father's treatment of Lady Annerley has never been supposed by the world in general, or the family physician in particular, to have been that which would stimulate a daughter's affection. " Besides," she goes on, " wasn't his risking his life to save mine in Egypt enough to make me give any amount of time and any amount of money and—anything else to save his—oh my God ! how he fought for me ! "

" Humph ! " says Dr. Lampson thoughtfully, " what took you to Egypt anyway ? Every one expected trouble there, and yet two days after your father's death away you sailed to plunge into war and bloodshed in Alexandria."

" I went there on business. Mr. Errol was going to Australia. I wished to see him before he left Egypt ; I had a message to send his father. Please don't cross-question me or I shall think you a lawyer, and my confidences to a physician will cease."

Lady Sarah says this last with a decided snap of both eyes and voice.

Lampson doesn't heed this, however, and goes on : " Who is his father ? "

" Mr. Ralph Errol of Melbourne ! "

" Ralph Errol! I believe I've heard of him ; one of their great capitalists out there. Humph ! sure of my fee on both sides of the house," grunts the doctor. " What the deuce has interested you in Ralph Errol of the antipodes ? "

" He—he took my father's place out in Australia," replies Lady Annerley, with a peculiar accent and hesitation in her voice, as she turns away and tries to look out of the window.

" Ah ! " remarks the physician, " that young man's father was your father, Sir Jonas Steven's, agent across the water."

" Yes, he represented my father's—banking interest," mutters my lady, whose eyes are gazing in a spasm of gloomy meditation over the bright waters of the Grand Canal that are gilded by the Italian sun.

She hardly knows what she is looking at, though the agitated splash of the water on the stones beneath seems to her no more rapid than the beating of her heart ; for this mention of her father has set some awful thoughts buzzing in her brain ; and if the doctor could only see her hands he would know that she was grasping the window-frame to support her body, which is trembling with some peculiar emotion.

Not noticing this, old Lampson grimly cogitates : "Rage destroys diplomacy. I'll get the truth of my lady by making her angry," and continues the conversation in rather a flippant strain : "Isn't it rather curious you knew all this ? My Lady Annerley was supposed to be devoted to the ball-room not the counting-house."

He stops here, for she turns to him and he sees her face.

"My father told me a great deal about his past life when on his death-bed," mutters Lady Annerley, in a broken and humble tone ; then all the humility leaves her voice and her manner, she strides to the would-be cynic and hisses in his ear : "Don't steal the secrets from the dead—you hear me ! *Let the dead alone !* "

"Curse it, madam ! You are pinching my arm ! " yells the doctor, for she has emphasized her last words by a very savage grip on the old man's biceps ; but Lady Annerley, thinking she hears a noise in the sick-room, has flown there, and Lampson follows her nursing his pinch and wrath together.

As he comes in she is gazing at the invalid, who is asleep, with a look that puts a new idea in the physician's head. And taking her on one side, he says : "You're very desperately in love with him ! "

Then she astounds him more by returning quite steadily : " The idea ! " but after a moment hides her head and begins to cry.

"Now none of this ! No sentiment in the sick-room ! No flirtation ! No marrying nor giving in marriage till Adonis is well."

"Marriage !—I ? You forget yourself, doctor ; I am only a widow eighteen months ! " The beautiful woman is attempting to be haughty.

"That's the usual time!" grins Lampson. "At twenty-
five, about eighteen months is the fatal period."

But she suddenly frightens him, for she towers over
him with flashing eyes, and cries: "Enough! No
more jokes about my heart!" Then goes away with a
blaze upon her face downstairs, where she says in a
broken voice: "Martin, I'm sick. Get me to bed!"
Which the maid does tremblingly, for she has an idea
that all fevers are infectious, and thinks: "If she
catches it, I'm a goner."

As for Lampson, he looks after the beautiful widow,
and this cynic mutters: "Poor devil!"

Family doctors as well as family lawyers know the
skeleton in the closet, and old Lampson is running Lady
Annerley's case over in his mind. At seventeen her
father had practically forced her to marry old Lord Annerley. For Sir Jonas Stevens had made his money as a
banker, and though knighted, worshiped the aristocracy
like a city alderman, i. e., with his whole soul. Viscount
Annerley was a relic of the Regency; had been a young
roué in the days of Beau Brummel, and even after his
marriage aspired to be an old roué. He hated his bride
because she despised him, which she did from the very
depths of her heart. Sir Jonas Stevens, her father, was
a man soured by something, no one knew what, and devoted only to accumulating great wealth. And from
seventeen to twenty-three the Viscountess Annerley lived
unloved by any man whose love she could return without
dishonor. Since then she has buried her husband and
her father, and with the old title of one and the grand
fortune of the other at twenty-five is one of the greatest
matches in all England.

With a husband who outraged her pride and a father
who cared not enough for her to shield her from the
attentions of the thoughtless or the vicious, no tinge or
speck of the slightest scandal has ever rested upon
Sarah Annerley's fame as a woman. Fitted to inspire as
well as entertain the tender passion, she has to this time
gone through life unloving.

It is probably some thought like the last which is in
the doctor's mind, as after looking searchingly at his
patient, and noting the great beauty of the young man's
features, fair curly hair, and the noble proportions of his

7

six feet of bone, muscle, and sinew, old Lampson says:
"George! in a month this chap 'll be an Adonis; then
she'll have her innings! Rather think young Errol
has wounded something else besides kangaroos and
Egyptians."

So as time runs on the Australian's convalesence becomes more pronounced, he gradually regaining his recol-
lection. For he recognizes Lady Annerley perfectly,
though he never clearly remembers the night before he
was stricken down, and has, to her great joy, forgotten
entirely the packet she gave him.

Lady Annerley has searched Errol's clothes and all his
belongings—everything that came with them from Egypt
—and it is not among them. Undoubtedly destroyed by
some accident, it can never come from Alexandria to disclose a secret that, since she loves him, must now be
dead.

Learning that his father has heard of his wound, the
young man often wonders why his governor has not
been able to run over to see him. At these times such
a peculiar expression comes over his nurse's face that
Lampson cogitates as he looks at her: "What's the
matter with my lady? Hang me if she ain't ashamed of
herself!" for he has known Sarah Annerley since she was
a baby.

To make up for his father's absence they give the patient a pile of telegrams and letters from the antipodes
over which Errol gloats, saying: "As soon as I am
strong enough I'll run over and see the old boy. He's
the finest gentleman, the truest father, and best friend in
the world. God bless him!"

These eulogies upon his father have a fearful effect
upon Lady Annerley. After one of them she spends half
the night pacing her room, fighting with her conscience,
crying: "If I told Charley he'd hate me!" Then takes to
cursing her father in a manner that would shock good
Christians if they heard her.

The strain on her mind tells upon her body; and one
morning after they have arranged a couch where the
ripple of the water is heard, and the patient can see the
Grand Canal, and Errol has strolled over to it and is
dividing his time by nibbling at grapes, nibbling at a book,
and interjecting an occasional glance at the beautiful

panorama before him, Dr. Lampson takes Lady Annerley downstairs, and says : "I've noticed you needed excitement, and provided it."

"Indeed, doctor, what have you prescribed?"

"Society! Girls! Your two great friends, Miss Ethel Lincoln and Miss Ida Potter."

"One the pet of the last London season and the other its goddess, the reigning American beauty. You've done very well, doctor," says Lady Annerley.

"Humph!" returns Lampson, proudly, "I always pre- scribe the finest medicines. The two were in Florence with some chaperon or other and Miss Lincoln's brother. I telegraphed them. They have accepted, deserted their chaperon for your care, and 'll be here"—looking at his watch—"perhaps in five minutes!"

"Then I must send my gondola for them."

"It has gone already, I looked out for that :—By George! what's that?" for a ripple of laughter comes in the hall doors opening on the Grand Canal, and Lady Annerley, crying, "The girls have come!" runs down the steps to the water's edge to see the prettiest picture in the world.

If one exclamation more than another excites the masculine mind, it is, "The girls have come!" The invalid upstairs hears it, pops his head out of the window, and sees the same picture. A street of living water, bounded by old *palazzos*, roofed by blue sky, gilded and made bright by a September Venetian sun, modernized by puf- fing steamboats, and made romantic by dashing gondolas. One of these lies alongside the steps immediately below him. Standing upon these steps is an Englishman of about thirty and a young lady, who has just gathered her skirts away from a splash or two of water churned upon the stones by the rocking boat. This position gives to her lithe and beautiful figure the pose of a Venus. The Australian has hardly time to appreciate her before a tiny scream or two comes to his ear. Looking into the gondola he sees a fairy in an agony of indecision, one tiny foot upon the gunwale of the boat, the other stretched out falteringly toward the steps, while an imploring voice is crying: "Arthur, please, help me! I shall fall in, and I can't swim!"

The gentleman addressed, who has been devoting all

his attention to the other young lady, turns upon her and replies sarcastically : " Ethel, stop showing off ! There's no man looking."

" Oh, what an insinuation ! A man to see my awkwardness ! A man—I should hope not—O-oh ! " This last exclamation, which is accompanied by a tremendous blush, is caused partly by the fairy's chancing to gaze upward and see Errol's admiring glance, and partly by her brother giving her a muscular yank, and jumping her upon the steps. She runs up these and disappears in the door to which the gentleman assists the other lady with punctilious deference and courtesy. Both the girls are dressed in most exquisite summer toilets and look like dreams—but the fairy—ah ! Errol gives a gasp of rapture.

" Any one could tell that brute was her brother, the way he pulled her out of the boat. Ethel—nice name ! When I am well, I feel as if I were just the man to assist Ethel out of gondolas ! " and the Australian stretches his limbs that have begun to throb with health again, and says : " Jove, I feel better already ! "

In the house, after the usual greetings, Miss Potter says, looking about and shaking her graceful plumage, for this young lady is rich enough and fortunate enough to be plumed by Worth, who feathers such birds very gorgeously, " Where is the hero ? "

" Oh, I've seen him ! " cries Ethel. " He's blonde and tawny and blue-eyed like a lion ! He looked at me as you pulled me from the boat, Arthur ! "

" Oh, you've got on that subject again, have you, Ethel ? " says the brother, snubbing the sister a little. For the two girls have heard about Errol in a long letter Lieutenant Potter has written his sister from Alexandria, and have been discussing the Australian's deeds of valor with an emphasis and enthusiasm that has made Arthur Lincoln by no means happy. He has been very much in love with Ida Potter for a long time, and consequently is jealous of everybody masculine, especially heroes.

" Well, he's very handsome, anyway. Snubbing me won't make him ugly," murmurs Miss Ethel.

" I'll show him to you soon, my dear," says Lady Annerley, proud of her champion ; for she is very fond of this bright-eyed, bright-mannered English girl, and has no idea how she will hate her afterward.

"When will he be put on exhibition?" asks Miss Potter with a little laugh.

"Between 2 and 4 P. M. Special tickets, and mind me, girls, no flirting with my patient," says Lampson grimly.

"I never flirt!" comes from both the young ladies at once; but Ethel laughs over it and Miss Potter says it very seriously, and then goes on quietly: "I don't believe in affecting love when I do not feel it—and feel it strongly."

"Do you mean that?" asks Arthur under his voice.

"I'm in the habit of saying what I mean!" returns Ida rising and going to Lady Annerley. But from this place of safety she gives the young man a veiled glance that sets him trembling, for during the last few weeks something in this catch-of-the-season's manner has set this young English barrister hoping for what rich dukes had hoped for in vain; for Miss Potter had been asked in marriage for her beauty rather than for her wealth, though her father's flocks and herds are said to be large as those of the patriarchs of old.

In a little time Lady Annerley takes them all upstairs to see Mr. Errol, and they find that young gentleman has somehow arrayed himself as if expecting lady visitors.

After a gasp or two at Miss Potter's loveliness, for no man could look at it unmoved, Errol turns to the fairy, who gives him an elfin gesture and murmurs: "Excuse my curiosity, my first hero!"

To this the young man answers: "I'm hardly strong enough to get up and make a bow to you, but—in Australia we sometimes shake hands."

"With pleasure," says Miss Ethel, and she gives hers to him, together with a very kindly glance from her blue eyes, for who can help pitying this great, handsome fellow as he lies upon the sofa so pale, interesting, and romantically wounded?

Holding this little right hand, Errol looks at the young lady's left, sees no engagement ring upon it, and gives a sigh of relief. Then with a slight pressure would imprison the other longer; but old Lampson, who takes wicked pleasure in making girls blush, cries out: "Ethel, let go that young man's hand ! Feeling pulses is my business, not yours ! "

At which the young lady gives a pathetic little scream, draws away her hand, suddenly crosses to the other side of the room ; but shortly after seems to wander back to the invalid's couch, and the two become very much engrossed in one another.

As for Arthur he gives a sigh of relief, for Miss Potter appears only slightly impressed with Mr. Errol, and goes out onto the balcony, where the setting sun comes in and tints this princess from the West whom nature has crowned with a beauty that is entirely indescribable but entirely American. For Miss Potter still keeps her Border-State accent and her Border-State manners. These have descended to her from her mother, who was of the blue-grass region of Kentucky, so famed for its lovely women.

Her Southern lisp has been called soft as the song of Italian opera ; her Border-State manners are said to be perfect as those of the ancient régime. She has such a pride in herself she makes everybody that bows to her do homage to the country which she represents and honors. In fact, she is, as Colonel Cottontree, the celebrated Texas diplomatist and statesman, who knows everybody of prominence on both sides of the ocean and who has given the daughter of his old friend her first launch into European society, says : " So cursed high, mighty, and aristocratic that the world bows down to her as the most fetching woman upon earth ; " this American beauty, who in the *salons* of London and Paris is *proud that she is American.*

CHAPTER IX.

HOME AGAIN !

A FEW days after this, Doctor Lampson having pronounced the patient safe, and bolted to his English patients, leaving as the only souvenir of his visit a large hole in Lady Annerley's bank account, they bring Errol downstairs, or rather he comes unassisted, for this great hulking fellow is beginning to be himself once more. The roses are coming into his cheeks and the power into his limbs, and his blue eyes sparkle with new-born health and happiness when they look on pretty Miss Ethel, who welcomes him with redder roses and brighter eyes than even she has ever displayed for his benefit before.

In fact, every one looks bright and happy this day, for Lady Annerley has made a little *fête* for the occasion, and Miss Potter and herself are in very fine feathers; though to the Australian the little English girl in her simple muslin frock, as he describes it to himself (which cost a thousand francs in Paris), is the most charming of the lot. So these two young people go to breaking my lady's heart by falling in love with each other.

Like most tragedies the thing comes about quite gradually, for it is difficult for Lady Annerley to believe that she is defeated by this *ingénue* of one season, who has only the fascination of her own dear little heart and fresh, youthful beauty with which to fight her battle. For, though her father, Percy Lincoln, is one of the great jurists of England and some day will probably be made for his services upon the bench a lord, the family, while closely connected with the best blood in Britain, are not very rich for the social station they occupy, and Miss Ethel's dower must be quite a modest one compared with Lady Annerley's grand estates and princely income.

So Sarah Annerley takes to watching these young people who are sometimes, she hopes, only playing passion, and at others so savage with each other that they make her joyous ; for my lady forgets that this is a first-love business, and therefore is at times a matter of jealousies, sighs, pouts, frowns, and even tears, as well as smiles, confidences, and subtle caresses. Errol, though nearly thirty years of age, is in the one grand passion of his life, and Ethel gives this man all the first pure love of a young girl whose cheeks have never been mauled by the advances of kissing school-boys, and whose heart has never been sullied, wounded, nor made languid by deceased flirtations nor amateur theatrical passions. Her father, Judge Lincoln, is devoted to his only daughter, and has kept her up to this time, as he does his juries, separate and apart from all outside contaminations and temptations.

This wretched business of Lady Annerley's is brought

to a crisis by an old adorer of hers, whose hand she has refused so many times she forgets the exact number. He is a young American who, in ample contrast to Miss Potter, is ashamed of his country—a creature of ferocious expression and feeble mind, who has red, languid, watery eyes.

These, together with a little bristly mustache, give to his countenance the savage look of a monkey in a rage, and when he parts his hair in the middle he is considered quite a killing fellow by young girls at germans and other adolescent amusements. No one would think him conceited, for the only virtue he publicly claims for himself is, " My sister married a lord !" However, he says this so often the monotony of it becomes terrible.

An ancestor of his fought at Bunker Hill, and another was on the staff of General Washington ; but their descendant has put on the chains they shed their blood to throw off, and bows down to and worships everything that is English, wishing with all his brave little spirit that he could use a single eye-glass with the languid air of a Guard's-Club swell, and his walk had the real Piccadilly stride about it.

This little wretch, who is a social sleuth-hound in his way, has somehow scented the party out, and drops in upon them full of London news, Paris gossip, and rumors from the Orient.

" By George !" he lisps, " Lady Annerley, we've all been talking about you. The Duc de Genlis Peragord spoke to me just *outside* the Jockey Club " (he has never been on the *inside* in his life). " Peragord said : 'Dubardu, how I envy that ah—ah—antipodes fellah, you know!' and I agree with him. How I wish I had been in ah— Egypt, you know, to have saved you from the awh— awh—crocodiles !"

Stifling a smile, Miss Ethel suggests that it was not crocodiles that attacked Lady Annerley.

" Noa !"

" It was an Eastern mob !"

" Oh, ah, yes, something wild and terrible ! Just the same I should have defended her ; something wild and terrific, like our cowboys. Oh, by Jove ! now I beg your pardon, Miss Potter, your father is a cowboy or something of that sort. I believe." For Ida has risen and is going out on the balcony, where she is shortly followed by Arthur.

A moment later there comes to them from the room: "By Jove! I never eat a beefsteak, but I think of Miss Potter's papa!"

This is followed by a ripple of laughter from the house, for the creature has the humorous methods of a monkey, and Errol and Ethel would laugh at nearly anything they are so happy, and Lady Annerley would laugh at anything because she is hysterically miserable, the manner of the Australian having been more marked than ever toward the English girl this morning.

"Shall I go in and stop him?" mutters Arthur to Ida savagely.

"Not at all, Mr. Lincoln. I find Mr. Van Cott amusing myself!" and to her adorer's astonishment Miss Potter laughs also, though in a peculiar and sarcastic way as if making fun of herself.

But here another remark of the facetious Van Cott, who has no idea his *bons mots* and *jeux d'esprits* are flying out of the window, comes to them and produces a terrible effect on both, as they hear him lisp: "Miss Ethel, Arthur very far gone?"

"Gone! What do you mean?"

"Why, on La Cattle Queen, of course. Ah, that gal knows what she is doing. She wants to catch the Honorable Arthur. She's playing her cards to become an English peeress!"

"Honorable Arthur? Who is he?"

"Why, don't you know? Good gracious! don't you *know?*" he shrieks excitedly. "You're the Honorable Ethel and he's the Honorable Arthur. Your governor's been retired and made a peer of the realm. I've got the *London Times* in my pocket. So glad to have given you the good news! Awfully jolly! congratulations!— Take the paper!"

Which Ethel does, and running out on to the balcony cries: "Arthur, see, papa's been made Baron Lincoln!" Then pauses astonished, for Miss Potter is at the far end of the veranda, and her little foot beating an impatient tattoo as she appears to be intensely interested in the dome of the San Marco. Her face is red and turned as much as possible from Arthur Lincoln's.

That young man has a horrible scowl upon his countenance, for he knows how these remarks have wounded
Miss Potter's pride and so far injured his chances.   He
says seriously: " Ethel, I'm afraid this promotion will be
an expensive one for all of us.   Father's salary as a
judge was greater than his pension will be as a peer."

This social elevation of the Lincolns brings about in
the course of the day several climaxes of passion that,
in the ordinary run of events, might have not occurred
for some time.   Miss Ethel turns and goes to Errol and
finds that gentleman has become quite distant in his de-
meanor.   For the poor fellow has always known that
Miss Lincoln has been greatly above him in the social
scale, and now is thinking as the daughter of a peer of
the English realm she is separated and set apart from
him by a class distinction that one unacquainted with
British society can hardly understand.   Errol's father
is simply a colonial merchant and sheep-owner, al-
beit a very rich one, and his son has seen enough of
English life to know that his suit will probably be considered presumptuous by the young lady's father ; consequently a proper pride comes to him and makes him
haughty to Miss Ethel herself.

Seeing her hero upon his dignity, his sweetheart, who
has a very high spirit of her own, becomes punctilious
also, and then sarcastic, asking him whether a longing for
native " damper " and kangaroo mutton is making him so
glum, and if Australian sheep-herders are not as wild,
savage, and uncouth as American cowboys?

These remarks make Errol very down-hearted, though
they amuse Mr. Van Cott greatly, and that young gentleman confides in Lady Annerley as follows :

" Jove, this is lovely !   Now she's the daughter of a
peer, blowed if Miss Ethel ain't going to throw the Australian over."

To which my lady replies only with a sad smile, for
she is afraid they are both too much interested for any
such good fortune as this to happen.

" Any way," Mr. Van Cott goes on, " Miss Lincoln
needn't think so beastly much of her father's new creation.   By Jove ! my brother-in-law, the Earl of Sandsdown, says that since the late additions to the peerage
it's becoming deuced vulgar to be a lord.   We, of the

old families, your ladyship and—a-hem!—myself, will appreciate the delicious wit of my brother-in-law, the Earl of Sandsdown."

"Quite!" says Lady Annerley very savagely. "My father was a city banker and bill-broker ; and yours, I believe, was an American, Mr. Van Cott, who made army contracts !" and leaves him speechless, but writhing with rage.

Miss Potter is in a rage also, for she has caught Ethel's remark about cowboys, and being wounded and feminine, turns about and stings her lover, by asking Van Cott rather pointedly : " How is the market for American heiresses ? What is the last quotation? You should surely know : your sister married a lord."

These remarks of the young ladies are by no means polite, and perhaps ill-natured and ill-bred : but Fifth Avenue, when it gets going, can do the rough-and-tumble act as well as the Bowery, though it does so in a different way. So they go on and make such a good, cutting, savage, sarcastic, *witty* day of it, that after dinner Errol and Arthur feel very glum, Ethel spiteful, Miss Potter sarcastic, and Lady Annerley up to anything the devil will put into her head, which he is quite sure to do as soon as he can think of something delicate enough, subtle enough, and cruel enough to be worthy of a highborn aristocratic sinner like my lady.

Under these circumstances it is not at all astonishing that Miss Potter thinks Lady Annerley's dinner bad, though the *menu* is excellent and the cooking in the best style of French art. She strolls out on to the balcony after dessert and has a luxurious cry. She has made the man she loves unhappy, and is therefore unhappy herself.

She is not allowed to enjoy this solo of misery long before a blazing cigar is poked through the open Venetian window ; this is followed a second afterward by Arthur Lincoln, who stands beside the girl and enjoys her beauty in silence, as Ida is busy smuggling away a last sneaking tear and says nothing.

After a whiff or two of his Havana, for the young man knows Miss Potter well enough to be aware that she has no objection to cigar smoke, he says rather sadly : " What a happy family we all were before that cad Van

Cott intruded himself among us, bringing with him the cares, jealousies, and ambitions of the outside world! "

" Yes, we—we were very happy here! " replies Ida, with a little sigh, looking at her shadow the moonlight makes on the water of the Grand Canal; and then more brightly : " So Venice is your Garden of Eden—little Van Cott your serpent," and with a little laugh, for she sees he has forgiven her all of her unkind words, and is regaining her spirits, "you and I are the Adam and Eve —oh, no ! I—I don't mean that ! "

She turns away with a blush on her face, and gazes at the water and passing gondolas and silent palaces ; but though she says no more, and dares not look over her shoulder, the blush deepens and deepens and becomes more red and bright and vivid, for Arthur is unable to withstand the beauty of Ida Potter, gilded by Venetian moonlight, and his arm is stealing round her waist—that waist that no lover's arm has clasped before. However, it doesn't do his chances any harm, for though her eyes flash and she is about to repulse him, before she can do so love conquers pride, she trembles under his embrace, and her beautiful head droops upon his shoulder.

He murmurs : " You love me ! " and is about to kiss her, but she breaks from him, and cries : " Not yet ! The man who kisses me marries me ! "

" Can't you see I want to do both ? " whispers Arthur, and would take her in his arms again, but she mutters hoarsely : " You shall do neither—*yet !* See my father ! "

" Why not now ? "

" *Never !* Until you see my father ! He will be in England within the month. *See my father !* "

This peculiar iteration, " See my father ! " makes the young man pause. He says, slowly : " I think I understand you, Ida. You fear your father will not think me worthy of you. I agree with him. I know you've refused much greater men than me—dukes and counts and all that, but you didn't love them, dearest ? "

" No—o ! "

" And none of them loved you more than I ! "

" I believe you, Arthur ! " mutters the girl, and his blood throbs to the sound, for it is the first time that she has used his Christian name.

" I have no doubt that a man of such aristocratic

tastes, habits, and associations, as your father must be, even though he has no title, may `expect a much grander name than ours for his daughter ! " he goes on gloomily.

She doesn't answer this, but in the moonlight he can see her trembling, shaking, and quivering with some uncontrollable emotion.

But now, looking at the lovely head that so lately nestled upon his shoulder, that shell-like ear in which a second ago he whispered, those coral lips so nearly kissed, this grand beauty that is almost in his hand, his ardor becomes too great to restrain ; he whispers : " Do you love me ? "

There is a sigh in the breeze ; it seems to say: " Y-e-s ! "

" You love me ! I have no fear ! You love me ! " he cries, and would seize her in his arms, but she breaks from him and fights him away, and cries, in a wild, frightened, desperate tone : " See my father ! Don't dare speak of this till you *see my father !* " and flies from him.

" Hang it ! I've no doubt old Potter is a dyed-in-the-bone aristocrat ! " mutters Arthur, " but I rather think the Lincolns have a fairly good family tree." Then he says, suddenly : " Confound it ! " for his cigar has been forgotten in his passionate excitement and has gone out.

Relighting this, he sits down, puffs rings of cigarsmoke round the moon, and thinks of the paternal Potter, but soon forgets all about him in contemplating the daughter.

" I—I nearly kissed her," he mutters, ,in a dazed, happy, dreamy way, and then, with sudden enthusiasm : " By Jove ! she loves me ! The dearest, sweetest, *most aristocratic* girl in the whole world loves me ! "

As for the lady, she goes away and mutters to herself savagely: "An aristocrat ? if he hadn't called me that I— I might have let him kiss me. An aristocrat ? I'm tired of the word ! "

And this is to a certain extent true. The girl's bearing and beauty are so noble, her whole attitude in life so confident and independent, and withal so modest and un-assuming, that European society, as it has looked upon her thoroughbred figure and blooded feet and hands, has said : " An aristocrat of perfect lineage and descent," and has desired to see the parents of such a child, and so expressed itself.

"I sigh for thy father, *ma chère*," murmured the old Dowager Comtesse de Saint Germain. "*Monsieur de Pottah* will remind me in his courtly manners of the days of my youth, when we danced *la minuette*."

"These old Virginia families, the Fairfaxes, Lees, Washingtons, and Potters, took some of our best blood out of the old world. Egad! I'm delighted they've sent a little of it back in you, my child," shouts out in his great, fox-hunting voice the ancient Duke of Sussexshire, gazing at the beauty. "It's perhaps curious to regain a lost art from America, but I expect the Chevalier Potter will bring back to us the stately bow of the Prince Regent and the *punctilio* of the Maccaroni. Ask your father to visit me as soon as he arrives in England."

These remarks always seemed to make Miss Potter blush and look more beautiful and aristocratic than ever.

Turning this over in her mind, the young lady comes into the grand parlor of the *palazzo*, where she meets Van Cott and Lady Annerley, who says with lips that tremble in spite of herself: "Have you seen Mr. Errol outside? I—I am afraid that the night air will be too damp for a convalescent!"

"The night air will also be bad for Miss Ethel. They'll *both* have colds," chirps Mr. Van Cott, and takes his leave. They go down to the front steps to see him into his gondola, for the young man lives at the *Hotel Barbesi;* and as they open the door they find the Australian and Miss Ethel seated close together in a *barca* moored to the stairs that Errol has hired for the purpose from some passing boatmen.

"We've been trying to make our silhouettes upon the water by the aid of the moon, only the mosquitoes wouldn't let us keep quiet. It's rather amusing!" cries the young lady looking slightly guilty.

"Yes, awfully jolly, and quite romantic!" echoes Errol, blushing a little, for his conscience sometimes accuses him of neglecting this woman who has nursed him, now that her aid is no longer a necessity to him.

"So I see," mutters Lady Annerley. "Quite romantic!"

"Y-as, romantic as anything!" laughs the facetious Van Cott. "To-morrow night, if the moon is fine, I'll come round and we'll experiment in silhouettes, you and I, Lady

Sarah." And after making some remarks he considers witty about "spoons," and "love's young dream," etc., etc., which put Lady Annerley on the rack, and make Ethel blush, and Errol want to punch his head, the creature is rowed off, his gondolier singing a *barcarol* as he drives the boat down the Grand Canal toward the beautiful church of *Santa Maria della Salute*, which glistens under the moon like white coral.

A moment after they all come in and there is a new and happier look on the faces of Ethel Lincoln and Charley Errol. Chancing to gaze at Lady Annerley, Miss Potter starts, for there is an unknown expression that she has never seen before on my lady's face ; but this is not at all curious, as Satan has just bethought himself and is putting into Sarah Annerley's head his newest, latest, and meanest invention in wickedness ; and, what is more, this woman, who has been good, noble, and generous up to now, has made up her mind to use it—if this little English girl drives her to it.

So the days run along, very fast and joyous for Ethel and Charley, but oh ! how slow and miserable for Lady Annerley, as she fights her game against fate, and does it badly.

At cards many play well for fun, few play well for stakes. So it is in the great struggles of life. The crack shot's hand often trembles when his existence depends upon its steadiness, and the veteran of the *duello* falls before the pistol of a tyro ; and in this case my lady, who has won many battles in the field of love, is so anxious and unnerved the cunning seems to have left her hand, and the novice wins the contest.

Miss Ethel's unstudied fascinations make her an easy conqueror, in this battle of the heart, over the enchantments of wit, mind, and experience, and greater, though more mature, beauty of Lady Annerley. Then one evening the climax comes—the blow falls.

It is October. The day has been perfect, as autumn days in Northern Italy generally are. The quartette, as they have got to call themselves, have, under the pretense of shopping, taken a gondola and sailed off into these streets of water, bounded by these gray old palaces from which modern life may sweep down the cobwebs, but cannot destroy entirely the romance. Lady Annerley, not having spirits enough to accompany them, is sitting alone, when young Van Cott drops in with the news.

"By George!" he cries, "I've spotted 'em at last! Australia's caught the little gal! It was so awfully dark in the shadow of the houses that, as my gondola passed another gondola, I heard two people, who shall be nameless, kiss each other."

"What do you mean?" gasps Lady Annerley.

"Oh, no scandal, I assure you—all proper—decorous— sedate! They're engaged, I know it!"

"Who's engaged?" This is a snarl, for Lady Anner- ley's temper has snapped its chain.

"Errol and Ethel Lincoln, to be sure."

"A-ah!"

But Mr. Van Cott runs on, too much engrossed with his story to notice that the lady he's talking to is nearly fainting.

"You see, to-day I—ah—saw the convalescent strid- ing along the Merceria as if he had an object in life once more; and sauntered after him. He sneaked into a jewel- er's shop—seemed to be ashamed of what he was doing. I knew the symptoms. Young men are always ashamed of buying the first engagement ring—the others come easier. 'First engagement ring,' thought I, and so I wandered in after him. When he saw me the chap posi- tively blushed and tried to hide it quick, but I had my eye on it. A big diamond and two smaller ones—cost £300. Look at Miss Ethel's finger to-night—you'll see it—third finger, left hand—engagement—I love you— fettered for life, and all that, you know."

"Would you please ring for a glass of water?" mutters Lady Annerley. "You are sure?"

"Water? Oh, certainly I'm sure! Charley and Ethel in one end of the gondola, Arthur and Ida in the other. Gondoliers in the middle feed to look up in the air for the pigeons of Saint Mark. I know the trick!" and he runs on in a sickening kind of way, and Lady Annerley, who listens dreamily to him, rather thinks this all a night- mare.

But she is suddenly awoke out of it with a start, for Van Cott thinks he has a good opening, and enthusi- astically cries: "~poons — four spoons — let's be six spoons—spoons all around!" and getting his arm about her waist, his red eyes become full of watery amative-ness as he gazes upon her loveliness, that even sorrow cannot dim, and murmurs : "Dearest Lady Sarah, you and I also—three engagements—three happy pair—three marriages—three——"

Here he stops and looks frightened, for she has risen and confronts him like a beautiful tigress. She has found something upon which to vent her pent-up rage and agony. She hisses : "You ! You dare ! You !"

"I—I—'pon my life, I didn't mean it ! You warn't half so angry the last time I asked you. Don't, don't carry on like that ! You're a regular bang-up Lady Macbeth. You—you frighten a fellow so. HELP !" For Sarah Annerley is nearly foaming at the mouth with rage.

His ludicrous terror checks her. After a moment she pulls herself together and says very coldly : "Pish ! You are not worth my indignation ! Let me give you a piece of information, Mr. Van Cott. After I refused you the third time I crossed you off my visiting list !"

"Oh, you did, did you !" he says down-heartedly, for the *entrée* to Lady Annerley's is very useful to all young men who wish to be fashionable ; and then he adds quite vivaciously, as if an idea has suddenly struck him : "But, by Jove ! I didn't cross *you* off mine !—See you to-morrow. Regards to the *fiancée !*" and goes to his gon-dola.

While being rowed away, a sudden light comes into his face, and he mutters : "My gracious ! If the widdah is not smashed on the Australian ! That's what made her so rummy to me. This is too rich for anything. Ha ! ha ! ha !" and this little exponent of the caddish civili-zation of the nineteenth century bursts into a shriek of laughter at the crushing and mangling of the heart of a woman who has been always kinder to him than he de-served.

And oh, how crushed and mangled it is ! Sarah An-nerley sits and thinks in the antique room, very silent, very quiet, save that occasional nervous wringing of the hands peculiar to despair. At last she cries : "I'll not believe it ! Gratitude should make him love me as it made me love him. His wounds for my sake, my fight-

ing death for him and winning him, gave him *to me !* It
was a ceremony. WE ARE HUSBAND AND WIFE ! Let her
dare to take him ! " Then she mutters : " It is not possible ; when he was weak he was mine, now he is strong
he will not desert me," and for a moment is happy and
does not believe.

But merry voices are heard in the hall and they all
come in to her, chatting and laughing and very happy.
She looks at Ethel's hand and it is there, flashing, and
glittering, and carrying despair and wickedness into her
heart—the engagement ring !

Following her gaze, Errol says : " Dear Lady Sarah,
Ethel and I have a little story to whisper to you ; one
with which we hope you will be pleased." Then he tells
her, and at last Sarah Annerley knows that Charley Errol
and Ethel Lincoln love and will marry—if Providence
and *she* will let them.

For Satan has been watching his opportunity, and here
whispers something in her ear that puts a smile of triumph in her face and strength of purpose in her heart,
that gives her power to return the compliments and good
wishes usual on such occasions.

This being over, she turns to Miss Potter, who has
been occupied at the piano with Arthur during this conversation, and says, perhaps a little maliciously, for she
is not inclined to be very kind to any one this evening :
" Shall I congratulate you also, my dear ? "

Whereupon Ida gives a blush, steps up to my lady,
and affects to laugh, but replies demurely : " Not at
present. Nobody has given me a ring yet ! " and holds
up a hand and arm as faultlessly white and deliciously
soft, rounded, lovely, and statuesque as anything ex-
hibited in the Louvre or dug up from Athenian ruins, to
remind us women were always beautiful. The hand has
no ornament whatsoever, and needs none ; the arm around
its glistening wrist, that would be colorless as marble were
it not for a blush that seems to have come upon it as the
girl speaks, for her face is rosy also, has a circlet of plain
massive gold to which hangs a single English sovereign
as a bangle.

Looking at this, Lady Annerley says : " Bracelets are
binding as well as rings ! "

" Then I was captured in my early youth," laughs Miss

Potter. "I've worn this almost as long as I can remember. Papa says it's my lucky sovereign. It's quite a family souvenir I believe. Its date is rather old—1849—long before I was born."

Under the excuse of showing the coin she gets near Arthur again, who whispers with a sigh of relief : "I've often wondered who put that bracelet upon your arm?"

"So you were jeal—" She checks herself suddenly, though her eyes seem to show the thought she has not expressed has made her happy.

"Jealous? Certainly! awfully jealous!" returns the young man. "When can I destroy my jealousy by a ring?"

She looks at him a moment and then says, apparently forcing herself to speak calmly : "I have just received a letter from America. Within the week my father will be in England. See my father!",

"I leave for England to-night!"

"Oh, not so fast!" says the girl. "Steamers never arrive in less than seven days, no matter how anxious we are, and a little more of your company, Arthur,—for perhaps after you see my father—I shall see you no more!" the last a little sadly.

"Do you think Mr. Potter will refuse me?" replies the young man in so scared a voice that Miss Potter laughs, though not very merrily. "I'm only a barrister now, of course, but, barring a republic, I'll sit in the House of Lords some day. I've not a great deal of money, but sufficient to support you ——"

"Oh, I've enough of that for both," she interrupts hurriedly. "I'd marry you if you were a beggar!"

"Would you? God bless you!" he cries and seizes her hand, but she pulls it away and mutters : "See my father, perhaps he'll—" Here she suddenly checks herself and running to Ethel cries, affecting vivacity : "Some music, miss ; show us the value of your two-guinea-a-minute lessons from Le Bellecord, the tenor!" and is apparently in high spirits for the rest of the evening on account of the approach of the paternal Potter.

During this episode of Arthur and Ida, the devil has been doing some fine work for Lady Annerley. A servant has brought in to Errol a telegram that has just arrived. Glancing over this the young man cries : "Glorious! My governor will be in London in a week. This is dated from Gibraltar."

".Coming home?" and they are all around him with questions except Lady Annerley, who has given a start and muttered to herself: "I have her!" for her rage is not directed against the man whom she loves, but the woman whom she hates.

"Yes, isn't it grand!" continues Errol in explanation. "The *pater* hasn't been home since he emigrated from England over thirty years ago!"

"Why, Charley, he'll be at the wedding!" suddenly cries Ethel; but this speech getting a burst of laughter from some of the rest she goes off and blushes by herself in a corner.

"Never mind, Ethel!" says her lover, blushing also, "we're ahead of some people we know," and he gives a look at Ida and Arthur, which makes them stop laughing and try to appear as if they did not understand him.

"What do you suppose has induced your father to take this step?" says Lady Annerley.

"You see, nearly a month ago I cabled him," returns Errol, "that I hoped to get married!"

"Oh!" cries Ethel, suddenly jumping up from her corner, "how dared you do it? What encouragement had I given you? Oh, Charley, how bold your father will think me!"

"Not at all. I only suggested that I had seen the girl —and she was not engaged!" returns her lover with a grin. "Upon receipt of the news, the old gentleman seems to have been anxious to bless you, and steamed for Europe."

"Would you mind my seeing the message?" asks Lady Annerley, who now suffers the agony of knowing that Errol has fallen in love with her rival at first sight.

"The rest of it is only—only private business!" mutters the Australian, a shadow coming over his face. As he says this he pockets the telegram.

"The rest is bad news," says Ethel, who has grown to read Errol's frank face very well in the last few weeks. "Oh, Charley!"

"It's not important enough to call bad news," returns the young man.

" Anyway, nothing can separate us now," murmurs the girl.

" Nothing ! " he repeats.

" We shall see ! " laughs Lady Annerley to herself, and the fiend inside her gives a hideous giggle.

"You will excuse me if I say good night. I—I am rather fatigued," she says after a moment, and then : " I presume I shall have to chaperon you girls back to England in a day or two," and bids them adieu.

As she gets to the door, Ethel runs up to her and takes her hand saying : " Isn't it lovely, dear Lady Sarah ? Just fancy, I'm going to marry the man who saved your life—my Charley ! "

But even her happy looks and trusting love do not turn Lady Annerley, who goes up to her room, and there her temper breaking its chain she acts like a mad woman, and laughs and chuckles ; " If I had told him in Egypt he'd be sure of her. Now Heaven has given me this to tear her from him ! God bless my father for his tale ! " Then the noise of music coming to her makes her wilder and more mad ; for it is Ethel's happy voice singing " Bonny Prince Charlie," which she rings out, putting as much love, devotion, and adoration in the beautiful old ballad as those did who, nearly two centuries ago, first sung the strain that meant death, woe, and despair to them who gave up their lives and blood in the battle and on the scaffold for the cause of " Bonny Scotch Charlie." As Ethel sings her love-song below Lady Annerley writes its requiem above.

This she does on plain letter paper and uncrested envelope, making an awkward attempt at a disguised hand, and addressing it very carefully to the Home Secretary of the English Government, London, and putting double postage on the letter, being desperately afraid it will in some way miscarry.

After it is finished she looks at it and says : " Charley, forgive me for the meanest crime on earth ! " Then hurries to finish the business before she can repent.

Wrapped in some dark covering, she glides down stairs, and passing the closed doors of the parlor, from which the song, laughter, and happy voices still come to her and make her cruel, Lady Annerley goes down the steps to the waters of the Grand Canal, and cautiously signals a gondola cruising about for a passing fare. It is rowed by two sturdy men, and as the night is dark one of the gondoliers holds a lantern up to light her steps as the other assists her into the boat. She passes over the gunwale and mutters : *"Piazza di San Marco !* Quick ! " and the lantern gives them a glimpse of her face.

The two men whisper together a moment : then one of them relinquishes his oar and stands just behind her, and though she cries to him to go back to his work, the fellow will not leave her side.

She cannot imagine the reason of this, but it is because the passions on her face have been so awful that the men think she means to commit suicide and fear she may drown herself.

Gliding over the calm waters the boat lands her at the *Piazza di San Marco,* and saying " Wait ! " she sneaks away into the darkness, trembling for fear some one may recognize her. Finding no one near her, for it is now eleven o'clock at night and the *Piazza* quite deserted, she steps up to one of the Government letter-boxes, and after a second's struggle drops the message into it. Then shuddering and ashamed of her own cruelty, she repents and would have it back again at any cost, as many have done before in that same *Piazza di San Marco,* centuries ago, after they had thrown the fatal accusation into the lion's mouth, and condemned some one once loved, now hated, to the Council of Ten, the dungeon, and the rack.

This whole business is so like that of ancient Venice, that this idea comes into her mind, and she gives a nasty laugh and thinks : " How history repeats itself," as she returns to the gondola.

She is quickly rowed home where, the lights being out, she steals up to her own apartments and goes to bed, but not to sleep ; and the next morning mutters, gazing in the mirror, but hanging her head: "Shall I ever be able to look myself in the face again ? "

But, notwithstanding, she contrives to look quite fresh this morning, though it is the first time in her life she has been compelled to the use of rouge.

A day or two after the whole party take the railway through Northern Italy and journey by easy stages *via* Turin and Mont Cenis to Paris, where ladies always find some shopping to detain them.

Here Arthur leaves them and goes on to tell his father what Miss Ethel intends to do and what he would like to do. His place, however, is taken by Mr. Van Cott, who runs against them in Paris

Finding Arthur absent, this young gentleman says to himself : " Miss Potter has thrown him. I'll have another try for an heiress ! By George ! I'll—it comes hard, but I'll sacrifice myself. For her dear sake I'll become a cowboy ! "

So, learning that the party are bound for England, B. Sidney Van Cott appears at the *Chémin de Fer du Nord* terminus, drops into their compartment, rubs his eyeglass, and exclaims : " By Jove ! Miss Potter, you reading a telegram ? "

" Yes," says Ida, an expectant happiness in her face, " it is from my father. He is in Liverpool, and will meet me at Folkestone. I haven't seen him for four years."

" That's awfully jolly. I'm going to London myself. I'll take charge of you to the dear papa ! " murmurs the little wretch, and he sits down and makes fun for the whole party till they come to the great quay at Boulogne.

Here Errol receives a telegram which makes him cry, " Hurrah ! "

This he answers, then takes it to the ladies and says : " My governor's in London. I wonder if he'll know the place, he hasn't seen it for so long ! "

Then the Channel steamer sails for England, on its deck Lady Annerley, her conscience crying out to her with every rap of her heart, which beats more wildly as she looks at Errol's happy face and thinks this is the last day he'll hold his head up among men. But conscience dies as she sees Ethel nestling her hand in his, a little serious expression on her face as she thinks how her father, the great judge, will receive her lover. Though, looking at the young man, pride and happiness come to the girl's eyes and she mutters : " Papa 'll love him too, no one can resist my Charley ! "

As for the Australian, hope and joy fill him also. He will meet his dear old father whom three months ago he had thought to see no more. And youth, health, and excitement getting the better of conventionality he hums :

"Home Again!" which makes Lady Annerley pant and sigh as she thinks how different it was when he last sang the tune in the house of Abdallah the Moor; where with danger and death about them she was happier than she is now.

But Errol still sings on, for though he has been born in Australia and lived a good part of his time there, the mother-country feeling comes to him as it does to all of true Anglo-Saxon descent when they look upon this cradle of their race, THE GREAT WHITE CLIFFS OF ALBION. So the ship foams her way to England this bright October day and dashes up to Folkestone Harbor ; then the great engines stop and the boat drifts in and some of those who stand upon her deck drift into the crisis of their lives.

_____

CHAPTER X.

THE HONORABLE SAMPSON POTTER, OF COMANCHE COUNTY, TEXAS.

ABOUT three o'clock on the afternoon of this same day, Police Sergeant Thomas Brackett, from Scotland Yard, glances carelessly over the file of telegrams for early delivery at the office of the West Cliff Hotel, Folkestone, England. Apparently impressed with an address on one of the envelopes he goes into the tap-room, takes a gulp of his favorite " 'alf and 'alf " to steady his ner es, and mutters to himself : " In the detective busines over thirty years, and this is the rummiest job of the lot ! "

After a moment's pause of consideration, Brackett, whistling to his dog Snapper, an exquisite little black-and-tan terrier composed of flashing eyes, flying limbs, pricked-up ears, and barking tongue, leaves the house, and walks along the cliffs to where he can sight the smoke of the steamer from Boulogne crossing the English Channel to connect with the tidal train for London.

It will not arrive for some little time, and the detective leisurely fills and smokes his pipe, sauntering along the road that runs across the cliffs toward Sandgate and Hythe. During the promenade, his dog makes excursions into the surrounding country, producing so much

noise in himself and excitement among neighboring cats
and canines, that, seeing a large bull-dog approaching, his
master calls Snapper to him and puts him in his overcoat pocket for safety.   This is easily done as the little
creature weighs only twenty-two ounces, half of which is
vivacious electricity.   Upon this, Snapper sets up a tremendous yell ; and after a moment's reflection the sergeant remarks : "I know what it is, Snapper! Them ·
darbies is cold," and appeases his little pet by removing
him to his other pocket.   For Snapper has been on too
many excursions with Sergeant Brackett not to know
that handcuffs are hard and cold pocket companions.

   Occupied between his pipe and his dog the picturesque
scene has no effect on the detective. The wide-spread-
ing view of the English Channel with the distant French
coast, the fresh green verdure of the surrounding Kent-
ish heights, and far below him the soft splash of the
waves upon the chalk-cliffs ; with, on his left in the valley, the busy commerce of the railway and shipping in
the port, all lighted up by a sunny brightness that seems
to be wafted by the breeze across the water and belong
rather to France than to England, would impress any one
but Sergeant Brackett.   He, however, with Anglo-Saxon
stolidity, proceeds to find a comfortable stile upon which
to sit, and produces a copy of the day's edition of the
London *Times*, through the columns of which he plods in
a dogged manner, reading over the advertisements as if
he had so much time to kill and meant to kill it.

   Suddenly, however, Brackett becomes an animated human being once more, and exclaims to Snapper, who is
now sitting beside him and licking his hand : " Rummier
and rummier! Darned if the lawyers ain't advertising
again for that Sammy Potts. Every detective in England has tried at odd times for the last thirty years to find
that individual and never a trace.   Wonder if they think
the newspapers is smarter than the police? Some of
these legal chaps is natural born fools."

   With this tribute to the detective force of England,
Sergeant Brackett relapses into the columns of the *Times*
once more. After a few minutes, every-day news and
commonplace information seem to pall upon his mind,
which appears to prefer the excitement of penny fiction
to the humdrum of penny news, and the detective sub-

stitutes for the paper a cheap novel bearing the blood-curdling title of *The Scalpers of the Far West*. This treasure of literature the sergeant had picked up at a news stand upon his way down from London, and had been longing to get a peep at its fascinating horrors; for Brackett enjoyed American border life in fiction and had read everything pertaining to it in literature from Mayne Reid's stories to *Texas Jack*—and what's more, believed what he read. As a matter of fact, the sergeant had at one time in his life thought of emigrating to America, and would have done so but for the curious ideas he had of American barbarism and the extraordinary belief he had of transatlantic blood-thirstiness, scalping, and general cussedness, engendered by these books.

Noting his master's preoccupation, young Snapper thinks this is his chance for fun, and makes off with great barking after a handsome brougham drawn by a pair of fine hacks and ornamented by a couple of elaborate flunkies that drives rapidly past from the direction of Sandgate. This awakens Sergeant Brackett; he calls his dog back and proceeds to the pier to await the arrival of the Boulogne boat; while the carriage Snapper had pursued stops in front of the West Cliff Hotel. Arthur Lincoln gets out of it, and is received by Lubbins, the head waiter of the establishment, with that abject humility and deference that only an English servant can assume when in the presence of his own to-be-fawned-upon aristocracy.

One can see *DeBrett's Peerage* and *Burke's Landed Gentry* in Lubbins' meek eye and obsequious bow as he says : " Yes, Mr. Harthur, *Lord* Lincoln is now in the reception-room hawaiting your coming."

" No, he's not, Lubbins," is heard in a kindly voice from the hall-way, and the next instant Percy Lincoln is shaking hands with his son. The moment's silent inspection of each other, natural to a meeting after several months' separation, being over, the elder man suddenly says to the younger, " Where's Ethel ? "

" Coming on the Boulogne boat with Lady Annerley and Miss Potter. I ran over last night ahead of them to be sure the villa would be ready."

" The tidal boat 'll be ' ere in twenty minutes, my lord," remarks Lubbins with another and even more

obsequious bow, rolling the word " lord " round his mouth
as if it were too sweet a morsel to let go easily, and emphasizing the title by an elaborate and elegant wave of
his napkin.

" Then come in and tell me all about your trip, Arthur," says the peer, and throwing his arm affectionately
around his son, leads that young gentleman into a little
parlor separated from the coffee-room of the hotel by a
hall.

As they enter, a voice with that curious twang peculiar
to the Southwestern States of America, loud but not harsh,
sonorous but extraordinarily soft at times, comes to their
ears from the coffee-room.

It says : " Lubbins, old 'os, is that 'ere lunch ready ?
I'm like ha Hindian on a U. Hess reservation—starving."

This thoroughly American voice and accent, mixed
with this abuse of the letter "*H*," peculiar only to cock-
neys of the most pronounced description, give such an
extraordinary effect to this speech that the elder Lincoln
smiles and the younger one laughs outright, whispering
to his father : " A rather curious character I should
think."

Lubbins ejaculates : " Yes, your worship ! " and after a
deprecating bow and an " Excuse me, back in a minute,
my lord," darts into the coffee-room.

Arthur Lincoln smiles after the departing waiter, and
remarks : " *He* knows."

" Knows what ? oh, ah, yes ; I forgot.   I suppose you
mean that Her Majesty's Government have for long and
distinguished services (I'm quoting from the patent of
nobility, Arthur) retired me from my judgeship to become Baron Lincoln of the realm and receive a pension.
I'm afraid there's too much honor and too little work in
the promotion."

His son replies : " But it is whispered at Westminster
that when our party comes into power you will be the
next Lord Chancellor."

" Ah ! our party hasn't come in yet," laughs Lord Lincoln, " so I'll take *this* arm-chair instead of the woolsack
for the present."

With this, the new-made peer selects the most comfortable seat in the cozy little parlor, and sinks into it
with the air of a man who may despise honors and pen-

sions theoretically, but who knows that practically they are very useful things in this selfish, struggling world.

As he sits there a bright ray of sunlight comes in the window, tinging his hair that is a soft, beautiful gray, and illuminating the finely molded head and strong, manly countenance beneath it. As he looks at him, the son cannot help thinking how proud he is of his governor.

The face before him is not only that of a great lawyer, but more and better than that, one of a good man, for the broad forehead, that betokens logic and justice and truth, is softened by a kindly expression of the mouth and eyes that indicates the more divine attribute of mercy. Percy Lincoln's record of thirty odd years upon the English bench has left him, all over Britain, the highest of reputations, that of a just and honest, but also kind-hearted, judge.

One of the most hardened criminals in England once said that he hated to be tried by Judge Lincoln, because his honor always looked at him in such a blarsted kind, downey, and merciful-like way that he had a sort of insane desire to peach upon himself and give away his pals and partners in the job. It is, perhaps, something of this kind of feeling that comes into the son's mind as he stands cogitating how he shall best make two confessions to his father, one for his sister and the other for himself. After a moment he concludes it is just as well to confess on his sister first and see how the governor stands it before he lets the cat out of the bag regarding himself.

Here Lord Lincoln breaks in upon his meditation, remarking : " You left Ethel in Paris. She has not written to me lately. This is unusual. What has she been doing ? "

" Shopping."

" Shopping ? "

" Oh, that's what all girls do in Paris, governor. Ida —that is, Miss Potter—" the young man checks himself rather suddenly, apparently a little embarrassed over his slip of the tongue on the name Ida.

" Well, Ida—that is, Miss Potter "—laughs the peer, imitating his son, who blushes slightly at this, " is a most fascinating girl. What was she doing ? "

" Oh, she—she was shopping also."

" And their chaperon, Lady Annerley, was she shopping, too? Was the young widow coming out of half mourning?"

"Not at all!"

"Affectation!" ejaculates Lord Lincoln. "No one ever supposed she loved her old husband."

"I suppose she'll make a love-match now."

"That rich young Australian, I understand," says Lord Lincoln, rising and trying to get a glimpse of the Boulogne boat out of the window.

"I don't think so," replies the son, rather hotly.

"Indeed ; why not?" says the old lawyer, cross-questioning the young lawyer. "Doesn't Lady Sarah love him?"

"Don't ask me to judge both a woman and a widow. Sometimes I think she almost hates him ; sometimes I fear she loves him!"

"*You* fear she loves him?" says Lord Lincoln, taking a quick glance at his son. "You don't love her yourself, do you, Arthur?"

"No, but I don't want her to love him!"

"Indeed! Why not?"

This is the young man's chance to do the confessing for his sister and he takes it. "Because the gentleman you have been speaking of is engaged to marry your daughter!"

The judge swings around from the window, gasps, "My daughter! Ethel?" and sinks into a seat. Being agitated he does not now select as comfortable a one as before. After gazing speechless at his son, who plays a staccato movement with his fingers upon the table, he gasps again : "And she consented, without consulting me?"

"Their engagement is subject to your approval. Mr. Errol will call upon you to-morrow!"

"Errol! That's the young man's name, is it?" asks the judge.

"Yes, Charley Errol. You must have heard of him before."

"It seems to me I have, somewhere, but never in connection with Lady Annerley. Everybody that hinted at the beautiful widow being in love with him seemed to envy the young fellow his powers of fascination for one of the catches of the matrimonial market, and rather sneered at him, calling him, 'Mr. Sheepfarmer,' 'Young Antipodes,' 'Kangaroo, Esq.,' and other jovial expressions of malice!"

"They couldn't say anything against him, morally or personally. Charley Errol is one of the best of fellows in the world. If any one decries him send him to me!" returns the son rather hotly, for Arthur Lincoln was of an impulsive nature, and, with the rashness of youth, was rather too ready at times to resent any slight upon either his friends or himself.

"So you're his champion and his ambassador—you know him well enough for that?" queries his father.

"We were together at Oxford and passable friends, but during the last two months in Italy he has captured me as completely as—as he has my sister."

"Then you think Ethel loves him—very much?" says the peer rather seriously and with a slight sigh.

For what father is not saddened by the news that the girl who has left him but a few weeks before almost a child with only him for her idol, will return to him with a woman's passion in her heart and another and stronger deity on the altar of her love? Percy Lincoln was too wise not to know that some day this must happen to his only daughter, but he had hoped that the day was of the future, not of the present.

As he is turning this rather bitter mental pill over in his mind, the American voice and Cockney accent come in through the partly open door of the parlor crying: "Lubbins, which 'll be here first, my lunch or that ere tidal-wave steamboat? It must have got snagged on the way from Bo-lo-*né* this afternoon; I'm getting as impatient for my darter as a cowboy is for whisky!"

Lubbins' obsequious voice soothes his impatience with, "Lunch is served, sir."

"Hurrah! Let me know when my daughter arrives. Now I'm on to the lunch like a praharee afire!" and a clattering of dishes, knives and forks indicates that the "praharee afire" will make very short work of the lunch.

Arthur Lincoln, with a rather disgusted shrug of his aristocratic shoulders, strides to the door and closes it with a bang, cutting short any more noise from the coffee-room, as his father says to him rather sternly: "How did all this happen, Arthur, and you never write me one word in regard to it? Neither did Ethel."

The last phrase has an implied reproach in it for the absent young lady at which her brother takes up her cause and does battle for it in these words : " Now, governor, don't fly up about the little girl ! It all happened so suddenly."

" Suddenly ? "

" Yes. You see when we arrived in Venice, Miss Potter, Ethel and I, a month or more ago, we met Errol at Lady Annerley's."

Here his father suddenly interrupts him with, " Errol ! I surely have known some one of that name," and appears to think deeply for a moment ; then quickly says : "Continue, please ! I beg your pardon."

"Well, he was an inmate of the house. He had been wounded nearly to death in defending Lady Annerley in Egypt, and she, in Venice, had nursed him to convalescence in a kind of motherly way."

" *Motherly !* A widow of twenty-five and a young man of—of any age ! " sneers Lord Lincoln, who does not seem altogether pleased with his son's story.

" Errol is about twenty-eight or nine, I believe," continues Arthur ; "but whether Lady Annerley's affection was motherly or not, Charley's was certainly not more than fraternal ; for the moment he saw Ethel it became a wonderful case of ' spoons ' upon his part, as well as on that of my sister."

" Then you think Ethel really loves him ? " says Lord Lincoln, who, though he detests slang, is in this case too . interested to pretend that he does not understand it.

" Loves him ? You know how proud she is ; if she did not love Charley Errol, do you suppose Ethel would let him—— " here Arthur pauses in a shame-faced· way, conscious from the expression on his father's face that he has told, perhaps, a little too much of his sister's story.

" You don't mean to tell me that he had the audacity to *kiss* my daughter ! " gasps his lordship.

" I'm afraid so," replies his son, after a moment's pause of consideration, conscious that he might as well make a clean breast of the matter.

The old man ejaculates " Good heavens ! " in such a

horror-struck tone that Arthur hardly chokes down a hysterical titter. For Lord Lincoln, though perfectly conscious that any other man's daughter would be kissed by her *fiancé*, scarcely deems it possible that any lover would have the audacity to offer a betrothal salute to his own pet lamb, that he has set apart from, and imagined more immaculate than the rest of the human flock.

"You see," continues Arthur in a slightly deprecating tone, " it was one night in Venice ; they had just taken me into their confidence ; it was moonlight, Italian moonlight. They were in one end of the gondola, I in the other."

Here the old lawyer entirely confounds the young lawyer, for he suddenly interrupts him by questioning. "Then who was in your end of the gondola? By George ! with your poetry one would think you in love yourself."

"Ida—that is Miss Potter," murmurs the son, suddenly blushing.

"Miss Potter !" returns his lordship, who apparently is anxious to get the conversation away from his daughter's kiss, " a lady from the ends of her thoroughbred fingers to the tips of her aristocratic feet ; every point about her shows blood. Her father is immensely rich, they say, pastures in Texas covered with cattle on a thousand hills. I have admired the young lady ever since she visited us with Ethel from Madame Beaumanoir's school. After me you will one day probably be a peer of the realm, and it never does a nobleman much harm to have a good •bank account. Miss Potter would make one of the best wives, best mothers, and most distinguished ladies in all England. I would not object to your marrying *her*, Arthur. Why don't you take my advice ?"

"I have ! "

"Eh ! what ! you don't mean it ! " says the peer, grasping his son by both shoulders, partly to keep himself from falling, for Lord Lincoln has got a most unexpected counter.

"Every word of it," returns the young man, with the enthusiasm of passion. " I don't care for her father's beeves, but I do care for his daughter. I love Ida Potter, and I've asked her to marry me ! "

"And she said—" suggests Lord Lincoln, for at the

end of his speech his son has turned suddenly away from his gaze.

"She said: ' My father will be in England in a week. Don't dare to speak of this again till you see him!' "

" What could she want to wait for?" cries the peer rather indignantly. " Most American girls would snap at an Honorable, as you are now, Arthur!"

"Perhaps she does not love me," suggests the son in a melancholy way, pulling out the fringe of the curtain of the window through which he is looking with an absent-minded destructiveness that would have driven the proprietor of the hotel to despair had he seen it.

" Pooh!" jeers Lord Lincoln. " You are too infernally modest. I've seen her look at you before you left England, two months ago, and the girl had already brought in a verdict in your favor. Hang it! it can't be that she fears her father will not be pleased with the alliance. Old Potter, I've no doubt, from his daughter's appearance, is an aristocrat, but he's got a very high social appetite if he can't stomach us!"

Any further eulogy of the Lincoln pedigree is cut short by the entry of Lubbins, who brings in some cigars and wine that the gentlemen have ordered. After the usual custom of waiters he leaves the door open, and there comes floating in after him : " Lubbins! a whisky and water, 'ot as the bilers of a Mississippi steamboat!"

" Disgusting personage that," remarks his lordship, rather angry at being interrupted.

" Very," rejoins the Honorable Arthur, who is rather aristocratic in his tastes.

" I'll close the door," suggests Lubbins, going out in response to the demand from the coffee-room. After a moment's pause Percy Lincoln, who has lit the end of his cigar with the calm, contemplative manner of a man upon the whole pleased with the news Providence, in the shape of his son, has just brought him, picks up the broken end of the conversation, saying :

" What is your future father-in-law's full name, Arthur?"

" The Honorable Sampson Potter," replies the son, rather proudly.

" Ah! one of their judges over there," suggests the peer, tossing his head in the direction of America.

9

"No, a member of one of their legislative bodies, I be-lieve."

"Ah! of course. As soon as you meet Mr. Potter ask him to visit us. I should like to discuss with him several of our international relations."

"I'll give him your invitation with a great deal of pleasure," assents Arthur, rising ; "but it must be nearly time for us to go down to the boat. Ethel will expect you, governor."

"I suppose her—her intended is dancing attendance upon the girl," says the peer, gulping a little at "the in-tended." "You'll have to introduce the young man to me, though the name Errol seems familiar. How long has his father lived in Australia ?"

"A number of years."

"Charles Errol was born there ?"

"Yes."

"And he is twenty-eight, you say ; then his father must have been out there nearly thirty years ?"

"Certainly. He's made an immense fortune in sheep farms. I've heard Lord Lansdowne speak of how mag-nificently he entertained him when he was in Melbourne, a few years ago. Charley Errol is his only child, so Ethel will have pots of money," continues Arthur, anxious to im-press his father with the strength of his friend as a mat-rimonial catch.

The young man would go on effusively, but here Percy Lincoln interrupts him with this astonishing ques-tion :

"Is the elder Errol so devoted to the antipodes that he has never returned to England ?" This is said as if a sudden idea has struck the questioner.

"I have never heard Charley speak of his father visit-ing England."

This apparently innocent remark has a great effect upon the peer. He almost staggers, and gasps, "Good heavens !" in a broken, pathetic kind of way.

The son does not notice this, for he is just looking out of the window at the steamboat bearing Miss Potter to his side. After a second he rather corrects himself by saying : "Mr. Errol's father is in England now !"

"A—ah !" this is a sigh of relief from the judge, "in England now ?"

" He will probably meet his son at this hotel to-night ! "

" Then it's all right."

" What do you mean ? " says his son, turning from the window and glancing at his father, the peculiarity in the tones of whose voice has caught his attention.

" Nothing, now ! " says the peer.   " Let's go down and meet the party."

With this the two men go to the front door of the hotel, the peer cracking one or two paternal little jokes such as old gentlemen indulge in when young gentlemen are rash enough to think of marriage ; apparently working him-- self up to the bless-you-my-children act of contemporaneous comedy upon his daughter's return.

About to get in his carriage, he says : " Errol, Ralph Errol, I think you said the father's name was ? "

" Yes, sir."

Here the ex-judge seems to meditate a moment, and then says : " I—I don't think I'll go down to the boat, I'm hardly up to the exertion ! "

" But Ethel 'll think it strange.   She'll fear you do not care to meet her lover ! "

" I do not care to meet her lover until he has consulted with his father.   I'll take our brougham and go on to the villa.   Hire a carriage and bring the young ladies after me ! "

Then Lord Lincoln steps into the carriage in an absent-minded way, while Arthur says " Home ! " to the coachman, and goes up the steps thinking, " What's come over the governor?   It can't be overwork, he looked hearty enough when I met him.   I suppose it's Ethel. I always feared it would break the old boy's heart to lose her. Egad, I have it ! " at length he mutters.   " *Pater* is afraid young Errol 'll want his wife to live in Australia. Glad the old gentleman seemed so well pleased with my matrimonial plans, however ! "   Turning over these things in his mind the young man has walked to the office of the hotel to arrange for a vehicle to take his sister and Miss Potter to Lord Lincoln's pretty marine villa, which stands about a mile from Folkestone, just where the white chalk cliffs descend to Sandgate.

While giving his order he is annoyed by the American voice and English accent that is now demanding in the next room : " Lubbins, a toothpick and some coffee-beans'

Scoot as if you were a Mississippi boat-race! My darter and the swells 'll be here in a minute ! "

In " scooting " for the coffee-beans Lubbins chances to pass very close to Arthur, who, being of a rather sensitive and refined nature, elevates his aristocratic nose and inquires *sotto voce :* " Who is that frightful creature with his disgusting manners and fearful English ? "

" Don't know, your honor," whispers the head waiter, " but he's very liberal with his tips, and 'as put 'is name down on the register, sir, last *entrée.*" As he says this, Lubbins, with an obsequious bow, places the book in question under Arthur's nose.

After gazing at it through his eye-glass for a second, such a fearful expression of anguish contorts the young man's face that Lubbins drops the volume and says faintly, " Police ! "

And the Honorable Arthur Lincoln in a kind of dazed nightmare reels out of the house and gasps with a kind of hysterical spasm, an indescribable conglomeration of groan and giggle : " The joke of the century ! Ha ! ha ! ha ! My Heaven ! *Despair and damnation !* MY FUTURE FATHER-IN-LAW ! "

For he has seen scrawled all over half a page of the hotel register :

The Hon Sampson Potter Comanche Conty Texas U.S.

CHAPTER XI.

HONOR THY FATHER.

.FOR a few seconds after this Arthur Lincoln stands in a sort of amazed coma ; then he suddenly mutters : " No ! No ! Impossible ! " darts into the hotel again, and gazes

once more at the register that Lubbins has replaced on
the office counter. Mr. Potter's chirography is as horribly distinct as when it first met his vision.

He sinks into a seat and faintly, in a broken kind of
voice, asks for water ; then, as the obsequious Lubbins
hands him the glass, gazing at him in deferential and
sympathetic astonishment, fiercely demands : " What the
devil are you looking at ? " in such a ferocious tone,
that the servitor addressed instantly remembers he has
business in the coffee-room, and disappears.

After sitting down a moment or two, Arthur springs
up and gets out of the hotel, but in a minute returns, a
horrible fascination having come over him, to inspect the
object that has produced such a peculiar effect upon him

Muttering to himself : " I'll obey her injunction. *I'll
see her father,*" he comes into the hotel in a kind of
sheepish manner, and carefully opening the coffee-room
door, glances round the screen that is placed before it—
drawing his head back · now and again whenever Mr.
Potter, who is dividing his attention between the *Morning Times* and his lunch, raises his eyes so as to make it
possible for him to see his observer.

The attitude and movements of the Honorable Arthur
Lincoln are by no means dignified, his dodging motion ·
behind the screen being very much like that of a cat
when on the lookout for dogs round the corner.

If the simile of the cat applies to Mr. Arthur Lincoln,
the analogy of the dog round the corner may equally suit
the Honorable Sampson Potter of Texas. He is what
might be called a mastiff and skye-terrier man ; that is, ·
one with the courage and faithfulness to trust of the
first-named animal, but also the unremitting wariness and
alert watchfulness of the latter. At present the mastiff
is eating ; the skye-terrior asleep.

If Arthur Lincoln has had a vague hope that Mr. Potter's elegance of appearance will contradict the peculiar
uncouthness of his diction, one glance is sufficient to destroy that idea. In 1882, the man before him conveyed
only vulgar barbarism to the mind of his English be-
holder ; though, had Mr. Potter arrived in London with
Buffalo Bill in 1887, he would have been regarded and
worshiped as the acme of wild Western elegance and refinement by the British public, for he is an almost perfect

picture of a Texan frontier ranger and cattle-man. His face, which is clean shaven, save a long mustache, is seamed with the wrinkles of hardship and the scars of encounters with both wild beasts and savage men, and has the peculiar red roughness produced by habitual exposure to the burning sun and chilling northers of Texas. His forehead would be that of a trusting, good-natured boy, were it not balanced by a nose of great size, power, and decision, and contradicted by lips of almost stern firmness, and a pair of eyes which have that clear steel-gray tint common to Brazilian diamonds of the first water and kindly men of very deadly dispositions—eyes that are sometimes mistaken for a little off color until the time of danger and death, when they beam and shine like the brilliants of Golconda. Over these features Mr. Potter wears a jet-black wig that is not ornamental, it being apparently of frontier make, as it has hair of several degrees of coarseness in its locks, and is so badly fashioned or carelessly put on, that it allows some of Potter's own straggling brown hair to show beneath it. The reason of its use is not easily apparent, as the hair it is intended to hide is only as yet slightly grizzled.

His suit of black broadcloth, fashioned in Southwestern fashion, seems too large for his thin, wiry form, for Potter is not a large man; though Brick Garvey, one of his old companions in the pioneer days of "The Lone Star State," had once said that "English Potter" (his *sobriquet* in those times) "never war a big man until he war fightin', then he war a giant!" Two large diamonds ornament his shirt, and another one his finger; he also wears a large California quartz abomination of a watch-chain, with one little gold coin dangling from it and making it by contrast appear even more clumsy and massive than it really is. A new necktie, white, old-fashioned, turn-down collar, and high cowhide boots, most elaborately blackened and polished from toes to tops, and into which his trousers are tucked, proclaim that Mr. Potter has made an elaborate toilet upon this gala day, when after four years' separation he will meet the daughter for whose education he has been willing to sacrifice even the joy of that daughter's companionship and the pleasure of her presence.

Having been compelled to silence for the last eight

hours, during which time he has left the Cunarder upon which he had this day arrived at Liverpool, and run across England to London, and from thence down to Folkestone, Mr. Potter has accumulated a great amount of compressed conversation. The cattle-king's kindly advances to conversation have not been well received by the traveling British public, and the frontier appearance and jovial prairie manners of the gentleman from Texas have caused one rural rector to refuse indignantly the offer of his pocket-flask, and a prim spinster of severe mien to request the guard " on no account to permit that red-faced ruffian to travel alone in the same compartment with her." Consequently the Honorable Sampson has had no one to talk with. He is now, however, making up for lost time on Lubbins, who is gazing open-mouthed at him with a mixture of admiration and terror, for since Arthur's extraordinary actions upon seeing his name, the head waiter is certain that there is some mystery connected with the gentleman eating lunch in the coffee-room.

All Mr. Potter's thoughts being on his daughter, his conversation is naturally upon the same subject.

" Look 'ere," he says, tapping the morning edition of the *Times*, which lies on the table before him. " ' Fashionable Intelligence.' Do you see ? Marquis de Saint Germon, Lady Longueville, and—by jingo !—Miss Hida Potter, U. *Hess*. That's my darter sandwiched in between a duchess and a potentate ! How's that for the Potter family ? "

" Very 'igh, your honor," remarks Lubbins, who worships the aristocracy also, and is now beginning to regard the man upon whom he is waiting as a kind of swell in disguise.

" And 'ere agin ! " remarks the Honorable Sampson, with a flush of joy. " Look at this : ' Movements of Noted Persons ' : Lady Saharah Hannerley, accompanied by the Honorable Miss Hethel Lincoln, Miss Hida Potter, the beautiful Hamerican heiress, the Honorable Harthur Lincoln, B. Sidney Van Cott, and Mr. Charles Herrol, arrived in Paris from Venice yesterday. Wonder which of these chaps his following my darter ? Put the gals ahead, the boys won't be far behind—not in Texas ! "

" I think the Honorable Mr. Harthur his the one ! " says Lubbins, with a chuckle. " ' E was halways a-run-

ning hafter her when your young lady was here a-visiting
his family."

" You've a level head, Lubbins. I've caught a suspi-
cion of that fact in my darter's letters. What kind of a
chap is the young man, anyway ?" says Mr. Potter, with
a wink, producing a packet of delicately tinted envelopes
directed in a beautiful and aristocratic female hand.

But Arthur sees and hears no more of this. He has
fled from the horrible desecration. Had he stayed to
look a little longer he would have seen another phase in
the gentleman he has been studying. After a few more
searching questions in regard to the character of the
Honorable Arthur, to which Lubbins replies, giving him a
rather fair reputation for liberality, and all the other car-
dinal virtues, for the son of the peer has been quite generous in his tips, which is the only standard by which
head waiters judge the morals and dispositions of men,
Mr. Potter rises, looks out of the window, and says,
suddenly : " What's the damage ? "

" Damage ? " echoes Lubbins, not understanding this
Americanism.

" Yes ; how much do I owe ? That 'ere boat's coming
in. Hurry, like a stampeded mustang ! My darter
mustn't be kept waiting for her daddy's four-year-old
kiss ! "

Thus adjured, the waiter bolts for the bill, while Potter,
sitting down to wait for him, gazes abstractedly at the
Times that still lies on the table before him. Something
in one of the advertising columns happens to catch his
eye, and the next instant the skye-terrier in him has
woke up and is reading the paper. It is the same advertisement that Sergeant Brackett had sneered at half an
hour before, but Mr. Potter reads it over and over again
so keenly and eagerly that when Lubbins returns with his
account, he abstractedly produces a sovereign, and says,
" Pay yourself ! " and goes on reading, speculating, and
making notes in his pocket-book, interlarding his labors
now and again with sundry exclamations such as " Snakes
and tarantulas ! " " Almighty curious ! " " Chaw me up ! "
" This is an eye-opener ! " and other kindred Western expressions of excited astonishment. Finally he cuts out
the advertisement from the *Times*, and takes the address
of the advertiser, which is H. Clarkson Portman, Solici-

tor, No. 33 Chancery Lane, W. C., London. He is so engrossed in this that Lubbins, after bringing back a pile of silver for the change and placing it in front of him, returns fifteen minutes after, and, finding the money still untouched, deftly pockets it, thinking Potter the most liberal man on earth.

Mr. Arthur Lincoln, having fled from the hotel, remarks : " She said : ' See my father ! ' Great heavens, *I have seen him !* " and for a moment has a wild idea of bolting to China, India, or any other place as far as possible from the paternal Potter. He hurries down the street toward the express train that is now drawn upon the pier awaiting the arrival of the Boulogne boat ; his eye follows the pier to the sea. The Channel steamer is just entering the harbor ; his imagination pictures the lovely being who has won his heart ; he murmurs : " She'd reconcile me to any father in the world ! " and then gives a kind of unhappy chuckle as he thinks: " The Honorable Sampson Potter of Texas will be a very bitter pill for my governor to swallow! " But for all that no more joyously expectant face and wildly beating heart has ever welcomed that Channel steamer than Arthur Lincoln's : and Heaven only knows what joys, and loves, and agonies have burnt recollections into the souls of men and women of that point for partings and for meetings, that platform for good news and for bad news, that place for the tearing apart of hearts, and the welding together of new ties and affections, that station on the highway of nations, that pier at Folkestone, England.

The deck of the steamboat is crowded, for the day is sunny as summer, and the sea unusually calm for the English Channel ; and, while waiting for the first rush of hurrying arrivals to pass him, Arthur Lincoln has time to put two ideas firmly in his head. It was not her fear of her father's refusing an alliance with him, but a fear that he would disdain a connection with her father, that had made Ida tell him to first see Mr. Potter before she would promise to be his wife. Conscious that he will lose her if he wounds the American girl's pride in the least, as he squeezes himself across the gang-way to the deck of the boat the young lawyer arranges his method of conducting his case ; which, like most legal expedients, is hardly fair for the party in opposition.

As he forces his way on, Sergeant Brackett, of Scotland Yard, is alongside of him.

The crowd have mostly landed, and Arthur has no trouble in finding the party who are not hurrying to the London train, as they intend to remain in Folkestone for the afternoon. Hastily greeting his sister, he says : "It's all right, little girl!" which makes tears of happiness come into Ethel's eyes, and causes the Australian to give his hand such a clasp that he knows the convalescent has entirely regained his strength. Then saying to Lady Annerley how kind she has been to take such good care of his sister, and with a " Helloa, Van Cott, my boy! Bound for London, eh! You'd better hurry and catch the train!" he starts for Miss Potter, who is in the rear of the rest.

Before he has time to address the American girl, Ethel has run back to him, and mutters anxiously : " Papa ! He's not here—he is angry ? "

" Not at all. Only too tired to wait for the boat. He expects you all at the villa ! " Then Arthur speaks to the party and says : " I've ordered refreshments at the West Cliff, and carriages to take you all out to Channel View. You mustn't refuse me ! "

" Of course not. I'll stay with you a week, old chappie. How is his lordship ? " returns Mr. Van Cott, seizing his opportunity, and inviting himself with a jump.

" Quite right," mutters Arthur, who hasn't intended to ask him, but is in too much of a hurry to discuss the question. Then he calls out : " Errol, you know the way, take 'em up to the West Cliff ! "

As the detective, standing near the party, hears the name Errol, he steps forward, about to address the young man, but, after seeing his face, stops somewhat astonished and, consulting his note-book, turns away and says nothing. But his eyes never leave the Australian, and, during the next few hours, though Errol does not know it, Sergeant Brackett, of Scotland Yard, is never very far away from him.

Ethel's turning back to her brother has left Errol alone. Lady Annerley has taken her place beside the Australian. Arthur, eager to get a word apart with Ida, suddenly utters : " Van Cott, you take care of Ethel," hands his sister over to the red-eyed youth, and is beside his divinity.

During these arrangements Miss Potter has stood, as
her lover thinks—for he has gazed at her several times—a
beautiful statue in gray, dashed with sea-green and white
foam, for that is the appearance of her costume, which is
some poetic creation of a great artist in Paris.   Though
the blushes have chased one another over her face in
waves of varied emotions, and her eyes, which are full of
anxious expectancy, have given him several veiled glances,
and her lips have trembled and once or twice opened as
if about to speak, to this time she has uttered not a
word.

Her parasol trembles nervously in her hand as he
approaches her, and she says : " My father !   He isn't
here to meet me also, after four years ?   Something has
happened to him ! "

" I imagine," returns Arthur, " Mr. Potter has mistaken
the time of the boat's arrival."

" Ah, you have seen him ? "

" Yes."

" Tell me, how is he ?   How did he look ?   Well ?
Happy ?   Joyous as I shall be at seeing him ? " and the
girl is about to run for the gangway.

" One moment," says Arthur, detaining her.   Then he
speaks aloud to Van Cott, who is moving off with Ethel,
and remarks : " Miss Potter has left her satchel down
in the cabin.   Don't wait for us ; we'll stay and find
it ! "

Here Miss Potter blushes, and Ethel laughs as Van
Cott mutters under his voice to her : " By Jove, that's a
stunner !   Ida hasn't been off the deck the whole trip ! "

He hasn't time to amplify this subject, however, for
Ethel, who sees Lady Annerley and her guiding star get-
ting too far away from her, now cries : " Come on !
Hurry, or we'll miss them ! " and figuratively drags Mr.
Van Cott off with her, leaving Arthur and Ida alone to-
gether.

" I think we'll be able to find your satchel in about five
minutes," says Mr. Lincoln, moving toward the cabin
entrance.

" Probably in much less time," returns Miss Potter,
dryly, " as I see my maid carrying it off the boat now,"
and then she bursts out: " How could you place me in
such an embarrassing position ?   Even while you were

talking my servant was flourishing it under your very
nose. Oh, Arthur !" This last is a reproach, but the young
man looks so contrite she smiles and says: " You would
like to see me alone ? "

" Very much ! ".

" Then I'll steal two minutes from papa for you.
There were only two people in the saloon the whole trip,
and they were seasick—probably it's empty now," and
she leads the way into the cabin, but as he follows her
down the companion-way she gives him a look over her
shoulder that makes the Honorable Arthur shiver, and
turning around upon him, says with haughty dignity :
" You say you saw my father ; did he accept your pro-
posal for his daughter ? "

If the young man had hesitated he would have lost
her, for even in his slight pause of a second the girl's
eyes are beginning to blaze and her breast to throb with
indignant pride, and she mutters: " Why don't you answer? You despise——"

But here Arthur, being a lawyer, and as such accustomed to suppress the truth or disguise it, with sudden
inspiration cries : " No ! your father did not refuse me ! "
And unable to control himself before this vision of panting beauty, mutters : " You said the man who kissed you
married you," seizes her in his arms.

There is a crush of lace and silk and satin and gewgaws as Ida Potter in one kiss, two tears, and several
blushes becomes his betrothed.

After a moment she draws herself from him, for there is
a noise as of some one's entering the cabin, and looking
up into his face with a trust that makes him ashamed
of his *ruse* says : " Arthur, what did papa say to you ?
Tell me ! "

" Well ! " returns the young man, dropping his eyes
under her glance, " to tell the ah—exact truth, he said—
nothing ! "

" *Nothing ?* "

" No ; the fact is, I didn't get a chance to speak to
him."

" *You did not speak to him ?* "

" I couldn't, I wasn't introduced ! "

" Then you only know his appearance, you don't know
his—his *peculiarities*. I had expected in this interview the

truth from you as a *man*, and you have given me the equivocation of a *lawyer!*"

Then with reproach in her eyes, but great dignity and nobility in her mien she continues: "You have made it necessary for the woman you profess to love to endure the humiliation of telling you with her own lips that her father is a man of but little education and what you and your class would call no breeding!" Here her voice softens and she goes on: "My father is a good man! Don't mistake me in this ; if his education were equal to his heart he might be Archbishop of Canterbury and do honor to the See. As it is you must now appreciate that he is not exactly the man to be the father of an English peeress, which your wife must one day be. You—you are released from your promise of marriage to me!" and turning her head away she utters in a broken voice : "Oh, it was a great mistake, my—my coming to England and loving you."

The young man, though much affected, has resolved with legal tact to let her make her speech, reserving the closing argument for himself, and here simply suggests : "And you forgive me?"

"Forgive? I have nothing to forgive ; only much to regret !" murmurs the girl.

"You *regret* my loving you?"

"I—I regret I did not have the strength to tell you of the barrier that society, that the world has set between us. At times—I—I have tried to treat you coldly, but it was too—too hard to destroy my one great hope, and I hesitated till—I—I had not the power. But now that you know the truth, the sooner we say farewell the better! Good-by, Arthur!" The girl turns to the young man whom she had one minute before called betrothed and had hoped to call husband, and tries to bid him farewell, holding out a trembling hand, gasping because she sees he is trembling also : "Don't think too unkindly of me, because I couldn't bear to tell you before !"

She is staggering from him, but he cries after her : "Do you think me so mean, that after I had gone on loving you for yourself, worshiping you for yourself, holding you as the one most noble woman on this earth for your own sake—— "

, She has turned back murmuring : " Arthur ! "

He pays no attention but talks straight at her, only with more enthusiasm, for he has the beauty of her face to inspire him. " That because of any accident of birth or education or refinement in your father, I could ever forget that you are the one woman in all this world that I will make my wife, and failing to gain you—I will wed no other ! "

" Don't speak so," she gasps. " You only make the parting harder ! "

" We shall not part ! "

" Think of your family—*they* will never consent."

" My father already loves you—you are my sister's dearest friend."

" But *my* father ! " cries Ida. " You have your pride of birth. I have my pride also. I love, I honor my father ! I will become a member of no family that does not honor him also ! He is the truest man upon this earth ! " And, fired with enthusiastic love, this daughter of uneducated old Potter looks like a princess of light, as her beautiful eyes flash and gleam like stars of truth in the gloom of the cabin.

Her enthusiasm is catching, for her lover cries also : " Then I know my father is man enough to honor him too ! Miss Potter," here he bows to her with the ceremony he would use to a duchess, " my father to-morrow shall ask from your father the honor of an alliance with his family. *Then*, Ida, what will your answer be ? "

The girl droops and trembles, and perhaps for a moment fights with herself ; but love conquers, and seeing this, he would take her in his arms again, but she stops him archly, saying : " Wait for my answer till then ! "

" Must I wait when I know all about your father's peculiarities, when I heard him talk for an hour before I came to you to get my answer ? "

" With my father's accent in your ears, you ask me to be your wife ? *You may kiss me at once !* " cries Miss Potter, and gives him so loving, true, trusting and unaffected an embrace that Arthur would have lingered over it forever, had not a loud, weather-beaten, tarry voice on deck yelled : " All ashore ! "

So the two run up the companion ladder into the sunlight, and on to the gangway, across which no fairer,

happier, more lovely creature ever tripped between boat
and shore than Ida Potter.   Notwithstanding Arthur's
ardent looks, she keeps her countenance very well, till
one tar standing by the gangway remarks to another :
" Look at her, Bill !   Ain't she sweet on him !   Blowed
if she ain't a bride !" and then—oh, the blushes !

CHAPTER XII.

MR. POTTER ENTERS SOCIETY.

RECOVERING from the embarrassment caused by this
remark Miss Potter soon nestles quite closely to the radiant Arthur.   They leave the railway station, and turning to their left walk up one of the streets leading to the
cliffs.   During this time she gives him a number of confidences that make the young man very happy as they
show him that the girl at his side regards him even now as
a member of her family.   She tells him that her mother,
whom she never saw to remember, was descended from
one of the old Virginia families who had taken part in
the first settlement of Kentucky in the days of Daniel
Boone ; and from there had, lured by the gold excitement
of the time, attempted to emigrate in 1850 to California.
Taking the Southern route by way of Texas, which at
that day was the home and favorite hunting ground of
the Comanche, the train with which they traveled had
been attacked by Indians and every member of the party
killed save her mother, who was but a girl, and an English boy of fifteen or sixteen.   This boy had saved her
mother's life in so gallant a way that it had made him
famed for courage even in that State, where desperate encounters and deadly combats at that time were matters of
every-day occurrence.
  Despite any difference of station or education, her
mother had loved and married him, and her means had
given Mr. Sampson Potter his first step in the race for
wealth.   She had died when Ida was born, in the dark
days of the Confederacy, when Potter had been brought
back from the front badly wounded, having been one of
the leaders in probably the most desperate charge ever

made in the war by Southern troops, *i. e.*, that of the Texans at the battle of Iuka.

Then the young lady says enthusiastically : " I have but two near relatives in the world, one of whom you have heard Lady Annerley speak, my elder brother, Houston, who is a lieutenant in the American navy and who headed the American marines that saved her and Mr. Errol at Alexandria ; a young gentleman who is wild, reckless, and sometimes rather extravagant—at least papa says so when he condescends to draw upon him, which is quite often ; but whom I love and honor because every one says he is an ornament to his service and his flag. The other is my father, whom I honor and love even more because he is just to every one and generous to every one save himself ; because in a State where it takes a truly brave man to always dare to do right, my father has a name which has become a terror to the lawless and wicked. As a ranger he defended Texan homes from Indians and bandits ; as a Congressman a whole railroad couldn't buy him ; and as a sheriff he never allowed any one to be lynched—and that's saying a good deal in Texas ! " adds Miss Potter so naively that this view of Texan justice makes the English lawyer open his astonished eyes.

After a moment the young lady continues : " Every one says that I get my face and my—well " (giving a pleasing little blush), " my figure, from my mother ; but I think my heart is nearly all from my father, who nursed me in his arms and was father and mother both to his little orphan, as he used to call me."

Any further eulogy upon the absent Potter is cut short by her hearing her father's voice coming from the open windows of the coffee-room. There is a rustle of silk, a flash of lace, and Ida has flown from Arthur's side up the steps into the hotel, and with glad cries, happy tears, and tender kisses, this goddess of fashion, refinement, and beauty is in the arms of the weather-beaten, woundscarred veteran of the plains and taken to his heart that beats only for her. Description would desecrate such a meeting.

Arthur thinks his presence would desecrate it also, and remains in the street ruminating upon his prospective father-in-law. His meditations are short, however, for

Lady Annerley and Errol approach him coming from the west, having apparently got past the hotel by some means. He looks at them in a lazy kind of way, and suddenly becoming struck with an idea, mutters : "By George ! my lady looks at Errol as if she loved him. I'm glad Ethel isn't here to see her. Strange ! I never noticed it before." And appears surprised, for at Venice and during their journey through France, Ida and Arthur and Ethel and Charley had lived their own selfish lives and loved their own selfish loves, and in their own great happiness utterly failed to note any signs of distress or suffer-ing in their hostess, who, to tell the truth, has concealed her misery by her pride ; though at times in the night, alone in her chamber, she has had some awful interviews with herself.

When she has left the railway she has led Errol purposely to the hotel by a roundabout way. She has something to say to him, and this is the only time to do it. She knows that this is the last moment in which she can do her duty ; if she does not speak now and tell him what she went to Egypt to confess to him, she can never-more do so in honor, *she dare nevermore do so at all.* While she is thinking this he gives her an opportunity to make her peace with her conscience and let him be happy.

"Dear Lady Sarah," he says, "I have been often wondering how I could best show my gratitude to you for the kind nursing you gave me which saved my life ! "

" Don't speak of gratitude," and she almost sneers at herself ; then mutters : " I had not been worthy the name of woman had I not done all I did after you fought so bravely, so nobly to save me in Egypt ! "

Thus the two get talking of the days in Alexandria and recalling the Arab boy, and Osman the dragoman, and Constantine Niccovie the Levantine, and she forgets, and for a short time is happy ; but he brings her back to reality with a start, for he suddenly says : " How did you first meet me ? I—I think I remember now you had something to say to me—something of importance ! "

And then she has a spasm of conscience and is about to tell him, but hears Ethel's voice behind them, and sees the face she is looking at turn and gaze backward and light up with a light her words and smile could never

bring to it, and she closes her lips and clinches her teeth
for fear that they may give this man a talisman against
the evil that will this day come upon him.

She is, perhaps, a little frightened, for what he says to
her shows that Errol has begun to remember Alexandria;
but all the same she will fight it out now.

So they come up to the hotel, she trying with all her
might to entertain him, and telling him that she is returning that evening to Boulogne, where she will stay
at the *Hôtel des Bains*, and where he must promise to
run over and visit her. She will be there a day or two
before returning to Paris.

To this Errol replies that he'll come over if his
fiancée 'll let him off, and so puts a dagger into Lady Annerley's heart.

Her lip trembles, but she contrives to mutter : " It 'll
be only for a day !" and turns away her head, to look at
the sea he thinks ; but it is to keep him from seeing
her tears. A moment after she says : " You'll promise to
come ? To-morrow, if possible ; remember, we have been
such good—friends ! "

" But Ethel——— "

" Ah, you are always thinking of her *now* !" Lady
Annerley can't keep the bitterness out of her voice.
Then she goes on : "I sha'n't have time to bid you good-
bye here ; and it will only take you a few hours."

"All right, I'll come to-morrow," returns Errol, who
fears he has wounded her in some way, and has a great
friendship for this woman who has done so much for him.

" You will ?   Promise ! "

" Certainly !   To-morrow," says Errol, " or any other
day you please. Why not? Ethel, thanks to you, has
the whole balance of my life."

" Has she ? " thinks Lady Annerley. " I wouldn't
change my chances for hers," and she makes herself so
affectionately pleasing and brilliantly cheerful, bringing
all the powers of her fine mind and cultured manner to
bear upon the Australian, that he is happy, though his
sweetheart is walking behind him with young Van Cott ;
and Miss Ethel seeing the young widow's attentions to
her idol becomes for the first time jealous.

This is by no means lessened by the remarks of the facetious Van Cott, who, being very savage at Arthur's tak-

ing Miss Potter away from him "just when she was beginning to love me, by Jove!" is determined to torment
his sister by all the powers of his little mind.

"Oh, ain't she gone on him!" he whispers. "Look!
there's a glance for you! I never knew my lady's eyes
were so beautiful before. She treated me awful; hope
she'll be kinder to him. By George! This last affair of
the widow's beats the rest; don't you think so, Miss
Ethel?"

"You believe she loves him?" gasps the tormented
one with such a piteous expression that if Van Cott had
any heart he would relent.

"I know it. 'Pon honor, I know it."

"Know it?" Here Ethel's eyes blaze.

"Y-as! I've proof of it. By George, do you suppose
unless Lady Annerley loved him, she would have refused
me!" he says with such an air of conviction, that, looking
at his imposing five feet two of figure and his weeping
eyes, Miss Ethel bursts out into a laugh, though it is not
a very happy one. Thus Mr. Van Cott, having sowed the
seed, circumstances coming after ripen it into a harvest.

So they all come to the hotel, and Arthur conducting
them, by the aid of Lubbins, into a reception-room, tells
them the carriages will shortly be round to take them to
his father's villa.

But the waiting is not altogether pleasant, for Van
Cott suddenly exclaims: "Where's Ida?" and this fa-
miliarity of appellation so enrages the Honorable Arthur
that he stops that young gentleman's searching for her
by saying sternly:

"*Miss* Potter is with her father, sir!"

"Oh—ah—y-as. With the awh—beefsteak man. I—
awh—beg pardon; mean cattle-king!" mutters Van Cott
meekly, and after a moment gets out of the room, for
Mr. Lincoln's eyes have grown quite savage.

Errol goes out also, but almost immediately returns
from the office with a message in his hand and says:
"Here's luck! I sha'n't have to go on to London. My
governor telegraphs me he'll be here on the afternoon
train to meet me," and going up to Ethel makes her very
happy by whispering: "I shall bring him over perhaps
this evening, and certainly to-morrow morning, to ask
your father for you in style."

Her blush is the only answer to this, but Lady Annerley a moment after says: " Don't fail to bring your father
to see me—you know where, Charley," and is rewarded
by a little sigh of misery from her young rival, who has
not yet learnt self-control in suffering. Seeing this, my
lady calls Errol " Charley " very often this afternoon, and
finds it a very effective weapon of punishment for Miss
Ethel Lincoln.

She is, however, quite anxious to know the exact train
upon which the elder Errol will arrive, and after consulting time-tables they all conclude that he will come on
the 6 P. M.   This will give her an hour longer in Folkestone without any chance of meeting the Australian's
father, for though very anxious to know the effect of her
cruelty, she cannot bear to see it. How to obtain this
information without compromising herself is now a problem in her mind.   This is soon solved, however, for she
notices the waiter. Every time Lubbins has brought in
refreshments his bow has been more obsequious to her
than to any of the rest, and his meek eyes have sought
hers in an appealingly humble manner.

" What does the man want of me ? " thinks her ladyship, and then suddenly remembers him and imagines
that he wishes her to recognize him. Lubbins is handing her a plate of cake and giving a more cringing
obeisance than usual, and catching him in the act she
says : " I have seen you before ! "

" Yes, my lady ! "

" I remember you ! "

" Oh, your ladyship ! "

" What is your name ? "

" Ah, Lady Annerley—Lubbins ; your ex-butler, Tobias
Lubbins, your ladyship." This information is all ac-
cented by bows, smirks, and flourishes of his napkin.

" Ah, of course, Lubbins, you were at my town,
house ! "

" No, your ladyship, at Brinksham, your Shropshire
estate."

" Precisely, so I thought. I require an English butler
at my hotel in Paris. I engage you ; make your arrangements, and report to me at *Hôtel des Bains*, Boulogne, to-morrow."

" But the proprietor of the West Cliff ? "

" Arrange the matter financially with him.   I will pay
for it ; I want you ! "

" Perhaps I'd better come to-night, your ladyship ? "
says Lubbins, who knows a situation in Lady Annerley's
house is much better than the one he has in the hotel.

" *To-morrow!* by the afternoon boat and not before !
You may go ! " returns Sarah Annerley in a tone Lubbins
has heard before and knows what it means.

" Yes, my lady ! " and as the waiter goes out of the
room she knows that the problem is solved ; that Lubbins, who has eyes in his head and uses them, and ears
in his head and uses them, and keyholes in his doors and
uses them, will be able, properly pumped, to give her all
the information she desires.

But she has no time for further thought, for Van Cott
comes staggering into the room, and after two or three
gulps, and being patted on the back, as the creature is
black in the face with laughter, he gasps out : " Oh
Lud, I've seen him ! When I first put eyes on him, oh
gracious, how he frightened me ! I thought I had a return of—of those awful——" Here he stammers and
blushes, for the young wretch has nearly made a horrible
confession on himself, but finally gets out : " You should
see him, he's a sensation ! "

" What have you seen ? " cries everybody in the room
except Arthur.

" Ida's governor ! Old Potter, the cattle-king ! He's
something you see on the stage and read about in novels ;
he's like THIS ! " and he goes off into an imitation of the
absent Potter that sends all but Arthur, who scowls at
him savagely, into a shriek of laughter ; for Van Cott,
like most persons of feeble mind, is a most excellent
mimic.

Lady Annerley finally says, in a tone of unbelief :
" You must exaggerate ! " and Miss Ethel cries : " Nonsense, the idea ! The father of Miss Potter must be a
gentleman ! "

" Well, just wait till you see him ! " mutters little Van
Cott.

But here an awful silence comes upon them all, for
Potter's voice is heard in the hall saying : " Lubbins,
you say the swells are in this har room ? " and the next
second Lubbins, who has been surreptitiously studying

up the hotel register, pompously announces : " The Honorable Sampson Potter of Comanche County, Texas, U. Hess, and daughter."

Then Ida walks quietly in and introduces her father.

Probably Arthur's love for the girl grows double as he realizes the cruel position in which she is placed, and ·notes the noble manner in which she makes almost a triumph for herself of what to any other girl in the world he imagines would be a total defeat.

She looks lovingly and encouragingly at her father, though he needs no encouragement, for old Potter is no more abashed in the presence of title than he would be in the society of Lubbins ; every one in the world to him is on a common plane save his daughter, and she is ahead of everybody.

He greets them all with a kindly smile, for they are his daughter's friends, and as Miss Potter, with a blush of love and affection, and perhaps pride, for she is certainly proud of her father, says : " Lady Annerley, Miss Ethel Lincoln, Mr. Arthur Lincoln, Mr. Errol, Mr. Van Cott, permit me to present my dear father," the old man takes up the strain and cries, jovially and unaffectedly : " Ladies and gents, I knows you hall by my darter's letters as well as I knows my own brand of cattle—your 'ands ! " Then goes about shaking and bobbing with unaffected Western grace.

After speaking to the ladies he comes straight to Arthur, and the young man can tell from Potter's manner that he knows the relation he wishes to assume to his daughter, for the pressure of his hand is kindly, the tone of his voice cordial, and the glance of his blue eyes friendly, though searching, as he says : " The Honorable Arthur Lincoln, I reckon ! My Ida has been talking you up ! "

Then he passes on to Errol, and Lincoln gradually grows to love him, for he is so good and so unaffected in his rude way to every one about him.

But though Potter speaks to them all he has but one being really in his thoughts. Every now and again Arthur can see the cold gray steel in his eyes glint and glisten as he looks after the beautiful figure of Miss Potter, who is now radiant ; as if he feared that this was a dream and he should wake up on the cattle range and find himself in Texas and the daughter of his heart in far-off Europe. Noting how his eyes sparkle with affection as they meet those of his daughter, and the unaffected heartiness of his manner, the young man reflects: " The Honorable Sampson Potter of Texas may make a much better father-in-law than many a penurious duke."

The Texan, after greeting Arthur, has turned to Errol. He looks at his face as if striving to call back something, then says : " Herrol, your face seems familiar like. Ever been in Texas ? "

" No, I am an Australian ! "

" Ah ! yes, I remember. My son wrote me about you from Alexandria. You're the young chap as saved the life of Lady Hannerley's thar. I've fit greasers and Injuns and grizzle bars, but never tackled the Arabesques and Mosoleums. You beat me thar ! "

At this little Van Cott cannot contain himself, and coming up to Mr. Potter, cries, imitating his accent quite correctly : " Them is my sentiments! Yes, siree, I'd 'ave liked to have tackled the Mosoleums myself ! Your 'and ! " and seizes Mr. Potter, who returns his grasp in a manner so warmly vigorous that the young gentleman gasps for breath, and his eyes nearly start from his head, as he says faintly : " Don't ! " For, presuming upon the cattle-king's amiability, Mr. Van Cott is beginning to play upon, and make jokes with him, as the little cur dog in the happy family sometimes does with the sleeping lion's tail, never dreaming that some day the king of beasts may get angry and roar, which will frighten the cur dog nearly to death.

" Young man, Hi likes your haccent. Hit's got the British ring to it. I emigrated from Hengland when a little shaver myself ! "

Which explains to several of them his peculiar use of the letter H. They all but Van Cott treat him very nicely, Lady Annerley insisting on his visiting her during the next few days, when she will be at the *Hôtel des Bains, Boulogne-sur-Mer*.

To this Mr. Potter says, " Whar ! "

" *Boulogne-sur-Mer*, the watering-place."

" Oh ! ah ! yes ! I reckon I understand you, Lady Saharah ! *Boulogne summers* and England winters. Quite right."

"I shall be delighted to see you!" says her ladyship, stifling a giggle as do most of the rest, and Miss Ethel coming to him, takes his arm, and smiling into the old man's face, asks him to tell them some of his adventures on the plains. Which Mr. Potter does with a gusto, vim, and appropriate action, taking for his theme the early days of Texas when he was known by his compatriots as "English Potter," and by the Indians and Mexicans as "the boy with no ha'r on his head." And so they pass a pleasant half hour till Lady Annerley rises to go and says she must catch the Calais boat; for having fired the petard, this great English lady is now desperately bent on running away from the explosion.

"You are going?" says Mr. Potter. "I'll see your ladyship safe to Dover. I've got a leetle matter of private business and one my darter particularly wants me to do in London to-night, so I've got to jump the train myself."

"My maid is with me. I need not trouble you!"

"We never call it trouble to take the gals about—not in Texas!" says Mr. Potter gallantly. "Besides, Ida thinks it important I get a new wig—though I ought to be a judge of the article, having worn one from boyhood up!"

"From boyhood?" yells Van Cott.

"I was scalped by Comanches when fifteen and have been bald-headed ever since!" remarks Mr. Potter proudly. "Like to see my head? It's a curiosity! I'll show it to you hall when I come back!"

With this he leads Arthur to the coffee-room and remarks, confidentially: "Hi'm coming down to see the peer to-morrow!"

"The peer?"

"Yes, your daddy. I've heard good reports of you, sir. You may 'ave 'opes!"

"Thank you, sir!" says Arthur warmly, and gets in reply a grasp of such unaffected vigor that he almost imitates Van Cott and says: "Don't!"

The two come out together on to the hotel steps, where the carriage is waiting, her ladyship seated in it.

Here Mr. Potter takes his daughter in his arms and kisses her with his whole heart, and which she blushingly returns, unmindful of the little crowd gathered about the West Cliff. For somehow Lubbins has spread the report of a distinguished Indian fighter who has been scalped being in the hotel, and quite a concourse of waiters, stable boys, and such like are gazing on Potter open-mouthed, among them Sergeant Brackett of Scotland Yard, his faithful Snapper by his side. Apparently Snapper admires the Texan also, for he runs up to him and licks his hand, bounding vivaciously into the air to do it. Then Potter makes the detective very proud, for he says : "Hello ! Darned if that ain't the cutest little brass-mounted dog I ever scratched ! " and he plays with the terrier while Lady Annerley motions Errol to her from Ethel's side, and says with marked emphasis : "You will remember your promise, Charley ? "

"Certainly, Lady Sarah ! "

And her ladyship looking at Miss Lincoln observes with pleasure that she has put another thorn in her side, for the English girl is thinking : "A promise—then there is something between the man I love and this fascinating woman, something in which I have no part."

Satisfied with her work, my lady next calls to Lubbins : "Remember, you will report to me to-morrow by the afternoon boat ! "

"Yes, your ladyship ! " bows Lubbins.

And Mr. Potter, getting in beside her, gives the whole party a kindly adieu, even calling Van Cott " *sonny*," an appellation which makes the little cad writhe, for one of the stable boys says to another : " Blest if he ain't his father ! " Then the carriage drives off, leaving Ethel, Ida, Errol, and Mr. Van Cott together on the hotel steps · and Sergeant Brackett gazing after the receding Potter with eyes enlarged by admiration and interest, for he has a new border novel in his hand and it is called *The Adventures of Sampson, the Scalper,* and having heard an account of the Texan from Lubbins, he thinks it Mr. Potter's life.

Shortly before they get to the railway, Martin, who is riding in front of them, suddenly gives a yell, and Lady Annerley looking up sees Mr. Potter carefully examining a tremendous Colt's cavalry revolver.

"What do you carry such a fearful weapon for here ? " asks her ladyship with a shudder, for she hasn't seen a firearm since she left Egypt, and this thing reminds her of the carnage and death of that awful time.

" 'Tain't exactly the thing for a ballroom, but it's kind of handy traveling. Thar might be road-agents about! I once had to kill three of them in a sleeping-car out West one night, and at critical moments it's vital to be sure of your pistol!" remarks Potter philosophically, replacing the weapon with extreme care. From this he goes on and tells Lady Annerley episodes of combats and wild life till they get to Dover, which is good for Sarah Annerley, as it keeps her from thinking, a thing that she takes to doing wildly when on the boat bound for Calais, and would repent and telegraph but for her memory of Ethel's happiness. But, tortured by conscience, she acts so strangely that Martin thinks her mistress' case the worst attack of seasickness she ever saw.

As for Mr. Potter, the railway to London that evening being free from road-agents, he gets to Charing-Cross Station, dines at the Langham Hotel, and then goes, late as it is, to see the lawyer whose advertisement he has read in that day's *Times*.

CHAPTER XIII.

THE RETURNED AUSTRALIAN.

POTTER and Lady Annerley having gone, Arthur naturally orders up the carriage which is to take Ida, Ethel, Van Cott, and himself to his father's home; for Errol has decided to remain at the West Cliff, at least until the arrival of his father.

While the carriage is coming round the Australian looks at his sweetheart and sees something in her face he has never noticed there before. He walks up to her, and getting her away from the rest of the party in one of the reception rooms, says : "Ethel, what's the matter? You look troubled."

Now, jealousy is a secretive passion that doesn't like the light of day, and Miss Lincoln promptly prevaricates by returning : "Nothing much! I—I was only thinking that I had better take off my engagement ring and keep it where papa will not see it. He has always had so much confidence in me that it would wound him deeply if he thought I had pledged my hand without his previous sanction !" and as she says this she gives Mr. Errol a twinge by transferring his sparkling diamonds from her finger to her pocket.

"But your brother said he had spoken to your father, and it was all right."

Her lover's tone is so sad that Miss Ethel, sorry for him, returns : "No doubt it will be, if—if you don't fall in love with Lady Annerley in the mean time."

But upon this last her voice, trying to laugh, falters, and becomes almost a cry.

"What do you mean ?"

"Why, you are going to visit her at Boulogne."

"Certainly ; after all that she has done for me I at least owe her politeness. Besides, I've promised !"

"Ah ! that was the promise I heard her mention. Charley, don't go ; it was wrong of her to ask you, knowing that to-morrow should be devoted to your formal engagement to me !" cries Ethel.

"But I owe her so much."

"And she owes you so much more. How close such scenes as you passed through must have brought you in Alexandria. Oh pshaw !—don't listen to me ;—what am I talking about ?" mutters the girl, checking herself and moving away from him.

But he walks after her, and turning her to him tries to look in her face, and says rather sternly : "Ethel, you surely do not fear I will fall in love with Lady Annerley ?"

"She is a young widow, and that's the most awful thing on earth," says the young lady quite sullenly, looking down and punching with her parasol the end of a little foot that is pushed from under her dress, and beating a savage tattoo upon the floor.

"Why, she's old enough——"

"To be mistress of the art of fascination ! She's twenty-five ; Cleopatra's age ! How you stand up for her !" cries Miss Ethel pettishly, forgetting that poor Errol has been rather decrying Lady Sarah's charms and she likening them to Cleopatra's.

Here the young gentleman rather astonishes the young lady, for he says : "My own, I am at last sure that you love me ; for the first time I see you jealous."

The surprises are not all on one side of the affair, how-

ever. For now she astounds him, anger begets truth, and
Miss Ethel's temper for the first time shows itself to
Charley Errol. She tosses company manners to the
winds and cries : " You are right ; I am jealous, and you
are wrong to make me so. Think how she strives to mo-
nopolize you ! Think how she calls you *Charley!* That
is my right only ; you are *my* Charley. What would
you think of Miss Potter if she called you Charley ? "

" You see, Lady Annerley got into the habit when we
were fighting for our lives in Egypt," Errol suggests
rather meekly.

" That's what makes it so terrible," breaks in the girl ;
" that's what frightens me. How she must have got to
love you when you fought like a Paladin of old to save
her life ! When I think how she must adore you I tremble ! "

" Tremble ! What do you mean, Ethel ? If you fear
my constancy you must despise me ! " and with this Errol
turns away from her.

But he does not get far when his sweetheart is round
his neck sobbing : " Despise you ? Oh, my love, don't
quarrel with me ! Go and see Lady Sarah. Of course
I can trust you. I must trust you, or else what is life
worth to me ? "

Charley Errol looks into her blue eyes, in which before
he has only seen laughter—the tears conquer him and he
mutters : " If I were to visit Lady Sarah now, I'd deserve
to be despised——"

" You—you m—m—mean it ? "

" Of course, you have my word," and he kisses her for
his reward. Here she breaks from him and runs to the
door, for her brother's voice is heard calling her from the
hall. At the door she pauses, laughs, and whispers :
" Your father will console you. Good-by, my Charley,
till to-morrow ! " and blowing a kiss to him, runs out
and gets into the carriage alongside of Mr. Van Cott,
who is moodily glum, for he sees Miss Potter occupying the front seat with Arthur, who is going to drive,
and hates him as his happy rival in the cattle-queen's
affections.

As they roll away Errol comes running out, and cries
to them that he'll be almost sure to bring his father
with him to see them this evening. A proposition that

gains him another smile from the lady in the back seat, who looks back and enjoys the sunshine of passion after its thunder-shower.

The road toward Sandgate, along which they drive, gives them a series of magnificent views of the English Channel, now extraordinarily quiet under the autumn breeze, and bright with moving sailing vessels and dashing steamers, while the whole scene is gilded by the setting sun.

The drive is only slightly over the mile, and Miss Potter and Arthur are in happy conversation as they turn to go into the lodge gates, that mark the entrance to the pretty gardens that surround Lord Lincoln's marine villa, most appropriately named " Channel View."

Upon these gates is seated a boy of about twelve, clothed in characteristic knickerbockers, though he wears an Eton cap. He has great, frank eyes, light flaxen hair, and is a washed-out masculine edition of Miss Ethel.

" Why, there's Teddy ! Stop, Arthur ! here's Teddy ! " cries his sister, as her younger brother, the Honorable Teddy Lincoln, comes running to the carriage.

" I've been waiting for you an hour," says the boy.

" Why, Teddy, you never did that before," says Miss Ethel, kissing the boy, who does not even look at her. " What a nice child ! "

As the Honorable Teddy scans the party in the carriage, he gives them all a sensation, for the tears of unutterable disappointment are in his eyes as he says, brokenly but savagely : " Where's Potter the Texan ? I've been waiting to see him an hour. Crabbe, our butler, has been in town and says he's a curiosity ! "

A silence falls upon the party, broken by Arthur trying to turn the thing off as a joke, and saying : " Well, Teddy, here's Mr. Potter's daughter, you know her. Won't she do as well ? "

" Do? How'll she do? *She ain't been scalped, has she ? * " cries out the boy, savagely firing a stone at a passing cur.

During the ride up the avenue Miss Potter says nothing, but there is a low giggling from Mr. Van Cott in the back seat that makes Arthur whip up the horses to drown his noise, though he would much sooner have turned the lash the other way.

Two minutes after this they are all at home, and Ethel,

in the library, sobbing on her father's knee, is whispering her confidences to the great lawyer about "her
Charley," while Arthur is waiting outside the door to
prepare the governor for the coming of the paternal Potter.

Left alone, Errol's eyes follow his betrothed till she is
out of sight, then his glance naturally turns the other
way to look for his father's coming.

He thinks he will go down and meet him, and actually
moves a few steps in that direction until, reflecting that
there are a good many trains from London to Folkestone
and he may have to wait for some time before the elder
Errol arrives, and even then miss him in the crowd, he
concludes it will be best to make things comfortable for
his father's reception and wait for him quietly at the
West Cliff.

Consequently he returns to the hotel, and stepping
past Sergeant Brackett, who had become restless on seeing Errol move, but is now apparently deeply interested
again in the adventures of *Sampson the Scalper*, he goes to
the office, engages two of the best bedrooms in the house,
and registering his father's name and his own, orders
dinner. Then the young man makes himself comfortable with a cigar and something drinkable before the
fire, and goes into a state of somnolent happiness; every
now and then waking up and going to the door of the
hotel whenever he hears the sound of wheels.

His father has been always very dear and close to him
as a boy, and since he has grown into a young man this
feeling has still existed and they have shared confidences
like brothers, as it would be good if more sons dared
do with their fathers and more daughters with their
mothers. Pondering on this, Mr. Charley does not go
to the door at the right time, and as he sits before
the fire, a pair of hands are clasped over his eyes and a
hearty, honest, manly voice says : "Guess who it is, my
lad ! " The next instant Charley Errol has sprung up
with a cry, knocking his chair over, and has his father in
his arms.

"You're all right ? " asks the elder Errol after the first
gush of greeting is over, looking at his son rather
anxiously. " No trouble from your wounds, Charley ? "

" No ; sound as a new sovereign," and Charley does a

little playful athletics.   Then he remarks, looking at his
father rather critically : "And you're not aged by a minute—the same dear old *pater.*   Do you know at one
time I hardly expected to see your face again ! "

"Yes, I know—I—I would have come to you after
that, but I received the news of your wounds by letter,
and before the letter came a cablegram arrived stating
you were out of all danger," replies Ralph Errol very
seriously, and then says, patting his son on the shoulder
quite proudly : "I'm glad to know my son did his duty
in that awful time so nobly.   The Australian papers
made quite a hero of you.   Lady Annerley whom you
saved is, I believe, the daughter of a gentleman who was
at one period of my life very kind to me.   People say
she is very beautiful.   Is she the lady whom——"

Here Charley jumps at the opening he has been longing for, and fishing out a photograph of Miss Ethel's face,
with which that young lady had favored him in Venice,
pokes it under his father's nose.

"Humph !   What is that ? " says the old gentleman,
wiping his glasses.

"That is the picture of the girl I love ! "

"Well, if I'm to look at the picture of the girl you love,
you'd better ring for lights.   This sunset gives her eyes
rather an unpleasant cast."

"Governor, you always did delight to chaff me," cries
the son laughing, but at the same time instructing Lubbins to illuminate.

This being done, he takes the opportunity of scrutiniz-
ing his father as that gentleman criticises Miss Ethel's
picture, and is quite happy to see the old gentleman
looking so well.   For Ralph Errol has the bearing and
culture of an educated gentleman, and is very much a
man of the world, considering his long and continuous
residence at the antipodes.   He is probably ten years
older than Mr. Potter, and is slightly bent by years, being
nearly sixty, and has the same jovial manner that his son
remembers when last he saw him ; though he notices with
concern that his father's eyes have a restless, uneasy look,
as if apprehensive of something or some one indefinite.

He has no time to note anything more before the old
gentleman remarks : " So this is the one you telegraphed
about.   She is rather pretty ! "

"*Rather* pretty?" retorts the son, in great scorn. "*Rather* pretty? Governor, your eyes haven't been failing you lately?"

"No, they're as good as they were twenty years ago!" laughs the father, and then he adds dryly, inspecting the picture again: "She has a nice nose!"

"A *nice nose?*"

"Well, *hasn't* she?" says Ralph with a chuckle.

"She has a nice nose. Nicer than any nose in Australia. By the by, how is Australia?"

"Oh, about the same as usual. Melbourne is a little bigger and a little richer—but I haven't had anything to eat since I left London!"

"I've thought of that," says the young man, and he rings the bell and orders: "Dinner at once!"

As this is being done, the elder is gazing from the window at his native land, and turns to his son, muttering: "So this is home. Does a man ever forget the place of his birth? To-morrow I'll run over to see the house in which I was born. Fourteen hours ago I landed and had England. Now, Charley, I have you and England together!" And there are tears in his eyes as Ralph Errol sits down opposite his boy and looks at him lovingly and proudly. After a moment he says, as if anxious to come to the subject: "Charley, who is the young lady?"

"The future Mrs. Errol?" says the young man, as if the title made him happy.

"I—I hope you haven't spoken to her," returns his father, hesitatingly.

"Oh, yes, I have!"

"But you received my cable?"

"Certainly, but had already asked her!"

"I'm sorry for that!"

"And why?" asks the son, anxiously.

"Because—because I believe in taking such important steps with deliberation." There is a hesitation that is almost embarrassment in the father's manner. "What is her name?"

"Why, I wrote you four pages about her!"

"The letter must have passed me at sea. Your telegram only called her the woman you loved. Who is she?"

 This question is put so nervously that Charley replies :
"You need not doubt the girl of my choice. Her father
is now Lord Lincoln, and has lately been retired from
his position on the bench."

"*Judge* Lincoln?" This with a gasp of astonishment.
Then the father asks in apparent incredulity: "And
he permitted his daughter to accept your suit?"

"Certainly. Why not? I speak to him to-morrow!"

"Oh, you haven't yet seen him?" the old man utters.

"No ; but I have not the slightest doubt he will accept me, especially when he sees you!"

"You must not speak to him to-morrow!"

"And why not?"

"Because I—I came over here to get some business
settled, and until that is done you must not see Judge
Lincoln," returns the father, getting up and leaning his
head over the mantel.

His tone is such that it alarms his son, and he cries :
"Is anything wrong in money matters? Tell me, dear
old governor, and I'm by your side!" And springing
up he puts his arm caressingly over his father's shoulder.

"No, we are richer than ever!"

"Then I cannot understand you. Explain!" says
Charley, turning away with a little anger in his tone.

But the old man mutters doggedly : "Let's have dinner. We'll talk the matter over to-morrow," and apparently would now put off the discussion.

"No! I'm too anxious to have an appetite. Please
explain now!" says Charley, attempting a laugh.

"I cannot explain for a few days—for some little
time!"

"Father, listen to me!" cries the son, coming again
to his side and speaking eagerly and excitedly. "I have
given my word to ask for her to-morrow. Dear old
governor, she'll think me a scoundrel!"

"Still you must not speak!"

"But father, why? If you are in trouble, I am your
son. Tell me ; surely I have the right to demand your reason when you ask me to do what must make the woman
I love doubt my truth to her. Tell me, dear old governor,
your reason!" and he would go on pleadingly.

But here his father turns his face to him and says
hoarsely : "*I will!*" and his face is such a one that the

son trembles as he looks at it. "I have come all the way from Australia to tell you—I—I—" Here the poor old man gasps and his face flushes with shame and is contorted with woe.

But at this moment they are interrupted by the door opening, and looking toward the, noise Charley sees Sergeant Brackett walk into the coffee-room, that has been empty to this moment, and place his dog in a corner, as if to put the little creature out of the way of danger.

As he does this Ralph Errol is muttering to himself : "No! No! My heavens! Tell my own son—I can't do it !" and sinking into a chair, is beating his hands together as if in despair.

Advancing toward the two, the detective with a deprecatory bow says : "Beg pardon, gents. You'll excuse me, sir, but I was directed to do this business polite. One of you is Mr. Ralph Errol, just from Australia. My name is Brackett, sergeant at Scotland Yard !"

"Scotland Yard !" This is a cry, and Ralph, pale as a ghost, springs up and gasps : "You—you come to——"

"Father, you have been robbed on shipboard I suppose," says the son. "I'll attend to the matter." And then, seeing his father staggering, runs to him and says : "You are faint. By George ! I should not have let you fast so long."

But Mr. Brackett continues in a dogged sort of way as if he didn't half like the job : "I have a warrant and instructions from the Home Office to arrest Ralph Errol !"

"Arrest my—my father !" cries Charley ; then he bursts out and laughs : "You are crazy ! He's the foremost man in Melbourne !"

To this Mr. Brackett says nothing, but is producing a document, when Ralph is between the officer and his son begging, pleading, crying : "Don't tell *him !* He is my son ! In mercy, don't tell HIM !"

But Brackett, having a heart, doesn't trust himself to look at him, and says sharply : "As a returned convict !"

"*A returned convict !*" shrieks the son. " My father? Speak ! Tell him he lies !" but not waiting for an answer he hisses : "You insulting scoundrel ! You dare to say this of my dear old governor ! I'll——"

And would do even more than he threaten~ for his

arm is upraised in his father's cause, when that father
staggers to him, and takes the power out of him body and
soul by muttering in a broken voice : " Stay ! The man
only does his duty and—tells you what I have never
dared to tell you, that your father is a ticket-of-leave-
man sentenced to transportation for life, forbidden to
return to his native land for the crime of burglary and
theft ! " and stands trembling and wringing his hands
and bowing his head before his son.

With these words the world seems to change to
Charley Errol, and no more be the bright place he used
to think it ; but looking on his father's face, from which
a pair of bloodshot eyes are imploring one word from
him to help him bear the shame and agony of the moment, something flies into the son's mind and he gives
his father hope and consolation, for he cries hoarsely :
" BUT INNOCENT ! "

" You believe it ! Thank God ! " and Ralph Errol is
sobbing in Charley's arms.

" I *know* it, dear old governor ! Your son, who knows
and loves you, couldn't believe *you* a thief ! "answers the
young man.

" I am a martyr to circumstantial evidence," mutters
the father. " Other men have said this, and lied, but I
say it, and it's the living truth, as I hope to see your
mother in heaven ! " Then looking into his boy's eyes,
Ralph Errol once more stands erect, and Sergeant
Brackett, who has drawn back a little from the interview,
sees rather dimly—for the old man's awful shame has
brought the tears to the detective's eyes—that there is
from now on no shrinking in the father's look, and that
his only fear had been his son would think him guilty.

After a moment the elder Errol continues, with grave
dignity, speaking straight at his boy as if he knew he had
little time to lose, for Sergeant Brackett is looking un-
easily at his watch : " Several times in my life I have
tried to tell you, but it—it was too humiliating to confess
to my son that the laws of my country had made me an
outcast and a felon, and branded me the convict and
the thief."

Here the son, who has become steadied by his father's
manner, returns : " But something, some one must be able
to prove you innocent ! "

"Only one man can, and I came over to find him, but now shall not be permitted," replies Ralph sadly. "But he has never been seen since that night ; he may have been the guilty party himself."

"His name ?"

"Look at the advertisements in the London *Times* since 1850 to to-day, also in those of the New York *Herald* since 1860, and you will often find the name of the office boy of Jaffey & Stevens—Sammy Potts !"

"Sammy Potts ! that's the man you want to find. Sammy Potts, I'll remember that !" mutters the son.

But here Mr. Brackett stops further conversation by saying : "Beg pardon, gents, but the night boat is about to leave for France. You can see my warrant," and shows them a document bearing her majesty's seal, which seems to Charley a great blur save the words : *Ralph Errol— ticket-of-leave man No.* 29,341.

These make him desperate, for they bring the truth to him, and burn it into his brain, that HE IS A CONVICT's SON.

"Your instructions !" gasps Ralph.

"Was to be very polite," returns Brackett, who knows that the person of his warrant is, though a felon, a man of consideration in the colonies, "but to see you left England to-night."

"I am at your service," says the ex-convict ; and supported by Charley he staggers out of the hotel, looking ten years older than when he entered it an hour ago. And so they come down to the pier, where the Channel steamboat is ready, waiting for the London train.

"You are coming with me ?" says the old man to his son.

"No; I stay here to prove your innocence. You were poor when convicted—we are rich now, and I'll buy the truth from somebody !" returns Charley Errol, who becomes firmest in despair ; for his bearing and manner now are the same as they were during that last night in Egypt. Then he goes on to the detective : "You have five minutes yet ! Answer my questions ! Wasn't it curious the Home Office should know so immediately of my father's arrival ?"

Mr. Brackett suggests that information has probably been furnished.

" Ah ! " cries the young man, "by some one who is afraid, father, of your being here ; who dare not let you live in England. *Perhaps the thief himself !* " and getting excited with this idea he cries to Brackett : " You are a detective to prove men guilty ; help me to prove one innocent. Here are your expenses ! Do your duty ; then find and report to me who lodged the information at the Home Office that drives my dear injured father again out of England ! "

" Where shall I report to you ? " asks Brackett eagerly, for he has filled the detective's hands with gold.

" Here at the West Cliff Hotel to-morrow."

" All right ; but we must get on board ! "

And Charley supporting Ralph to the steamer, which is now receiving its crowd from the train, the old man whispers : " Oh, my boy, if I could have seen my birthplace ; but when I pass that gangway I leave my country forever—and you—my disgrace falls on you ! "

Then his son feels a tear-drop on his face that makes him desperate. He returns : " Father, you shall come back to England, no more a ticket-of-leave man, but honored and respected by the world who drove you from it ! *I swear it !*" Next he says hurriedly, for Brackett is pressing them over the gangway : " Who can give me the details of your trial ? "

" It was over thirty years ago. My lawyer is dead."

" Then to what *living* man who is just and knows can I apply ? "

" To the judge who tried and sentenced me ! "

" His name ? " cries out the son, for the crowd has forced him from his father and back upon the pier, but Ralph Errol hesitates and does not answer.

" *His name ?* " shrieks out the son, desperately ; for the gang-plank is taken up, the signal bell is ringing, and the boat is steaming away into the night for France ; then out of the darkness, floating upon the sad splash of the sea, comes his father's voice and strikes him with despair, for it answers : " PERCY LINCOLN ! ! "

And the young man cries : " My God, HER FATHER ! How shall I tell HER ? "

BOOK III.

A WOMAN'S BATTLE.

CHAPTER XIV.

ALL FOR MY DARTER!

MR. POTTER arrives at the solicitor's office, in London, at nearly nine o'clock that night, and naturally finds Mr. Portman hasn't been there for several hours. He then obtains the address of his residence from the directory, and is driven to his house, some miles away in Pimlico. This takes considerably more than an hour, and arriving there at almost 11 P. M., he has some trouble in arousing the housekeeper, who comes to the door in dishabille and a bad temper.

"I want to see H. Clarkson Portman," says Potter.

"It must be important business, waking a body up at this time of night!" remarks the woman, regarding the American with rather suspicious eyes.

"It is—there's a thousand pounds in it." And he shows her the advertisement, which he has cut out of the *Times.*

"Well, you'll not see Mr. Portman till to-morrow night; he was just called by telegram to Boulogne, and left twenty minutes ago."

"All right! I'll leave a letter for Portman!" says Potter, and coming into the house he tells her to give him the "fixins" for a note. This being done after some little grumbling by the woman, he writes a laconic letter of three words to the solicitor, and giving it to the housekeeper goes out upon the door-step and says:

"Tell Portman I'll call on him when I return to London in a few days ! " With that he shouts to the driver, " Langham Hotel like Jerusalem ! " and so drives away, the woman calling after him that her master may not be back till the day after the morrow.

Returned to the Langham, Potter meets his old Texas friend, Colonel Cottontree, and the two have a confidential chat in the American corner of the smoking-room, chiefly discussing the new acquaintances Potter has made during the day, at Folkestone ; Cottontree, who knows nearly everybody in the swim of European society, or American also, for that matter, informing him incidentally that Lady Annerley is the daughter of the great London banker, Sir Jonas Stevens.

Whereupon Potter breaks out into exclamations of surprise and joy, declaring that this same Jonas Stevens once did him the best turn in his life, and that he's going over the next day to Boulogne to thank her ladyship for her father's kindness to a poor English boy.

After that the conversation drifts over to the Lincolns, the colonel telling the Honorable Sampson that though he knows Miss Potter is too good for any one but an angel, still, for all that, she mustn't wait till she goes to heaven to wed one. That Arthur Lincoln is now a rising barrister, and at his father's death will doubtless be a lord.

" That's better than a duke," answers Potter. " Thar was two dukes running arter her, and I was scared she get sweet on one of them. I can stand a lord, but hang me if I don't draw the line at dukes and dudes ; I've read so much about 'em in the Texas newspapers that I'm cursed if I don't hate 'em both. This whisky here, Cottontree, don't seem to be up to the strength of our old Kentucky bourbon ! "

To this the colonel laughingly assents, and the two go to bed, but early the next morning take the train for Folkestone and Dover, Cottontree being bound for Paris, which is for the present his home. At Folkestone, Potter says adieu to the colonel and engaging a chaise, drives over to " Channel View," stopping *en route* at the West Cliff, and going in to get a light for his cigar.

The morning is a beautiful one, and at the lodge gates Potter thinks he'll enjoy a walk up the avenue leading to the villa. He gets out of the conveyance, and telling the driver to come back for him in a couple of hours, valise in hand tramps up to Lord Lincoln's doors.

His progress up the avenue, however, is by no means unnoticed or unattended. The Honorable Teddy has heard that Potter, the scalped, is to arrive that morning, and, together with most of the children of the neighbor-hood, has been awaiting the coming of the curiosity.

Preceded by a white-headed urchin, a semi-idiot, who is nicknamed the "Cow Face," from his resemblance to that animal, they all follow Mr. Potter in a solemn, open-eyed, staring procession.

At first they keep at a respectful distance from this bloodthirsty warrior of the plains, of whom Teddy has told them stories of his terrible ferocity that have made their young blood run cold in their veins. But curiosity getting the better of fear, the nearer they come to the house the closer they approach Mr. Potter.

At first the Honorable Sampson does not notice them, for their steps are cautious, and they would not for the world do anything to anger or enrage him, considering under these circumstances he would not permit them to live a minute. But at last the "Cow Face," noticing the monster is absent-minded, rashly actually imitates, be-hind Mr. Potter's back, the operation of scalping as he imagines it would be performed, which so excites his companions' risibles that they can't help tittering and giggling, though they know this places them in mortal danger.

Mr. Potter, however, thinking of his daughter, goes along very peacefully until, hearing one of these giggles more pronounced than the rest, he suddenly turns round and catches the "Cow Face" in the act.

"Run for your lives!" shrieks the Honorable Teddy, and so they all do except the "Cow Face" who is nearest to Potter, and too frightened to move his limbs.

"What do you want, little boy?" says Mr. Potter, pleasantly.

"I—I—I didn't mean anything—I—please——"

"Well, don't—don't get skeared. What can I do for you?" repeats the Honorable Sampson, seeing the child is very pale and trembling.

"I—I wanted to see your hat off," gasps the boy des-perately, but picking up a little courage, for the ogre has not yet killed him. "Teddy Lincoln said you'd been scalped and was a curiosity."

"Wall, now, I declar," says Mr. Potter, "if this scalping business don't make me celebrated most everywhere!" Then he takes off his hat and his wig too, and shows the astonished rustic a sight that makes the boy have awful dreams for a week, after which he gives him half a crown and tells him to buy some candy. This being watched from places of distant safety by Teddy and the rest, the "Cow Face" is the hero of the juveniles of the neighborhood, and shines with Mr. Potter's reflected light for many a day.

Without further adventure the American reaches the steps leading to the villa, where his beautiful daughter comes down to him with a rush, and gives him several tender kisses despite the presence of two magnificent flunkies who are hurrying after her, and the Honorable Arthur who makes a background. The next instant the flunkies have despoiled Mr. Potter of his valise and overcoat, and Arthur is asking him if he has breakfasted, and being answered affirmatively, suggests that he shall take him into the library and introduce him to Lord Lincoln, Miss Ethel being with some friends in the conservatories.

After a few moments' conversation with his daughter, Mr. Potter says to Arthur : "All right ; I'll tackle the peer now!" Then whispers to Ida : "What are you looking nervous about? I ain't skeered of a lord no more than I am of an Injun," and so is shown into the library.

The nervousness is all on the part of Lord Lincoln, who awaits Mr. Potter's coming with awe. His son has told him of the eccentricities of the American ; in fact, Arthur, with the instinct of a lawyer, has drawn his future father-in-law's picture with the tact of a diplomatist. In his description, Mr. Potter's extraordinary idiom, rude manners, and barbarous gaucheries are all eccentricities peculiar to the Wild West ; eccentricities, nothing more.

Suspecting some such thing, Miss Potter has had an interview with Lord Lincoln herself that morning, and told him in an unaffected but by no means self-assertive manner the fair, square, plain, unvarnished truth about her father ; neither disguising his failings nor extolling his virtues, and ending by saying : "Like many more

in our country of great social surprises, my father has
given up his chance in life for the good of his children.
That I may wear the dresses of a duchess and ride in
my liveried carriage, he has driven cattle on the plains,
and has exposed his life to all the dangers of a semi-
barbarous existence. My happiness has been his happiness and his pride shall be my pride, and though I love
your son very deeply, I'll enter no family who does not respect him as if he were the first gentleman in England ! "

"And so they shall, my dear ! " returns Lord Lincoln,
wiping a tear out of his eye. " For no one could be the
father of such a girl and not be a good man."

"You—you are very kind ! " murmurs Miss Potter,
and his lordship's tears taking all the pride out of her,
she goes up to the old gentleman and gives him a very
sweet kiss that she had intended for her father, and so
leaves the ex-judge with a much better appreciation of
what the Honorable Sampson really is than his son had
given him.

But though prepared in a manner for the Texan's appearance, Lord Lincoln cannot restrain a shiver as he
hears Mr. Potter's voice in the hall and mutters to himself: " Good heavens ! The awful man at the hotel ! "

However he hasn't much time for reflection, for Mr.
Potter enters the room, and in the enthusiasm of the
moment, not waiting for Arthur to introduce him, seizes
his lordship's hand exclaiming : " Peer, how are you ? "

"*Peer ?*" gasps the nobleman astonished, for he has
never been so addressed before.

"Yes, that's what you're called, ain't it ? Peer of the
realm ? I used peer because we'll probably be connected
and I thought it would be more social." Then the
Texan addresses the son and says: " Harthur, I would
'ave knowed Peer was your daddy anywhar."

For Mr. Potter's use of the letter H when excited is
awful ; in quieter moments he is more conservative.   .

"Won't you be seated ? " says Lord Lincoln rather
awkwardly, for his senses have nearly left him under Mr.
Potter's attentions.

"Certainly ! Anything to accommodate ! " and the
American helps himself to an arm-chair and says, offering a Havana : "'Ave a cigar, Peer ? I always like to
smoke over my business. I can recommend these ; my

son sent 'em to me from Cuba. Put some in your pocket,
Harthur, my lad. My darter won't object. I trained
her when a baby on my knee to the hodor of the weed."

Thus urged, his lordship accepts and Arthur takes
Potter's advice and two or three of his cigars, for he has
smoked one of the Texan's the day before, and has been
longing for another like it ever since. After lighting up,
however, the young man watching his opportunity whispers to his father : " Remember, I love his daughter," and
leaves the room.

Looking after him Potter remarks : " A pretty likely
boy ! Won't he and my darter make a team? Eh,
Peer ! "

At this Lord Lincoln smiles for he is very proud of
his son, but with a lawyer's caution replies : " Before
we proceed, you will excuse me asking you a question,
Mr. Potter, as to your family. Any one about here can
tell you all about the Lincolns, but you come from a
distant country and I should like to know a little of your
family history."

" That's natural !" says Potter, " and I'll tell you my
life. I was born in England, of no family to speak of ;
my parents died before I knew 'em. I was educated at
a Blue Coat school, hemigrated to Texas at fifteen, started
across the plains on the gold fever to California. Our
train was *massacreed* by Injuns and I and Ida's mother
was all that was left alive. I saved the gal, but was
scalped doing it. Like to see my head ? It's a curiosity !"

" Not at present ! " gasps Lord Lincoln.

" All right, then I'll go on. The future Mrs. Potter was
of very high breeding ; the blue grass blood of Kentucky
flowed in her veins, her relations had all been killed, and
I was the only one left to protect her. And I did, and
loved her and married her and settled down and built a
log-cabin, and then after a while Houston, that's my boy.
was born, and then came the war, and I was a colonel in
the Confederate service——"

" A colonel ! you never use the title ! " interjects the
Englishman.

" No, I'm one of the few man as fought in the late
unpleasantness as don't have a military orniment to my
name. After I was elected to hoffice, I found Con-

gressmen were scarcer than colonels, and I dropped the colonel and took the honorable. D'ye see, jidge—beg pardon, I mean Peer!" returns Mr. Potter. "Wall, I came back from the front one time desperately wounded, and found my wife was dead, but 'ad left me a little baby as her momentum upon earth!" Here the old man stops speaking and turns his head away as if seeing something in the far-off past, and his eyes are red as he looks again upon the Englishman whose face is also sad, for this has made Lincoln think of his wife who has passed away from him.

After a moment, however, he says : "I beg your pardon. What did you say your wife left you? I hardly caught your last."

"I said she left me her momentum, her image, Ida Potter, and I allowed as I would live my life for the daughter as I would 'ave lived it for the mother. Then I looked around me and I seed ten thousand acres of land and two thousand head of cattle, hall for the little baby, Ida Potter, of Potter's Cross Roads, Comanche County, Texas ; and ten years arter I gazed about me and diskivered two hundred thousand acres of land and twenty thousand head of cattle, all for my darter, Miss Ida Potter, of Potterstown, Comanche County, State of Texas ; and twenty years afterward, jist a month ago to-day, I squinted around me and surveyed five hundred thousand acres of land, and fifty thousand head of cattle and half a bank and half ha hopera-house and half a railroad, all for my darter, the Honorable Miss Hida Potter, of the metropolis of Pottersville, Comanche County, State of Texas!" As he says this, Mr. Potter, who in imagination has gradually grown with his town, stands beaming with excitement and gazing at his hearer. Then he remarks : "How does that strike you?"

"You seem to have done remarkably well," returns Lord Lincoln ; "but who has the other half of the railroad, bank, and opera-house?"

"Them's for my son! Them's for—my—son," repeats Mr. Potter, proudly ; "but bless my heart! I know I'll cheat the boy in the division. I love him, but Houston's a man and can take care of himself, and boys get away from us—but it's the darters, Peer, they get into our old hearts. You've a sweet little gal yourself!"

"Yes, and she'll marry too, and—go away from me. Don't say any more, Potter—you break my heart!" interrupts Lincoln, his eyes getting weak at the thought of his Ethel's blue eyes and sunny hair going to far-away Australia. And then these two old fogies look at each other and fall into each other's arms, and burst into tears, but respect and love each other, and are great friends ever afterward.

"Now, Peer," says Mr. Potter, getting control of himself first, "I want you to meet me on the matter between us, not as a lord to honorable, but as man to man, each a working for the happiness of his child."

"And I will do so. No one could listen to your story and see your great love for your daughter, and not respect you, sir." And rising from his seat Lord Lincoln says : "I am proud to ask from you the honor of your daughter's hand for my son!"

"Granted, Peer, granted!" replies Potter, and then says : "Let's go out and see the young folks!"

This they do, and Ida, who is walking with Arthur, perceiving the two patriarchs of their families coming toward them arm in arm, whispers to her sweetheart : "I knew they'd love each other. See, am I not superstitious? I'm wearing my lucky bracelet," and shows him the band of gold and sovereign bangle that the young man has noticed in Venice. "This generally brings me good fortune."

"Indeed! Is it a charm?" asks Arthur, taking hold of it for an excuse to press the white arm it ornaments.

"I think it one—don't kiss it, Arthur. They're near—they'll see you!"

But Arthur's lips are too close to the lovely wrist, and as he kisses he notices a little cross upon the sovereign and calls her attention to it.

"Why, it's just under the 8 and 4 of the date. I never noticed it before. I'll ask papa about it some day—but now I have to fascinate your father, and you have to captivate mine."

With this she turns to Lord Lincoln and takes his arm, leaving her father and Mr. Arthur to become better acquainted.

A little time after this they go in to lunch, where Miss Ethel joins them, looking distressed and disappointed, for she has been all the morning in a summer house that commands a view of the Folkestone road, looking and longing for the sight of Charley Errol, who comes not ; and Mr. Van Cott and the Honorable Teddy joining them from the billiard-room, the party find themselves complete. In fact, altogether too complete ; for Master Teddy, who has been permitted the pleasures of the adult table in honor of Mr. Potter's visit, contrives to make two remarkable *faux pas* that produce unexpected effects in the far-off future.

First of all, in the jovial unconcern of youth, he incidentally calls little Van Cott a dude.

"Oh, he's a dude, is he ? " says Mr. Potter in an awful tone of voice, glaring so strangely at the unfortunate Van Cott that he squirms in his chair, though every one else bursts into a laugh.   "A dude ! I've never seen one afore, but I've read of them.   Thar was one down our way once, but he got lost somewhar before he got to my place.   He was never found."

This last Mr. Potter utters very solemnly, and though he does not mention the subject again, from this moment he begins to despise, loathe, and hate Mr. Van Cott. For the name having been just coined, every would-be humorist of the day in America had been shooting his bolt at the tribe ; and had made the name of dude a title of contempt and derision, especially in the extreme West, where they never saw the article, and judged of it only from what the newspapers said about it. As for Mr. Potter, he regards dudes in the same category as he does Indians, greasers, and rattlesnakes ; that is, things to be killed on sight.

"Now, I appeal to you all, especially the ladies, is it not perfectly fearful of young Master Teddy to call me a dude ? " cries Van Cott.

"Can't you stand a little truth ? " says Potter, looking at him with scorn.   "You're as tender and as touchy as a newspaper after it's slandered every man in the community except the editor ! "

"You don't seem to like newspapers," suggests Lord Lincoln, wishing to change the subject.

"No, sir ! I ran for Congress once and one of 'em called me an alias," returns Potter snappishly. "Of course I had the editor out."

"Papa ! don't—don't, please, tell us any of your awful duels ! " cries his daughter, remembering with a shuddei the stories of her father's deadly pistol.

"This wasn't so bad," says Potter with a grin. "Lord bless you, he looked so young that I pitied him and only shot him through the arm, though I was most certain it would lose me my election."

"A deed of mercy lose you your election?" echoes Arthur, astonished.

"Yes. You see the boys didn't look at it in that way : they kinder thought I had lost my nerve, and couldn't shoot any more, and so went back on me." And Mr. Potter goes to eating in a savage manner, thinking of the wrongs he has received from the press, as what American politician has not ?

A few moments after this, Mr. Potter is giving a general dissertation on some scientific subject, when the Honorable Teddy, who during the meal has been gazing at him with open-eyed, open-mouthed curiosity, and has for the first time in his life been unable to eat, suddenly petrifies everybody by asking : "Say, when the In dians scalped you did they *take out the brains ?* "

This remark seems so horribly appropriate, for Potter has been in very deep water upon the scientific question, that every one stops eating and there comes a cruel silence, broken only by a snicker from Van Cott. Then Arthur without saying a word ejects the youthful seeker after knowledge.

Meantime catching Van Cott's giggle, and not liking to be laughed at by a dude (as which Mr. Potter now regards him) the frontier warrior turns an awful eye upon this snickering civilized creature and says : "Young man, don't play with me ! "

"N—n—no—I won't ! " gasps Van Cott, his laugh dying away in a peculiar choking gurgle, and the whole party are relieved when the meal is over.

Mr. Potter soon recovers his good humor, and tells them he is going to Boulogne to thank Lady Annerley for past favors.

To which his daughter makes no objection, imagining it is for that lady's chaperonage of her upon the Continent ; though both Arthur and Ethel look serious at the mention of her name, Arthur, because he sees that his sister fears her influence on Errol, and Ethel because her Charley has not yet come to see her father.

As they are all assembled to bid Mr. Potter good-by she ventures to ask him rather tremblingly if he has seen Mr. Errol that day.

"Why yes," he replies ; "saw him at the hotel at Folkestone as I drove over."

Then noticing the anxious glance of the young lady, and remembering his daughter has told him that Ethel is in love with the Australian, Mr. Potter proceeds to figuratively drive a nail in that gentleman's coffin. He takes Lord Lincoln aside and says to him : "Peer, I've heard as how young Errol is a sparking your daughter ; now, being as it were one of the family, I wants to warn you of him."

"Why, what has he done?" asks Lincoln, looking very serious.

"Last night at the 'otel I saw him fresh and hearty; this morning when I came from London he looked gone up, couldn't gaze me in the heye—seemed ashamed like. Now thar's only one thing does that kind of business over night and that's too much whisky !"

"Potter, you must be mistaken !" gasps his lordship.

"Not at all ! We have whisky in Texas, and I know the effects of it." And with a farewell kiss to his daughter, Mr. Potter gets in the carriage that has come for him, and drives off for Folkestone on his way to Boulogne.

CHAPTER XV.

AN ENGLISH JUDGE.

THE library of Channel View is upon the ground floor, and French windows make it easy of access from the terrace, which leads down to the gardens at the back of the house. Soon after Mr. Potter's departure, his daughter wanders into this room, and not finding interest in any of the law-books with which its shelves are crowded, passes from it into another and smaller apartment where novels and lighter literature abound. This apartment is only separated from the other by a curtained arch, and sitting down to read, for Arthur is at present occupied with his father, after a few minutes Miss Potter gets a surprise and then a shock.

Lord Lincoln comes into the library. Actuated by Mr. Potter's remarks, he has just had a little conversation with Arthur, and asked that gentleman some rather pointed questions about young Errol which have set his son to grinding his teeth, as he sees his sister's pale cheeks and suffering eyes ; for he attributes the tardiness of Ethel's lover entirely to Lady Annerley.

This interview is broken up, however, by Miss Ethel herself, who comes running to her father, a pretty blush upon her face, and whispers : " Papa, go into the library, he's coming up the lawn. I saw him with an opera-glass."

" He—who ? " says the peer, not catching her meaning for a moment.

" Why, my—the gentleman I—I spoke to you about! Papa, what makes you ask such horrid, searching questions ? I'm not on the witness-stand ! " laughs the girl, who is now as happy as a bird in summer.

" Oh ! ha—Mr. Errol ! "

" And I wish to say just one word more about my Charley, I love him ! " and with this she playfully shoves Lord Lincoln into the library, and as she does so, her father knows she tells the truth, and prays that Potter may have been mistaken.

" You told me that twenty times last night ! "

" Did I ? " This is in a tone of astonished reflection. " Then," she says, with great decision, " I tell it to you again ! So I hope you'll help him on a bit. You know it must be very embarrassing for a young man to ask the father."

" More so than it is to ask the daughter ? " returns the father, patting her cheek.

" Oh ! very much more so ! " This is said contemplatively. " You see he hasn't the inspiration—that's *me !* " and she looks at her father archly and laughs.

" Then the inspiration had better be present ! "

" Ough ! I couldn't think of that ! But wait till you see my Charley ; no one could resist my Charley. When he says : ' Darling, I love you,' you'll kiss him—I mean I'll kiss him—oh ! what do I mean ? " cries Miss Ethel,

getting red in the face at some of the thoughts in her
head.

"Do you think he'll dare address *me* in that way ? "

"No, not if you look as solemn as that ! But, papa
dear, don't keep him long from me.   Just give him your
blessing and send him out into the garden, and I'll—I'll
do the rest.   See, isn't his engagement ring pretty? "
And, rather trembling at her audacity, Miss Ethel flashes
Errol's diamonds into her father's face.

"And you wear it before my consent is received ? "
says her father with a little tremble in his voice, for this
is the first tangible evidence that his daughter has set
up a newer and a stronger idol in her heart.

"Because I know you'll give it ! " And the girl, seeing she has wounded him, tries to apologize by kisses.
Then, after a moment she cries : "He'll be coming. Remember I'm in the garden," and gets to one of the windows, then turns and throws her father another kiss and
laughs : "No one could resist my Charley !" and flies to
hide her blushes and her love from the man coming up
the avenue.

Here Miss Potter, who has heard but little of this interview, for it has been carried on mostly in an undertone
between father and daughter, would come out.

She is about to do so when somebody staggers into the
library from one of the French windows, and she hears
a voice which she knows but hoarse and changed, and
then Percy Lincoln answering him, and as he does so, his
voice becomes grating and harsh, for he suffers too.
The words they say drive her back.   And as they go on
she, standing there behind the curtains, her eyes filled
with sympathy and horror hears things that make her
start and writhe, and at the close she could cry out and
groan and moan like the other two ; for from one man's
agony comes another's woe, and then from that a woman's fears and tremblings, and almost despair.   For this
is what they say.

It is Errol's voice speaks first :

"You are Percy Lincoln, once judge of the Queen's
Bench ? "

"And who are you ? " cries the peer, for the creature
before him is unshaved, and his clothes, though good, are
those of a man who has not been to bed, his linen dirty

and unchanged, and he has matted hair and blood-shot eyes that have a hangdog look about them and seek the floor.

"I am Charles Errol, son of Ralph Errol, the convict, whom you sentenced thirty years ago as a thief and burglar, but I didn't know it till last night!"

"My heavens, how ill you're looking, my poor boy!" and Lincoln would ring for assistance and refreshment, but the other stops him saying: "No—she'd come in, and I couldn't look at her!"

At this there's a gasp, "My daughter!" though Errol appears to hardly hear it, and goes on: "That's why I sneaked in here. I haven't slept! All last night I was thinking—thinking—thinking that I was a convict's son, that when to-morrow's sun arose I couldn't look you or any other man in the face, for I'm not accustomed to this shame! My father hid it from me. Oh! if he had not!" Here the poor fellow pleads: "I wouldn't have brought sorrow into your family. But now I appeal to you, not as a father, but as a lawyer. You have left the bench! My father says he is innocent. I believe him! Aid me to prove it for my sake, for your daughter's sake."

"Good heavens! Ethel!" mutters the judge, beginning to tremble. Then he says, forcing himself to calmness for her sake: "Do you know the circumstances of your father's conviction?"

"No!"

"What date was it?"

"Somewhere about thirty-two or three years ago!"

And Percy Lincoln, staggering to one of his book-cases, looks over his bound journal of cases tried before him, and finally, in the record of the year 1850, "THE QUEEN VS. RALPH ERROL!" stares him in the face. Then getting to his desk again, he reads this memorandum, and begins to remember something of that curious case. "Burglary and theft," he mutters; then gives a flash of hope to the creature who is hanging on his words, for he says: "I charged in favor of the prisoner!"

"God bless you for that!"

"But the jury thought him guilty! Try and calm yourself so as to listen to me!" And Lord Lincoln, restraining his own agitation, reads Errol these notes upon his

father's case : " ' Ralph Errol, age twenty-five, married,
clerk of Jaffey & Stevens, bankers, Fleet Street, London.
Charged with stealing on January 6, 1850, A. D., one
hundred sovereigns, purposely marked to detect thief.'
My notes are very complete. I have even on this page an
accurate description of the marked coins—look ! ' "

Placing the book before Charley Errol, the judge
reads on : " Each sovereign was of the coinage of 1849,
and was identified by a cross placed between the figures
8 and 4 in the date."

At this, if they were not so interested they would hear
from the room where Ida Potter stands a little cry of surprise ; for she is gazing astounded at the coin upon her
bracelet.

" The prisoner was arrested on board the Australian
packet, and on his person, or disposed of by him and recovered, were seventy of the one hundred marked coins.
The remaining thirty were supposed to have been taken
by his confederate, the office boy, who disappeared the
same day—Sammy Potts ! "

Here the listening woman reels and mutters a cry of
dismay, though it is under her breath.

"Sammy Potts !" says Errol hoarsely ; "that's the boy
my father mentioned."

But the judge reads on : " Jonas Stevens, the manag-
ing clerk of Jaffey & Stevens, testified sovereigns were
marked to detect thief, as firm had lost £5,000 before
by similar thefts, undoubtedly made by some one in their
bank. He appeared friendly to prisoner and said what
he could for him."

"You see, he thought him innocent," interrupts Errol.

"This journal does not say so ! " remarks the lawyer,
who goes on reading : " The inner door of the office had
been forced. The jury found a breaking and entering,
and convicted on second count—burglary. Prisoner
when about to be sentenced made the following remarkable statement : He had intended to emigrate to Australia, but knowing his wife's parents would object to their
daughter leaving England, had secretly taken passage for
Melbourne, collected his savings, one hundred sovereigns, resigned his position at Jaffey & Stevens, placed
his money in a bag in his private desk at bank. Went
home, returned the next morning, found office door open,

took his bag of sovereigns, and went on board the vessel where his wife met him ; before sailing, was arrested and dragged back, to be convicted of stealing his own property or what had been *substituted* for it. Concluding said : ' Find Sammy Potts, the office boy, who slept in the building and has so mysteriously disappeared, and against whom a true bill has been brought as my accomplice—find the other thirty marked sovereigns, and you'll have the clew to what makes me a criminal and drives me a convict from the land of my birth ! ' " then Percy Lincoln closes the book.

" This Jonas Stevens who spoke for my father—yes, and did more than that ; for here is his name attached to a number of the advertisements for Sammy Potts," bursts in Errol, showing the lawyer a lot of the papers he has obtained from London, " where is he ? "

" Dead ! "

" Ah ! death cuts me off everywhere ! "

" He became the great banker, the late Sir Jonas Stevens."

" The father of Lady Annerley ! That is why she was so interested in me ; she might aid—— "

" She can know nothing of importance," returns the judge calmly but sorrowfully. " At this late date your case is almost hopeless."

" It shall not be hopeless ! " cries out the Australian with the ardor of youth. " Name any fee you like, but help me to prove my father is a wronged man ! "

" Any fee ? " mutters Lord Lincoln, and begins to think.

" I am imploring you not only for my sake, but for your daughter's—her happiness —— "

" Her happiness ! " gasps the peer, and then, after a moment, he says slowly : " Young man, I'll take your case ! "

" Heaven bless you ! "

" But you must pay my fee ! "

" How much ? "

" It is not money ! "

" Not money ? "

" I want my daughter's happiness ! " cries the peer hoarsely. " I shall prepare a paper and you must sign it ! " and with that he sits down and writes very rapidly.

" My God ! I know what you're going to do. You're

going to ask me to give her up," cries back the young
man, wringing his hands and sinking into a chair and
gazing at the father of his loved one who' is going to take
her from him forever.

And as he sits there, his back to the window, Miss
Ethel puts her head in and cries : " Papa, you are keeping Charley very long ! "

At her voice the two men shudder and gaze at eacl,
other, but neither dares look at her. Then, though she
does not come in, she breaks her lover's heart, for she
tosses some roses playfully over him and laughs : " I'll
be found in the garden," and goes off singing in merry
contrast to the poor wretch, who snatches up the flowers
and gasps : " Perhaps after to-day this is all I'll have left
of her ! " then covers them with kisses and crushes
them into his bosom.

By this time his lordship has finished writing and
says, " Listen ! " and then very solemnly reads to Errol
something that sounds to him like a death-warrant, for it
is : " I, Charles Errol, do hereby release Miss Ethel Lincoln from any promise she has made me, and consent
never to speak to her again."

" Sign that and keep it ! " cries the peer, "and I'll labor
for your father till the day of my death ! "

" You—you wish to separate me from your daughter's
life ? "

" Entirely ! "

Finding no mercy in the old man's tone, the younger
one breaks out in despair : " Thirty years ago you sentenced my father to banishment ; to-day, for being his son,
you sentence me to worse ! Your daughter loves me ! "

" That's the reason ! " says Lincoln with a groan. " I
will not have her life wrecked by marrying the son of a
criminal ! There's not one chance in a thousand of proving your father's innocence ! "

" Then give the son that chance also ! " shrieks out
Errol. " I have everything on earth to make your child
happy, save family honor ; if I regain that, and lose her,
I have nothing *but* honor. Pity me, pity her, give me
the one'chance in a thousand ! "

This last is said in a way that affects the father very
deeply. He begins to reflect that his daughter loves the
young fellow who is before him, more agitated and more

broken than if he were sentencing him to death. Looking at him, and seeing how he suffers, he imagines his
Ethel gazing at him with the same despair, and after a
moment's consideration he says : " I will give you the
one chance ! " then tears up the paper.

" I !—I ! " Errol's eyes beam with hope.

" For I believe you love my child ! and now your word
of honor as a man, that, till I give you my permission, you
will not speak to her ! "

" God bless you ! it is yours ! " and Charley seizes his
hand.

" On your honor as a man ! " says the father solemnly.

" On my honor as a man ! " returns the Australian,
looking Lord Lincoln straight in the eyes. " But you
will work for my father's good name ? "

" Yes, and for my daughter's happiness ! " and the
lawyer rings the bell and orders his carriage.

" Where are you going ? " asks Errol, who now for the
first time since the night before seems to have regained
thorough command of his senses.

" To London to read up the complete record of your
case ! Where can I communicate with your father ? "

" In Boulogne ; they ordered him out of England last
night ! "

" Last night ! Humph ! curious the Home Office got
the information so suddenly. I must investigate that ! "
says Lincoln, who is now becoming interested in his
case as a lawyer.

Here a servant · enters and says : " A man named
Brackett wishes to see Mr. Errol ! "

" This is Mr. Errol," replies the peer, and then takes
Charley aside and asks : " Who is Brackett ? "

" The detective who took my father out of England. I
hired him to discover if any one informed the Home Office
cf my father's arrival."

" Quite right," returns the lawyer. " If he has discovered anything, let me know at once. My London address
is 'the Carleton ! ' "

" Won't you see him ? " asks Errol.

" No—at least not at present. I don't care about being
known as your counsel in this matter. Even if you
prove your father's innocence, the only way he can
now be set right before the world is her majesty's free

pardon, and as the judge who presided at the trial, my recommendation will have greater weight if I do not act publicly as his lawyer. See this man here, and telegraph me what he says. Then, for God's sake, get away without letting my daughter see you!"

With this he turns to the servant and says: "Show Mr. Brackett in!"

"What shall I do then?" asks Errol hopelessly.

"Devote your time to finding those thirty marked sovereigns, and if alive *Sammy Potts!*" says his lordship hurriedly. "I'm afraid it's your father's only chance!"

Then Lord Lincoln, with a very grave face, goes out to his carriage, passing Sergeant Brackett, who is coming in preceded by his little dog, and who pulls off his hat to the peer and says: "Morning, my lord!"

Arrived at his carriage Lincoln mutters to the footman: "To the London train! tell 'em I'll be down to-night!" and drives away, turning over in his mind how he shall break the news to his daughter, whom he is for the first time in his life not anxious to see.

"Well?" says Charley, hurriedly, as the detective comes in.

"Well!" returns Brackett, lifting little Snapper into a chair.

"How did you leave my father?"

"In Boulogne, at the *Hôtel d'Angleterre*. He was as happy as could be expected. He told me to say so to you."

"Yes, the dear old governor always remembers me," mutters Errol, and thinking of his father's disgrace and humiliation, his son's lip trembles, but after a moment he says: "Go on!"

"Well, I returned to London last night, and this morning—I have rather a pull on one of the clerks in the Home Office—I got a look at the letters."

"The letters?"

"Yes, there was two of 'em, and I then found out who sent the information that your father was expected from Australia."

"His name?"

"Not his, but hers—Lady Annerley!"

"Lady Annerley? She's the dearest friend I have on earth! You are mistaken, sir!" returns Errol, sternly.

"You can't calculate on widows or women, sir," mutters Brackett, respectfully but firmly, "and I'll prove it."

"That she would deliberately injure me in this cruel way—I'll not believe you!" says the Australian very warmly.

"But you shall, sir!" exclaims Brackett, who has dogged blood in his veins. "Knowing its importance I telegraphed in your name to her, and received for you in answer this telegram, and as it was important followed you with it from the hotel at Folkestone."

Then the detective, handing him a telegram addressed to Charles Errol, the young man reads:

"Your message received. Don't fail to come to-day, as I leave Boulogne to-morrow.. SARAH ANNERLEY."

After looking this over once or twice Charley carelessly drops it on Judge Lincoln's desk, and says: "This explains nothing, and by no means proves your story."

"Go to Boulogne, sir—see her, and pump her in person," suggests Brackett, eagerly, and seeing Errol hesitate, he clinches the matter by adding: "I'll swear it. Why, she even sent a letter from Paris the day before yesterday. I got a copy of it before I came down to nab your old man. It's in my pocket-book!" With this the detective shows Errol the following:

"To THE HOME SECRETARY OF THE ENGLISH GOVERNMENT, LONDON:

"The ticket-of-leave man, Ralph Errol, will be in Folkestone to-morrow afternoon."

Then he says: "The post-mark of that letter was Paris, October 14th. Was Lady Annerley in Paris then?"

"Certainly. We had just arrived from Venice!"

"And the post-mark of the first letter sent the Home Secretary was Venice, October 9th. Where was her ladyship on that date?"

"In Venice."

"Do you see? Two places fixes her pretty well. Besides who could have learned your movements? Please go over and pump her, and I'll follow you in a few hours with a *fac-simile* of the letter she wrote from Italy."

Thus adjured Errol answers: "Very well; but until

you do prove it, don't accuse Sarah Annerley of such a crime against me. Brackett, let us go ! "

" All right ! " says the detective, then calling to the dog, "Stop biting that tidy, Snapper," he departs for Folkestone, followed by his pet.

Errol sets his teeth and follows the detective, groaning to himself : "What will Ethel say to my deserting her without a word ? "

He goes out of the library, forgetting in his excitement Lady Annerley's telegram, and not noticing the rustle of a dress behind him. For Miss Potter, who has been panting like an imprisoned dove and waiting for him to go away, staggers out of the little room, and with a very pale though determined face seizes upon the record of THE QUEEN VS. ERROL, and reads it over, comparing the coin upon her bracelet with the description in the judge's journal, muttering : " Identical ! the same ! " Then she cries : " The name in my father's Bible—Sammy Potts ! There's an indictment for him as a felon ! " and claps her hand to her heart as if she were wounded. But after a time she mutters : " My father, a thief ? Absurd ! I'll follow him and ask him how I come to wear a portion of the plunder that made Ralph Errol a convict."

With this she gets out of the room, calls her maid, and leaving a note for Arthur saying business has compelled her to follow her father, walks down the avenue and meets Lord Lincoln's carriage returning. This she stops and orders the coachman to take her to Folkestone, which the man readily does as he knows her very well. So, attended by her maid, Miss Potter gets to the railway station, and finding the boat from Dover to Calais sails the earlier, seats herself in the train to the former place and proceeds to Boulogne.

Errol, after walking gloomily alongside the detective for a quarter of a mile in silence, suddenly pauses and says : " Brackett, go on to Folkestone and get me a ticket. I'll be after you in a few minutes."

" You'll be late for the boat ! "

" I can't help that," returns the young man. " I've left Lady Annerley's telegram behind me. I must get it at any cost ! " And he, unheeding the detective's remonstrances, resolutely turns back toward Lord Lincoln's villa, passing the carriage that is bearing Miss Potter on her way to ,Boulogne. Neither of them sees the other, both being too occupied with their meditations, for Errol has just now thought: "My Heaven! what will Ethel imagine if she sees Lady Annerley's telegram?" This idea sends him into a run.

As for Mr. Brackett, he trudges on toward Folkestone, muttering : "I'm afraid Lady Sarah ain't going to help him much to his father's innocence. I rather think it's jealousy or some other cat-like female notion for the son made her ladyship peach on his old man !"

Now all this is very wise for Brackett, but he is shining in reflected light. The elder Errol had given him more money in Boulogne, and Sergeant Brackett had with it hired the brightest mind upon the London detective force, and so far has been acting under his advice. Later on, when unexpected and trying circumstances arise, Mr. Brackett is by no means so shrewd, and gets into very hot water. The sergeant has been sent down by the Home Office to do a nasty, cruel piece of business for them in as kind a way as possible, for Brackett is a man with a tender heart despite his official duties, though he is generally and justly regarded at Scotland Yard as the fool of the force. However, he whistles to his dog, and getting to Folkestone buys Mr. Errol a ticket to Boulogne, being quite capable of such duties.

Returned to Lord Lincoln's house, Errol enters the library cautiously to obtain the telegram.

While searching for this, which is not a rapid job, as Miss Potter has in her hurry and excitement made a litter of the papers on Lord Lincoln's table, he is horrified to hear the Honorable Teddy crying outside: "Come, Ethel ! Quick ! Your young man has been looking for you all over the garden and can't find you ! He's in the library now !"

Knowing the terrible embarrassment of meeting her, he leaves the telegram unfound and starts for the window, but as he does so Arthur comes in through the door leading from the house and says to him : "Ah, Charley, my boy ! How did the governor meet you ? All right, ch ?" To which Errol returns : "Yes—but I must go now— but before I go—" and would explain to the young man, but Ethel enters and running to him cries : "Why didn't you come to me in the garden ?"

" You were going without seeing my sister ? " remarks
Arthur rather curiously. For he is in by no means a good
humor, having just got his *fiancée's* note, and having heard
his future father-in-law made fun of by Van Cott by insinuations that he cannot resent, for they were something
in this form : " By Jove ! isn't Miss Potter a noble girl ?
She really loves and is proud of her father. Isn't it beautiful to see ? " etc., etc.

Miss Ethel does not pay any attention to this ; she is
questioning with both eyes and mouth : " What did papa
say ? "

" He's gone to London," stammers Errol.

" Charley, what is the matter ? " cries the girl. " Why
don't you answer ? Oh, papa can't have refused ! "

Here Errol astounds both brother and sister by saying
doggedly : " I—I haven't asked him."

" Not asked him ? " At this Ethel's lips begin to quiver
and tears to gather in her eyes, that become reproachful.

" Then what the devil did you come here for ? " asks
Arthur very savagely, for he has now got something to
vent his anger upon ; and hasn't been very much pleased
with Errol's conduct in regard to Lady Annerley the day
before.

" I—I can tell you nothing ! " mutters the Australian,
whose soul cries " No ! " to the thought of telling the
woman he loves that he is the son of a convict.

" I insist on knowing ! " returns Arthur. " Your presence here, if you did not speak, is an insult to my sister."

But Ethel cries : " No, no, Arthur ! Charley loves and
could not insult me ! "

And her lover groans : "*I* insult *you?*" for the girl
has kept on begging him, as he loves her, to tell her why
he has not spoken.

On this Errol steadies himself and says to her, holding
her eyes with his : " I entreat you to believe me without
speaking. Ethel, will you trust me if I am silent till I
return ? "

Looking in his face the girl believes, and murmurs :
" I love you and I'll trust you ! "

But here Arthur comes between them and says : " As
this young lady's brother I ask an explanation *now !* You
are going—where ? "

" To Boulogne ! " replies Errol hoarsely.

These words horrify his sweetheart and she cries out : "To Boulogne ? After your promise ? Why, you gave me your word you would not go and see Lady Sarah ! "

Now this makes her brother white with rage, and he says sneeringly : "And you demeaned yourself, Ethel, to ask a promise that would not have been necessary *if he loved you ?* "

To this insinuation Errol does not reply ; but taking Arthur aside whispers to him : " If you insist on knowing, that book on your father's desk will tell you why I cannot speak to your sister ; but for God's sake don't tell her ! " then turns to go.

After a second's search, finding no book, for Miss Potter has dropped it on the floor, Arthur picks up the telegraphic message, and glancing over it, cries : " There's no book !—but this telegram from Lady Annerley, which says that you are a scoundrel ! "

" A scoundrel ? " echoes Errol, coming toward him ; but Ethel shrieks : " No ! no ! " and gets between them, while her brother addresses her in these words : " My sister, this man gained your love ! Was to-day to ask your father for your hand. Yet to-day crosses the Channel in pursuit of Lady Annerley and her money ! This telegram proves it ! "

Here Ethel gasps out, " Charley ! " looking unutterable reproach.

This look maddens both the brother and the lover, and passion takes the place of judgment.

" Ethel, don't believe him," mutters Errol, and then shouts out : " Arthur, you'll repent this ! "

" Then speak ! " cries the brother.

" Tell her I am——*I cannot !* "

" Then neither will I repent THIS ! " and with his glove he slaps the Australian's face. Then sneers : " Are you a coward ? "

For the mental shock of this terrible insult before the woman he loves has staggered Errol, though he is now growing larger and his eyes are beginning to have the look they had when he was condemning the Armenian and the Greek to death in Egypt.

" No ! " he cries hoarsely, and springing toward Arthur there might have been murder done in Judge Lincoln's house that day. But almost blinded by rage, Errol can

still see the face of his lost love as she sinks between him and his foe crying piteously : " Arthur, my
brother ! Charley, my lover ! " and holds her little hands
between these two men that have now become wild
beasts. Chastened by the suffering of the last day Errol
looks at Arthur and makes him ashamed.

For he gasps : " YOU ARE HER BROTHER ! " Then
staggers out of the room and leaves the house.

CHAPTER XVI.

A WESTERN CYCLONE STRIKES MR. VAN COTT.

VAN COTT has suddenly disappeared. An hour or so
after this Arthur leaves also, for it is not pleasant to be
alone in the house with a sister who, instead of looking
admiringly and lovingly upon her protector and avenger,
shudders and says : " You struck him in my presence,
and he did not return the blow because I am your sister
and he loved me. Ah ! that was true nobility and noble
manhood ! "

At these times her eyes are so reproachful that Arthur
is glad to get away from them, and thinking of his absent sweetheart, without saying a word to Ethel bolts for
Boulogne, in pursuit of Miss Potter, in a very savage and
uncomfortable humor.

To do this he goes *via* Dover and Calais, and Miss
Ethel discovering it some time afterward, becomes impressed and terrified by the secresy of her brother's
movements. She thinks he has gone after her derelict
Charley to bring him to another account at Lady Annerley's in Boulogne. Desperately fearing that these
two men she loves will do each other mortal injury when
unrestrained by her presence, poor Ethel, pale with terror
and chaperoned by the old family housekeeper that she
presses into her service, flies to Folkestone and then
takes a tidal steamer for Boulogne, where Lady Annerley
awaits all comers, to do battle for Charley Errol's hand.

So it comes to pass that, an hour and three-quarters
after this, landing on the quay at that town, Miss Ethel,
with a trembling voice, accosts the Honorable Sampson
Potter. He has strolled down to watch the steamer come

in, having failed to find her ladyship at home, as, expecting Mr. Errol's arrival, she has denied herself to everybody else.

"What's the matter, little one ?" asks Potter, who sees
in the girl's pale face signs of the trouble and misery in
her heart.

"Have you seen anything of my Cha—, I mean Mr.
Errol ? I am afraid they'll meet, and oh ! I must stop
it." Here Miss Lincoln can say no more, for tears choke
her.

But being petted and soothed and comforted by the
old Texan, who, like most good men, has an immense
capacity for protecting beauty in distress, Miss Ethel
swallows her tears and gasps: "Dear Mr. Potter, can I
rely on your aid ?"

To which the old gentleman replies very solemnly :
"As if you was my own darter ! "

Thus assured, dear little Ethel tells her pathetic story,
emphasizing its passion by vivid blushes and its sadness
by tender tears. At the close, as she tells him that the
two young men had a fearful quarrel, and her brother
struck the man she loves, Mr. Potter horrifies her, for he
says anxiously : "Great gosh ! a blow passed—how long
ago ?"

"Three hours ! "

"Then it can't be possible that both can be *alive !*"

"Ah ! you *know*—*!*" This is a scream of agony
from Ethel, who fears her Arthur and her Charley have
already met in this French city, where the duello is not
yet a thing of the past, and that Mr. Potter has seen it.

"No, I know nothin' definite !" says Potter, who has
a very serious face. "But a blow couldn't pass three
hours without somebody dying—not in Texas ! "

"But not here ! " replies Ethel. "Men do not kill
each other for mere blows here ! "

"Then what the deuce do they kill each other for ?"
asks the Texan, amazed.

She does not answer this, but goes on very earnestly :
"You must save them from themselves—your daughter
loves one ! "

Here Mr. Potter starts and mutters : "Good heavens !
my Ida ! I must find Arthur before an accident—*if he's
alive.*"

"You don't think him *dead?*" cries Ethel, for the terrible manner of the old man frightens her.

He turns away his face and doesn't answer her, for his thirty odd years in Texas make him think it very probable that Arthur is dead. As he says: "When one young man strikes another it's a tarnation serious business. If possible we must find 'em."

"They—they came to Boulogne!"

"Then they've come here to— We must find 'em and stop 'em afore——"

"Before what?" cries Ethel.

"Afore they slaughter each other!" And before Ethel knows what she is doing he has her in a carriage and is driving at racing gait up the quay for the town, not noticing the piteous calls of her chaperon, whom Potter has left astounded and terrified upon the pier. This individual now follows them in full cry; for she is an English woman who has never been out of England, and such women usually regard the French as barbarians and cutthroats. The ride is a short one. They dash up the *Quai Bonaparte,* and crossing the bridge called *Du Barrage,* make for the *Hôtel des Bains,* where Mr. Potter shrewdly imagines at least one of the young men will be found.

Miss Ethel finds time, short as it is during the ride, to whisper to the old man who sits at her side that if they fight, her Charley will surely kill her brother, for the girl has heard such stories from Lady Annerley of Errol's prowess in Egypt that she thinks her hero invincible.

To this Mr. Potter replies, trying to soothe her—the girl being in a fearful state of nervous agitation—that he's sized up Arthur, and that he looks pretty quick on the trigger.

"Oh, yes," she sobs, "but no one would resist my Charley. . But he knows I love my brother. I'll sacrifice my pride and beg him to spare Arthur, for if they fought I should be lost to him forever!"

"That's a prime idea—if he loves you!" returns Potter.

"*If* he loves me?" and there is so much trust and belief in the girl's eye that the Texan makes no more suggestions of that kind, though, as he turns the affair over in his mind, he becomes gradually convinced that Errol is a scoundrel and has been captivated by Lady Annerley's magnificent beauty ; that lady's charms having made a great impression upon Mr. Potter `the day before. Carried away with his subject he unconsciously remarks to himself : "Oh, these widders, these young and plump widders, they're powerful players in the game of match-in' !"

Which gives Miss Ethel another spasm of blushes and agony and shame, for unfortunately she hears him, and guesses what he means.

Arrived at the *Hôtel des Bains*, to their astonishment they find neither Arthur nor Charley ; but after looking about the office, halls, public parlor, and every place where young men would probably be, Mr. Potter encounters, to his joy, Lubbins, the ex-head-waiter of the hotel at Folkestone.

That worthy has just reported for duty to Lady Annerley upstairs, and been deftly pumped by her of all he knew of what occurred to Charley Errol and his father after she had left England the evening before. From him she has learnt enough to know that the catastrophe she has prepared has taken place and caused the man she loved misery and despair.

Meager as Lubbins' information is, it has left Lady Annerley in a fearful state, and she is now in her parlor, at one moment crying to herself in triumph : "The man I love is separated from the woman who came between us !" and the next cursing herself for the misery she has brought upon her idol, or, as the mood takes her, muttering : "I will make amends ! Charley, when you know how dearly I love you, you will forgive me—even *this !* "

Notwithstanding this, Lady Annerley has no thought of repentance and confession, though she has some terror. She has been reading the advertisement in the *Times* for Sammy Potts, the office boy of Jaffey & Stevens, but upon consideration she concludes there is no fear of his being found after thirty years' disappearance and silence.

After a moment's examination, to be quite sure of his man, Potter cries out heartily : " Hello, Lubbins ! what's made you a Frenchman ?."

To which Lubbins replies, with an obeisance, that he now has the honor to be in Lady Annerley's service ; but that her ladyship is not at home at present, for Lubbins remembers that she only wishes to see Mr. Errol, and is very prompt in his lies, telling some of them before he is asked.

" All right," says Potter; "now I want you to make yourself real smart and useful," and giving him a donation he takes him to Miss Lincoln and tells him to see that she has a nice little dinner. To which poor Ethel, whom misery has deprived of appetite, says appealingly : " Please, nothing for me, I couldn't eat now ! "

But Potter remarks to her, affecting sternness : " No man nor woman can do honest work in this world unless their stomach and vittals is comfortable. Lubbins, see that she dines—get waiters ! I don't speak this French lingo, and find myself sometimes out a leetle in addressing the natives."

Then he takes Miss Ethel aside and says : " You stay here to head off either of 'em that may come to see Lady Saharah, and I'll go out and track 'em, and, if in this neighborhood, I'll find 'em. Don't get anxious or be skeered of her ladyship, and you'll come out right side up ! " So Mr. Potter starts on his travels, first however telling Lubbins to get any mortal thing the young lady wants and chalk up the damage to him.

Taking a bearing by the sun, after the method common to cattle-men, Mr. Potter lays his course up the quay and toward the bridge leading to the railway station, as he imagines, by some chance, neither of the young men has as yet arrived.

This is true as regards Arthur, who has taken a longer route, and the train from Calais has just deposited him in Boulogne. Coming out of the station he meets, to his astonishment, their old housekeeper from Channel View, that Miss Ethel has taken as her chaperon. She has followed Mr. Potter's carriage to this point, and is now making up her mind in what direction to continue her movements. The woman is decidedly uneasy in the jabbering foreign crowd, and hails Mr. Arthur's unexpected appearance with exuberant joy. She hurriedly tells her young master of Miss. Ethel's sudden journey to this place, at which Arthur's face assumes almost a sneer, though it is a very angry one ; for he imagines his sister has thrown away her pride and come in pursuit of

her recreant swain, to plead with him to give her back
the affection which Lady Annerley has stolen.

"Come with me, I know where to find her!" he cries
hoarsely, and followed by the woman, is soon over the
Pont du Barrage, and before he is aware almost into
Mr. Potter's arms. This gentleman cries out: "Hello,
sonny!" and pounces upon Arthur with such effusion
that the young man gasps under his treatment: "One
would think I had risen from the dead."

"And so you have. I'd given you up for gone. Many's
the fine young face I've seen go under the prahairie
sod to the pop of a six-shooter out in Texas. Ah, this
duhello! the duhello is a nasty business!"

"What makes you think I'm going to fight a duel?"
asks Arthur.

"Now it's no good putting on hinnocence," returns
Potter. "Your sister told me hall," and he gives the
young man a synopsis of what Miss Ethel has said to
him, and telling the housekeeper, who has been staring
at him, where she will find her mistress, drags Arthur
into a neighboring *café* and wine shop.

Here he says sternly: "Now, my boy, if you want my
darter I ain't agoing to have you risk making her a
widder in feelings before she gets a husband in reality.
Arthur, you mustn't fight him!"

"I've been thinking of that matter, Mr. Potter, and
have determined to see Mr. Errol again and ask an explanation, and if wrong—" here the young man hesitates,
but Potter puts the distasteful word into his mouth. He
says: "Hapologize! Hapologize! That's right, my son.
But, Arthur, it seems a needless question to ask, but here
people are so curious. Are you harmed?"

"Armed?"

"Yes, harmed, well harmed! 'Ave you a self-cocker?
A man is only half a man without a self-cocker, nowadays. If you're quick on the trigger, it gives you the
drop!"

"I never carried a pistol in my life!"

"And you struck him and wasn't harmed? Great
gosh, how rash!" Mr. Potter rolls his eyes in awful astonishment.

"Would you have had me stand by and see the anguish in my sister's eyes, and let the scoundrel who had

won her heart pass away to pursue this widow, unpun-
ished?" cries Arthur, working himself up into a rage
again at the remembrance of Ethel's wrongs.

"And he did that? Why he wouldn't be let live—
not in Texas!" Here Mr. Potter becomes excited also
and cries enthusiastically: "Arthur, if you hadn't hit
him, you shouldn't have my darter!" Then he thinks
of what Ethel has said, and mutters: "Still, you may
have been hasty. Your sister believes he loves her!"

"Then why did he refuse to speak? No, I know I am
right!"

"Then don't apologize! Harm yourself. For my
darter's sake, harm yourself at once!" and Potter's voice
becomes pathetic as he whispers: "Don't let him see
you before you're harmed; go and get a gun at once!
Promise me, as you love my darter, to go and get a gun
at once!"

Thinking to pacify the old man, who is now so anxious
for his safety, Arthur gives the promise and turns to go;
but Potter runs after him, and mutters: "He may be
laying for you. I once knew a chap as was perforated
while he was buying his pistol. Take mine!" And forces
into Arthur's hand the terrible weapon that he habitually
carries.

"I don't expect such immediate danger. This is Europe," mutters the Englishman, who thinks from the size
of the revolver it will be nearly as inconvenient to carry
as a cannon.

"You shall take it!" commands Potter. "Take a
fine sight and it's certain death. And if you see him
coming for you with a double-barreled shotgun, don't
let him get nearer than seventy-five yards; take a rest,
and this is good for a hundred. Take that pistol. Do
you suppose I could look my Ida in the face if I'd let
you go out to be potted without a gun?"

"Your daughter—have you not seen her? She's here!"

"In Boulogne? Did she come over to stop the fight,
too?"

"No. She came before the quarrel. She wrote me
it was for your sake!"

"Ah! she can't keep away from her daddy now she's
got him again!" cries Potter, delighted. "She's probably at my hotel. I told her I'd stop at the Pavilion. It's a

good way out of town, and city noises bother me at nights. Take that pistol, or I sha'n't be easy about you, and go up and see that Errol, and if he don't come to terms, let daylight through him !"

Thus adjured Arthur goes out toward the *Hôtel des Bains*, leaving Potter, for the first time in thirty years, without a "gun " in his pocket.

A moment after this the Texan remembers himself and mutters : " Here I have been exciting Arthur to homicide when I should have been doing a parson's work and pouring ile on the troubled waters. Potter, you ain't to be trusted. This 'ere cowboy spirit will rise up in you and must be put down. You make those boys shake hands !"

Actuated by this motive he runs out into the street, but to his disgust is pounced upon by little Van Cott, who prances up to him in quite an unusual state of excitement, calling : " I've been looking for you, my dear Mr. Pottah !" Then having got alongside of him, languidly holds out a feeble hand, and lisps : " Ta-ta !"

After a moment's pause of astonishment, Mr. Potter mutters to himself, savagely : " Oh, it's the dude !" and then says aloud gruffly : " Oh ! it's you, is it ?"

" Yas. I've been looking for you everywhere. Your daughter told me to see you. Ta-ta, my boy, ta-ta !" goes on little Van Cott, quite excited and very happy.

" My daughter sent you to see me ?"

" Yas. She desired me to awh—interview you—to awh —demand her hand in marriage."

" In marriage ?" glares Potter, his eyes rolling in savage astonishment. " Ye ain't lying to me, ye little imp ! "

" No—it's true. 'Pon honor, it's true !"

And so curiously enough it is. For poor little Van Cott, having learned that Miss Potter had left Channel View hurriedly, has imagined that it must be on account of some break with Arthur. Thinking that probably he may now stand a chance of success with the American heiress, he has followed her rapidly to Dover. Being fortunate in catching an express train, he has overtaken Ida at that place and journeyed to Boulogne *via* Calais in her company ; though she has protested at his coming, but in rather a half-hearted way, because her mind has been so occupied and troubled by the curious discovery she has made in Lord Lincoln's library in regard to her father.

The little chap is bent on pleasing her, and finally, for his antics are quite as amusing as a monkey's, the girl gives him a melancholy smile or two, which so encourages him that on the train between Calais and Boulogne Van Cott actually asks her to marry him, calling her his " deah gal ! " " his floweret of the West," and other endearing terms that put Miss Potter in a fearful rage.

She becomes so malicious that a diabolically cruel idea strikes her. She gives Van Cott a grin that is almost a scowl, and says to him : " Sir, the man who wishes my hand must first apply to my father ! "

" Oh, rapture, my own love ! " cries Van Cott in delight, and would, filled with ardor and joy, embellish his suit with some little practical caresses, but there is something in Miss Potter's eye that stops him. So postponing his Romeo attitude for the present, Mr. Van Cott, on arriving at Boulogne, cries : " I'll see papa, deah—won't keep you waiting long, pet ! " and starts in pursuit of the paternal Potter, while the young lady looks after his retreating figure, and grimly wonders how much there will be left of the creature after Sampson has finished with him.

On Mr. Van Cott's declaration Potter stares at him a second in unbelief, and then says hoarsely : " 'Ello, here's more bad luck." The next instant the little chap thinks a locomotive has seized him, for Potter grabs him by the collar, and runs him through the wine-shop and into a little private room at the rear of it where there is a small table and chair or two, and sinking into one of these gasps out at him : " 'Tain't possible ! "

" Yas, perfectly possible. She has at last brought me to book ! But I wish you'd be more careful of my cuffs, they're quite crumpled," returns Van Cott, who imagines that Potter's " 'Tain't possible ! " means that he cannot believe in such good news.

" Never mind your gewgaws," says the Texan. " It's quiet and retired here. Tell me all about it—and if it ain't the truth——"

Here Mr. Potter's jaws snap ominously, for he can't believe that his daughter would have sent any one to him on such an errand, she being engaged to Arthur

Lincoln ; least of all this little creature, whom he now regards as an abomination.

"Oh, yas ! it's all settled.   She brought me over as her escort to Boulogne."

"You don't say !" interjects Potter grimly, and then mutters, looking at the mass of good clothes and fine linen standing before him : "She must have been hard up for a young man !"

"Now," goes on Van Cott, who doesn't seem to see that the paternal Potter is in a very savage and un-Christian condition of mind, "I presume you'll make the settlements all right.   You know I'm brother-in-law to Lord Sandsdown, and we *old* families always expect *new* ones to do the liberal !"

"And my darter consented to marry you ?" grunts the old man, who still will not believe.

"Well, not exactly yet ; but she told me to come to you and you'd fix the matter with me."

"And so I will !" And a grim smile illuminates the scarred and battle-seared features of the frontier warrior.

· "But from her manner, Ida——"

"*The Honorable Miss Potter, sir !*" This correction is emphasized by such a tremendous thump on the little table that an empty bottle and some glasses upon it dance a jig, and several waiters come to the door expecting an order, but the appearance of Mr. Potter is such that they all go away again without saying a word.

"Of course, the Honorable Miss Potter," says Sidney, rather nervously now,. "would be pleased to marry into a family like mine !"

· "She would, would she ?   Are you American or are you English, Mr. B. Sidney Van Cott ?"

"By birth, unfortunately, I am partially American ; but by association and marriage English, decidedly English ; my sister married a lord.   But my exact nationality would require consideration—I will meditate upon it !"

"Then I'll tell you without meditation," cries Potter. "You is a nobody from nowhar.   That's what you is !"

"Sir, please be calm !" murmurs Van Cott, edging toward the door.

"You is ashamed to be Hamerican and you hain't Henglish! ' yells Potter, beside himself with rage.   "And you 'ad the impertinence to think the Honorable Miss Ida Potter of Comanche County, Texas, would marry a mixture of nothings like you ! "

" Sir, this insult——"

" That's right, now you're talking up to me. Now we'll get to business soon ! " says Potter, the light of battle coming into his eye.   " Yes, it is an insult for you to put your no-nation eyes on a praharie flower like the Honorable Miss Ida Potter."

" Is it ? " cries Van Cott, who has got very angry and like most men has some kind of courage in his blood when roused.   " You're a nice man to talk to me !" and he flashes out and gives Mr. Potter his opinion of him, telling him how vulgar he is and that he can't speak the English language, and has come over here to humiliate his daughter.

At this, Potter cries out, very hoarsely and trembl- ingly : " My God ! you—you don't think she's ashamed of me—her daddy." And wipes his eyes that have got red at the thought, but goes on very humbly that he knows the difference between himself and his darling Ida, and that if he thought his presence had hurt her feelings or humiliated her among the grand folks she was running with, he'd go back to Texas, where people honored him. Then bursts out : " Don't I know she's as far above me as the sun's above the earth ? Don't I groan at not being up to her level all the time ? " and tears coming into the old man's eyes, he blubbers like a baby, for Mr. Van Cott has found the only flaw in Potter's armor.

" Yes, and you refused me, when I would pick her up out of the gutter and make your daughter a lady ! " says Van Cott very. pompously, who now thinks he has found the whip-hand of Potter, and begins to be very high and mighty with him.

" *Pick my daughter out of the gutter ?* MAKE MISS POTTER A LADY ! " This is a scream like that of a cata- mount from her father, and with it comes a new and awful light into the Texan's eyes at the slur upon his god- dess.   He doesn't speak loud any more, but says very quietly : " Young man, don't speak of my darter, if you love your life ! You'd better go away ! "

This look makes Van Cott nervous.

" I'll—I'll send a friend to—to you—to explain ! "

mutters Sidney, who thinks he had better be going and gets nearer the door.·

" A friend ! that's right ! that's spunky ! " echoes Potter. " That's well said ! "

Thus encouraged, Van Cott thinks, perhaps, the old man is simply testing his courage, and says, returning a step and trying to look threatening : " I would chastise you, sir, but——"

" CHASTISE ME ! "

" I'd fight you, but the duello is nowadays obsolete——"

" NOT IN TEXAS ! " says Potter, and looking at Mr. Van Cott to be sure he doesn't get the drop on him, he reaches back and for the first time in thirty years finds that he hasn't got a " gun." Then, being a man of lightning thought, cries : " Ah, would you ! " and the next instant poor little Van Cott thinks himself in the grasp of a hurricane, and gives a shriek of horror, for he finds himself flying through the air out of the window, which is open, the day being mild, into the back-yard of the place, where he lands upon a manure heap, to the salvation · of his bones and ruin of his garments. Potter grimly looks at him as he struggles among the hens and fowls, who make quite a row at his intrusion, and mutters : " The little varmint ! He was going to wing me with a derringer through his pants ! " For Van Cott had unfortunately at the .critical moment put his hand into his pocket, reaching for a handkerchief with which to wipe his eyes, which were watery with impotent rage and passion.

After a second's consideration Potter mutters : " That nothing has made me so fightin' mad. I feel just as if I was back in Texas. ' Pick my daughter out of the gutter ! Make Miss Potter a lady ! ' I'll fix myself at once ! " Then making for the first gun store he sees, he selects with great care a murderous-looking, old-style Colt's revolver, fired by old-fashioned percussion caps.

The Frenchman who waits on him speaks a little English, as do most tradesmen in Boulogne, the town having so many Anglo-Saxon inhabitants and so much British trade. To this man Mr. Potter explains that he never uses cartridges, as he don't trust his life to the carelessness of New England factory gals, and he likes to know what's in his gun when he pulls the trigger. Then, loading the weapon carefully, he goes into a little shooting

gallery attached to the shop and proceeds to test it ; and
finally getting the pistol sighted to his liking makes such
wonderful practice upon the projecting pipes, hanging
balls and jingling bells with which the place is adorned,
that the proprietor rushes excitedly into the street, and
telling his neighbors of the wonderful shot that is in his
gallery, the place is soon filled with a little crowd of admiring spectators.

ı Among them chances Sergeant Brackett, who has just
come over to Boulogne, followed by his faithful Snapper.
This pistol practice of Mr. Potter impresses the detective
greatly, for he has been amusing himself with a copy of
Solomon Sure-eye, the Dead Shot of the West, and the
Texan's feats with the pistol remind him of the redoubtable Sure-eye's tremendous efforts with firearms at op-
posing gamblers, cowboys, and red-skins.   Little Snapper
also enjoys it, for he barks so furiously and wags his tail
so joyously at every report, that Potter's attention is at-
tracted to the tiny but vivacious creature.   He asks the
dog's name, and on being told pats him on the head and
yells : " Hi, Snapper ! Rats ! " and laughing at the animal's desperate search for the same, gets into a conversation with Brackett about his little pet.

Brackett, proud of his noticing the animal, tells
him several anecdotes of Snapper's acuteness and faithfulness, how he has scented him out in all kinds of
places.   That once on a job, when he was shadowing
a man suspected of cracking a till in Birmingham, the
cunning cove inveigled him into a vacant house and
locked him in, and would have got away ; but Snapper was
on the outside, and set up such a yelling and scratching
that the neighborhood was aroused and let him out just
in time to nab his man boarding a train for Liverpool.
" But I must be going, sir—business—sarvant, Mr. Potter," and Brackett, who fears he has lingered too long,
starts off in search of Mr. Errol.

Looking after him, the Texan mutters : " From his
talk that fellow's a detective.   Yes, and a cursed poor
one, too ! Knew my name—but that's natural ; I'm gin-
erally pretty wall celebrated wherever I am."

So Mr. Potter goes to shooting again and takes another pistol, and getting to his work with a revolver in
either hand, makes such a breakage about the gallery

that the proprietor wishes to engage him to give a public exhibition.

This last is witnessed for a moment by poor Van Cott, who has telegraphed for more clothes. Hearing the noise he looks in for a moment, and seeing Mr. Potter split a card flies away for his life, and skulks about in the remote parts of the town till it is time for him to catch the Paris train. He thinks Potter will not be apt to find him in that big city. During this time little Van Cott trembles and has cold sweats, and dodges hastily around corners, for he imagines this target practice is for him, and he murmurs wofully to himself : " My Gad, he'll shoot me with a pistol ! "

The revolvers suiting him, Mr. Potter thinks he will take them both, and buckling them on to him remarks : " In deference to the decrees of society, since I came over here I've only worn one gun and felt but half a man ; now I'm two-handed again. I feel as if I war in Texas and going on the war-path ! " Which coming out of the shop he does, and at the *Hôtel des Bains* encounters for his first opponent a woman who, on the very first round, discomforts and figuratively rescalps Mr. Potter, nearly wounding him to death.

CHAPTER XVII.

WHICH LOVES HIM BEST.

LEAVING Mr. Van Cott at the railway station in Boulogne to discover and disclose his matrimonial intentions to Mr. Potter, Ida has taken a carriage to drive to the *Hôtel du Pavillion*. As it is on the sea, and distant from the main part of the town this occupies some little time. Her father, on leaving Lord Lincoln's house, had told her that he would probably stop at this hotel, especially if he remained over night in France ; consequently she expects to find him here. The clerk informs her very politely that her father has honored them with his patronage and engaged a room, for Miss Potter's name is well known in this fashionable caravansary. Having shown her to a parlor, the young lady spends a quiet hour awaiting the Honorable Sampson's return : for the season is at its close and the house nearly deserted by the devotees of fashionable salt water. .

During this time of waiting an agony of curiosity as well as dread is in the girl. Every time she looks at the marked sovereign that dangles upon her white wrist she wonders why these coins, which had driven the father of poor Charley Errol a convict from the land of his birth, should be considered by her father a signal of his success in the world. For Mr. Potter wears a duplicate piece upon his watch-chain, and she knows her brother, the lieutenant in the navy, has another, which the Honorable Sampson had given him and told him, "to clinch to for luck ! " Then, thinking of the indictment for felony hanging over the office boy who disappeared the day Errol was arrested, and who she now is convinced is her father, by an involuntary movement she is about to conceal the coin, and has even taken off the bracelet to hide it from view. But here an invincible pride comes to her, and she feels it would be a slur upon her parent, and mutters to herself : "Thank Heaven, I love my father too much to doubt him ! My father a thief ? Impossible ! " With this she puts on the bracelet again so that it is very prominent and everybody can see it, and flashes the sovereign in the air to attract notice, and thinks to herself : "That's confidence in my father's honor ! "

But tired at length of delay Miss Potter at last makes up her mind to search for Mr. Potter in the town itself. She orders a carriage and says to the driver : "*Hôtel des Bains*," for she imagines the Honorable Sampson has found his call upon Lady Annerley so pleasant he has prolonged it. She knows what a tender spot the paternal Potter has for pretty women, and that he had been greatly impressed with the widow's magnificent beauty the day before.

Consequently, a few minutes after Mr. Potter had left that hostelry in pursuit of Arthur, his daughter goes into the *Hôtel des Bains*, and finding Lubbins in the hall, tells him to take her card up to Lady Annerley in a tone which makes that servitor forget to lie and say her ladyship is not at home. Walking into the public parlor to await the answer, Miss Potter finds poor little Ethel, who hasn't been able to eat any dinner, and who, in answer to the American girl's cry of astonished surprise, runs to her and murmurs with trembling lips : " You are in Boulogne on the same errand as I ! "

" What errand?" says Miss Potter, more astonished.

Here Ethel adds to her surprise, for she returns : " To prevent the man that I love and the man that you love meeting each other with deathly hate in their hearts."

This speech, coupled with the girl's manner and appearance, frightens Ida. She cries out : " What do you mean ? I cannot understand you ! Quick ! tell me ! What new complication—" and gets a shock. For Ethel gives her a short account of the quarrel between the two young men, and at the end dismays her, for she says : " Then my brother struck the man I love."

" And Mr. Errol—what did he do to the man that *I* love ? " comes from Miss Potter's pale lips.

And she trembles, for she knows the awful ending that such affairs have in Texas, and the memories of her youth come home to her.

" He held his hand and did not return the blow."

" God bless him for that ! " cries Ida.

" Because he said the man you love was my brother ! "

" How truly noble ! " murmurs the girl then and she exclaims : " But I will repay him for it all, this very day ! " and after a moment inquires if Arthur is surely in Boulogne.

Which being answered affirmatively, she tells Ethel that she must stay at this hotel and keep Mr. Errol, who will certainly call upon Lady Annerley.

" You think he will visit her *now ?* "

This last is so pathetic that Miss Potter says very impressively to the girl : " It is because he loves you, Ethel Lincoln ; never doubt that Charley Errol loves you. I will find and bring your brother here, and he shall apologize to a noble gentleman for a cruel wrong."

" You think my Charley noble ? " asks Miss Ethel, brightening up at the comfort of these words.

" I know it. Noble because he loves you well, but loves his word to your father and his honor as a gentleman better."

This is the kind of consolation Miss Lincoln likes, praise for her hero. She says purringly : " Thank you ! You like my Charley ? "

" I *love* him ! "

" O-o-oh ! "

" As a brother ! " returns Miss Potter, with a faint
smile on her face, hurriedly going out in pursuit of Arthur.
For she is exceedingly anxious for her *fiancé* to make
amends for his injustice to Mr. Errol and put a stop to
an affair that belongs to a class of which her Texan memories give her even now a trembling horror.

In her hurry Ida entirely forgets the card she has
dispatched to Lady Annerley, and that lady being rather
surprised at her visit, and thinking the American girl
may have some information about Charley Errol's movements, makes up her mind to see her. Reserving her
own private parlor in which to receive Mr. Errol when
he arrives, she comes downstairs into the public one,
expecting to see Miss Potter. For a moment she looks
about the room, and finding no one apparently in it, goes
toward a bay window at the end of the apartment.
There to her astonishment she comes upon Miss Ethel,
who, seeing her enemy, and being reassured by Miss Potter's words, prepares for the combat ; though it is very
much like a female dove pluming herself and sharpen-
ing her mild beak to do battle with the magnificent but
naughty hawk. For Lady Annerley is in a toilet de-
signed for the insnaring of Mr. Errol, and is an alluring
mixture of black satin, sparkling diamonds, dazzling
neck, white arms and flashing eyes ; and Miss Ethel's
now pathetic beauty and pretty but modest traveling
dress are by no means so commanding.

On first seeing each other both ladies have a blush ;
though Miss Lincoln soon loses hers and becomes pale.
Lady Annerley's remains, rouge being stronger than
blood.

They greet each other with the usual compliments of
the season and without any great embarrassment, though
Miss Ethel trembles and shrinks a little under her ladyship's kiss ; for these two have been great friends before
they knew Charley Errol. And now Ethel, comparatively
sure of the young man's affection, is inclined to be generous to her unsuccessful rival ; while Lady Annerley,
not guessing what has occurred since she left England,
knows that her only consistent conduct is that of friend,
not rival.

She says : " I see you loved France, my child, well enough to revisit it. Why did you not tell me you were coming ?" Then she forces herself to smile and utters playfully: " I presume Mr. Errol is one of the party ? "

" Oh, no," returns Miss Ethel. " I am in Mr. Potter's party !" and doing a little stronger acting causes herself to laugh and say airily : " You see, I gave Charley a—a half holiday, to see his father."

" A-ah !" echoes her ladyship consideringly. Then looking at the girl, she knows Charley Errol has not yet had enough strength of mind to tell his sweetheart his father is a convict.

At this moment Lubbins brings to her a card. Glancing at it Sarah Annerley imagines Satan has put a trump into her hand, and proceeds to play it.

She says to Lubbins : " Wait a moment, and then show the gentleman here."

" I thought, my lady, it was to your private parlor ! "

" HERE ! ! "

" Yes, my lady." And Lubbins disappears.

Then she turns to Ethel and says : " Would you mind occupying that bay window for a moment ? I expect a visitor."

" Of course not, " replies the girl, and sits in it, thinking to herself : " If it were Charley she'd surely have him asked to her private parlor." Then she says aloud : " This view of the quay will interest me for half an hour if you take that long."

" It will be only for a moment, and I'll draw the curtain so we won't disturb you," mutters her ladyship. " The gentleman's card says he calls on business ! "

With this Sarah Annerley moves the heavy draperies, shutting out Miss Lincoln from the sight of any one in the room. Then she laughs to herself : " I'll kill her love—it will be a mercy to her. She'll hear every word, and know from Charley Errol's own lips that he's the son of a criminal. He shall see whether her baby passion is worth to a man who suffers more than that of a woman who by suffering has learnt to love." And scowling at the curtain, she hisses between her clenched teeth : " I'll break your heart ! "

But here a smile seizes upon and illumines her face, and she flies toward the door, for she hears a coming

step she knows and waits for it, murmuring tenderly :
"He's coming—Charley's coming ! " For she hates Ethel
Lincoln, and would torture her forever, and loves Charley
Errol, and has tortured him, but only to gain him ; and
this torture being over, is anxious to take him to her, and
soothe his woes.   Such are the curiosities of passion.

A moment after this she cries : " Welcome to Boulogne,
my dear Mr. Errol! " and is shaking hands with the
young man.

Mr. Errol looks better than he did in the morning, for
he has got to hoping again, now he has Lord Lincoln's
assistance.   He has just been to his father and told him
this, considerately keeping from the old man, however,
the fee he has paid for that lawyer's services.

Still there are enough traces of suffering in his face to
make Lady Sarah suffer also, as he looks at her rather
searchingly, for he remembers Brackett's injunction, and
says :   " Lady Annerley, the business on which I called
to speak to you is of the greatest private moment."

"Business?   I had hoped you called for pleasure."

"Until this business is settled," returns Errol gloomily,
"there can be no pleasure for me."

" Then sit down," mutters her ladyship nervously, for
though she has no fear he suspects her in any way, still
she is very anxious to know how she can aid him.   Then
sinking into a chair, and motioning him to another, she
says : " I'll listen."

He does not accept her invitation, but repeats : " This
business is of a most *personal* nature," and looks about
the room suspiciously.

"Ah ! " replies Lady Sarah, taking the hint. " My private parlor is at present engaged, but my servant will see
that we are not interrupted here."   Going to the door
she finds Lubbins quite near it, and tells him to see that
no one comes in without informing her, then repeats her
invitation to be seated, which Mr. Errol now accepts.

Being very anxious for Miss Ethel's benefit to bring the
scene to a climax, Sarah Annerley now makes herself as
agreeable and fascinating as she can, all the time plying
him with such questions as : " How did your father enjoy
his voyage from Australia?   You had not seen him for
two years, I believe?   What a cordial and delightful
meeting it must have been ! "

During these questions Charley Errol is thinking · "It is not possible she can be such a hypocrite."

Finally she tells him he is not looking well, and says : " I presume you must have sat up talking with your governor all last night ? "

This brings speech to his lips ; his eyes become full of agony, and he mutters : "Yes—all last night I *suffered!*" ·

"Suffered ? Mr. Errol—Charley, what trouble can you have, with everything to make you happy—engaged to a beautiful girl ? "

Here he gives a cry that makes her feel for him, and she has sympathy in her eyes as she says : " But in any· —in all misfortunes you know you have my lo—, my friendship. You know that, don't you, Charley ? "

" I want more than your friendship," the young man says hoarsely.

" More ? " there is joy in Lady Sarah's voice.

" I want your aid ! "

" Aid ! I do not understand ! "

" Last night my father was again exiled from England ? "

"Your father ! Exiled ! " She is very much astonished and cries out : " Impossible ! For what ? " thinking he will tell the girl in the bay window.

Here he frightens her, for he says, looking at her searchingly : " Lady Annerley, do you not know ? "

But she forces herself to meet his gaze and returns : " I know nothing except your father is an old Australian, who returned to England last night." Then she asks again for the benefit of the girl in the bay window : " For what was he exiled the first time ? " ·

But he disappoints her once more, for he mutters : " My father's tale is too sad a one to repeat—if you do not know it ? "

" *If* I do not know it ? Why did you think I knew it ? "

" For two reasons. First, in Egypt—— "

" In Egypt ! " This is a cry.

" Yes, my memory is coming back to me. Last night I was thinking about it. You said something of my father."

" Yes ! " she returns. " I did say something of your father. You asked me if you died to send him the news—but I didn't let you die—*did I ? Answer me that*

14

first, and make insinuations that you know to be cruel afterward!"

The thought of her kindness to him makes him tender to her, and he says rather shamefacedly : "Lady Sarah, I would say nothing to you on this subject, but the detective who is investigating the affair——"

"Ah !" this is partly a gasp of dismay and partly a cry of rage.

"Declared to me that you were the person that sent the information to the Home Office that caused my father to be again expelled from England."

The tone in which Charley Errol says this is so apologetic that it gives the woman, hanging on his words, courage. She cries haughtily : "He dared accuse me of that?" Then her eyes become soft, her tone appealing, as she says, her heart in her mouth : "And you, Charley, what did you say?"

"What did I say?" cries Errol, the memory of her kindness coming to him and the enthusiasm of his great friendship for her carrying him away : "I said I would never believe such treachery of the noble woman who had been my devoted nurse, and whose father had been my father's fast friend in his great trouble."

"When did you learn that?" she questions anxiously.

"My father told me not an hour ago ! "

"Ah ! all that binds us closer now."

"It does," cries Charley. "We're firmer friends than ever ; and, oh, my heavens, how I want them now !" Then she, holding out a sympathetic and beautiful hand to him, this poor, tortured, shamefaced creature seizes it, calling her "his good angel," which makes conscience give her another thrust.

After a moment, however, they both become calmer, and she says : "Thank you for doing me justice," and then suggests rather nervously : "but the detective——"

"Oh, I left him in England some hours ago ! "

And she mutters to this : "Thank Heaven !" But it is only a speech of the mind and he doesn't hear it, for Lubbins has come hurriedly in and announced that "a man named Brackett insists on seeing Mr. Herrol."

Before Lady Annerley can interpose an objection Errol tells Lubbins to let him in.

"Who is it ? " she asks.

"The detective we were just speaking about. He must have some new information."

And asking her to excuse him a moment the young man turns to Mr. Brackett, who comes in whistling to Snapper, while Sarah Annerley trembles and gasps to herself : " If he should discover? My heavens ! If Charley should discover ! " This thought overcomes her and she sinks into a chair, for upon the entrance of the detective she had sprung to her feet almost as if to run from the apartment.

" The proof you demanded, sir ! " says Brackett shortly, holding out to Mr. Errol a letter.

This the young man does not take, but turns and says: " Lady Annerley, this man again repeats his assertion."

" And, Charley, you let him do it ? "

This appeal Mr. Errol cannot resist, and replies to Brackett determinedly : " I cannot believe you ! "

But here her ladyship interrupts further discussion by crying : "Lubbins, put that dog out ! " for little Snapper has crept quietly up to her and surreptitiously licked her hand. She is venting her spleen against the detective on his pet.

Lubbins, cautiously approaching the little creature, as if he dreaded hydrophobia, Mr. Brackett says : " Bah ! Snapper won't hurt either of you," and picking the dog up gives it to the servant and tells him to hold it in the hall till he comes out. This Lubbins does, Snapper transferring his caresses from Lady Annerley's hands to the ex-waiter's face, and her ladyship suggesting that Mr. Brackett had perhaps better take out his dog himself.

This makes the detective angry, and he determines to put in practice a trick that wiser heads than his have suggested in London.

He says : " In a minute, if your ladyship will do me the honor to answer a few questions." This is uttered very respectfully, for Sergeant Brackett would have been deferential to a peeress even while clapping the bracelets upon her wrists.

" A dozen, if you dare ask them ! " sneers Lady Annerley, rising, and like a good many clever women, letting her temper get the better of her at precisely the wrong moment.

"Then," says Mr. Brackett, tapping the letter he still carries in his hand, and catching her ladyship's eye, "you deny, Lady Annerley, that this letter, which is a *fac-simile* of the one received at the Home Office from Venice, is in your handwriting?"

"Of course I do!" cries Lady Sarah, getting very frightened at the word Venice.

"What?" says Brackett, confidently, "when it has your signature attached to it?"

This is a barefaced falsehood and it makes her wild with rage. 'She shrieks out: "It is a lie; there was no signature to that letter!" Then pauses and turns pale, for passion leaves her and reason comes back to her with a shock.

Mr. Brackett says quietly: "You are perfectly right, my lady, there is no signature to this letter." And handing it to Mr. Errol he remarks: "You see, sir, she knows all about it. I shall await your orders at my lodgings," then goes out on tiptoe. For when the detective stops speaking the silence is like that of the tomb, and this man and woman are looking at each other in a way that impresses Sergeant Brackett.

This silence continues after the detective has left the room; it is first broken by the woman, for Lady Annerley, angry with despair, visits her wrath upon the first object at her hand, which is the Australian. She cries out to him in reproach: "And—and you, Charley Errol, who called yourself my friend, allowed that man to trick me out of my secret—thus——"

On this the man, who has given a hasty glance at the letter, for he can hardly still believe the truth, wounds her with these words: "And you, Lady Annerley, whom I once thought my friend, why have you hated me?" And she calls out: "I hate *you!*" and sinks down upon a sofa and gasps "*you!*" but still looks him in the face.

"Oh, what a hypocrite you are!" he goes on with a fearful reproach in his voice. "After professing the greatest friendship for me you sent this cruel letter that has driven my father an exile from his birthplace and separated me perhaps forever from the girl I was about to marry! Your true reason—Sarah Annerley, your true reason for *this?*"

"My true reason?" she cries, and then groans, looking

straight at him : " Heaven help me ! What shall I tell
you now ? "

" I ask you *why*? "

" Why ? " she cries and looks at him, a new light coming into her face which makes him stare amazed. Then
she pants : " Can't you guess ? I—" and here hesitates,
and real blushes cover her, making her more beautiful
than ever ; but she forces herself to go on : " I did not
wish you to wed the girl you were about to marry !
Charley, don't look me in the face and I—I will tell you.
What else could separate you from the girl you were
about to marry ? "

This brings a cry from him, for he now begins to know.

But she keeps on, not noticing : " A desperate woman
cares not for her means. I knew but one thing could do
it and I did it. Her father's family pride will never
permit his daughter's union with what you are. I am
my own mistress, wealthy and independent of the world.
I could forget your shame, for I—oh, Charley, I lo——"
And would complete the word but, covered with shame
and humiliation, this great English lady cannot speak it,
and, turning away, falls down upon a sofa, not looking at
him.

To this Errol, very pale, whispers : " My Heaven, you
love *me !* " for at last he sees.

At these words she turns upon him and cries: " How
dare you say it ? You have not yet said you love *me!*"
and then clings about him, for pride has been destroyed
by passion, and gasps : " How could I help it, I, who saw
you fight for me in Egypt ! " and then begs him: " Don't
investigate ! Don't try to prove your father's innocence,
and by it proclaim his shame ! Think, *know* that here is
a woman who will cast her lot with you ; who will leave
England, where society would not tolerate you, for your
sake ; who offers you your *one* chance of happiness ! "

But he cries back to her : " My one chance of happiness ? I have but *one*, and that is to right my father ;
to make his name so high in honor that the woman I love
will share it with me ! For if I do not gain Ethel Lincoln I am unhappy forever ! "

Then, in his imagination seeing the pale face of the
girl he loves as she sank down in sad appeal between
her brother and his righteous anger, he struggles and

breaks away from Lady Annerley's pleading arms. Then
he thinks it all a dream, for he hears : "Charley, you
shall gain me ! That woman's arts shall not part us !"
and looking up, startled and astounded, sees the same
sweet face of his love and imagination. For Ethel Lincoln is standing between him and Lady Annerley, who
starts back, screaming in a half-scared voice : " I had
forgotten her ! " In the delirium of the confession of
her passion, brought about by Mr. Brackett, her rival's
presence has passed entirely from her mind.

Ethel's face is no longer sad nor her eyes pathetic ;
the first is radiant with trusting love, the second sparkle
with indignant fire at Lady Annerley. The dove is about
to battle with the hawk.

"You overheard——" mutters Errol.

" Enough to make me love you more than that woman
ever could ! "

This confidence and trust of the girl in her sweetheart's
affection makes Lady Sarah very bitter toward her and
she answers: " We shall see how much you love him.
Do you know what this man is ? "

" Yes.   He's the man I love ! "

Then Lady Annerley goes on. in quiet intensity to
the girl, who stands like a statue listening to her. " Do
you love him well enough to—to take the taint of his
family upon you ; to turn your back upon your friends
to be disowned by your brother and your father ?   Then
if you do—take him ! for the man you wish to marry
is—— "

She has to pause here, for now Errol is screaming at her
in a voice that would be loud were it not hoarse with despair : " Mercy ! Don't ! Don't tell her of my shame ! "

But she mutters : " Forgive me, Charley ! " and then
cries out louder than he : " Is the offspring of a *ticket-of-
leave man ;* the SON OF A CONVICT ! "

At this the statue falls down at the feet of the suffering
man, gasping : " Charley, tell her it is not true ! "

And the man, turning his face away and bowing his
head, whispers : " I cannot."

The awful shock of the revelation crushes the girl.
She hides her head also.

" You see which loves you best, " says Lady Annerley
in a sneer and triumph that become Dead Sea fruits upon

her lips ; for here the girl staggers to the man and clasps her arms around him and soothes him, crying "*I* do ! For if he is all this, he is still the man *I love !* Don't heed her cruel words when my arms are round you !"

And bringing to this poor, tortured fellow the love of the wife instead of the love of the maiden, his agony becomes less and tears soothe him and give him rest.

A moment after he says very quietly but very sadly to the girl, forcing himself to be calmer as he sees she is giving way, and putting her gently from him: " But, darling, I must heed them ; they are the words of the world, and we can't escape them !" then suddenly cries to her : " Oh, don't make my task too hard ! Don't make me forget in the magic of your embrace that every word I speak to you now breaks my word to your father !" For she has got to him again and her arms are holding him once more.

These he unclasps gently, and getting before her ladyship, who has watched all this with varying hope and fear, he says quite gently, though there is a little tremble in his voice : " Lady Annerley, you have conquered. You have parted me from the being I love most upon this earth !"

And my lady mutters to herself : " *At last !* "

Then Errol articulates, though the speech is hardly audible : " Ethel, there is but one chance you will ever hear my voice again in this world, and that is the chance of proving my father's innocence !"

And Lady Annerley cries : " Then your parting is *eternal !* "

This word breaks the spell. The scene, which was quiet with despair, now becomes a wild protest against it.

Ethel echoes : " Eternal !" and runs to Errol, crying : " Charley ! Don't leave me *forever !* Think how much I love you ! Know that if the world drives you from it, I will go with you !"

" Don't torture me," gasps Errol, hoarsely.

" That where your home is, mine shall be also !"

While she says this Charley is trembling in the girl's embrace, whose proffered sacrifice for him makes her dearer than ever.

He mutters : " Oh ! how you tempt me ! Pity me ! Don't make my duty too hard !"

Then struggling away from her, he cries : " *I'm not*

selfish enough to accept your social suicide !" and turns to stagger off.

But catching him before he reaches the door, the girl begs and pleads with him : " Charley, do not desert me ! " then screams hysterically: " DON'T LET THAT WOMAN TRIUMPH ! "

It is October, and the hotel having but few guests, so far no one has noticed what has been going on in the parlor, but Arthur, who has just come to the house, hears his sister's cry and strides into the apartment. He drags her to her feet, saying in a sarcastic voice : " What ! Humiliating yourself again—before your rival ! Ethel, I despise you ! "

" No, no ! he loves me ! " gasps Ethel. " You owe him reparation."

But the victory in Lady Annerley's eyes makes the young man hardly heed his sister's words, and he mutters : " Reparation to *him ?* When I hear you cry, ' Do not desert me !' and see that woman's eyes blazing with triumph ! " Then dropping the girl upon a sofa he advances to Errol, who has drawn himself up and uttered : ' For God's sake, don't touch me again. If you do, by Heaven, I'll forget she is your sister, and remember only that I am a man ! "

The first is said almost pleadingly, the second in that awful low tone that comes to men when they are going to kill each other, and the next instant Mr. Potter's prophecy would have probably been fulfilled, were it not that now there comes the flurry of a light dress, and in a flash Ida Potter's beautiful face, radiant with anxiety, is between the awful passions of these men.

She has seen Arthur enter the hotel and hurried after him. She cries " *Stop !* " in a way that makes both of them pause ; and then, turning to Arthur, says : " Here is a gentleman to whom you owe apology."

" Without an explanation? Never ! " replies her betrothed, doggedly.

" Then I will make it for you ! " cries Ida, and she turns and gives the Australian a look of confidence and respect that sends the blood coursing through this poor, humiliated fellow's veins again as she says : " Charles Errol, Ethel's brother does not understand your cruel position —but I do ! For my sake pardon and forgive him ! "

Here Arthur mutters to her : " Ida, this is humiliation !
You shall apologize no more ! " and would stop her.

But she waves him away, and with a face beaming with
generous enthusiasm cries : " I.will do more than apologize ; I will repay—for, Charles Errol, I give you back
hope ! "

" Hope ! " echoes the young man, and strides up to her
uttering hoarsely : " What do you know of all this ? "

Then she makes them all astounded, for she says :
" In the *Times* of yesterday there is an advertisement for
an office boy—missing for thirty years."

On this Lady Annerley suddenly, in an awful voice,
cries out : " Good heavens ! " and begins to tremble.

" What would you give to find him ? "

" Everything on earth ! "

" He has disappeared ! He is dead ! Impossible ! " interrupts Lady Sarah.

" Then I will bring him to you ! "

And now Sarah Annerley cries : " He dare not return !
He fled from an indictment for felony thirty years ago ! "
But Ida only sees the Australian gazing at her and hanging on her words as if the breath of life were issuing
from her lips, and turning on Lady Annerley cries back
at her : " But is innocent ! I know it ! "

" And how will you prove that ? "

" *By asking him !* "

" Asking *him ?* " This is a cry of surprise from all of
them, even Arthur.

But Miss Potter returns : " Yes ! Do you suppose I
fear the ordeal ? When my father left England, thirty
years ago, to win fortune in America, he was the office
boy you seek ! "

Then Errol mutters : " In Heaven's name who's
guilty ? "

And Ida cries : " SHE KNOWS ! " and stands like the
statue of truth over Lady Annerley, who has collapsed
upon a sofa with a faint gasping that seems like : " Don't
tell him ! Don't tell him ! "

Thus they all leave her and coming out encounter
Lubbins, who says nothing, though his eyes are very big.

Before they are away from the hotel, however, Miss
Potter tells Arthur, who wonders if they are all mad,
enough of the truth to cause him to beg Errol's pardon

and shake hands with the young Australian, who bolts
off to his father with the joyous news of Sammy Potts'
being found.

Arthur escorts the two girls back to the *Hôtel du Pavillon*, where they will stay for the night and expect to
see Mr. Potter, but he has not arrived. Here Ida, telling her lover all she knows of the case of the elder Errol
and her father's connection with it, he looks very solemn,
for an indictment for felony always seems serious to an
English lawyer.

He says to the girl : "You should have told Mr. Potter of this first."

"What ! Do you suppose I doubt my father's innocence ? Do you imagine I could see the agony in poor
Charley Errol's eyes and hold my tongue, when that
woman dared me ?" replies Ida airily.

"Innocence is sometimes difficult to prove !" mutters
her lover, and then asks anxiously at the office for Mr.
Potter. They have not seen him, and he waits and waits
until tired.

It is now seven o'clock and Arthur, hearing a rumor
that makes him shudder, comes in with a disturbed face
to the young ladies, and says he will go into town and
hunt up Ida's father.

"What is the matter?" returns Miss Potter to him,
here noting his expression. "Why are you running away
without any dinner?" for that meal has just been announced.

"I—you see your governor may have gone back to
England to-night ! "

"Nonsense ! I saw his old valise in the office. I'd
know it anywhere by the two bullet holes in it !" asserts
the girl.

"Still—I—I think I'd better make sure ! "

"Make sure of what ? You've heard something !
You sha'n't go till I hear it. If it's about my father, I
demand to know it !" and Miss American has got in
front of the door.

"Well, I'm afraid your information to Lady Annerley
has got your father into trouble. There is a rumor in
the hotel that Mr. Potter has left town."

"Very well. Go and see. I'll keep dinner for you,"
returns Ida, with an absolute faith in her father's probit-

and safety that astounds the young-man. For she going back to the table, he notes even as he leaves the room, has lost none of her appetite, and eats as if she enjoys the meal much more than poor Ethel, who even now is by no means in a buoyant mood.

The dinner passes, eight o'clock comes, then nine ; and now Miss Potter gets a little anxious, not for her father's innocence, but for Arthur's safety, in whose ability to knock about the streets of this French town she has by no means the supreme confidence she has in her father's.

At ten o'clock Arthur comes in, and now his news startles even her ; as he with a scared face announces that there is a warrant out for the arrest of Sammy Potts, and a requisition on the French Government has come over to the detective for his body. That hearing of this, Sampson Potter had fled by train toward Paris pursued by Sergeant Brackett, and that he, Arthur, has telegraphed to Lord Lincoln, who will be over in the morning.

Now no girl could hear such a report of her father without some uneasiness, and it is not decreased by Arthur's moody manner. For that young gentleman has got very solemn, and is now making remarks about boys of tender age not being responsible for their actions ; that no child is legally liable ; that some of the worst lads he has known have become the noblest men ; that he himself as a child had been a fearful thief at cake and jam ; that a man should not be held to account for the transgressions of babyhood, etc., etc.

One of these reflections intended to soothe his sweet-heart coming to her ears, this very proud young lady flashes up to her lover and frightens him by saying : " No more of that, Arthur, if you want to marry me. No insinuations that by any possibility my father, boy or man, could ever take anything that wasn't his, or any undue advantage of any man !"

In which she does the absent Potter more than justice, for the Honorable Sampson was considered the very keenest man in the West on a cattle trade, and in a horse transaction was regarded as a living terror by his friends in Texas.

Having thus vindicated her father, Miss Potter goes

to bed, where femininity gets the better of pride and she cries and sobs: "Oh, my Heaven! I, who should have warned my father so that he could prove his innocence, have betrayed him to his enemies!" But though she tosses and writhes, no doubt ever enters the girl's mind of old Potter's entire guiltlessness.

And now pride comes back to her again, for Ethel knocks on the door of her room and being admitted, snuggles herself up to Ida in bed and thinking to soothe her says: "Ida, dear one, I've been praying for your poor father, whom the detective is following to arrest."

"Have you?" says Miss Potter. "I'VE BEEN PRAYING FOR THE DETECTIVE!"

CHAPTER XVIII.

POOR OLD POTTER.

ON leaving Errol and Lady Annerley Sergeant Brackett goes to his lodgings in a humble hotel upon the quay, and gets an awful surprise. Awaiting him is a packet from the English Government marked "immediate." On opening this the detective gives an amazed gasp of horror, and drops the packet on the floor as if it had been an infernal machine.

Then mutters: "It ain't possible!" but looking it over again there is no doubt of the genuineness of the documents contained in it. These consist of a warrant for the arrest of one Samuel Potts *alias* Sampson Potter, indicted for felony; also a requisition in proper form upon the French Government for the extradition of the aforesaid criminal; as well as a letter from Scotland Yard telling Brackett not to leave the matter to the French *gendarmerie*, but to see to the execution of the warrant in person, and if possible bring Potts *alias* Potter to England without appealing to French law; warning Brackett, however, to be exceedingly careful of his own personal safety in the affair, as from various inquiries hastily made said Potts or Potter had the reputation in America of being a most determined and bloody criminal as well as a fearfully dangerous man to encounter.

"Dangerous!" ejaculates the detective, with a shiver. "*Dangerous!*" It's most like murder to send me on such business. A man with a family!" and then turning to his dumb friend for consolation, as many of us often do, he mumbles: "They're tired of paying your old master's salary up at the Yard, Snapper, and want him wiped off the roll." A remark that is more true than the sergeant imagines. To this Snapper responds by licking Brackett's face with his tongue and vigorously wagging his tail as if he were glad of it. Which the poor brute isn't, as he loves his master with all his warm little heart, and would follow him through the world for-ever; a devotion that Snapper has an opportunity some-what later that day of proving, to Brackett's misery and despair.

After a little time the detective pulls himself together and looks over the documents again. They are official and correct in every particular, a blank space, however, being left for a further description of Potts *alias* Potter, which Brackett fills up with the words "Dangerous, bloodthirsty, and to be approached with caution." Thinking, in case he should be fortunate enough not to find Potter and so let him escape, they will tend to excul-pate him (Brackett) in the eyes of the English police offi-cials.

For now what he saw in the shooting gallery comes to him with awful significance, and he mutters: "My Lord! he was preparing himself for me. God help my family!" and contemplates telegraphing his resignation to Eng-land. But after a moment a brilliant idea shoots through his mind, and that is, he will spread the report he has a warrant to arrest Potter as a criminal, and so warned the Texan may leave the place and permit him, Brackett, to live. For the sergeant has become so imbued with his favorite border literature that he wouldn't give a penny for his chance for life in an encounter with Sammy Potts *alias* Potter. A brutal English burglar or French escaped galley slave, the detective would have met with courage and equanimity; but this scalping Western ruffian, this bandit of the plains—the thought of meeting him in com-bat makes Brackett shudder as if he had the ague. Even this afternoon he has read a work of fiction called *Potts the Pirate of the Prairies,* and conceives the horrible atrocities of its gory hero to be nothing more than the life and adventures of Sammy Potts.

" How in the name of bad luck did the authorities drop on him ? " mutters the detective, as he goes out to spread the report.

But this is easily accounted for by the fact that Mr. Potter had left a letter for Mr. Portman, Errol's advertising solicitor, stating the fact that he was Sammy Potts, and on his return to England the next morning that gentleman had communicated with the British police authorities, with the before-stated result.

It does not take long to circulate a rumor that any man is a criminal, and Mr. Brackett's statement is soon flying about Boulogne. It reaches the *Hôtel des Bains*, and is instantly carried by the excited Lubbins to Lady Annerley, who has been in a state of semi-coma since her interview with Errol. She hurriedly sends word to the detective that she must see him.

If Potts can prove his innocence, it will disclose to Charley Errol a treachery on her part, unutterably more cruel, cowardly, and dishonorable than the mere betrayal of his father's presence in England to the police, of which at this time he only thinks her guilty. The contemplation of the contempt and loathing this will arouse in the heart of the man she loves makes her shudder and thrill with horror. And she lies upon a sofa, when unobserved, moaning and wringing her hands, and when Lubbins or her maid is present forcing herself to an unnatural calmness.

A few moments after this the ex-waiter comes up more excited than ever and ejaculates : " The Honorable Sammy Potts—I—I mean Sampson Potter, to see your ladyship ! "

" Did he seem agitated ? " asks his mistress with a start, struggling to a sitting position upon the sofa.

" Hon the contrary—werry cool and *dilettante !* "

" Quick ! show him up ! " and Lubbins with a bow leaving the room Lady Annerley pulls herself together for a last and mighty struggle to seem less than a fiend in the mind of the man she loves. If Potts can't prove his innocence and she can induce him to fly, all may be well ; if not——

But Mr. Potter now comes in and genially remarks : " Warm evening, Lady Hannerley, warm evening ! " re-

moving his hat, producing a red silk bandana, and wiping
his wig.

"Mr. Potts—Potter, won't you be seated?" murmurs
her ladyship, who has risen to receive him, stumbling a
little over his name.

But he doesn't notice this, and beams upon her: "Won't
you? Ladies first! No man sits when a lady stands—not
in Texas."

Then very gallantly placing her in a chair, the old
frontier gentleman's eyes grow big at the beauty before
him, for Mr. Potter is not accustomed to ladies in evening dress, and the fair arms and neck of Lady Annerley,
together with her flashing diamonds and exquisite toilet,
have set his ancient heart to beating as he gallantly mutters: "Great Scott, your ladyship is like a *sireen* of the
night!"

Not heeding his compliment, Lady Annerley, desperately anxious to get to business, asks him if he has seen
his daughter this afternoon.

To this he replies "No;" but that he hears she is in
Boulogne, and that he will get on her trail as soon as he
has finished up a leetle business that he has called upon
her ladyship to transact.

"Business with *me!*" she cries, and going quickly to
the door she locks it.

"Hello! What's that for?" ejaculates Mr. Potter.

"I have a servant that has ears!"

Here she gets a surprise, for the Texan suggests:
"Than you'd better open it agin, for the more 'as heerd
me say what I'm going to, the prouder you'd be, Lady
Saharah."

"The prouder I'd be?"

"Prouder than if you was a Hinjin with a red
blanket."

"I don't understand!" gasps her ladyship, for a moment wildly thinking that Mr. Potter's intentions are matrimonial, as his eyes follow her in a peculiar grateful way,
and she remembers his remarks about her being a *sireen.*

He undeceives her, however, in a moment. "Until
last night, Lady Sahara," he says, "I never knowed you
were the darter of Hold Ginerosity himself!"

"Old Generosity!" echoes Lady Annerley, very much
astonished.

" Yes. The late Sir Jonas Stevens—the noblest man that's buried, and that means a great deal more than the noblest man who lives !" cries Potter, his eyes blazing with grateful enthusiasm.

" Noble ? " gasps Lady Sarah, who now half thinks Potter crazy, but after a moment says, suggestively : " You have not had many dealings with him ? "

" But one—and that branded him Ho. J.—Hold Ginerosity. Your father was very kind to me, and you have been very sociable to my darter, and I thanks you for it. Generous blood will tell. Your father was my worship. I prayed for your father ! "

" Prayed for my father ? " the tone of this is faint with astonishment.

" Prayed for him ! " repeats Potter, every fiber in his body showing he means what he says. " Prayed for him every night in my life till I grew out of the habit of praying at all ! " Then he pauses, and dashes two tears out of his eyes, and now goes on more slowly. " After thirty years death has cut me off from thanking your daddy—the great banker—and so now I've come over to Boulogne to thank you as the darter of the best friend I ever had."

" Friend ? " returns Lady Annerley, who finds it very hard to believe any good of her father. Then a sudden light flashing into her eyes she asks excitedly : " What did he do for you ? " and gets this ambiguous answer.

" What did he do for me ? He made the *pigmy* Sammy Potts into the *giant* Sampson Potter ! "

She doesn't say anything to this, she is so crushed at finding that Potter has no fear of his identity being known, and therefore that he must be able to prove his innocence.

He, however, doesn't give her much chance for comment, for he goes on rapidly, warming to his subject: " I'll tell you how it was : One winter morning in 1850—I, the little office boy of Jaffey & Stevens, as slept in the office, was awoke one morning by seeing your father—he was cashier of the bank in them days—putting sovereigns into a clerk's desk."

She says nothing to this, knowing what is coming, though her lips form the words : " Ralph Errol's ! "

" He was paying him back wages, he said, as the clerk was going to Australia early that day."

" And then ? "

Here Potter fairly gleams at his listener, who sits gazing at him as if he were a basilisk. " How generous he was ! Your father asked me if I'd like to hemigrate also and become a man ? The Californy gold fever of 1849 was in my blood, and afore night I found myself bound for New Orleans with thirty sovereigns in my pocket—A LOAN FROM YOUR NOBLE FATHER."

Here she interrupts him with : " A loan ! Do you think I'll believe this likely story ? "

" You won't take my thanks, Lady Sahara ; that's true generosity ! " returns Potter. " But I'll make you take 'em ! "

" And how ? "

" By proving that your father lent me them ar thirty sovereigns ! " gleams the Texan on her with grateful eyes, and she cries at him : " Proving it ! you sha'n't do it ! "

" You're too good-hearted and modest," he says after a moment, for her manner surprises him. " But I'll make it clear to you. Do you see this sovereign, Lady Annerley ? " With this he holds up the coin upon his watch-chain. " Every time I look at it I utters a blessing upon your daddy. My son sports one similar for luck, and my darter dangles one from her wrist because I've told her to."

Looking on this coin Lady Sarah notes with a start it has the peculiar mark her father spoke of in his death-bed confession.

" You've no doubt seen Miss Potter's," says that young lady's father, complacently.

" Yes ! " mutters his listener in a kind of a daze ; then she suddenly continues : " But that does not prove you received them from my father ! " and after a moment suggests : " I want better evidence."

She says this quite persuasively, but if Mr. Potter could have known what was in Lady Annerley's mind at the time he would have taken her glistening white throat into his hands, strangled her, and thus made an end to the interview.

As it is he paralyzes her, for he returns : " Then I'll

15

give it to you," and producing an old weather-beaten
leather wallet from his coat pocket, fumbles in it for a
document of some kind, while she gasps to herself :
" *Written evidençe !*" and nearly faints.

Mr. Potter, however, is too busy to notice her. He is
rummaging over the contents of his pocket-book, which
contains some greenbacks, English bank-notes, a New
York hotel bill receipted, a few doubtful pennies and
coins he has been unable to negotiate, and one or two
laundry lists, all these scented with a lot of fine-cut chew-
ing tobacco that has insinuated itself from his pocket.
At last he finds what he is searching for, and holds up a
half page of paper yellow with age, the ink of which is
faded from the same cause.

" Thar," he cries, " is the receipt of your daddy for the
return of them thirty sovereigns·he loaned me ! "

And she gasps : " No ! no ! " and were she not seated
in a chair would fall down.

" Your daddy was as difficult as you to get to acknowl-
edge his generosity ! " remarks Mr. Potter. " I had to
write to him twenty times to get this document—for my
first object in the New World was to return his noble loan
in the Old. But at last, in 1857, I was shipping hides to
London and had an agent, and as I made a point of it,
and sent the agent to him, your father inclosed me, under his own seal, this," and she looking contrives to read
the following :

> " LONDON, July 15, 1857.
> " £30——
> " Received from Samuel Potts thirty pounds (£30), with interest
> to date from January 6, 1850.
> " JONAS STEVENS."

" You, see ! " cries Mr. Potter triumphantly. " That
ar date, January 6, 1850, was the last day Sammy Potts
was in England."

" Yes," murmurs Lady Sarah, half sarcastically, " I
presume that was a hard document to get from my
father ? " Then a rapid look at the persistent and determined Potter makes her admire her father's acuteness
in seeing it was safer for him in 1857 to send this receipt
to far-off Texas than to have London agents running
after him and tendering him thirty pounds from Sammy
Potts, a boy only seven years before advertised for all

over England as connected with a great crime ; and he
the close-fisted Jonas Stevens, astonishing the agents by
refusing the money.

Her father's acuteness makes her have confidence in
her own. She carelessly hints : " I presume that's all the
proof you have ! "

" Why yes, ain't that enough ? " returns Potter. " I
fished that out of my trunk last night to bring it over to
you."

Here Lady Anneriey cries to herself : " Thank God ! "
And then asks aloud : " What did you intend to do with
it ? "

" I intended to frame it and give it to you, that you
might place it on a pedestal in your father's honor."

" For my father's honor let me make a better use of it.
Can I ? " asks Lady Sarah, fascinating him by her beautiful eyes.

The honest old gentleman bows to her with back-
woods grace, and this great English lady takes from his
hand the document and mutters : " True generosity con-
sists in forgetting the kindness. My father would
wish his also forgotten ! " THEN SHE BURNS UP IN A
LIGHTED TAPER UPON THE TABLE NEAR HER THE ONLY
EVIDENCE THAT STANDS BETWEEN THIS POOR OLD MAN
AND A BRITISH PRISON.

While he smiles at her and says, as the last ashes fall
upon the floor : " My dear, you're just like your dead
daddy—both noble ! "

" Noble ! " she cries to him, and there is a wildness in
her eye that makes Mr. Potter astonished, for she is in
her mind cursing herself as the most infamous thing on
earth ; but there is triumph in her look also. She knows
that there is but one salvation for the man standing before
her, he must fly, and thinks joyously : " Charley will never
know my father committed the crime that made his father
a convict, and that I knew it, and yet made him, innocent
as he was, again suffer the shame and agony of exile ; " and
last of all, that the elder Errol can never prove an unjust
conviction, and the man she loves is separated from
Ethel Lincoln forever.

She contrives to turn the conversation upon some light
subject, however ; thinking all the time how she dare tell
this old man who looks at her admiringly the awful thing

she has done to him so that he may escape in time ; but has no opportunity, for he has got upon the subject of his daughter, and is thanking Lady Annerley for her kindness to that young lady.

At this moment Lubbins knocks at the door, and she going to it, her face changes to an ashy pallor, for he announces that Sergeant Brackett is downstairs to speak to her as she requested. She mutters to her servant to keep the detective below, and now she is forced to tell Potter that he must fly.

She comes to him and hurriedly says : " There is an English police officer below. Take my advice ! Go quickly without the man seeing you ! "

" Why ? " returns Potter, staring at her, for her manner is significant.

" Because he will arrest you ! "

" Arrest *me* ? That's startling ! " mutters the Texan, feeling to be sure his pistols are all right. " Arrest the Honorable Sampson Potter ! " He repeats this last as if it were incredible, and the flame of battle begins to light up his eyes.

Here Lady Annerley figuratively knocks him down, pistols and all, for she says : " Not *Sampson Potter*, but *Sammy Potts*, against whom thirty years ago an indictment was found by an English jury for stealing thirty sovereigns marked to detect theft ! "

" TARANTULAS ! " This is a whoop that resounds through the room, re-echoes through the halls, and reaches Sergeant Brackett. He has never heard a war-cry before, but read of them. He knows the Texan is upstairs, and hastily and tremblingly descends to the reading room, and Potter, though he does not know it, is safe from immediate arrest.

" Counterparts of the one on your chain ! " mutters Lady Annerley, playing with the coin and showing him the distinguishing mark, for after giving the whoop Mr. Potter has begun to rub his head as if dazed.

" But you, Lady Sarah, know and can prove that I am innocent," he says to her after a long pause of thought.

" I know that thirty years ago," she returns pointedly, " a jury convicted Ralph Errol of stealing seventy of those marked coins, and made him a convict ! "

Here Potter mutters :   " Ralph `Errol ! " and seems to
be recalling something, for he now suddenly cries out : " I
—I remember the man now !   Good Heaven !   *The clerk
your father was paying back wages to that morning!*
Then, by Jupiter ! Ralph Errol is innocent also ! Your
father was putting them in his desk !   Thar'd been big
money stolen before—and they marked to detect theft !
Then your father, Lady Annerley, was the thief óf 'em
all !   Your noble father, Hold Generosity, *put his crimes
on both of us !* "   With this he gives her a look that makes
the woman before him cringe ; then mutters as in a dream :
" And Errol suffered the prisonship and the penal settlement, and poor honest little Sammy Potts was made an
infamous habsconder."
    " How will you prove all this ? " sneers her ladyship.
    " How ! by producing——"
    " Your only written proof is burnt ! "
    Here Potter frightens her by crying : " By you ! oh ir-
famy ! by *you !* " and half draws a pistol, but puts it
back and looks at her, muttering between his clenched
teeth :   " If you war a man ! "
    " Yes ! " returns Sarah desperately, " you'd murder
me as you did your other victims ! "
    " Madam ! " says Mr. Potter solemnly, with a profound
bow, " in my time I have *killed* many men, but never
murdered one.   But if you war one, I'd execute you with
no disturbing conscience !   As it is, I'll tell the jury on
you ! "   This is said with his old-time frontier jauntiness,
but it is the last speech he makes in this interview as a
Texan.
    After this, as she holds up the awful certainty of Eng-
lish justice to his eyes, he thinks of his daughter, and
the more humble spirit of the office boy, Sammy Potts,
comes to the fire-eater Sampson Potter.
    From that time on she crushes him with awful facts
and things he had forgotten.
    He mutters to her : " I'll swear to the jury your father
loaned the coins to me ! "
    " You won't get a chance !   Prisoners are not permitted
to testify in English courts ! "
    " Great Scott ! I forgot that ! "
    " Besides," here her voice is very slow, cutting and
sarcastic, " Sir Jonas Stevens was for twenty-five years

a great banker. During that time the business world knows that he never lent one penny without undoubted and ample security. Do you suppose the jury would believe on your mere word, against the record of a lifetime, that he loaned thirty pounds to a *starving office boy!* Oh no! Old Generosity did not do business IN THAT WAY!" She emphasizes this last by a nasty little laugh.

"No!" groans Potter. "Because Hi caught 'im putting his crime on Ralph H'errol he lent me hinfamy and despair. You can halways borrow them without collaterals." For as he becomes more English in feeling he throws his *h's* about with more Cockney eccentricity. Then he turns to her and mutters: "Lady Hannerley, you destroyed the evidence of it—but it is not too late to do justice now."

"It is too late for me to do anything but save you from an English prison."

"An Henglish prison!" shudders Potter, as he remembers how he feared them when a boy; but here suddenly an awful thought shoots through him and he screams out at her: "MY DARTER! This will break her heart! My darter, Lady Hannerley, MY DARTER! They'll despise her for her daddy's sake. Lady Sarah, repent, confess!" and goes about in such a despair that she shudders and trembles and half repents.

But he goes on: "Think of my darter! How would you feel if you loved a man to have your daddy's shame exposed to him?"

And she cries out as wildly as he, taking the words out of his mouth: "To HIM! To THE MAN I LOVE! No, no; I won't have that! I WON'T HAVE THAT!"

Then the thought of Charley Errol coming to her, from this time on she is adamant. She says very coolly now: "Mr. Potts, you had better fly! Escape from English justice; *it never forgets!* Last night Ralph Errol returned to England as an Australian magnate; last night Ralph Errol as a ticket-of-leave man was again driven an exile from his country to Boulogne;" and then cries out English justice to him, till the natural respect all Englishmen have for law, and the certainty of speedy conviction and punishment to all criminals, rich or poor, high or low, which, unfortunately, does not exist in

America, comes back to Mr. Potter, and he gets nearer every minute to the days of his youth.

Seeing the effect of this upon him, she says to him : " You must fly at once to Paris, then on to Marseilles, where you can get a steamer for Havana, New Orleans, or Galveston by to-morrow morning."

" And then——" mumbles Potter, who hardly thinks for himself now.

" I care not where, so long as you are not seen again," and Lady Sarah, taking Mr. Potter to a smaller door in . the room, opens it, and showing him a back stairway says, looking at her watch : " The express train will leave for Paris in fifteen minutes. In the hall outside my room is a detective armed with a requisition from the English Government ; but by this you can avoid him. Have you money enough for your flight? It would not be safe to visit a bank in Paris. Permit me," offering him money.

He looks at her for a moment, though in a dazed condition, and says : " No, thank you, my lady ; no more loans from the Stevens family !" then staggers out.

But suddenly returns, and touching her on the shoulder as she looks at him with triumph, whispers to her in a voice she hardly knows, it is so husky and broken with misery : " One half second, Lady Annerley, before I, an innocent man, fly as a criminal !—Think that to protect your dead father's name you are destroying two living ones." For at this time Potter believes filial devotion to be the motive of this lady's atrocious conduct. " Think !" he repeats impressively, " that when you burnt my proof of innocence in that flame, you not only destroyed the happiness of my darter and the man she loves, but the union of Ethel Lincoln and the man who loves her !"

" Oh ! that was why—" she gasps. And he gasps back at her : " Confess ! In justice to the living, in mercy to us all !" and here something springs into his brain and makes him as near lunacy as a sane man can be, and he shrieks: " My God ! don't let my darter when she lays down to-night think the daddy she has loved and honored since she was born *a thief* and *a scoundrel !* " And if it had been Sampson Potter who said the words, he would have killed Lady Annerley as he uttered them;

but being now only poor frightened Sammy Potts, he merely pleads to her.

But his torture makes her suffer, and she cries back at him to go before she has the officer to put the manacles upon his wrists.

And getting a little spirit he mutters: *"But when I return!"*

At this she in haughty triumph—for she has now thrown all conscience to the winds—laughs at him and cries: "Ah, you dare not!"

"But if I do, I'll bring you what you want least in all this world, and that is *justice!*"

"Beware of that yourself. *Justice!* ENGLISH JUSTICE! Quick, if you want to catch the train! The detective 'll telegraph! Disguise yourself!" she cries.

And so, crushed by sudden calamity, the savage hero of the prairies, who entered this room as *Sampson Potter* the Texan ranger, staggers out of it flying from English justice, the bogey of youth, in spirit as well as name the meek little office-boy, *Sammy Potts.*

BOOK IV.

Mr. Potter Takes the War-path.

CHAPTER XIX.

THE AWAKING OF THE LION.

Poor old Potter having disappeared, Lady Annerley, radiant with triumph, sends for Sergeant Brackett. That worthy enters very cautiously, being shown in by Lubbins, and is quite relieved to find no one in the apartment but Lady Annerley. In fact he had hesitated about coming up until assured by the ex-waiter that her ladyship was alone.

Not knowing where Sergeant Brackett had obtained the inspiration by which he had exposed her, Lady Annerley has a much higher opinion of the detective's acuteness and determination than he deserves, and has sent for him to try and bribe him to permit Mr. Potter to escape unarrested.

She proffers the officer a seat, and telling him she has a favor to ask of him, finds that, persuaded by her, he may consent to permit Sampson Potter to escape his eye that evening, because the disgrace and shame of the father will break that lovely American girl's heart, and he (Brackett) has a heart also.

After discovering the detective's views on the subject of arresting Mr. Potter, Lady Annerley, however, makes a great mistake.

"I presume when your ladyship told him his boyish crime was discovered, Potter, the Texan, took very high ground," remarks Brackett. "I heard an exclamation of his downstairs. He's a little inclined to be blood-thirsty, I am informed!"

"Bl..odthirsty!" cries Lady Sarah, laughing. "Sampson, the Texan, might be ; but Sammy, the little office boy, was very meek." Then to show her own brilliancy she gives Brackett an account of how suddenly, crushed by the discovery of his boyhood felony, Potter, the Texan, had become frightened of that fearful English justice he remembered in his youth as Sammy Potts, the office boy, and had fled timidly from the awe-inspiring detective. "At this very moment I expect he's trembling, and looking round corners for the awful English policeman."

Here Mr. Brackett becomes awful, indeed ; for springing, up he says determinedly : "Which way did the infernal scoundrel go? I'll have the darbies on that Sammy Potts inside of five minutes!" and would start off very savagely on his mission, but Lady Annerley throws herself before the door, crying : "Let one victim escape!"

"Losing a criminal looked for thirty years! It can't be done, your ladyship," mutters Brackett, and would push past her.

"It shall be done!" she returns, twining her arms about the detective and holding him with hysterical force. "How much money will bribe you to let him fly?"

"Don't tempt a poor man!"

"One hundred pounds!"

"I darsn't listen to you!" and Brackett gets from her.

But while they have been struggling Lady Annerley has been thinking. She says : "Go, you idiot!"

"What do you mean?" returns the officer, taking a last look at her before pursuing Sammy Potts.

"I mean that if you overtake that man—that awful, bloodthirsty Texan—you'll be dead the minute he sees you ; that's all. I saw his pistols!"

"So did I!" says Brackett, returning with a shudder.

"And wanted to prevent his having another murder on his soul, and for his daughter's sake would have spent a hundred pounds to save your life!"

"You have saved Sampson Potter, for his daughter's sake," returns the detective. "I had forgotten Miss Potter. I'll—I'll take your hundred pounds; I've a heart, Lady Annerley—and couldn't you send Lubbins for a drop of brandy?"

Here Mr. Brackett sinks into a chair, a cold per-

spiration upon him at the thought of what he has escaped.

"I'm glad I induced you," whispers her ladyship, and
ringing the bell, sends Mr. Lubbins for what the detective wants ; then, producing a purse filled with Bank of
England notes, gives the sergeant his hundred pounds.
A little sneering smile is on her face while doing this,
for she knows that this bribe to permit the escape of a
fugitive from justice must bind the detective to her interests, soul and body.

Her smile would hardly be as light, however, and
Brackett's tremors would be more intense and his perspiration would be colder, did these two think that there is
but one thing standing between them and death, and that
is the restraining influence in his mind of his daughter ;
for through the door *Sammy Potts* had fled in terror five
minutes before *Sampson Potter* is glaring at them, a drawn
pistol in his hand.

This has all been brought about by a simple revulsion
in his nature. *Sammy Potts* fled from English justice :
but getting to the bottom of the stairs, his mind, that had
been confused by this sudden and crushing blow, begins
to become clear. He commences to think, and as he
thinks becomes the Texan once more. He remembers
his daughter, and that if he flies it will be considered a
proof of his guilt, and determines to come back and, as
he puts it to himself, "face the music ! " Then he mutters : " Arrest the Honorable Sampson Potter ? Will
he ? " and getting very angry at the idea, concludes he
will make it a personal matter with the detective.

Returning up the stairs he reaches the door, and seeing Lady Annerley's smile of triumph and the money
transaction between her and Brackett, he imagines it is
some payment in behalf of a conspiracy against his proving
his innocence, and were it not for the thought of how it
would affect his daughter, the payment would have been
completed between two corpses.   ·

As it is, he watches them with a very evil eye, as
Lubbins brings in Mr. Brackett's brandy and a telegram
to Lady Annerley.

The first of these produces an apparently pleasing effect
upon the police officer ; the second nearly sends Lady
Annerley into a swoon.   ·

She takes it nonchalantly in her hand as if it were hardly worth reading at the present moment, even is about to lay it down ; but reconsidering the matter, tears open the envelope, and glances over it carelessly. As she gazes, there comes such an awful horror into her face that Potter as he looks at her starts ; then uttering a faint cry, half gasp, half moan, Sarah Annerley falls down in a chair. Brackett and Lubbins both run for water and revive her. She looks at the detective, and suddenly forcing herself to strength, after a moment's thought hurriedly writes a few lines and directs them. Then she says : "Sergeant Brackett, this is a matter of life and death with me. Can I depend upon you?"

"I am at your ladyship's service."

"Very well ; here is all the money you can possibly need. Go to Paris at once, and immediately deliver this note to the gentleman to whom it is addressed. In return he will give you a packet ; deliver it to me in person, and for it I will give you five hundred pounds cash !"

And giving the detective the money for his expenses and the note, she says : "Lubbins, go and get a cab for Sergeant Brackett !"

This the servitor does. Then she whispers in such a low voice to Brackett that Potter, at the distance he is from them, cannot hear it ; but it is to this effect, that the officer is first to obtain the packet called for in her letter at any risk ; but in case he is waylaid, pursued, or followed so that it is impossible for him to deliver the packet to her, he is to destroy it in any way he can.

She would say more, but during this time an idea has flown through Potter's mind, and to their ears comes his awful voice crying : "*That letter and telegram, or your lives !*"

At this, with a shriek Brackett bolts through the other door that is open ; but would have fallen dead upon the threshold, had not Lady Annerley sprung between the Texan and the detective crying hoarsely : "Kill me first ! I don't want to live !" Which is quite the truth, this telegram has made her so miserable.

Potter is compelled to lower his pistol or shoot her, and Brackett escapes down the stairway, flies into the cab, and drives for the railway station.

The next instant, with a snarl of rage Sampson Potter

lays his hands in violence for the first time in his life
upon a woman. He cries: "Rattlesnakes and centi-
pedes!" and seizes Lady Annerley by the wrists, for she
has flown back to the table and is burning by means of
the lighted taper the telegram.

Without any ceremony he crushes the fire out with his
naked hands, then, holding her two little wrists together
in one strong fist, with the other opens her delicate
fingers, and though she struggles desperately and vicious-
ly, takes from them the remnants of the dispatch and
tries to read them. While she, reduced to woman's last
weapons, bursts into tears and calls him a coward.

There are only two words that he can distinguish, for
Lady Annerley had fought to destroy the message with
her whole heart, but these are enough to astound him.
The first is its address, Paris ; the second, part of its signature, which he gazes at amazed, for it is that of his son,
the lieutenant in the American navy.

"What deviltry have you been working on him?" he
cries to her. But she answers only by sneers and mocking
laughter, and mutters : "Why don't you kill me? Coward, look at your marks upon my wrists!"

Then he suddenly cries to her : "By the Etarnal! You
want me to miss that Paris train!" and bolts from the
room, leaving her astonished at his acuteness, but also
wringing her hands and muttering despairingly : "When
I had made it certain that nothing could now show my
awful baseness to my love, to have this, the thing I had
thought destroyed in burning Alexandria, the packet
I gave to Errol, arise to strike me down forever in his
heart!"

Mr. Brackett being incited by Lubbins' remark of
"Quick! He's coming downstairs!" drives to the
railway station shrieking to the hackman : "*Vite! Allez!*"
and various other French terms, till that individual says
sternly : "Begorrah, one would think yer was ashamed of
your own language!" Though he remarks soothingly on
being paid his fare at the depot : "Mayhaps your *parlez-
vousing* did *shove* us on a little faster ; the horse is
Frinch!"

Not stopping to discuss the philosophy of this proposition, Brackett is about to hurry into the crowd, thinking
that if pursued he has less chance of detection in the

throng ; when the hack-driver stops him by : " Is this your baste ? " And looking down the detective sees poor little Snapper come panting along, running with all his small might and main after his master.

" Lord ! I must have been frightened to have forgot him ! " mutters the sergeant, picking up the little crea- ture and putting it in his overcoat pocket. Then diving into the station he buys his ticket for Paris, and hurries to the train. Selecting a compartment with only one vacant seat he takes it, knowing that Potter, if following him, will at least be compelled to occupy another. As dogs are not allowed in passenger carriages, Mr. Brackett keeps his little pet in his pocket, soothing him to quiet and sleep by giving him one of his hands to lick, which Snapper does with much vigor, gusto, and affection. This continues till the train, giving a whistle, gets under way, and seeing nothing of his awful pursuer, Sergeant Brackett feels relieved and begins to go over in his mind his instructions from Lady Annerley.

In this, however, he is mistaken, for at the very last moment a cab, its horses in a foam, dashes up to the ter- minus, and Mr. Potter, yelling to the driver : " Pay you when I get back ! " bolts for the train.

Unheeding the execrations of his cabman, who, not understanding English shrieks after this frontier robber in French, Mr. Potter forces his way to the train and boards it just as it moves out of the depot, not noticing though nearly running over, little Van Cott, who has come there with the intention of going to Paris to escape him.

On seeing his dreaded enemy, the poor fugitive gives a frightened shudder and concludes it is best not to go, at least upon that train ; then, noticing the downcast though excited appearance of the Texan, a new idea comes to him. Muttering to himself : " By George, I've run old Potter out of Boulogne ! " he makes up his mind to re- main in town over night, and going up to the *Hôtel des Bains*, takes a dinner and drink or two with great enjoy- ment. These so excite him that he begins to persuade himself that it is owing entirely to fear of his mighty self that the Texan has fled in such a hurry, and he makes a night of it ; his last distinguishable words to the waiters as they put him to bed being : " I—awh—hic—would have

spared the old man for his daughter—she's—hic—a
duced fine gal !"

Mr. Potter, jammed in between an Alsacian who speaks
German-French, and a Magyar whose dialogue is Hun-
garian-German, finds that he can gain little information
from either as to the route to Paris or how he shall proceed after he gets there.

Fortunately, finding in his pocket a guide-book that
Colonel Cottontree had advised him to buy in London
the night before, he looks this over, and coming upon a
bill of fare in conjoined French and English thinks rather
contentedly that they can't starve him as long as the
waiters can read. Then his commissariat arranged for,
like other great generals Potter proceeds to lay out the
plan of his campaign.

He doesn't know where his son is to be found in Paris,
otherwise he would drive to his address at once. The
young man's last communication was a letter sent to the
address of his London bankers and received by him on
his arrival from America. The place from which it had
been mailed Mr. Potter forgets, but imagines it was
Genoa, and thinks that too far off to trouble his head
about, as he knows it is in Italy or Africa, or somewhere
down south.

Then the guide-book reminds him of Colonel Cottontree, and he thinks that if any one can find his son on
sudden notice in Paris Cottontree's the man, and so
arranges in his mind this plan of action : First, to make
sure that Brackett is on the train ; if so, to follow him cautiously, being certain that he will lead him to his son ;
second, should he by any chance lose track of the detective,
to go to Colonel Cottontree and get him to find the lieutenant for him. For Mr. Potter is now morally sure that
this telegram from his son is vitally connected in some
unknown way with the motives and action of Lady
Annerley ; though, rack his brain as much as he likes, he
cannot guess how. So he dismisses the matter from his
mind muttering : "Tarnation ! This beats the fifteen
puzzle—this does !" Referring to an invention that
made a number of sane men lunatics about that time,
and for which Mr. Potter has a profound admiration.

During these reflections the train, which is a tidal express connecting with the Folkestone boat, and which

reaches Paris in a little over four hours and a half,
dashes up the valley of the Liane.

Mr. Potter consults his watch and discovers it is just
after 5 P. M.; then examines his guide-book, and with
some careful study concludes that it should arrive in
Paris about half past nine, and will probably stop at
Abbeville, Amiens, and Creil before reaching the French
capital. He is not very sure of this, but has a kind of
hazy idea this will be about his schedule, as he terms it.

He makes up his mind to become certain at Abbeville
that Brackett is on board, and the train stopping at Mon-
treuil Verton a moment, he nearly has an accident, as
alighting for that purpose he is almost left behind; the
halt being only for a few seconds. At Abbeville he makes
the attempt again, but as Brackett keeps close in his
compartment, and it is now considerably after six o'clock
and growing dark, does not succeed. But Brackett from
his seat sees and recognizes Mr. Potter with a shudder,
as the Texan strides up the platform glaring into the
carriages.

All this trouble and non-success makes his pursuer very
angry; the continual Babel of French and foreign languages, none of which he can understand, aggravates and
annoys him; enforced silence makes him feel very helpless and irritates him; and by the time the train runs
into the brightly lighted station at Amiens the American
is in the worst humor he has been in that day, which is
saying a great deal. He glares impatiently out of the
window of his compartment, for the guide-book suggests
refreshments at this place, and refreshments always mean
delay. And now he is determined to find the skulking
varmint if he's alive and about.

In this rather difficult matter, in a large, pressing,
surging crowd, he is aided by accident. Mr. Brackett has thought the matter over, and concluded it may
be safer to visit Paris by another train rather than the
one that carries Mr. Potter. As soon as his compartment
is opened he has sprung from it and is making for the
exit to the station. The Texan, locked up in his compartment, sees him, and feeling very much like a chained rat-
terrier smelling a fleeing rat, raises such an awful hub-
bub for the guard to open his door that the gatekeeper
in charge of the exit hears the row, and thinking it an

escaping pickpocket closes the doors, and Brackett cannot leave the station.

This movement has been noticed by Potter, and the moment he gets out of his carriage he charges to the exit, and remains there cutting off retreat, while the detective buries himself deeply in the crowd, and slinking back to another compartment, thinks in a downcast mood how he will escape Mr. Potter in Paris. He makes no attempt to leave the train at Creil, and so pursued and pursuer come into the great illuminated *Gare Chemin de Fer du Nord* at an hour when Paris is full of light, life, and that vivacity of movement and action for which the capital of France is noted.

CHAPTER XX.

A NIGHT IN PARIS.

MR. POTTER alights with a very serious task before him ; that is, in a vast and unknown city, ignorant of its language, geography, and customs, to follow a man who is trying to avoid him, and losing track of the man to obtain an interview with his son, with whose habits, usual re. sorts and address, in this new and unexplored metropo. lis, he is entirely unacquainted. No person is by education and accomplishment less fitted for such a labor than Mr. Potter; and yet no man, by natural shrewdness, wiry physique, and undaunted determination, better equipped for its successful performance than the Texan. He mutters to himself : " I've tracked Injuns on the prairies, and can trail a policeman in Par*ie !* " For he has been trying to increase his French vocabulary in the past few hours, and has added " Par*ie* " to the list.

However, the crowd is so vast that there is great danger of his never even beginning the trail ; for after leaving the train he has found it impossible to get his eye upon Brackett ; but at last, as he is swept out of the terminus, he catches sight of little Snapper frisking about, delighted to escape from the detective's pocket, and is horrified to perceive the sergeant about to get into a cab. If Potter spoke the language of the country. to call an-

other cab and bid the man follow. Brackett would be the
work of an instant ; but the Texan, with a groan, realizes he doesn't speak French well enough for such intri-
cate instructions.

Brackett has stepped into the cab with Snapper ; the
driver is about to whip up ; in another moment he will
be gone. With a quickness born of despair Potter lifts
up his voice and hails the departing cabman. Though
half a hundred jehus try to seize upon him for their
own, he bolts through them, pursuing the cab on foot,
the driver of which, with Parisian shrewdness, preferring
two fares to one, pulls up his horse, and with a smile on
his face waits for the Texan to overtake him.

This he does ; but as he comes along Brackett puts out
his head, and seeing him, bolts from the cab and goes hurriedly along the street on foot, and Potter, noting this, goes
on after him, caring nothing for the excited and astonished
exclamations of the unfortunate driver who, bereft of both
fares instead of gaining another, follows along also, with
varying polite entreaties and passionate blasphemies.

So they make a curious procession, Sergeant Brackett,
with a pale face, marching on the sidewalk at the front ;
little Snapper dancing along all about his master ; and behind them Potter the Texan, with a grim and determined
scowl upon his countenance, though there is a twinkle in
his eye that sometimes rolls itself back toward the hackman. This gentleman drives close to the curbstone and
just at the American's rear, at one moment piteously
begging : "*Eh, bien, messieurs ! Vous m'avez pris !
Gardez moi ! Je suis engager. Faites votre course avec
moi !*" waving his hand, and smiling a Gallic smile ; at
the next bursting forth into "*Sacré cochons !*" and other
more awful Parisian execrations which he makes vivid
with a gesticulation wild as that of a jumping-jack and
peculiar to the *boulevarts*.

So they come along the *Rue Saint Quentin* to the *Rue
de La Fayette*, at the corner of which the driver can follow no further, for he goes into a kind of French frenzy,
and explodes into a million of wicked vocal fireworks.

Turning along this street Sergeant Brackett follows it.
as well as Potter can make out from a hasty glance at
the moon, which is now up, in a generally southwesterly
course   and he is nearly right, for the detective has been

in Paris before, and is going toward the *Place de l'Opera* and fashionable *boulevarts*.

The night is a beautiful, balmy, autumn one, and Paris is in its glory. The shops are well lighted, and as they come near the public centers the crowd grows larger and Brackett more difficult to keep in sight. In fact, were it not for Snapper, who dances about in the gaslight, Potter would have lost the detective long ago.

This the Texan perceives, and mutters : " A few more *parley vous* and I'm a goner ! " but now finding in his pocket a piece of forgotten cord that had been economically put by from some dry goods package, a flash of hope comes to him. He runs quickly forward, and seizing little Snapper, who is by no means afraid of him, remembering him as the man who made nice noises in the shooting gallery, ties this string to the terrier's collar, for he is determined *to track Brackett about Paris by scent,* and here is the hound ready made to his hand.

Missing his dog the detective looks back, and partly seeing, partly guessing Potter's design, and knowing Snapper's acute powers, now hurries forward with a speed born of despair. In this way they go over a mile, and now approach the *Place de l'Opera*, the crowd every moment becoming larger and giving Potter more and more trouble. And here a cruel accident happens to the Texan ; Snapper, his hound, who has been running up to this time stanch and true, encounters and must stop to smell another terrier, which delays him so much that, taking advantage of a string of carriages, Brackett crosses the street, gets them between him and Potter, and now entirely disappears.

Almost forcing his way through the crowd the Texan crosses also, but after looking about a little time without success, mutters to himself : " If it hadn't been for my darter I'd have let daylight through that policeman long ago ! "

Then he resigns himself to the guidance of little Snapper who goes smelling about, and to Potter's delight takes up a trail which leads through the *Place de l'Opera.* At the end of this Snapper comes out on the *Boulevart des Capucines,* and Potter of Texas gives almost a gasp at Paris at night in its glory.

The lighted *cafés,* the numerous carriages, cabs and

omnibuses, the gayly dressed men and women—the whole holiday appearance of everybody who is out of doors this night—and this is one of Paris' out-of-door evenings—amaze the Texan, who has never seen the like before and thinks it a kind of dream of fairy land. He mutters something about a town on a picnic, and then more gloomily makes a remark about a needle in a haystack.

Noting that even Snapper, disconcerted by the unusual scene, can apparently follow his master no further, he picks up the dog and puts it in his overcoat pocket, for the string attached to the little creature's collar ties, entangles, and trips people up, and they do not like it. Thus jostled by the surging throng, and far from his bearings and moorings, Mr. Potter lifts up his eyes despairingly and stands gazing around for an American face, knowing fun and his countrymen are never very far apart.

But after waiting a few minutes none seem to come along, and being extremely hungry, Mr. Potter looks about him for an eating-house, and finding the *Café de la Paix* right beside him, enters that gorgeous restaurant.

He returns the waiter's polite smiles. Then one suggesting : "*Cabinet particulier!*" nods his head and mutters : "*Oui!* Bring it quick !" and is immediately shown upstairs into a private room in the *entresol*.

"They're remarkably polite," thinks Potter ; "must have heard of me somewhere ; perhaps they know my darter. She's been humming about these regions."

He is, however, brought from these reflections quite suddenly. The waiter, after a preliminary flourish, produces a bill of fare and pushes it under Potter's nose.

"I thought I ordered something downstairs," mutters the old gentleman ; but the servant apparently insisting, he produces his guide-book and selects from its bill of fare in joint English and French what he wants, pointing out the dishes to the waiter. Next getting hold of a wine list he puts his finger on *Veuve Cliquot* and says : "That's the ticket ! That'll knock the blues out of me !" Then to indicate speed, he, by gesticulation, shows himself to be very hungry, by compressing and rubbing his abdomen.

This, combined with the Texan's morose but excited expression, makes the waiter frightened ; he thinks Potter very sick and is about to rush for a doctor; but at last understanding, and word being brought to the office that there is an American in the establishment, Amadie, a *garçon* who thinks he speaks English, is sent to Mr. Potter, who now gets what he wants and makes a very fair meal of it, only being seriously interrupted once, and that is by Snapper.

Being hungry, also, when the meat is brought on, the dog becomes so fearfully restless and whiningly uneasy that Potter, thinking the beast smells his master, jumps hurriedly up, searches the room, and wanders savagely about the passage-ways. Noting at last that Snapper only becomes excited as he approaches the provisions, Potter, with a sudden guffaw, guesses the trouble with the dog, and transfers him from his pocket to the dining-table. He and the intelligent little creature take their meal together, Snapper performing such tricks of gastronomy, and using his teeth so vigorously, his eyes so thankfully, and his ears so vivaciously that he literally eats his way into the Texan's big heart. But now Potter looks at his watch; it is after ten o'clock, and he feels he must be moving.

In fact the whole performance so far has been a rapid one. Brackett had come most of the way down the *Rue de La Fayette* at as near a run as a walk could be, and Potter has been waited upon quite promptly and eaten with American rapidity, but he feels that it is absolutely necessary to find Colonel Cottontree at once. So, after paying his bill, he stimulates Amadie's English by a couple of francs, and showing the waiter his friend's card, says: "Cab." That worthy reads the address, No. 34 *Boulevart Malesharbes ;* then delights Mr. Potter by running out onto the sidewalk with him, calling a *voiture*, and giving the necessary explanations to the driver.

The Texan is now whirled along the *Boulevarts des Capucines* and *Madeleine*, and turning a corner, in about three minutes is at his friend's address. But here another obstacle confronts and confounds the wanderer. Colonel Cottontree is out, and so is his servant. Potter, after great trouble, jabber, and gesticulation, discovering this from the *concierge*, concludes not to wait for his friend, as he knows Cottontree is an all-night man, never returning to his domicile till the small hours of the morning.

Entering the cab again he calls out savagely, " Back ! Home ! " for he·has an idea born of desperation to once more consult Amadie, the waiter.   Not understanding his order, the driver thinks he can do no better than show Mr. Potter the sights of Paris, and proceeds, in spite of growls, imprecations, and. threatenings, to give that gentleman a drive in the *Champs Elysées.*

Here the Texan, though foaming at the mouth with rage, gazes around in a kind of astonished ecstasy.   The flaring gas jets, electric lights, sparkling fountains, and beautiful and elegantly costumed women make this pleasure garden of Paris seem like a fairy *fête* this perfect October evening to his frontier eyes.   He mutters to himself faintly : " Great Scottie !   I'll come back here if I live."

Then thinks : " This is too gay and festive a spree for *all* our boys to be out of it," and disregarding ·the dissenting gestures of the driver, he jumps out of his cab, and would proceed on foot, hoping to meet some face that looks as if it came from across the Atlantic, or to hear some words that have a meaning to his mind, did not Snapper at this moment astonish him.

He had placed the little dog beside him in the cab, and Snapper had enjoyed the picturesque sight also.   Potter upon alighting is about to replace the animal in his pocket, when with a low cry the terrier flies suddenly into the alluring entrance of a *café chantant,* and bolting after his whilom pet, the Texan finds himself in the *Des Ambassadeurs.*

No one demands an admission fee, and Potter amazed beams upon the gorgeous scene murmuring :   " I've heard the Français were great at doing the polite ; but curse· me if I ever guessed afore this they was so all-fired generous!"

Then pursuing Snapper, who is about to run down the aisle, he picks him up and secures him in his pocket, and next utters a grunt of surprised delight, for there, a dozen rows ahead of him, is Sergeant Brackett, of the British detective force, about to leisurely sit down and gaze at the fascinating pirouettes of a ballet-girl performing on the stage of this open-air theater.

This unexpected good fortune comes about from the

simple reason that Mr. Brackett, having called upon Lieutenant Potter, has found that young gentleman out, and is now killing a little time before calling again. It makes the Texan, however, feel so comfortable, that, after resolving to quietly wait and follow the sergeant out, and then if he again attempts to run away, let daylight through him, he sinks into a chair, and a waiter being already at his elbow, orders a drink.

Brackett, interested in the ballet-girl, has not observed how the affection of his dog has once more betrayed him to his enemy, and would probably be entirely defeated, but now the peculiar customs of the place come to the detective's assistance, and again save him on this night in Paris.

The entrance to this Temple of Thespis, Terpsichore and Thalia is free, but it is the habit of every one entering its open portal to order a drink, cigar, or something of the sort, the price whereof varies with the location of the seat the individual selects. To those near the stage the charge per drink is three francs, about the center of the house the tariff falls to two francs, while to people seated modestly in the rear the price is only one franc for the same liquor or cigar.

The visitors apparently pay for refreshments, but really pay for seats.

Now Mr. Potter has taken a chair in the modest rear of the place, and his first drink only costs him one franc. But, partly to get a better view of the performing ladies, whose charms begin to appeal to his gallant Western heart, and partly to keep a closer look-out upon Brackett, who has also moved his seat apparently to more closely inspect the allurements of the stage beauties, the Texan begins to move about in a free and easy way from one unoccupied chair to another. And now his drinks begin to rise in price in a manner that astonishes, irritates, and makes combative Mr. Potter, who is very generous, but doesn't like to be imposed upon as a fool and won't be swindled nor robbed.

As his second waiter charges him two francs for the same bad whisky that a moment before had cost him but one, he begins to get angry ; and when the third insists in an impudent and threatening way that whisky has gone up once more, and the tariff is now three francs per glass, and would almost use force to collect it, Mr. Potter astonishes the *Café des Ambassadeurs.*

The lady singing upon the stage stops her song with a fearful shriek, the orchestra gives one discordant bray and is silent, the spectators arise in dismay, for the Honorable Sampson has carried the waiter, a brawny Alsacian, into the center aisle of the establishment, where he can have more room for the business, and is literally wiping the floor with the unfortunate Frenchman, whose voice rises up over the tumult in piteous appeals of agitated terror.

But Potter here suddenly leaves his victim and would bolt for the door himself, for Brackett has seen and recognized him, and with a wild look upon his face is flying out.

Impressed by Potter's efforts to escape, several of the fighting brigade of the establishment, that in American slang would be termed "bouncers," bar his way to the door, and would now proceed to take vengeance upon this disturber of the festivities.

Seeing this the Texan raises up his voice and cries, with a very dangerous look upon his face : "If thar's any American round, for God's sake let him come quick, BEFORE I KILL ALL THESE WAITERS !"

Here a voice answers him in English : "I'm an American and I'LL SAVE THE WAITERS !" And Mr. Potter perceives a young gentleman in elaborate evening dress forcing and elbowing his way through the crowd.

His appearance causes a buzz ; the ladies gleam on him in admiration and the men gaze upon him, with perhaps a little envy. He is one of the Paris celebrities of the day. He calls out something in French and the waiters all murmur : "*Le Prince de Baccarat!*" and bow down to him and are saved.

"I'm right glad you come!" says Potter. "I should have turned loose on 'em in a second, and then they'd have thought the siege of Parie had begun again."

"Yes. I knew I had to speak quick," says this young gentleman, who has traveled over Europe and America, and understands the man to whom he is talking. "I'll arrange this affair for you," and he explains to Mr. Potter the peculiar custom of the place that had enraged him.

Then he turns to the proprietor and soon settles the matter with him and the attendant *gendarmes*, and Mr. Potter finds the way open for him to pursue Sergeant Brackett once more.

" Can I do anything else for you ?   You don't seem to understand the language, and I always like to assist my traveling compatriots.   Permit me ! " and with this the young man gives the Texan his card.

" You're almighty kind, Mr. Deucey ! " returns Potter, "and if you could take me to my son I'd bless you to my dying day.   It's a matter of life and death, and almighty quick life and death too ! "

" Who is your son ? " inquires his listener, getting serious, for Potter's tones indicate he means what he says.

" Lieutenant Pottei of the U. S. Navy."

" I know him." returns young Deucey, and, being a man of action, hurries the old Texan through the crowd, and at the entrance pops him into his own private carriage, and getting in beside him, tells his coachman : " Press Club, like lightning : " Then he takes a long look at Potter, and with a surreptitious whistle says : " So you're Miss Potter's father ? '

" Yes ; and I'm mighty glad to meet you !   I was most despairing," murmurs the Honorable Sampson, gazing at his guide with affection.

And glad he should be, for Providence has been kind to Mr. Potter at last.   He has fallen in the hands of the man probably best fitted to smooth his road in Paris for him, *Le Prince de Baccarat*, a young American gentleman, on whom at this time the Goddess of Fortune is smiling so kindly that she has made him almost a millionaire by his winnings at this most desperate of games.   A man who hazards a million francs on the turn of a card is a hero on the Parisian *Boulevarts ;* everybody knows him and he knows a good many of the everybody.   He has had dinner at the Press Club the evening before with Lieutenant Potter, and is aware that gentleman has his rooms in that building.   He speaks French like a native, and under his guidance the carriage flies up the *boulevarts*, and passing the Opera House, they alight and enter the magnificent Press Club, now blazing with light and just beginning to assume its usual all-night gayety and brilliancy.

Chaperoned by Mr. Deucey, the doors fly open to Mr.
Potter, who might have knocked on them forever on
his own account. And without any of the delays and
formalities that would, under ordinary circumstances,
have taken place, they go up the grand stair-case and
the Texan enters the *baccarat* room. Thus vouched for,
the waiters bow to the ground before him, and though
his wild Western costume seems in curious contrast to
the brilliant evening dress that every one else wears, Mr.
Potter strides through the room, commented upon but not
hindered, and yells : " Houston, my boy ! at last ! "!

And Lieutenant Potter, who is just about to sit down at
one of the tables, returning : " Great heavens ! Is that
you, dad ? " they immediately seize each other's hands
and nearly wring off each other's arms.

CHAPTER XXI.

THE PACKET FROM EGYPT.

" I've got life and death business with you, lad," whispers Potter.

"Then come this way ! " says his son. And Mr.
Deucey suggesting a private room, the two Potters go
into it. Here the old man says : " Lady Annerley—
what did you telegraph her about ? "

"Why," returns the young man, " I arrived at Paris
yesterday, and having a packet to deliver to her—— "

" What packet was that ? "

" One that she had given young Errol before he was
wounded. One he had promised to return to her."

" Ah ! " This is a snort of perception from Potter.

" I called at her hotel here, and she not being in town
obtained her address at Boulogne and telegraphed her I
would go there in person to-morrow to deliver it. She
had seemed to value it very much, and had sought all
over Abdallah the Moor's house for it in Egypt," he continues.

" That packet contains your father's salvation from the
state's prison ! I've got that she-devil at last ! " cries
Potter in triumph. " Give it to me ! "

" I can't ! " returns the son with a white face ; for either his father is mad or means what he says.

" Can't ? " shrieks the Texan. " Why not ? "

" Because five minutes ago I received a written order from Lady Annerley, and delivered it to her agent."

The last words of this speech are not heard by the elder Potter. He has sprung out of the room to follow the detective ; but a moment after he returns, seeing the hopelessness of immediate pursuit. Then he takes his son aside and mutters : " He'll be going back on the railway to Boulogne. If that packet gets into her hands I'm a convict ! Your daddy, your innocent daddy, boy, is a convict, and you and your sister disgraced ! "

Here young Potter, who, when he met his father a minute or two before this, was smiling, utters a low cry and his features twitch with sudden anguish, for he knows his father, and, persuaded he is not mad, believes him.

His naval promptitude of action comes to him. He springs into the hall, sends a waiter for a cab, and asks young Deucey, who has waited outside to see if he can be of any assistance, for the manner of the two men shows the affair is serious: " What railways go to Boulogne ? "

" The *Chemin de Fer du Nord*—but after passing Creil there are several roundabout roads and branches, one by way of Calais, besides the direct route."

" Are there any others ? "

" None but those so circuitous that they need hardly be considered."

" Can you tell me the time when the next train leaves the terminus ? "

" No, but I'll find out." And after consultation with the railway guide he says : " 11.05, and you can catch it if you drive fast."

" Much obliged. You'll excuse our going ? " returns young Potter, and he gets his father, who has remained in the private room, but now comes out of it with a look upon his face that makes Mr. Deucey shudder, though at *baccarat* he is considered to have very strong nerves.

" God bless you, sir ! " mutters Potter, wringing that young gentleman's hand. " You've been kind to me when I needed a friend, and I'll come back to Paris and see you if I live ! "

" Will you ? " returns *Le Prince de Baccarat.* " Then
I'll show it to you."

And Potter whispering to his son he'll explain matters
as they go along, they spring into the cab and are driven
to the railway station as fast as a French horse can carry
them.

In the cab the lieutenant tells his father what he knows
about the packet taken from the body of the dragoman,
Osman Ali, by the sergeant of marines, and delivered to
him.

The old man gives his son his early history and relates
the wondrous tale of that afternoon, the young man staring
at him astounded. Then he concludes with these words :
" I've thought the whole tangle out.   You say she went to
Egypt immediately after her scoundrel father, Sir Jonas
Stevens', death ?   Looking into God's eye the dying thief
confessed to save the living convict.   Lady Annerley
went to Alexandria to tell Charley Errol *the truth.*   THAT
PACKET IS THE CONFESSION !   But after he fought for
her, she grew to love him and feared he would despise
her for her daddy's awful crime against his father, and
wanted it back again.   That packet is my only chance
before an English jury, and whether the detective lives
or dies—boy ! do you mind me ? *lives or dies*—that
packet must never reach Saharah Hannerley's hands ;
otherwise she'll burn it, as she did that receipt, and
your daddy's a goner."

" I understand," mutters the lieutenant, with quite a
sad face ; for though he would not admit it now, Lady Annerley's magnificent beauty had made such an impression
on the young man that, hearing Charley Errol was going
to marry an English girl, he had got leave from his ship
that was stationed at Nice and ran up to Paris, with a sneaking thought in his mind of capturing the beautiful widow
himself ; hence his immediate call and prompt telegram.

Then Potter suddenly suggests with a shiver : " Do
you think he can have mailed that packet to her ? "

" No," returns his son ; " for she knows that we could
make such a showing by to-morrow morning that no post-
office in France would deliver it to her without examination. She wanted to make absolutely sure of it and destroy
it herself."

Here both Potter and his son fail to give Lady Annerley's acuteness due credit. They do not guess that her foresight had suggested that, in some way unknown to her at the time, Potter or his son might guess the importance of the packet ; and she had instructed Sergeant Brackett, in case of close pursuit and in danger of losing it, he is to destroy the document.

By this time the Potters are at the railway station. They leave the cab, and, the lieutenant speaking French, have no trouble in buying tickets for Boulogne. The depot is well lighted, and after getting inside, the two have time to make a complete search of the train ; looking carefully into every carriage, in spite of the annoyance and protests of the guard, who, however, is too tired and sleepy to give them any great amount of hindrance. There are but few passengers, and these mostly local, upon this late train, as it stops at all the stations on the road and is a very slow affair, laying over at Amiens for several hours.

They have two minutes left for consultation before the train leaves. " You are sure he is not on the cars ? " says the lieutenant. " I only saw the man for a minute and might miss him."

" Perfectly sure. I didn't see him and his dog didn't smell him," returns Potter, fondling little Snapper, who is ensconced comfortably in his pocket. " Is there any other train for the cuss to get to Boulogne on ? "

After consulting the time-table hurriedly, the lieutenant replies : " No ! this train, though it will lie over in Amiens, will be the first by at least an hour to put a man in Boulogne. None of the expresses leave till to-morrow morning."

" Then he's on board of this—somewhar. He's not going to let me head him off at Lady Hannerley's door," cries Potter.

" Well, if he is not on the train now he has had no opportunity of getting on it since we've been talking," returns the young officer ; for the two have held this conversation near the entrance and kept a sharp lookout upon all new-comers, which are not very many at this time of night.

" He must be on the train somewhar," returns Potter, doggedly, " and I'm going on it."

" Very well," says his son ; " I'll go with you."

"Then," whispers the father, " sonny, he is not to get to that woman with that packet *alive*. Them's my orders !"

"All right. Let me have one of your pistols—you always carry two."

"You ain't harmed?" gasps Potter, astonished. " Haven't I always told you to carry a gun? You never know when it may come handy."

"You have two," repeats the lieutenant.

"Yes, but I may need 'em both. You see, I may have to stand off the local police."

"For God's sake," mutters his son impressively, " re-member that though you may kill a few *gendarmes* you can't whip the whole of France," for the young man knows that his father is now in a deadly humor, and fears he may do something very rash.

"Yes, I know that," says Potter. "But I believe I could give a very good account of myself." With this modest speech he hands his son one of his pistols. And the guard crying "All aboard !" they jump into a first-class compartment and the train rolls out of the Paris sta-tion.

Being a local, it stops for a few minutes at Saint Denis, on the outskirts of the city, and among the peo-ple boarding the train is a sailor, who goes quietly into a third-class carriage.

The two Americans discuss the affair under their breath as the train slips along the rails, and getting all the details the lieutenant looks even more serious than before, and becomes as angry and excited as his father. He mutters to the old man : " Don't you fear if I put my eyes on Mr. Brackett. He'll no more escape me than he would you." Then giving his father's hand a silent squeeze, the tears come into the young man's eyes as he looks at old Potter's now almost despairing face.

"If I don't get square on this matter, don't you think she deserves killing ?" asks the father, as if for advice.

"Yes," replies the young man ; " but don't you do it. Remember Ida."

"My God, don't talk of *her !*" mutters the Texan, the water getting near his eyes.

"Have you telegraphed her ?"

"No."

"Then she may be anxious. Hearing of your sudden departure from Boulogne, she may fear you to be——"

"A thief? Not she! Houston, don't slander your sister; that gal's the truest grit of any of us!" says Potter with a stern voice, interrupting him.

But the train here stopping at Chantilly, Potter continues: "If I don't get something soothing, I shall break right out to cursing. There are ladies in the carriage, Houston; I'll get into another one and smoke a cigar. Come along."

"No, thank you, dad. I haven't got over the shock of what you told me yet. I'll stay here and think it over."

"Very well," returns Potter, and he leaves the carriage and goes to a third-class compartment, where he lights up, and the smoke rather seems to soothe matters for him.

The lieutenant turns the affair over and over in his mind, and the more he thinks of it the more serious and horrible its consequences seem to him. He becomes so engrossed in this matter that the train stops at Creil and then goes on again as far as Clermont before he thinks of rejoining his father. He now imagines he would like a cigar also, and leaving his luxurious first-class compartment goes to the third-class one he saw old Potter enter; but he does not find him. Then he looks through all the third-class carriages and finally all the others twice and carefully, but without success. *Sampson Potter of Texas is not on the train.*

Hastily questioning the guard, that official is not sure, but thinks he saw a sailor at Creil leave the compartment the lieutenant indicates; and that after him rather hurriedly came a man answering to the description given to him of the elder Potter.

The lieutenant hastily questions the guard as to the possibility of returning to Creil; but finds there is no passenger train for nearly two hours; then, thinking the matter over, concludes to go on to Boulogne at once, so as to prevent Sergeant Brackett delivering the packet to Lady Annerley if by any accident he escapes his father.

He has no fear for the old man's personal safety; in fact, he unconsciously repeats his sister's ideas on the subject, for he once or twice says to himself with a sickly

kind of a laugh: "God help the poor detective!"
But he is very much astonished and surprised at what
has occurred, and indulges in a continuous brown study
until he reaches Amiens.

Here he gets a much greater astonishment. He is
compelled to lie over at this place for nearly three hours,
and being too excited to sleep remains about the *buffet*
and station. Some two hours after his arrival a telegraph official, noticing his foreign appearance, approaches
him, asking if his name is Lieutenant Potter ; and on
being answered affirmatively, takes him to the telegraph
office, where he receives a message.

This he opens hurriedly, glances it over, stares at it,
and then demands that they repeat the dispatch back to
Creil and see if it is correct.

This is done, and being answered "O. K !" Lieutenant Potter reads it all over again, and, his eyes big with
surprised astonishment, mutters: "What the deuce can
this mean ?" For the telegram received by him reads :

"CREIL, *October* 17, 1882, 2 A. M.
"To LIEUTENANT POTTER, U. S. NAVY, ON THE ROAD BETWEEN
HERE AND BOULOGNE :
" There's the devil to pay. Meet me Boulogne Dépôt, at 9.25,
morning train. Have arrested Samuel Potts, and am bringing him
along, gagged, and guarded by two *gendarmes.*
"SERGEANT BRACKETT,
" *British Detective.*"

CHAPTER XXII.

THE FLIGHT OF THE DETECTIVE.

WHEN Sampson Potter leaves his son at Chantilly and
transfers himself from a first-class compartment to a third
class in order to enjoy his cigar, he is nearer to despair
than he has ever been in his eventful life. The whole
awful affair has come upon him so suddenly and unexpectedly that he is partially in a dazed condition. As
long as he had his enemy, the detective, in sight, he was
hopeful and alert ; now, his opponent having disappeared,
he smokes his cigar in a dreary, despairing sort of manner,
and thinks it a cursed bad one, though it isn't. From
this, however, he is awakened by Snapper. The train has

hardly left Chantilly before the dog makes him angry by suddenly, without any apparent cause, trying to tear the lining out of his overcoat. He says savagely: "Hi, Snapper! Quiet!"

But Snapper won't quiet.

He now makes a frantic attempt to walk off bodily with both Potter and his overcoat along the seat of the carriage in the direction of the other side of the compartment. To move at all he has to do this, for, there being a large overhanging lapel to the Texan's grea. warm pocket, Snapper has been buttoned in, partly for his security and partly for his comfort, as the night has been growing chilly and is now cold. These silent but desperate efforts are repeated so often that Potter looks round to discover the cause, and thinks : "We must have rats aboard ! "

But discovering no rodents, he gives a sudden stare ; for Snapper is trying to bite his way out of the pocket in a frantic and determined manner, and all the time straining his little strength to crawl toward the other side of the compartment ; and an idea suddenly has flashed through Potter's brain : " *If it ain't rats, it's his master !* "

The Texan is now awake and peering with his ferret eyes into the gloom of the compartment, which is partially illuminated by an oil lamp.

The seat Mr. Potter is on is the one next to the locomotive ; and, as is common in all third-class carriages, runs entirely across the compartment. There is only another bench to examine and that is the one opposite him. Upon it sit a French peasant woman of about fifty and three men; two of them small shopkeepers and apparently friends, as they are talking together ; the other, a sailor by his dress, who is trying to decipher a French newspaper that he holds quite close to his face. After looking them all over, Potter gives a disappointed sigh and relapses into gloomy meditation. Sergeant Brackett is not in the carriage.

But he has hardly time to settle himself back in his seat, when Snapper makes a more vigorous attempt, if possible, than ever to escape from the overcoat and get toward the other side of the car. " Curse it ! I wonder if he'll be quiet if I take the little cuss where he wants to go," thinks Potter, and transfers himself to the other end of his bench, where he says : " Now I reckon you'll give us a rest, Snapper. If you don't I'll cuff you ! " for the dog's uneasiness annoys the Texan in his present irritable state.

But the demon of unrest seems to have entered the little beast's body ; he now makes a charge to cross the car. This would put him right in the lap of the sailor. Potter instinctively looks over, and his gaze becomes petrified. He can't see the whole of the tar's face for the newspaper, but upon the weather-beaten forehead, though the night is cold and chilly, he observes a great drop of perspiration slowly gather. Then Snapper gives a frantic whine and the perspiration falls with a little splash upon the newspaper the sailor reads.

And as the perspiration drops, so does Potter, as he sinks back in his chair in amazed astonishment and mutters : " Wall, I'm darned ! "

Potter's sensations overcome him ; Brackett's are even more horrible. For the sailor is the redoubtable sergeant, who has decided to use the consummate arts he has read of in great French detective stories to baffle his pursuer.

This idea came into his head while flying from the *café chantant*, and as soon as he obtained the packet from Lieutenant Potter he drove to a theatrical costumer and there donned the disguise of a sailor, the woman in charge kindly making his face up for the character, supposing him going to some fancy ball. Retaining only his overcoat, and leaving orders for his other every-day garments to be forwarded to his address at Boulogne, the sergeant had found that he had sufficient time, and had driven out to Saint Denis to board the train there, considering that course safer than going to the main station of the railway in Paris.

Seated in his third-class compartment, with his packet secure in his inner pocket, he had felt safe in person and in purse, for he had considered Lady Annerley's five hundred pounds as good as earned until he saw the remorseless Potter enter the carriage to enjoy his cigar.

After that, for a few blessed moments he has been comparatively sure he would not be recognized ; but from the instant Snapper has begun his extraordinary performances, he has regarded himself as lost, knowing and even cursing the devoted love of his pet that is betraying him. His nervous agony has become so acute that when Snapper actually brings Potter opposite to him, the tell-tale perspiration will show, to his undoing.

"Good Lord!" thinks Brackett, as the Texan utters his suppressed exclamation; "I'm gone now!"

And so he would be if Potter were really sure. Then the detective would never pass out of that car alive with that packet in his possession.

But the arts of civilization are not those of barbarism, and the old frontiersman does not know that many costumers in Paris keep open to a late hour for the convenience of masked balls. He might even suspect the dress, but the sailor's face seems genuine, Mr. Potter not knowing the wonderful art of facial make-up, and the extraordinary power of grease-paint properly applied. And he mutters to himself: "If I was real certain"—reasoning that he cannot shoot a man just because a dog wants to smell him, and determines to test the identity of the sailor by every means in his power.

First he tries conversation, addressing him in English; but the man only smiles at him a blank smile. Then he releases Snapper from his pocket, and when that little beast, with a cry of joy, jumps into the sailor's lap, with tail and cars and body all wriggling ecstasy, the sailor pets the pretty creature, fondles it, lets it remain in his lap, chirps to it, and smiles blandly upon it, which amazes Potter, who had expected him, if Brackett, to repulse it. For the detective has just now done, as men with small brains sometimes do, a very smart thing.

Inspired by success, for he sees that now Potter begins to be in doubt as to his identity, the sergeant proceeds to a master-stroke. With a forced smile, which his painted wrinkles make hideous, he suddenly places Snapper in the pocket of his overcoat that he knows the dog doesn't like, the one with the cold handcuffs in it. From their chill and hard encounter Mr. Snapper recoils, whines, jumps out of the pocket, and, looking reproachfully at his master, goes back to Potter, whose pockets he knows are warm and comfortable, and have no chilling iron or steel inside them.

This seems to settle the matter, and the Texan, muttering to himself : " Great snakes ! fooled hagain ! " relapses into his seat as the train runs into Creil, the time from Chantilly to this place being only about fifteen minutes.

Creil is a great railway junction, no less than five lines coming into the station, and here Brackett determines to leave the train and try to take some roundabout route to Boulogne, anything being preferable to Potter's close proximity.

This he does with considerable coolness ; for he waits till the train has but a minute or two longer to remain before he gets up and steps out of the compartment.

Now the very act of the sailor's going arouses Potter's suspicions again ; besides Snapper, missing his master's presence, is apparently anxious to be after him.   All this, coupled with the fact that the Texan has noticed that the man's ticket is for Boulogne, sets the frontiersman to thinking.   He gets out of the carriage also and stands waiting ; if the sailor returns to the train he has probably mistaken his man ; if not, he will follow him.

Thirty seconds after this the train steams off into the darkness, and Potter now hurries into the railway refreshment *salon* where he saw the sailor disappear.

But half a minute is a long start, and the Texan cannot discover the sailor in the *buffet*.   He rushes out of the exit from the station to the town ; no sailor.   But here he begins suddenly to run, for Snapper, who has somehow got out of his pocket, sees a carriage, and is flying up one of the deserted streets of this little French town in pursuit of it.

He runs silently after the dog, taking care not to overtake him, and finding no difficulty in keeping up to him ; for this old man of the prairies is as wiry as many a college athlete.   He is soon rewarded.

Snapper, bounding along two or three minutes, overtakes a cab that is driving ahead of them, and jumps up and barks.   Then a head is put cautiously out of the window and apparently does not see the Texan, for a voice that makes Potter's heart bound with joy says : " Hi, old doggy ! we've both run away from the beggar ! " The cab door is opened, and Snapper springs into the arms of his beloved master.

On this the Texan, increasing his speed, also overtakes

the hack and swings himself up alongside of the driver, to that individual's anger and fright; for he begins to cry out French oaths and to attempt to knock the Texan from the box.

"Shut up!" mutters Potter with sententious sternness, "or you're cold clay!"

But the man only screams the louder.

"You don't *sabé* me, Frenchy!" returns the Texan in terrible earnest. "Perhaps you *sabé this!*" And he claps his pistol to the forehead of the fighting Jehu.

The effect of the revolver is instantaneous and tremendous. The hackman gives a shriek that would raise the Seven Sleepers, and springs over backward, falling off the carriage box, while, approaching noises warning Mr. Potter of pursuit, he whips up the horses, and goes at a terrible gait for a minute or so. Then he suddenly pulls in the animals panting on their haunches, springs off the box, opens the cab door, and jabbing his revolver against Sergeant Brackett's heart says: "That packet you got from my son—or you're dead!"

All this has curdled the blood of the detective. He has heard the struggle on the box and what he supposes is the hackman's death-cry, and would have sprung out of the carriage himself, but the fearful speed has deterred him; therefore he has used the time in another way.

He now mutters faintly: "You can kill me, but I haven't got it."

"Not got it?" screams the Texan. "Great Scott! my darter!" and for a moment feels sick; for at every mishap in this whole affair Mr. Potter thinks of his daughter, and it causes a weakness that no disaster to himself could bring him.

Just here Sergeant Brackett astounds Mr. Potter; for he mistakes tenderness for nervousness, and says in a stronger voice: "Samuel Potts, I arrest you in the Queen's name! I've a warrant for you and requisition on the French Government. You'd better not resist, I hear *gendarmes* coming!"

"'Ave you?" mutters the Texan, grimly. "Show me the documents!"

"Here they are!" And Brackett hands Potter two official papers, which the Honorable Sampson hastily examines by the light of the carriage lamp, while the ser-

geant proudly produces a pair of bright handcuffs, and
arranges them for Potter's wrists.

" Yes, these are O. K. ! " returns the Texan, pocketing
the documents.

" Then, Samuel Potts, you're wanted ! Hold up your
hands ! "

" Hold up *yours* ! "

"*My Lord* ! "

" Hold up your hands ! Now handcuff yourself, or
I'll riddle ye ! Quick ! "

" *My God* ! "

" No back talk ! You'll be dead before you hear the
click of the lock ! This gun's a self-cocker ! That's
comfortable ! " concludes Mr. Potter, as Sergeant Brackett, with a smothered moan, sinks back in the hack handcuffed by himself with his own handcuffs, the most
thoroughly astonished and dismayed detective that ever
shadowed a criminal.

" Now the key to these bracelets ! " demands Potter.

" I—I've dropped it. I haven't got it."

" The key, or you won't have. time to say your
prayers ! "

" It's—it's in my trousers pocket."

" All right, I've got it ! " mutters Potter, giving the
handcuffs an extra snap to make sure they are well on
Brackett's wrists. " And now that packet you got from
my son ! "

But before either of them can say more the hack is surrounded by *gendarmes*, headed by the driver of the cab
that Potter had so summarily dismissed from his box.

Mr. Potter, remembering his son's advice, doesn't try to
whip France ; but having made up his mind how to
act, stands unmoved till the sergeant of the *gendarmes*
comes up to him. Then he silently hands that officer
the two warrants ; and while the French policeman examines them by the light of the coach lamp, points to
the name of Sergeant Brackett in the French extradition
document, and pats his own breast.

" A—ah ! Monsieur le Sergeant *Gendarme* Brackett ! "
says the Frenchman, giving him a polite bow ; for he
reads and understands the requisition on his government,
which is in his language, and guesses what the warrant
for Samuel Potts, which is in English, must mean.

"*Oui!*" returns Potter, effusively, and then points with his finger to the name of the criminal in the French document, indicating the handcuffed Brackett as the man.

"A-ah ! *Le voleur !* Samuel Pot-tes !" says the French police officer, and his men drag from the carriage the detective, who is trying, in very bad French, to explain to them his identity.

"He is handcuffed !—DISGUISED !" says the sergeant of *gendarmes*, in French, after a moment's examination of the paint on Brackett's face, that now is being made into streaks by the perspiration of surprise, agitation, and misery.

And now, somewhat to Potter's relief, the hackman, who has been looking at him searchingly, suddenly turns round and recognizes Brackett as the man who threatened to shoot him in the dark with his pistol, and goes into a frenzy at the unfortunate detective, calling him "*Assassin! Meurtrier! Le vieux larron!*" and other French expletives indicative of Brackett's supposed crimes.

So they all come along to the police station carrying with them their prisoner, whom they have shoved into the hack again, and who occupies his time by shaking his handcuffs at Potter and screaming an unintelligible mixture of French and English out of the window. The cab-driver's story has made them all think the detective dangerous, and they pay no attention to his ravings.

At the police station, despite his struggles and im. precations, they run Sergeant Brackett into a dark cell, lock him in, and leave him.

Then Potter proceeds to grease the wheels of justice, giving the hackman a twenty-franc piece, and indicating by signs that he is to remain with his carriage outside. Next he sends out for lots of wine to a neighboring *café*, and immediately becomes popular with the French police. A man who speaks a little English is found to act as interpreter, and Potter, rewarding him for his trouble *in advance*, his story, as the man relates it to the sergeant of *gendarmes*, is perfectly satisfactory. Then he leads that officer away, and silently holds out a hundred-franc note.

"*Ah, monsieur, n'importe!*" says the sergeant of

gendarmes, with a shrug of his shoulders, but takes the money.

And now Potter says through the interpreter that he's going in to search his prisoner; for all this time, though compelled to postpone action, he has had but one thought on his mind—the packet.

The cell door is unlocked, and without much ceremony or gentleness he examines Brackett from head to heel, and to his horror finds *nothing*. Then he falls to begging the detective to tell him for his daughter's sake what he has done with the packet. And getting no answer, for his manner is almost that of a crazy man, and now *Brackett dare not tell him*, he wastes no more time in threats, and goes hurriedly out to examine the hack, having an idea that perhaps the detective may have concealed the packet there. Making this examination by the aid of a carriage lamp, he finds some scraps of paper that frighten him. He hurriedly takes them into the police office and inspects them. They are in a feminine hand, and he turns pale and white, and drops of agony come out upon this strong man's brow, as he mutters faintly : " My God ! My darter ! " For he knows *the last proof of his innocence in the world is destroyed ;* but still thinks only of what it will bring to her.

Then he suddenly springs up and through the interpreter offers great rewards for pieces of this document the criminal has destroyed ; and they all take lanterns and go out upon the road over which the hack has passed, Potter showing them where search should be made.

After a little time the French *gendarmes*, the interpreter, and also the hackman, who all take a hand in this business, begin to bring him scraps of paper similar to those he has found in the carriage ; he paying for them according to size, five, ten, fifteen, and even twenty francs.

These stimulating rewards make the men very eager, and they find a good many pieces, some of them quite large, for Brackett has done his work in a hurry and there has been but little wind this night.

So they work on for hours, going over the same ground many times, till at last a *gendarme* brings him a large piece of paper, and Potter looking at it gives a yell of joy, and hands the man a five-pound note. For it is the entire wrapper of the packet, addressed in Lady Annerley's own handwriting, and has been only unfastened, having the ribbon with which it was secured attached to the paper; and a cunning idea has sprung into the old Texan's mind.

After a little more searching, they make up their minds they can find no more, and return to the police station, all the rest very happy, but Potter in an awful mood. He instantly arranges by the interpreter to transfer his prisoner to Boulogne by the express train that passes through Creil early in the morning, arriving at its destination between nine and ten o'clock.

Then he goes in with a white face to Brackett and whispers to him : " You don't know what you've done, but *I* do ! You pray God all night that this matter turns out right, for if it don't I'll kill you ; and I never told a man that yet without he was dead when I said the last word. I'll do it any way if you open your lips to a living human—till I've settled *her !* "

With this he gags Brackett to make sure of his silence, and goes out and puts on his revolver again ; for on visiting the detective Potter had left his pistol outside, for fear that he would kill his enemy, which would have destroyed the plan he had in his mind. Then he telegraphs the lieutenant.

So, aided by the sergeant of *gendarmes,* Mr. Potter follows out the dispatch he had sent to his son, and arriving at Boulogne, meets the young man at the depot. Where, having got Mr. Brackett into a cab, they drive him to a room the lieutenant has engaged in a little out-of-the-way hotel on the quay, and Potter and his son have a long conversation.

Which the father ends by saying : " It's a desperate dodge, but I think it'll *break the slate !* "

CHAPTER XXIII.

THE APOTHEOSIS OF SAMMY POTTS.

WHILE Mr. Potter is arranging to "break the slate," his friends are having an exciting time in Boulogne, where Lady Annerley, though suffering the tortures of

Hades, is also distributing misery and despair to such of the Texan's adherents as come in her way.

She has had an awful night of it, however, and though in no fear of bodily harm, has probably suffered more than her emissary, Sergeant Brackett, at the hands of the French *gendarmes* and the ferocious Texan.

Her conscience has been crying out at her with every beat of the pendulum : " You have kept one innocent man in exile, and perhaps condemned another to prison to the dishonor of their families and the ruin of all who belong to them !—and for *what ?* To retain the respect and perhaps" (for she still has wild dreams) " gain the love of a man whom you are now torturing and degrading by means of his father's shame, ignominy, and despair ! "

She has but to open her mouth and they will all be happy—save herself. But at this the vision of Errol and Ethel at the altar comes to her and she cries out wildly : " No, no ! Fate joined us in Egypt ! I'll not lose his respect—the *chance* of his love ! Though it is torture to remain silent, it would be more to confess. I have burned my bridges ; I am silent now *forever !* "

So the morning opens for her, and at about ten o'clock, she having just made an affectation of eating breakfast, the obsequious Lubbins brings to her Mr. Charles Errol's card, and she says : " At home to him ! Here, in my private parlor."

The young man has heard the rumors of the night before from Arthur of the flight of Potter the Texan, upon the discovery that he was the missing Sammy Potts, and of his pursuit by the London detective, Sergeant Brackett. He has not seen Lord Lincoln, who has arrived upon the morning boat, and is now holding consultation with his son and daughter at the *Hôtel du Pavillon.* This information has been conveyed to him in a little note from Ethel in which she writes : " You have promised not to speak to me ; but I have *promised* to love you to the end of my life, and I'll keep it. Ida is the only calm one in our party. She seems to fear nothing for her father, but a great deal for the detective who is trying to arrest him. Her confidence in her father's honor has produced the greatest admiration in my father. Give your poor father *my love*, and say I wish to call him *father* also—*soon !* "

A note filled with such passages as this would give hope to any lover; and Charley Errol would be more calm this morning were it not for his father.

The elder Errol has endured banishment for thirty years with equanimity and dignity at a distance from the land of his birth. Having placed once more his foot upon his mother country, he longs for it as for his life, and spends hours on the beach gazing at the dim white cliffs, and muttering in a broken voice to his son: "Charley, take my bones to my old home; they'll let them rest there—soon! The disgrace and shame of thirty years ago have come all back to me. I can't look men in the face. I feel like I did when they first put the convict's garb upon my body and the felon's chains upon my limbs!"

This kind of thing has made young Errol desperate, and he has come to Lady Annerley to try and force the truth from her; for he has been thinking through the night; and suffering stimulating his faculties, begins to remember something of what she had said to him when she first met him in Egypt.

As he comes in, unheeding the pleading glance of the woman whose beauty is now made pathetic by despairing love, the look upon his face is stern. He coldly says: "You hardly expected me again, I presume, Lady Annerley?"

To this she begs: "Please don't use that tone to me. I don't deserve it—from you! Charley, you came——"

"To wring the acknowledgment of my father's innocence from you!"

"From *me?* I—I have never said I thought your father guilty!"

"No? Then prove him innocent! I've been looking at his face, that can't bear my glance because the world calls him a felon. You can remove that shame—and, Lady Annerley, you shall do it!"

But she confounds him by saying: "And what do I know? Only that your father is a convict; and if I used that knowledge to separate you from Ethel Lincoln—you know the reason"—then cries to him: "Charley, why are you so cruel to me? You—you would be different to me—if you knew how you fought for me—if you remembered Egypt!"

Then he cries back at her : " I do remember Egypt ! "
Her voice and bearing have set his memory going and
the past has come to him again, for he says hoarsely :
" What did that packet contain you told me to treasure
as my life—the one you gave me to send my father?
The truth was in that packet ! Tell it to me ! *That
truth I will have !*"

This astounds and terrifies her—he is beginning to remember—but it also makes her cooler. She draws herself up and says to him cuttingly : " Ah, yes, Lord Lincoln has been telegraphed for ; he is here to part his
daughter from the convict's son. That is why I must
make your father innocent ! "

At this he looks at her astonished, for it is the only
cruel speech she has ever made him in all the suffering
her passion for him has brought to her. He mutters :
" Lady Sarah, you're a different woman to the one who
nursed me to life in Italy three months ago ! "

" That was before her baby face came between us ! "
cries her ladyship, hoarsely.

The agony in her tone makes him contrite, for he remembers Lady Annerley's kind nursing, and fears he
may have given her cause to think she at one time had
his heart. He says half apologetically : " You—you
never thought I loved you ? "

This remark adds to the agony of love the agony of
shame. She sneers : " Ah, what a generous question ! "
Then droops her head and answers it sadly : " No ! She
could awaken a passion I could not touch," next says
hoarsely : " That's why I hate her ! "

" I had supposed your pride—" murmurs Errol ; but
gets no farther, for she cuts him short by wringing her
hands and crying out : " Pride is for those who think, not
those who feel ! Pride was for yesterday ; to-day I've
only passion and despair ! Charley, forgive me for the
sorrow I've brought again upon your father ! " and Lady
Annerley is at his feet sobbing. " Oh, if you knew how I
suffer, too—seeing you turn from me who had given you
back your life ! " For the anguish in her face has made
him look away from her. " You said that before *she*
came—in Venice ! " She rises and gets near him again
with these words, and seeing no response in his eyes
goes into a spasm of horrible despair, crying out : " My

God ! How cruel you are to me ! Some day you'll know the difference between a young girl's rose-leaf passion and the love of a woman who has all her life hungered for affection and never found it—in father—in husband —*in any one !* Some day you'll know !—*some day ! some —day !* "

The last of this is uttered as if it were the sigh of a breaking heart. Her suffering makes him forget his own. He does not look at her, for fear she will see sympathy and mistake it for love. Giving one quick glance at him, and noting this, Lady Annerley sinks into a chair and hides her head in her hands, which tremble and shake as if she had the ague.

Upon their silence breaks Miss Potter's voice, coming in through the parlor door. It says, in cutting tones : " Lubbins, it is unnecessary to say Lady Annerley is not at home. I heard her voice distinctly."

This diversion is just what her ladyship wants. She is afraid of herself—afraid that the suffering of the man she loves will overcome her resolution. She springs to the door, opens it, and says : " Please come in, Miss Potter ! "

Whereupon Ida enters, light, brilliant, carefully and beautifully dressed as ever, though perhaps she would be slightly paler did not excitement give her a little additional color. She is followed by Mr. Arthur Lincoln, who looks much the worse for the trouble of the last few hours and who begs her to be calm.

Miss Potter, however, is calm ; she bows coldly to her ladyship, gives Errol her hand, and then says : " Lady Annerley, it is reported in Boulogne that you are the authority for a statement that my father is a fugitive from justice ! " This is in a freezing tone, though Miss Potter's eyes have a dazzling sparkle.

" Well ! " remarks her ladyship, with equal coolness, for she is afraid of nothing this day except the suffering face of the man she loves.

But before she can say more Charley Errol turns to her with a last pleading glance and mutters : " You— you won't tell me, Lady Sarah ? "

She does not look at him but gasps : " Why do you torture me with questions ? " Then venting her misery upon Miss Potter, she cries : " Ask *her !* She said she could give you hope ! Ask the daughter of the convict who has fled."

" You mean my father ? " says Ida, her eyes beginning to blaze.

" Yes ! " desperately.

" I am *not* the daughter of a convict ! "

" Not the daughter of a convict—*yet!*" sneers her ladyship.

" You have no retraction to make ? "

" No retraction—but plenty of *proof!* .Your father proved it himself by flying ! "

" Flying ? My father never in his life fled from anything ! " and Miss Potter affects a laugh.

Here Lady Annerley astonishes her, for she lies to her being in that kind of a mood she will stop at nothing. She says : " I saw your father fly for Paris."

" You saw him ? "

" Yes ! The moment he heard his *alias* had been disclosed by you—that you had betrayed and ruined him ! "

" But it was you who feared that revelation ! " cries Ida, her eyes beginning to look like old Potter's when he arrested the detective. " Lady Sarah, my father shall return to make you fear again. I swear to you ! " And wishing to avoid profitless discussion the young lady turns toward the door, but Sarah Annerley whispers to her : " If he does, I swear to you I'll have your father in an English jail."

Both Errol and Arthur start at this, and Mr. Lincoln says : " Lady Annerley, such words are not warranted unless you have certain proof ! "

" Proof ! I have *conviction!* " returns her ladyship, whose eyes are now riveted upon Miss Potter's wrist. " His daughter's wearing some of the very plunder on her arm ! "

At this Ida astonishes the two men even more than Lady Annerley, for she comes back, light, airy, almost laughing, and says nonchalantly : " Oh, you're referring to my lucky coin, the marked sovereign ! " and holds her dazzling wrist high in air, jingling the bauble in Lady Annerley's face.

This astounds Lady Annerley, but it horrifies the two men, for they recognize the bangle she displays as one of the marked coins.

Arthur gasps : " Ida, what does this mean ? "

Lady Sarah cries : " Dare she say who gave her the stolen goods ? "

" Yes," answers Ida proudly. "My father! my father! do you hear me? *My father!* My father does not decorate his daughter with baubles that will make her *blush!* My father——"

But Arthur stops her by saying with legal caution : " Then for your father's sake don't tell her any more ! "

And Charley Errol mutters with a sigh : " Miss Potter, I'm sorry for you ! "

These remarks and the way they look at her astound and horrify the girl ; she stands gazing at them astonished ; then indignation comes into her eyes ; she pants out : " Why, you all seem to think my father guilty ! "

And the subject warming her blood and enthusiasm making her eyes blaze with trusting faith, she pours out to them : "I've known his love for twenty years, and though every jury in the world and every judge on the bench cried : ' Guilty ! *Guilty!!* GUILTY ! ! ! ' I would cry: ' INNOCENT ! ' "

As the other three stare at the girl a soft feminine-masculine voice comes to them and makes them all turn suddenly about and see Mr. Van Cott. That young gentleman is faultlessly arrayed and looks very pale after his " night of it." He has come quietly in past Lubbins, who has been too intent upon the scene in my lady's parlor to do his duty outside of it.

Mr. Van Cott says : " Pardon my entering unannounced, Lady Annerley, but I feared Miss Potter might be anxious, and came to tell her that story of her father's flying to escape arrest is all beastly rot."

" Not fled ! " cries her ladyship.

" Oh, yes ; he's gone safe enough, but he didn't fly from the law. He fled from——"

" What ? " says Ida.

" From me ! "

" From *you?* " gasps the girl, amazed, as indeed so are all the rest.

" Yas ; I and your father had an interview about you, Miss Ida ; you know the reason ! " Here he gives her a significant ogle that makes the young lady struggle between rage and a smile. " Your father was insolent to me and I was compelled to threaten to chastise him ; and fearing me—for my manner was very determined— he has doubtless fled. But you can tell him he may re- turn ; I won't hurt him, for your sake ! "

He puts another ogle to the end of this, but Miss Pot- ter does not see him ; she is looking behind him with a flood of joy in her eyes, and crying : " My father ! " . For a voice outside is saying : " This way, Peer ! "

Then she runs to the door sobbing " At last ! "

For the strain being over something has given way in this tortured heart that has flaunted her father's banner of innocence so jauntily in all the uncertainty and anguish of the last twelve hours, and Miss Potter, who carried herself so airily with her father fled, is now panting and crying on her father's breast, who is here to fight his own battles.

Old Potter, however, does not kiss her ; he simply pats her shoulder in a soothing kind of way, and looking at Lady Annerley, says sternly : " Ida, who's been making you cry ? "

" Father, that woman says that you are a thief ! " whis- pers his daughter.

" Hida Potter ! " returns her father solemnly, putting her from him, and looking her in the face, "did you be- lieve her ? "

" No ! "

" Then kiss your daddy ! " Which this goddess of fashion does to the old frontiersman as if it were a boon most precious.

Then he hands his daughter to Lord Lincoln, who has come in with him. This gentleman, assisted by his son, comforts and soothes her, for the girl is almost hysterical now. While Mr. Potter walks up to Lady Annerley—who since his entrance has become like a marble statue— with blazing eyes, that now and then involuntarily turn toward Charley Errol, as he looks on silent and aston- ished.

" Lady Hannerley," says Potter, " did you dare to tell that gal her daddy was a habsconder and a thief ? "

" Certainly ! " replies her ladyship, coolly, though there is a little tremor in her voice.

" Then either you or Hi kicks the beam this trip, and I reckon it's you ! " answers Mr. Potter, and turns toward

Lord Lincoln, muttering apologetically : " Peer, it's the second time in my life I ever threatened a woman ! "

" And it shall be the last ! " replies Lady Annerley, who will now destroy this man who can tell her secret, whether they believe him or not. " For when you leave this room you shall be a prisoner ! " Then she adds sneeringly : " You boy felon !" and walking across the room, touches a bell.

On which Ida screams out : " You sha'n't call my father that ! " and comes toward her, but the Texan says sharply : " Your dad can do his own fighting ! Lady Sahara, you're making me feel just like a Comanche Injun ! "

Here Lubbins comes in, and Lady Annerley sneers : " When Sergeant Brackett returns tell him that the felon for whom he has a warrant is here."

At the mention of the detective's name, Potter goes into such an awful scream of laughter that he gives them all a start, and a second after a sensation.

He cries : " Is that your proclamation ? I would have let you come down easy off your roost, but you won't have it ! Charles Errol, *I've something for you !* " and placing his hand in his breast pocket, draws out a document. The minute the Australian's eyes fall upon it he cries hoarsely : " *My God ! The packet she gave me in Egypt, and stole from me when I was wounded !* " and would seize it.

But Lady Annerley is between them, begging, beseech-ing, imploring : " Remember your promise ! Charley, in mercy—in pity to the woman who loves you—remem-ber your promise : ' If we both *lived* you would give it back to me ! ' "

" A promise ? Then I'll keep the thing myself ! " mut-ters Potter, putting the paper back in his bosom.

But Errol cries to him : " It is mine ! It holds my father's honor ! "

" And it holds mine also ! " returns Potter. " I've 'ad an awful time to git it, and I'll protect it with my life, and open it, and read it aloud to you, and the judge—beg pardon, Peer—and the man who stays me is a very dead man ! "

And taking the packet from his pocket again, quite slowly, is about to tear it open, when Lady Annerley's arms are clutched round his, and she sobs, though her eyes have no tears : " In mercy ! The man I love would think me worse than I am. Give me that packet back, and I'll tell him—all !—and the truth—but in my own way—as—as—my heart is breaking now ! "

" That's fair ! " says Potter, with almost a sigh of relief.

Then she droops her head, and murmurs : " Send them all away."

The Texan returns : " The judge'll stay for his family interests. I'll stay to protect my own, and you can have it out with the young man ! " And in a second he has Arthur and Ida from the room, little Van Cott having grown very pale, and quietly and silently stolen away as soon as Mr. Potter came in.

Then he whispers hurriedly to Lord Lincoln : " You told me as we came here you could take a deposition good in England. Write what she says down, for the Lord's sake ! "

Sitting at a table at the back of the room, Percy Lincoln writes hurriedly the words that now pass from the woman to the man who has been gazing in silence at her.

After a gasp or two—for her lips though they open give forth no sound—Sarah Annerley forces them to do their office, though her voice seems to have changed and become harsh and discordant since she last spoke. And these are the words she utters :

" I—I stood by my father, Sir Jonas Stevens', deathbed, and listened to the confession of a dying thief ! "

On this there is a start from two of the men.

Errol cries in an amazed voice : " Your father ! my father's friend ? "

Lincoln springs from his seat murmuring : " Are you sane ? Your father—Sir Jonas Stevens—the great financier, the respected banker ! "

But she cries at him : " Don't interrupt me ! you distract his attention ! If he doesn't listen to me, how will he ever forgive ? " and gazes once more at Errol as if to drive her words home to his heart.

While Potter whispers to the judge : " For all our sakes, don't do anything but write her words on paper."

She begins to speak again, punctuating her revealings with tearless sobs.

" My father swore to me that while a young man he had stolen from the bank he was yet a clerk in a number of sums of money. The bank was determined to find the culprit. For his own safety he suggested that certain sovereigns be marked so that if stolen they could be identified, knowing that Ralph Errol was secretly going to Australia. On the morning of his departure he was about to place them all in Errol's desk in lieu of the savings your father, Charley, was to carry with him. He had not completed this when he was seen by the office boy, to whom he gave thirty of the coins so as to aid him to emigrate to America. That boy, Samuel Potts, took them innocently as a loan from my father, whom years afterward he repaid. *That was my father's crime!*"

To this Errol says nothing. His eyes have a far away look and are full of tears, his lips are trembling ; he is thinking of *his* father's years of miserable shame and cruel punishment. He doesn't seem to hear her.

Then she mutters hoarsely : " You know the truth now ! Give me the packet !" and turns to take it from Potter's hands.

But he whispers to Lincoln : " Swear her to it, judge ! Swear her to it on the Bible, for the Lord's sake !"

The Texan's manner impresses the judge, who hands her the statement he has written out and says : " Lady Annerley, sign your name to this."

And she doing as he asks, he takes her oath that it is true.

Then she mutters again : " Give me that packet !" which Potter does with a triumphant chuckle which she does not heed, for she cries to Errol : " Now LISTEN TO MY EXPIATION !

" On my father's death I immediately telegraphed, and found that you were in Egypt *en route* to Australia. Disregarding the warnings of my friends and my own safety I hurried to Alexandria. There I waited—after all had fled—endangering my own life to do you justice ! You remember I tried to tell you, but you wouldn't listen, you were thinking how to save my life. Ah, how you did save ! How you fought for me ! Can't you remember ? Charley, *my* Charley, can't you remember ! My God ! How nobly you fought for me and made me *love you!*"

Seeing he makes her no answer, she goes to him in a piteous, begging, pleading way, and touching his arm, trembles in fear of a repulse, and says humbly, in one long,
sighing whisper : "Charley—can't—you—remember?"

Her manner and despair make tears come into the eyes
of the judge who has sentenced fellow-men to death,
and the frontier warrior who has butchered his foes without sorrow or remorse.

But Errol simply says, not looking at her : "I did my
duty ! How have you done yours?" Then gazes at her
sternly, for she does not answer the terrible accusation,
and cries : "*How have you done yours?*"

And now the scene becomes cruel, for she shrieks out
at him : "My God ! Don't look at me in that way !
Have *some* pity ! How could I tell the man I had grown
to love better than my life that *my* father had made *his*
father an outcast and a felon for over thirty years ? You
would have despised me for my father's crime, and hated
me—as you do *now !* Don't think me all bad. I did the
other sins when jealousy drove me mad. My Heaven !
He don't even believe !"

This last she screams in a kind of despairing appeal to
the world. Then seizing Errol and forcing him to look at
her agony she whispers : "I intended to tell you the
awful story at the first, but I'll prove that to you. That
you shall know. That you shall believe by *this !* This,
that I had meant for you to read if they killed me in
Alexandria. This, that none but you shall ever see, for
it tells of—of how much I adored you then—the first,
the only love-letter I shall ever write—THIS !"

And she tears open the packet Potter had given her,
and is about to hand it to Errol ; but gazing at it her
face changes from awful despair to amazed astonishment. She gasps : "He would never have known if I
had not confessed ; now he'll never believe *all !*" Here
the passion of a tigress comes upon her ; she screams,
"Tricked at the last ! Betrayed by *you !*" then, staggering toward the Texan, utters an awful choking shriek
and falls like a dead woman at his feet, the pages of
the open packet scattering about her senseless form.

Picking one of these up, Lincoln says astounded :
"Why, they're blank !"

"Yes !" remarks Potter. "Ye see, judge—I beg your

pardon, Peer—I couldn't get enough of the fragments to make sense. Her emissary had destroyed the document, though he'd left the wrapper whole, and so I tricked her and busted the slate!" and stooping down would pick Lady Annerley up.

But Errol is before him and lifts her very tenderly, for the memories of Africa are back in his heart as he looks upon this woman who has sinned so against him, and mutters, "Poor devil!" So, placing her inanimate form upon the sofa, he gives this woman who has broken her heart over him his first and his last embrace.

Lady Annerley's shrieks have drawn Arthur and the rest to the door, and Mr. Potter, calling his daughter to him, says : "She was once kind to you, Ida ; give my lady what care you can. Thar's been a funeral of a heart in this room."

Going to her, Miss Potter cries out : "How she must have suffered ! She's grown old since I saw her last. Father, what have you all done to her?"

"No more than justice demanded," returns the old man. "Quit moralizing, and bring her to!"

So with the American girl's kind arms about her Lady Annerley is borne out of the room, punished by the fact that she never knows the man she has wronged and loved forgave her.

While this is being done the men hold a hurried consultation, Lord Lincoln telling them that his resignation from the bench not being as yet accepted, and no successor to the office having been appointed, Lady Annerley's affidavit taken by him will be sufficiently binding for the purpose he shall use it, that is, to quash the indictment against Samuel Potts, and to make such representations to the Home Secretary as shall obtain the Queen's free pardon for Ralph Errol, and so much reparation as it is possible to make for the stigma placed for over thirty years on an innocent man.

In conclusion Lord Lincoln says : "The judge who sentenced your father shall be the first to call upon him and offer him his sympathy and apologies. And as for any injustice or wrong done to you by any of my family, I can make an atonement that you, at least, Mr. Errol, should think sufficient; for my daughter, who has been the joy of my life, will now, I presume, become the blessing of yours. You've been a good son, and that is the best guarantee you'll be a good husband. Come, let us go to your father !"

Then Lord Líncoln puts his arm over Charley Errol's shoulder.

But Potter stops him by saying : " Peer, I shar'n't go back to England till you get that ar indictment squashed ! I don't want to be arrested, and I'll take my darter and have a quiet time in Par*ie.*"

At this Miss Potter comes running to her father, and says : " Of course I'll go with you ! Dear papa, I'll never leave you till——"

Here the Honorable Sampson makes Arthur and the girl blush, for he cries : " Till the weddin' ! We'll get the trousseau in Par*ie.* Par*ie* is the place for trousseaus ! Peer, you'd better send that little darter of yours along with us !"

But Errol here mutters to Lord Lincoln : " Think of my father—of his uncertainty—his agony ! Come ! we must tell him at once."

And the two are about to leave together ; but on getting to the door the judge suddenly pauses, and turning to the Texan, who stands with his daughter's arm around him, says : " You'll excuse my asking you a lawyer's question, but how and why did you change your name ? "

" How ? " returns Potter proudly. " By act of the Texas Legislature ! Why ? Because the Democratic Party thought *Sampson Potter* a more high-toned name to run for Congress than *Sammy Potts.* That's what makes me Mr. Potter of Texas."

FINIS.

PRINTED BY J. S. VIRTUE AND CO., LIMITED, CITY ROAD, LONDON.